Jam & Roses

MARY GIBSON was born and brought up in Bermondsey, where both her grandmother and mother were factory girls. Her first novel, *Custard Tarts and Broken Hearts*, was selected for World Book Night in 2015, and she is the author of four other novels: *Jam and Roses, Gunner Girls and Fighter Boys, Bourbon Creams and Tattered Dreams* and *Hattie's Home*. She lives in Kent.

By Mary Gibson

Custard Tarts and Broken Hearts
Jam and Roses
Gunner Girls and Fighter Boys
Bourbon Creams and Tattered Dreams
Hattie's Home

Jam & Roses

Mary Gibson

First published in the UK in 2015 by Head of Zeus Ltd

This paperback edition first published in the UK
in 2018 by Head of Zeus Ltd

9 7 5 3 1 2 4 6 8

A catalogue record for this book is available from
the British Library.

Paperback ISBN 9781788543859
Ebook ISBN 9781781855904

Typeset by Ben Cracknell Studios, Norwich

Printed and bound by CPI Group (UK) Ltd, Croydon, CR0 4YY

Head of Zeus Ltd
First Floor East
5–8 Hardwick Street
London EC1R 4RG

WWW.HEADOFZEUS.COM

Dedicated to all the Bermondsey girls, and boys,
past, present and future.

'We are the Bermondsey Girls!'

June 1923

Milly Colman and her workmates linked arms as they walked, three abreast, along Tower Bridge Road. Throwing her head back with a bold grin, Milly suddenly started up a song and the others bellowed in unison: '*We are some of the Bermondsey girls, we are some of the girls! We spend our tanners, we mind our manners, we are respected wherever we go . . .*'

They were singing because it was Saturday afternoon and, until Monday morning, they were free of the factory. It was time to have fun. After a week at Southwell's jam factory, hulling strawberries till their fingertips bled red as soft fruit, Milly felt she deserved it, they all did. Vans and carts from Kent, crammed with strawberries, had been arriving daily for over two weeks. There was no shortage of overtime and the factory had even taken on extra hands to make the most of the brief strawberry season, when the fruit had to be sorted, hulled and boiled into jam, before it spoiled. The sweet strawberry scent of the Kent countryside now hung over the whole of Dockhead, vying with hops from the Anchor Brewery, cinnamon and ginger from the spice mill, and the less savoury aromas of the tannery. The strawberry glut meant that the girls all had extra money in their pockets, even after handing over most of their wages to their mothers that dinner time.

'*When we're walking down the Old Kent Road, doors and windows open wi-i-ide. If you see a copper come, hit 'im on the 'ead and run. We are the Bermondsey girls!*'

They roared the last refrain even louder, breaking ranks for no one, so that some of the shoppers thronging the pavement had to hop quickly out of their way. A few older women looked at them disapprovingly as they careered along the street, and as one respectable-looking couple crossed the road to avoid them, Milly heard the woman mutter, 'Common factory girls, what can you expect?'

'We're as good as you, any day!' Milly offered loudly, so that the woman ducked her head and hurried on. Milly felt affronted. When did it become a crime to be happy? They might be loud, but they weren't scruffy. They'd all been home to change from their work clothes and Milly was proud of the new summer dress she'd made for herself. With its scoop neck and long white pointed collar over the pretty blue print, it was actually the height of fashion, and who was to know it was made from an old dress from Bermondsey clothes market that she'd unpicked and re-used?

Yet not everyone scorned them. There were others, often the elderly, who smiled indulgently. Perhaps they knew themselves that after working ten hours a day, six and a half days a week, every little scrap of leisure time was to be savoured to the full. And in an often ugly world of close-crowded houses, packed with too many bodies for any privacy, sometimes happiness had to be found wherever it could. If that was on a crowded shopping street, so be it.

And, as usual, given any disapproval, Milly's bravado only made her all the brasher. 'Where shall we go first, girls?' she asked her friends Kitty Bunclerk and Peggy Dillon in a deliberately loud voice.

'Manzes, I'm starving!' Peggy said.

'You're *always* starving, we can go there later, look at the queue!' said Milly, pointing to the shuffling line of eager diners that stretched back from the pie-and-mash shop to the street corner.

'Well, I can't go round looking at stalls on an empty stomach. Come on, girls, the queue's moving.' Peggy let go of Milly's arm and headed towards the shop.

Tower Bridge Road was lined with stalls selling all manner of fruit and vegetables, household goods, and oil and paraffin, and at this end was the Bermondsey second-hand clothes market, known simply as the Old Clo'. The stallholders were calling out their wares and Milly would have preferred an hour in the fresh air, wandering from stall to stall, before surrendering to the steamy heat of the pie-and-mash shop. But this was the girls' traditional Saturday dinner-time treat and so they tagged on to the end of the queue, which was indeed moving quickly. Thankfully, the shop's front window, which stretched its entire length, had been opened up to let in some air, and the smell of parsley liquor and vinegar caught in Milly's nostrils. Oh well, perhaps she was hungry after all.

Sawdust covered the shop's tiled floor, and a white marble counter ran the length of it. From behind the counter, four equally big-bosomed women, in green-splashed white aprons, served at a frenetic pace, screaming their orders down a dumb waiter to the kitchen below. 'More pies! More liquor! More eels!' The insatiable Saturday morning crowd had the air of not having eaten for a week.

'Pie, mash and liquor, three times!' Peggy gave their order and a white-aproned woman piled their plates with deep, oval meat pies and dollops of mashed potato, before ladling over bright green parsley liquor.

They were lucky to find a marble-topped table near the back, which had just been vacated. This was never a leisurely lunch; people tended to eat fast and get on with their precious Saturdays. But Milly loved it here. The bustle and life, the thick steam from the green-encrusted liquor pots and the delicious gravy smells that wafted up from the pies, all spoke of Saturday freedom.

3

She liberally doused her dinner with vinegar, and lifted the first delicious mouthful.

'Mmm, taste that, Kit!'

But her workmate was a fussy eater, though how she'd managed that, in a houseful of seven children, Milly couldn't fathom. Kitty was a skinny girl who seemed to live on air.

'It's all right, but I don't know why everyone raves about it,' Kitty said, putting delicate forkfuls into her mouth.

'I should think you'd be glad of a change from bread and drippin', that's all you get in your house, innit?' asked Peggy, shovelling in another mouthful.

After a few more forkfuls Kitty pushed her plate away and Peggy, who could always find room, asked, 'Don't you want the rest? I'll 'ave it.'

'Peggy, you gannet,' said Milly. 'It's a wonder you're not half the size of a house the way you pack it in.' Milly looked on in astonishment as the girl devoured the rest of Kitty's dinner.

'Comes of starvin' as a kid,' Peggy said solemnly. She was also from a big Dockhead family, but her father had rarely been in work and Peggy had grown up used to going without. Where Kitty had learned to eat less, Peggy's appetite seemed to have grown in proportion to her lack. 'My dad says I've got hollow legs.' She smiled.

While they waited for Peggy to finish, Kitty went to get them three mugs of dark brown tea.

'You meeting Pat tonight?' she asked Milly, as she slid the mugs across the marble table.

Milly shook her head. 'He's working.'

'Oh, *working*. Moonlighting more like!' Peggy said.

Pat Donovan had managed to buy his own lorry by the time he was nineteen, largely on the proceeds of stolen goods. He was one of Milly's drinking pals at the Folly, a pub her father never used. The group of friends would often go to dances at Dockhead Church Hall, but over the past couple of months Pat had begun to single her out to be his partner, and almost without realizing she had a choice in the matter, it seemed accepted that they were courting.

'It might not be an *honest* bob, but at least he's out earning something. He's a grafter!'

Peggy was silenced, perhaps thinking of her own father, whose working day consisted of walking down to the call-on gates at Butler's Wharf in the hopes of getting some dock work and then walking home again, disappointed.

'Well, you might as well come with us to the pub then,' Kitty said.

Milly agreed and stood up abruptly. 'Come on, Peg!' She had waited long enough for Peggy to scrape the plate clean. She pulled it away, leaving Peggy with her knife poised.

'Oi, I haven't finished!'

'You have now,' Milly said, pulling her up. The girls pushed through the crush at the door and out into the bright day.

'First stop, the Old Clo'!' said Milly.

The market was crammed with people; there was barely enough room between the stalls for the crowd to get through. Trousers, suits, dresses and coats were piled high, and it took a lot of patience to discover anything decent amongst the dross. Milly loved to root around, picking up old garments made of good material that might have been overlooked simply because they were out of fashion. While she was sorting through one stall, Kitty and Peggy went off in search of stockings and underwear. After half an hour they met up with their spoils. Milly held up a coat of navy-blue wool. 'What do you think of this?'

Kitty wrinkled her nose. 'Looks like my mum's!'

'Use your imagination! Feel, it's lovely material! I'll make it into a wrap-around.' She produced another threadbare jacket with fur trimming which was still in good condition. 'I'll take the fur off this one and make it into a collar!'

Kitty's eyes lit up. 'You couldn't make one for me an'all while you're at it, could you?'

After strolling the length of Tower Bridge Road, and examining every stall, Milly still didn't want to go home. Her father, only ever known as the old man, would be rolling in from his lunchtime drinking session about now. Sometimes he fell into bed, to sleep the rest of the afternoon away, before getting up for his evening at the pub. Other times he would sit slumped in his armchair by the fire, like some sleeping dragon, ready for Milly or one of her two sisters to trip over his outstretched legs. Then he would roar, flicking them with the back of his hand. She suggested they get a tram down to Greenwich Park.

'I can't go, got to look after the kids this afternoon,' said Peggy, 'but I'll meet you at the Folly tonight. Cheerio!'

As Peggy left them, Milly spotted a tram. 'Come on, Kit, we can still catch it!' The girls ran at full pelt, hopping on to the back board, just as the tram pulled out into Grange Road. Settling breathlessly down on the top deck, Milly took off her cloche hat, letting the breeze lift her hair. Turning to Kitty, she asked suddenly, 'What do you think of Pat?'

Perhaps she had caught her friend unprepared, but Milly felt her hesitate.

'He's nice enough, I suppose, but . . .'

'But what?' Milly pressed.

'Well, he's never going to be much good, is he?'

Milly was surprised that she didn't feel more hurt at her friend's assessment.

'What, because he's on the fiddle?'

Kitty shook her head. 'Who's not? It's not so much *that* as, well, you must have heard about the girl from Rotherhithe?'

Milly shook her head. 'No, tell me.'

But just then the tram came to a halt and they clattered down the stairs. As they passed through the ornate iron gates, Milly prompted her friend.

'Go on then, what about the girl from Rotherhithe?'

'He got her up the duff and then sodded off.'

Milly could certainly believe it. Pat's hands were continually wandering to her dress buttons after a night at the pub. But so far she'd always been able to slap him down and keep him in order. Her physical strength was useful for more than hefting baskets of fruit or seven-pound stone jam jars.

'Well, he won't do that to me!' she said grimly.

'Just be careful, Milly,' her friend said. 'I've noticed these days you get pissed as a puddin' when you're out with him. Sometimes you can't even walk, let alone push him off!'

'Oh, I can look after myself!' Milly laughed, then grabbing Kitty's hand, she began running towards the boating lake.

Milly spent the next hour rowing them round the lake, making sure she splashed Kitty liberally for her assertion that she was turning into a drunk.

'Come in, number nine! You'll tip that boat up!' The boat keeper had seen her antics and was frantically waving them in, calling their number on his megaphone. Milly gave one last thwack with the oar and as the spray flew high over the boat, glinting in the late afternoon sun, she saw a rainbow form. Taking it as a good omen, she put Kitty's suggestions about Pat firmly to the back of her mind, and rowed hard for the bank.

'You're banned!' the boat keeper said as they tumbled, giggling and soaking wet, out of the boat. He was a grey-haired, well-groomed military-looking man, with one arm of his park keeper's uniform pinned up, a not unusual sight since the war. Now, in spite of his ire, he offered them his single hand, helping each of them out of the wobbling boat.

'We're only having a bit of fun!' Milly protested, looking down at her wet feet. 'Nobody got drownded!' Milly smiled as winningly at the boat keeper as she knew how, which seemed to do the trick.

'I'll give you drownded! Clear off, you cheeky minx.' He smiled and the two girls sauntered off down the gravel path, back to the park gates.

'Oh, Kitty, don't you just love to see a bit of sky!'

In Dockhead, where Milly lived, every vista was sliced and slashed by rooftops, chimneys and brick terraces; even the river was largely obscured by slabs of warehouses, and Milly instinctively sought out any open spaces. Now she led her friend off the path, on to the grass, where ancient chestnut trees were all that obscured the sailing clouds. She tipped her head back and began to whirl round, spreading her arms wide, so that the treetops spun in and out of view and she could drink in the cobalt, cloud-painted sky. From here, at the top of Observatory Hill, she could see the Thames snaking away below her, she could pick out the chimneys, belching smoke from Bermondsey factories, and could name each of the crowded docks upstream. She felt alive, full of an irrepressible energy, and began hurtling down the steep hill at breakneck speed.

'Careful!' Kitty called after her.

'Keep up, Kit! I can't stop now!' she called as she careened towards the lower path. At the bottom she pulled herself up short, skidding to a halt on the gravel, while Kitty tottered down gingerly behind her.

'We haven't all got your legs!' she complained as she reached the path.

'Come on, old gel, let me help you home!' Milly scooped Kitty up, swinging her round, ignoring her squeals of protest. If only she could stay out here forever, Milly thought as she whirled, and never have to go back home. For though the Great War had ended all of five years ago, peace had yet to find its way to the Colmans' little terraced house in Arnold's Place.

When she arrived home Milly's high spirits were immediately squashed. Her mother was laying the table ready for the old man's dinner. She was a slight, faded woman in her late forties, but looked older by a decade. Her broad pale face, betraying her Irish descent, creased into papery crinkles as she smiled at Milly. But from the cupboard under the stairs, which led to the tiny coal cellar, came a low snivelling

8

'Why's Elsie in the coal hole?' Milly asked. Her youngest sister, Amy, was never consigned there, so she knew it must be her middle sister, Elsie, undergoing one of her father's punishments.

'Ohhh, I'm sick of it. She cheeked the old man. She never learns.'

Milly dropped her purchases and opened the cupboard, to be confronted by Elsie, an angular thirteen-year-old, her face streaked with coal and tears.

'Why d'ye cheek him, you dozy mare?' Milly asked.

Elsie's skinny frame shook with tremors of small sobs. 'I didn't cheek him. I just said I'd dreamed he was dead . . . which I did!'

Milly raised her eyes, muttering, 'We've all had that dream,' as she pulled her sister out of the cupboard.

'What if he comes down?' Elsie whispered fearfully.

'He's snoring in the bed, it's shaking the bloody ceiling. He won't know any different,' Milly said, wiping her hands of coal dust.

'Jesus, you look like a minstrel. Go and wash your face and hands.' Their mother sent Elsie to the scullery.

'Why did you let her stay in there?' Milly asked accusingly.

'Truth be told, love, I had such a job getting him upstairs to bed and then I was so busy – I forgot all about her! God forgive me.'

Seeing her mother's stricken face, Milly immediately regretted her question. After all, she thought guiltily, while she'd been larking around in the park, her mother had been contending with all the miseries Milly had been avoiding. 'Oh well, Polly Witch *will* tell us her dreams, won't she?' Again came a stab of guilt; it was easier to blame Elsie than the one person who deserved it.

Just then she heard thudding upstairs, followed by a burst of phlegmy coughing from her father. 'I won't need any tea, Mum, had pie and mash with the girls.' And hastily picking up her purchases, she dashed upstairs to her bedroom, before the old man came down and ruined her good mood entirely.

*

Everybody called it the Folly, though its real name had been lost in time, hidden beneath the thick grime that obscured the painted sign above its door. Situated at one end of Hickman's Folly, it looked from the outside like a conventional spit-and-sawdust pub, but the attraction for Milly and her friends was its unconventionality. No one could see in through the windows, veiled as they were with a film of soot, the door was ill-fitting and the exterior betrayed its years beneath peeling layers of paint. Only the bills, plastering the walls like mismatched wallpaper, hinted at its new identity. The latest advertised a night of jazz music from the resident pianist, and therein lay the attraction. By far the best thing about the Folly was Maisie, the pianist. Unlike Harry in the Swan, whose repertoire was restricted to the old tunes Milly's mother liked to sing, Maisie was up to date with all the latest jazz music from America. So long as she always had a full pint glass on top of the piano, she would play all night, and so the younger residents of Dockhead gravitated towards the pub.

It had been a fairly sedate night and Milly and Kitty were trying to liven things up, singing along happily to 'Ain't We Got Fun'.

'There's nothing surer, the rich get rich and the poor get
   poorer!
In the meantime, in between time, ain't we got fun?'

They'd just reached the end of the chorus when Pat walked in, with a tall, fair young man Milly hadn't seen before. Pat made his way over to their table and unable to be heard above the din, mimed a drinking gesture. Peggy and Milly's arms shot out as one, holding up their empty glasses to be refilled.

'Good job I've already earned me bunce tonight!' said Pat, shaking his head. But as he went to the bar Kitty's face fell.

'Well, that's the end of *our* fun for tonight.'

'What's the matter with you?' Milly asked. 'He's all right. At least he offers to buy a round. Shove up.'

Milly made her friend scoot along the bench so there'd be room for Pat and his friend.

'It's just that he takes over,' Kitty whispered, 'and you go all soppy round him, you don't act like yourself at all and it's not even as if he's your type.'

'How do you know what my type is?' Milly snapped. The truth was, she didn't know herself what 'her type' was, so how could anyone else? Surely she wasn't the only one who went out with a feller just because he asked, rather than because she felt much interest? Anyway, how would she know if she never tried?

'Just don't let him keep buying you drinks all night, he's got a wad of notes there the size of me nan's feather mattress!'

Milly had noticed. Pat wasn't averse to flashing his money about, when he had it.

'Oh, Kitty Bunclerk, you're worse than me mother. Shut up now, here he comes.'

Pat came back with the drinks and introduced his friend, Freddie Clark. Pat had mentioned him before as a 'business partner', though Milly had never met him. The men settled down happily in the midst of the girls.

'I thought you'd be out all night?' Milly said to Pat.

'I did too, but my mate Freddie here turned up sooner than I expected. He got some lovely stuff from Atkinson's factory, didn't you, Fred?'

Freddie lifted his glass. 'We should give the girls some samples, mate, before they all go!'

Atkinson's was a Bermondsey perfume and cosmetics factory, situated next to Young's glue factory, an incongruous but convenient location as gelatine from the bone yard ended up in many face creams. Milly had worked there for a while, when she first left school. It had been one of her favourite jobs. Proud of her shapely, long-fingered hands, at Atkinson's she could dip into the moisturizer all day and come home with the soft hands of a lady, instead of a factory girl. Now, looking down at her rough, chapped knuckles and swollen fingers, she wished she still worked there.

'Here y'are, girls.' Freddie dug into his pocket and brought out three small bottles of perfume. 'California Poppy, you'll be smelling like a field of flowers!' He smiled and Milly noticed that Kitty didn't decline. In spite of her criticisms of Pat, she allowed the boys to buy several rounds and by the end of the evening they were all the best of friends, singing along with Maisie.

'Look for the silver lining, when e'er a cloud appears in the blue, remember somewhere the sun is shining, and so the right thing to do, is make it shine for you . . .'

When last orders were called and they all tumbled out of the pub into the cool summer night, the sound of their loud goodnights echoed in the street and Pat caught Milly's hand, asking to walk her home. As the friends went their separate ways, Milly wasn't so tipsy that she didn't notice Kitty walking unsteadily up Hickman's Folly, in the company of Freddie Clark.

Pat put his arm round her, which was welcome, if for no other reason than that the night had turned chilly.

'Shall we walk down to the river?' he asked, and partly because she didn't want to bump into her father coming out of the Swan at the opposite end of Hickman's Folly, she let herself be guided down Jacob Street, to the little jetty at the back of Southwell's jam factory. It was a secluded spot, bounded by Southwell's warehouses and with only the dark river to witness their kisses. But as Pat became more passionate and his hand strayed to her dress front, she remembered the girl from Rotherhithe, and using more force than she intended, shoved his chest with the flat of her hand, sending him toppling backwards.

'Hold up, Milly, you'll have me in the river!' His alarmed face was comical and Milly laughed.

'Oh, don't look so grumpy!' she said, dragging him back into her arms. 'But I'm not as easy as the girls from Rotherhithe!'

'You shouldn't believe everything you hear,' Pat said, tight-lipped.

She kissed him lightly on the cheek and spun round. 'No one's said nothing to me, must be your guilty conscience. Come on, walk me home.'

At the corner of Arnold's Place she let him kiss her goodnight but after he left her, standing beneath the gas lamp outside Mrs Knight's, she heard footsteps behind. Turning to see why he'd come back, she felt a ringing blow to the side of her head that sent her spinning against the wall. Her cheek grazed sooty brick, and for a moment the gaslight seemed to pale. Her fingers scrabbled for the window sill as she tried to steady herself.

'You little slut!' It was the old man. Grabbing her by the shoulder, he frogmarched her towards their front door.

'What? I've done nothing!' Milly pleaded, but his hand was a vice and she couldn't wriggle away.

'You dare show me up, letting him paw you in the street like a prossie! Get in there!' He flung her into the house but she was ready for him now, and the minute he released his grip she leaped free, bounding up the stairs. She was in the bedroom with the chair firmly jammed under the handle before he could catch her. Holding her breath, her head pounding and blood trickling from the graze on her cheek, she waited. But she heard no following footsteps. *Too pissed to get up the stairs*, she thought, *probably conked out in the kitchen*. Turning towards the bed she shared with her sisters, she heard Elsie's sleepy, sweet singing voice coming from the bed: '*Every morning, every evening, ain't we got fun . . .*'

Milly groaned and, slipping off her frock, made her way gratefully to the bed. She got in beside Elsie, who allowed her to snuggle up in the warm spot she'd made.

'Did he get you?' Elsie asked drowsily.

'Nah, too slow.'

'Good.' Elsie yawned.

'Good,' Amy echoed from the other end of the bed, gripping Milly's cold foot with her small warm hand.

13

If only it could always be like this between her and her sisters, Milly thought as she drifted off to sleep, but she knew the fragile threads that bound them together tonight could so easily tear apart, and tomorrow they would be at war again.

2

The Set of Jugs

June 1923

'Gawd, *Jesus*, Mary'n Joseph, bless us'n spare us'n save us'n keep us! Don't you know the war's over? I leave you for five minutes!'

Ellen Colman stood at the kitchen doorway. She was holding a matching set of three blue willow-pattern jugs, the largest in one hand and the two smaller hooked into the fingers of her other hand. She watched as her daughters fought, entangled in a struggling mass of flailing arms and legs. 'Why can't you three just be friends?' she said in exasperation.

Milly Colman's grip on her sister did not relax. Holding Elsie at arm's length, she looked calmly over at her mother, tightening her strong fingers around the younger girl's pale skinny wrist. Elsie launched herself forward, kicking out furiously at Milly's shins. But her fragile frame was no match for Milly, who at seventeen was tall, powerful and swift. Effortlessly she held Elsie at bay, while Amy, the youngest of the Colman sisters, attacked Milly from below, darting around her legs like a snapping terrier and pinching her calves whenever she got close enough. Milly fended her off with one leg, while balancing perfectly on the other.

'It's not me!' Milly protested. 'It's her.' She gave Elsie a shake. 'She's a nutter!'

'Well, you shouldn't have called me "Dolly Daydream"!' Elsie gasped, her energy all but expended against Milly's immovable force. Elsie's sharply jutting pixie chin was the last lingering

15

evidence of her defiance and Milly judged it safe to loose her grip. Then, with a careless shove, she propelled her sister into the quicksilver path of Amy. The collision winded the nine-year-old, who bumped down on to the rag rug, gasping for air. The enmity between the Colman sisters, now only evident in their glares, seemed to fill the room with its fizzing energy.

'You wear me out,' said their mother, wearily stepping over Amy, before placing the three jugs on the kitchen table. She was careful with them, for they were the only matching crockery she possessed. 'Three boys I managed to bring up, gawd rest their souls, without 'apporth the trouble you three give me.' At the mention of her sons, Mrs Colman's slight form seemed to flicker like a dying candle flame. She crossed herself.

Milly blanched at the gesture. 'Don't do that,' she said flatly, reaching for her mother's hand. Then defiantly, 'Anyway, Wilf's not dead!'

Her youngest brother had been the only one of the three boys to return from the war. He had quickly re-enlisted, posted to the Gold Coast.

'No, but he might as well be dead for all we'll ever see of him again. He wasn't back home a week before he got fed up of you girls rowing and gawd knows what. No wonder he thought he might as well stay in the army!'

This was a fiction Milly couldn't allow her mother to get away with. 'Don't blame us! You know it was the old man drove him away,' she said.

Mrs Colman pursed her lips and chose to ignore Milly's last remark. She sighed heavily. 'It's what I get for having girls, I suppose.'

'Well, I didn't do *nothing*!' Amy sat pulling at the rug with sulky fingers. As the youngest she often got away without a telling off, but not today.

'Don't you play the innocent, you always have to put your two penn'orth in, don't you?' snapped her mother. 'Anyway, I don't care who started it, you're all as bad as each other.'

She picked up the largest of the jugs, shoving it into Milly's hands.

'Go down the butcher's and get me six penn'orth o' faggots and pease pudding for the old man's tea.' She held out the medium-sized jug to Elsie. 'You, stop your snivelling, take this down the Swan and Sugarloaf for his pint of bitter.'

She held out the smallest of the jugs to Amy, who had turned a defiant back on her mother and was now kicking the brass fender. Ellen Colman pulled her up by the back of her dress. 'I've just about had enough of you an'all. Go to Hughes the grocer's and get a penn'orth o' jam in this.' Handing her the jug, she placed a penny into her daughter's other hand. 'And hurry up, all of you, or the old man'll be screaming for his tea and then you'll be for it.'

The three girls made a dash for the passage, each vying to be the first through the front door. Milly emerged triumphant into Arnold's Place, swinging the large china jug loosely at her side, closely followed by Elsie, a head shorter, who cupped her jug like a chalice. Amy skipped along behind, attempting to balance the smallest jug on her head.

'There goes the set of jugs,' said Mrs Knight to Pat's mother, old Ma Donovan from Hickman's Folly. The sisters might look like a set of three, as they processed in descending order beneath the glimmering gas lamp, but in truth they were as mismatched as all the rest of their mother's crockery.

'Better move yerselves, girls, before the shops shut!' Mrs Knight called out to them, but as she passed by, Milly heard her mutter to old Ma Donovan, 'If that vicious old bastard Colman gets home and there's no tea on the table, them girls'll know all about it!'

Milly smiled and waved the jug threateningly at Mrs Knight. 'Let him just try it!' she said defiantly, but in spite of her bravado, the memory of that last blow to the head he'd given her made her quicken her pace. The old man's temper was best not roused, especially not on a Friday night, when he was looking forward to a drink at the Swan and Sugarloaf with his mates.

Arnold's Place was a long, narrow row of two-up two-downs, facing each other across a paved alley. The light struggled to edge its way into the houses by day, and by night its dimness was relieved only by the single gas lamp, attached to Mrs Knight's wall. Clustered beneath the lamp now, children played a ball game, while a baby in a battered old pram screamed with excited laughter every time the ball arced over it. Mrs Knight and Mrs Donovan, arms crossed over their pinafores, looked on, seemingly unworried that the baby would come to harm from the wooden cricket ball.

Milly hurried towards Dockhead. She could hear her sisters following, but didn't slacken her pace until she passed Hughes the grocer, then she allowed herself a brief look back to make sure Amy had gone in for the penn'orth of jam. Elsie would have the furthest to go, right to the end of Arnold's Place and the pub on the corner of Hickman's Folly. Milly was already in the butcher's when Elsie ambled by. Her bobbed straight hair framed her face like a pixie cap, and she had that dreamy look on her face. She would take all night, Milly thought, and then they'd all have to pay for it when the old man was kept waiting for his beer.

While Barnes the butcher was filling her jug with hot faggots and pease pudding, she tried to remember what today's argument had been about. Nothing really, that was always the way. Elsie talked rubbish sometimes, and it annoyed her.

I'm going to be in the films when I grow up. I'll be on at the Star and you can all come and see me. That's what she'd said, and when Milly, who'd worked at Southwell's jam factory on and off since leaving school three years ago, told her not to be a Dolly Daydream, that she'd be a factory girl same as everyone else, Elsie had flown into one of her mad fits. When she got like that, all Milly could do was fend her off. Now she felt sorry about the fight, mostly for her mother's sake. She had looked so weary.

'And an extra one for the prettiest girl in Arnold's Place!' said the butcher.

She came out of her musing, to see Barnes beaming at her, ladling the extra faggot into her jug.

'How's your poor mother?' he asked. For some reason Mrs Colman's name was always prefixed by 'poor'. Perhaps because of her two dead soldier sons, but there wasn't a house in Arnold's Place who'd escaped that sort of grief. No, Millie thought bitterly, it had more to do with being married to the old man.

'Not too bad, Mr Barnes. Can you put this on the slate?'

Barnes looked up sharply as he put a large dollop of orange pease pudding over the faggots.

'Only till tomorrow . . .' Milly lied, crossing her fingers behind her back. She was going to confession tomorrow anyway. He turned to the slate.

'Just tell your mother it's addin' up,' he said, and she smiled gratefully as he handed her the jug. He'd tied oiled paper over the top, but the smell of the faggot gravy wafted up tantalizingly as she hurried home. The lion's share would go to the old man, but her mother would mix up what was left in some onion gravy for the rest of them. It was already beginning to get dark when she reached her front door, and she prayed he wasn't home yet. Her mother, who was stirring the gravy on the range, spun round as Milly entered.

'Thank gawd you're back with the faggots! Run and get Elsie for me, love, while I put these on.' She jerked her head towards the scullery. Milly heard sluicing sounds coming from the stone sink. 'He's home.'

Thrusting the jug into her mother's hands, Milly turned on her heel and ran. Her father's targets were usually the ones nearest to hand, and Milly didn't want him venting his displeasure on her mother. Amy would be all right, still small enough to find a corner to roll into and hide. Milly sped all the way back to the Swan and Sugarloaf before she finally found Elsie. The pink bow in her hair was slightly askew, giving her a disturbingly lopsided appearance. Her dress didn't help matters; a worn cast-off of Milly's, inexpertly shortened by her mother, it drooped at the front. Milly wished she'd done the sewing herself. She would have made a much better job of it. It looked a disgrace, but Elsie's imagination had no doubt transformed it into a ball gown because she was walking in stately fashion, holding the beer jug like a bouquet, nodding and smiling graciously to imaginary crowds on either side.

'Oi! Cinderella!' Milly shouted in her strong, rather throaty voice. 'You're not going to the soddin' ball – get a move on, the old man's home!'

Elsie, shocked out of her daydream, started forward in a half walk, half trot which had the beer slopping over the edge of the jug.

'Give us it here. There'll be nothing left of it by the time we get home.'

She carefully took the jug from Elsie, who didn't protest, and soon Milly with her steady, long strides had outstripped her, managing to spill not one drop of beer on the way.

When she slipped into the kitchen, her father was already sitting down to his faggots and pease pudding. He looked up briefly.

'Put it there.' He jabbed a finger next to his plate. Setting the jug down on the table, which she noticed had been covered with a clean cloth, she went to fetch the old man's glass. Her mother stood stirring faggots in the stew pot, her face tight and body held rigid over the range. He must have started on her already. For Milly, it was never a dilemma. If she could only ever protect one person in the house, it had to be her mother. Amy largely escaped his rages, so quick on her feet she could easily evade a kick or a jab, and Elsie could always retreat into that fantasy world of hers after a hiding. But her mother . . . she insisted on standing like a punch bag between the old man and her children. She never seemed to think of protecting herself. Milly always had to do it for her.

Her father had scrubbed himself pink, his dark hair brushed back from his forehead, his drooping moustache trimmed. Part of his redness was due to his drinking habits. But he had shaved carefully with his cut-throat razor and had already changed out of his work clothes. After a day at Bevington's, the leather mills in the Neckinger, he would come home with the stink of lime and chemicals clinging to him, and though he wore a thick apron at work, his clothes always seemed to smell of dead animals. His hands would be stained black, red or green, depending on what dyes he'd been mixing that day. Demanding scalding water and lots of carbolic soap as soon as he came in, he sometimes scrubbed his hands till they bled. Milly had to give him that, he was a scrupulously clean man. But she thought any other virtues must have passed over him in the womb. The good fairy never waved any magic wand over the old man's crib, she was sure of that.

After downing his pint of bitter, he wiped his moustache with the back of his hand and stood up. Milly kept herself stationed between him and her mother, but he seemed calm enough as he pulled his jacket off the hook and jammed on his flat cap, though Milly knew he was always unpredictable. As he passed, he shot a hand out over Milly's shoulder, grabbing her mother's hair.

'Don't serve that shit up to me again, you get enough house-keeping to give me a decent, cooked dinner after a day's work.' Milly felt her mother flinch as he tugged harder. Fortunately, his thirst outweighed his displeasure and he stalked out, only to trip over Elsie, seated on the front doorstep. Milly heard him stumble, then his growled 'Dozy mare!' and the thud of his boot connecting with Elsie.

Her sister came in whimpering and nestled into her mother's worn pinafore, like a small child. She looked up. 'He's messed up me grotto!'

Grottos were the latest craze with the children of Arnold's Place, who would put flotsam and jetsam, and 'precious' objects, into artistic arrangements laid out on the pavement. Some pretty shells from the seafood stall, pebbles or blue glass polished by the Thames or pieces of driftwood gleaned from the foreshore, anything to bring a splash of beauty into the slate-grey street.

21

'Remember the grotto' was every child's hopeful refrain to passers-by, who would toss a halfpenny into their laps. But Elsie didn't care about the pennies; she always built her grottos for love.

'Oh, Elsie, you're too old for street games, and anyway you shouldn't be making grottos on the doorstep, love!' her mother said gently.

'I was only practising.' Elsie sniffed, holding out a handful of beads from a broken bracelet. Milly recognized it instantly.

'That's mine, you thieving little magpie!' She made a grab for Elsie, while Amy dived to scoop up the scattered beads bouncing across the lino.

'Mine now!' Amy piped up triumphantly.

Their mother threw the ladle into the stew pot. 'Gawd, *Jesus*, Mary'n Joseph, bless us'n spare us'n save us'n keep us, as if I didn't have enough to put up with!'

Her voice suddenly broke and she bowed her head over the pot. 'What with *him* always at me and my boys gone, all gone . . .' Ellen Colman took in a shuddering breath and Milly was at her side, drawing her mother's heaving shoulders into her strong embrace. 'Oh, it'd be different if the boys were here,' Mrs Colman moaned hoarsely.

Milly squeezed her tighter and gazed over her head at the photograph of the three sisters, ranged like a set of jugs. It had its mirror image at the opposite end of the mantelpiece, with a photo of three little boys in an almost identical pose – her brothers Charlie and Jimmy, now lying dead in Belgian graves, and lastly Wilf, still soldiering under a baking African sun. None of them would be coming home again. Perhaps her mother was right. If only her brothers had been in the house, the old man's reign of terror might have been curbed, yet she doubted it. Wilf *could* have stayed home after the war but he'd run from his bullying father, and however much her mother might hope for his return, he was as dead to them as Charlie and Jimmy.

As Ellen Colman tried to stifle her sobs, Milly saw that Elsie and Amy were staring at her, motionless as crouching statues now, looking up from the floor with anxious faces, all trace of their argument vanished.

'Don't cry, Mum,' was all she said. 'The boys ain't coming back, but you've got me, I'll sort the old man out, I can fight as good as any man!'

Her mother straightened up, rubbed at her face, then put a hand, still wet with her own tears, against Milly's cheek. Suddenly she smiled. 'Kill 'em an' eat 'em, you would . . . that's my Milly.'

The Letter

August–September 1923

A dank mist hung heavy over Arnold's Place as Milly left the house and began walking towards the river. She was on the early shift at Southwell's, only a ten-minute walk away, on the riverside by Bermondsey Wall, which was a blessing on such a chilly morning. She pulled her coat closely around her, surely summer wasn't over already? If only the letter would come. Every year it was the same. The neighbours would stand at their doors, calling out to each other, 'Had your letter yet?' The letter from the farmer meant five precious weeks in the real countryside, away from the roofs and chimneys that blocked out all but a pitiful patch of the Bermondsey sky. She couldn't wait to breathe fresh air instead of choking smoke from dozens of factory chimneys. She longed for that first sharp scent of acid green hops as she stripped them from the bines. She didn't even mind her fingers turning black; it wasn't much different from the purple or red they were normally stained, from sorting fruits at the factory. The greatest blessing of all, though, was having a break from the old man; he stayed at home, working and drinking. But it wasn't every year your family was chosen to go to the hop fields, sometimes the harvest was poor and the farmer didn't need so many pickers. And this year their letter hadn't arrived.

Turning into Jacob Street, she joined a stream of other women and girls heading towards the factory gates. Two tall chimneys with *Southwell's* painted on them were already spewing smoke into the pink-tinged sky, and a low rumble, like thunder beneath her feet, came from the great steam engines in the factory basement, which heated the boiling pans and drove the machine belts. Milly would be working in the picking room today. She sniffed to see which fruit had already been started. Blackcurrants! Her fingers would be stained deep purple by the end of the day.

The yard was surrounded by four six-storey buildings. Two were warehouses, the others housed the picking, boiling, filling and finishing rooms. Beyond the buildings she glimpsed the river, where the factory's own wharf was jammed with lighters and barges delivering sugar and fruit or being loaded with stone jars of the factory's preserves. Southwell's didn't just make jam. There was marmalade in the Seville orange season, candied peel and pickles, and even Christmas puddings.

'Mind yer back!' a stores man shouted at her. Looking up quickly, she saw a trolley loaded with sugar sacks trundling towards her on one of the tracks that criss-crossed the yard. Leaping over the rails, she side-stepped into the path of another trolley, full of stone jam jars, coming from the opposite direction.

'Oi, Milly, wakey, wakey!' Two young men, working above her at a first-floor loading bay, shouted a warning. Dodging the second trolley, she waved up at them gratefully.

'You coming to the Folly for a drink tonight?' One of the boys, a drinking pal of Pat's, leaned further out of the loading bay.

'Might do if I live that long!' She hurried on, through the double doors. The truth was that she was tiring of spending her nights drinking at the Folly with Pat. This morning she had a head full of cotton wool and the last thing she felt like was another drinking bout. Bounding up the stone stairs two at a time, in an attempt to shake her sluggishness, she reached the top floor with her head thumping. Once in the vast, high-windowed picking room, she wrapped a coarse, green apron around her and pulled a white hat well down over her head. She hated the hat, it squashed her dark, wavy hair, so that she emerged at the end of the day looking like a wet seal. She made her way through rows of wooden bins and chutes, full of tumbling fruit, till she reached her own picking line where, with a hundred-odd other girls, she would spend the next ten hours sorting through blackcurrants. Her cheerful good morning was echoed back by all the girls within earshot, as a whoosh of steam from the boiler room fired up the de-stalking machine. It chugged into life, belts whirring and blackcurrants flying, their stalks plucked off at lightning speed. The new machine, installed only last year, now did the work a hundred girls would once have done by hand. Blackcurrants tumbled like black pearls down wide wooden chutes as Milly began her day's work. Standing next to Kitty, she soon got into a rhythm, fingers flying, hands a blur, so that she hardly registered what she was doing as her hands moved automatically, picking and flicking away the bad fruits into a wicker basket beneath the chute. The other part of her mind concentrated on what Kitty was saying.

'My mum's got her letter. Your mum got your letter yet?' Kitty asked.

Milly shook her head. 'I don't think it's coming this year.'

'Well, I'm not going, what do you want to give up a good job for, just so you can spend weeks on end in a bloody tin hut in the middle of nowhere?' said Kitty. 'And the money's piss poor. I can't see the attraction meself.'

'If you had to live with our old man you'd see the attraction.' Milly pulled a face, making Kitty laugh.

'Well, you're doing yerself no favours picking hops, love, are you. That's what makes the beer that turns him into such a mean bastard!' Kitty grinned.

'You've got a point there, Kit, but I need to get away for a bit . . . he's getting worse, and being on my own with him, well . . .'

Kitty shot her a look. 'Sorry, love, you know you're always welcome to come round to us to get out of his way.'

The Bunclerks' crowded home in Hickman's Folly had often been a temporary refuge from her own warring household when she was growing up, but with nine people and only two bedrooms, Kitty's offer was kind but impractical.

'Thanks, Kit, but I need to get right away.'

As the noon hooter signalled their release and the clattering machinery belts came to an abrupt silence, Kitty linked arms with her.

'If only I had the money and could get a place of me own, I'd be off like a shot,' Milly said as they joined the crowd of women jamming the stairwell.

Kitty laughed abruptly. 'Do me a favour, you'd *never* leave those sisters of yours!'

She was about to protest, but in the face of Kitty's knowing look, she held her tongue. Milly's hard exterior might fool most people, but her friend had known her too long to be taken in.

'And I'll tell you another thing for nothing, if you'd only let them see how much you think of them, they'd give you a lot less trouble.'

Milly shook her head. She'd stopped trying to fathom why, when she held a hand out to her sisters, it was usually firmly slapped away. But all she said was, 'I doubt it, trouble's their middle names.'

The girls made their way to the dining hall. Always referred to as 'the mess room', it was a long, low-ceilinged room, full of wooden benches and tables, where workers who didn't want to go home for lunch could eat their sandwiches and drink their bottles of cold tea. They found a bench and Kitty returned to the subject of hop-picking. 'But what if you can't get your job back this time?'

Milly shrugged. 'I can always get another factory job.'

And in past years she always had, if not at Southwell's, then at Hartley's or Peek Frean's. She could even go tin bashing at Feaver's. And though some considered hopping harder work than the factory, for Milly, it was her only holiday and she was determined to take it.

That evening when she returned home she found a large wooden crate half-filling the tiny kitchen. Mounted on four wheels, with two broomstick handles nailed to one end, it was a rough-and-ready handcart. Her mother stood over it, smiling.

'The hopping box!' The sight brought a sudden smile to Millie's face and she threw her arms round her mother. 'You got the letter!'

'Yes, love, we're going to Horsmonden, same farm as last year.'

Milly pulled away, looking puzzled. 'What's the matter, you don't look very pleased about it?'

Normally the packing of the hopping box filled her mother with a rare excitement.

'I'm pleased.' Mrs Colman hesitated. 'But . . . well, it's just we've got to shift ourselves now, doesn't give us much time to fill up the hopping box.'

Just then Amy came in from the scullery, carrying a roll of lino almost as tall as herself. She tripped over the rug and Milly dived to catch her just in time.

'Here, give me that.' Plucking the lino from Amy's hands, she transferred it to the box.

Amy scowled. 'I was doing that!'

'Don't start as soon as Milly gets in, she was only trying to help.' Her mother gave Amy a warning look. 'Go and see what's happened to Elsie, she's probably fallen down the privy!'

Milly peeped into the box, which was already half full. There was a bolt of tough ticking material for making mattresses, some old cooking pots and crockery, a roll of wallpaper and several tins of food.

'I don't know what you're worried about. You're getting on well!'

The mere sight of the box filled Milly with anticipation. It was tucked away in the backyard all year, a promise of escape. Some women filled it up gradually over the year, but Milly's mother was too superstitious for that, and always waited for the farmer's letter to arrive first. The box had to carry everything they'd need for a five- or six-week stay in the wooden hopping hut. Some families stayed in the same hut each year and even took their own furniture, but the old man wouldn't have that.

'Oh, Mum, I've been dreaming about it all day. I can't wait!' said Milly as she took off her coat and set about slicing cold meat for the family's tea. When Mrs Colman didn't answer, Milly looked up, but her mother avoided her gaze. 'Oh, love, I should've said something earlier, but I kept thinking he'd change his mind.'

'What do you mean?' Milly found she was forgetting to breathe. 'What's happened?'

'You can't go hopping this year,' her mother blurted out in a rush. 'The old man won't have it. Says you've got to stick at Southwell's.'

'Can't go?' Milly's throat tightened and she was shocked to find herself on the verge of tears. Even she hadn't been aware just how much this meant to her. It didn't help that Elsie and Amy were giggling over the hopping box, impervious to her disappointment.

'But he's let me go hopping the last three years and I've *always* got another job after. Why can't I go this year?'

Her mother shook her head. 'He says our hopping money's not enough and Southwell's is too good to give up. He says there won't always be other jobs to walk into.'

Milly left the meat unsliced. Ashamed of the tears pricking her eyes, she walked to the shelf and took down the smallest blue willow-pattern jug.

'I'm sorry, love, don't get upset—'

'We've got no pickle for the meat. I'll go to Hughes,' she said, hurrying out before her mother could see the tear trickling down her cheek.

In the street, she brushed it away and set off for the grocer's, sprinting as fast as her long legs could take her. If only her feet had wings attached and she could fly up above the streets and docks, high over the Thames, eastward over London till she reached the green hop gardens of Kent. But that was stupid thinking, the sort that got Elsie into so much trouble. She slapped to a halt outside Hughes, chest heaving, clutching her ribs where a stitch had caught her suddenly.

She hated going into the grocery, for Hughes was a superior man with a stony face, full of unspoken criticism. She'd known him since childhood, but he never smiled at her. Even the way she asked for jam or pickle seemed to draw a withering look from Hughes. He wasn't from around Dockhead, but however much he disapproved of the 'Bermondsey Irish' who lived there, he didn't seem to mind taking their money. The Colmans were Bermondsey Irish, Milly's mother one of the descendants of Irish navvies who'd come over a hundred years earlier to build London's first railway viaduct. The little Irish community, sometimes just called 'the caddywacks', had clustered around St Saviour's Dock, forming an enclave within Bermondsey. Hughes was definitely not a caddywack and he let you know it.

'Two penn'orth o' pickle, please!' She defiantly banged her mother's precious jug on to the marble counter before realizing it wasn't Hughes standing behind it. Instead there was a young man she judged must be in his mid-twenties. She thought there was a resemblance to Hughes, the same fresh colouring, neat ears and nose, but there the likeness ended. He had a pleasant oval face and clear blue eyes, with eyebrows that slanted upwards like little wings. He raised one of these now to comical effect.

'Someone's not happy!' he said, smiling at her.

'Sorry,' she muttered. 'I thought you were Hughes.'

He chuckled. 'He has that effect on me as well, sometimes,' he half whispered. 'But I am a Hughes too, Bertie Hughes. I'm his nephew.'

'Ohh,' Milly said, taken aback by his friendliness. 'I didn't know he had any family. He doesn't live round here.'

Bertie Hughes carefully weighed Milly's jug and then spooned the mustard pickle out of a seven-pound jar on the counter.

'No, we come from Dulwich way. I've been working in the Camberwell shop, but he's moved me here for a few weeks, says he needs a holiday.'

'A holiday? Lucky sod. Probably just wants to get away from the Bermondsey rough,' she said bluntly.

He grinned. 'Probably.'

Then she had to laugh with him. For some reason the encounter with Bertie Hughes had lightened her mood, and she left with the beginnings of a plan to ensure she would still have that 'holiday' of her own.

But for her plan to work, she would need her mother's help. And so, that evening after the old man had gone to the Swan and Sugarloaf and her sisters were in bed, she sat opposite her mother in the quiet kitchen. Without the tension of her father's presence or the conflict with her sisters, this was always Milly's favourite time of the day. Ellen Colman had been struggling to darn one of the old man's jackets; her weak eyes meant she wasn't a good needlewoman.

'Here, Mum, I'll do it,' Milly offered. Taking the needle carefully from her mother's hand, she decided to broach her plan. 'What if I just go hopping for a week?'

Her mother began shaking her head.

'Mum, just listen a minute. Southwell's will let me have a week off unpaid, and what if I promise Dad I can make more picking than I'll get in wages?'

'Twelve bob? You'll have to pick ten hours a day to do that!'

'No, I won't, don't forget what I do all day! My fingers are twice as quick as yours. I'll do it easily!' Her mother must know it was true; everything Milly did was swift and deft. Often when they sat sewing in the evening she would catch Mrs Colman watching her. 'It's a wonder you don't stab yourself, the speed you go at!' her mother would say.

'So, Mum, will *you* ask him?'

Mrs Colman shifted in her seat and Milly felt a blush rising to her cheeks, feeling cowardly for asking her mother to do it. But if she suggested it herself, he would never listen.

Her mother considered for a long moment, while Milly's blush deepened. She was praying silently her mother would agree.

'I'm not promising nothing, so don't get your hopes up. But all right, I'll ask him.'

Milly dropped the darning, and flung her arms round her mother, squeezing her tightly. 'Thanks, Mum,' she said, kissing her on the cheek.

'That's all right, darlin', I know how you love it down hopping.'

Sitting her rangy body on her mother's lap, she hooked her long legs over the arm of the chair. Milly rested her head against her mother's as she had when she was small.

'Get off me now, you're squashing me half to death, yer great lump.' Her mother shoved her off, but not before planting a kiss on her cheek.

Milly suffered a whole week of gnawing anxiety, while her mother waited to pick her moment. It wasn't until the hopping box was full to bursting and the day for the family's departure to Kent had arrived that Mrs Colman found the courage to speak to the old man. It was Saturday afternoon, pay day, when her father felt rich, with his suit out of the pawnshop and a pocket full of change for his bet and beer. They were all sitting round the kitchen table after their dinner of mutton stew, one of the old man's favourites. Milly gave her mother a meaningful look and a small nod towards her father. The old man didn't approve of talking at the dinner table and propped a little bamboo cane by his plate, to keep his children in order. She and Amy had long ago learned to keep their thoughts to themselves at family meals. Elsie's knuckles, however, were permanently bruised, as a sharp rap from the cane regularly failed to halt her unruly thoughts from tumbling out. Milly's mother took a deep breath, and her cough broke the silence.

'Me and the kids'll be going tonight then.'

The old man grunted, 'Well, make sure you're quiet, I don't want you waking me up at two in the morning.'

Milly thought it highly unlikely that anything would wake him after his Saturday night pot full, and anyway, the family knew the drill so well, it was like a military operation. They'd be out of bed just after midnight, last-minute items packed into the hopping box and the girls bundled up in layers of clothing. They would creep out of the house, in time to catch the four o'clock 'hopping special' train from London Bridge. The old man never usually stirred.

'I was thinking it'd be good if Milly could come for a week, though, it would do me a turn, helping with the kids,' her mother said lightly.

Clever Mum, Milly thought, *don't for an instant let him know how much I want to go.* Her father said nothing. His thick, leather-tanned fingers rolled the cane back and forth across the table.

'I've already told you, woman,' he barked, 'she can't go, we need her wages!'

Milly jumped. 'But I'm the best picker down there. I can earn more than twelve bob, easy!' she blurted out.

The old man's coal-dark eyes lit with a slow burning ember, then suddenly the cane flashed in the air, whipping down across her hand. Stifling her cry as pain shot up her arm, she stuffed her hand under her armpit. The two younger girls sat stock-still and her mother shook her head imperceptibly. The fight was over as far as her mother was concerned, but for Milly it was only just beginning.

That night she didn't sleep. As her sisters' breathed and snored beside her in untroubled slumber, Milly lay awake, watching the moon move slowly across the sky. At two o'clock the door to their bedroom creaked open and her mother crept over to the bed.

'I'm sorry, love, once he's made up his mind . . .'

'Don't worry, Mum, you did your best.' Her mother had taken hold of the damaged hand, and Milly winced. She hoped he hadn't cracked any finger bones, for her work depended on her nimble fingers. She eased herself out of bed, nipping across the freezing lino, to pull on her stockings and clothes. She'd promised her mother she'd help get the box and her sisters to London Bridge. If she couldn't go herself, she'd still have the thrill of the excited crowds as they jostled along the platform, jamming themselves and all their chattels into the too few carriages. She helped Amy get her things together, but the child was sleepy and truculant, and as Milly brushed her hair the younger girl squealed. 'You're hurting me.'

Milly tapped her on the head with the brush. 'Shhh! You'll wake him up, then you'll be staying behind with me! Do you want that?'

Amy shook her head and followed meekly as Milly led her sisters gingerly down the creaking staircase to the kitchen, where their mother had a single candle burning. Bundled into their coats, they left quietly, Milly carefully closing the front door behind them. Their mother took Amy's hand and Elsie followed with a bundle of clothes under her arm, while Milly trundled the hopping box through the silent, moon-streaked streets, past Dockhead to London Bridge.

Once in Tooley Street, they joined scores of other families making the same pilgrimage. It seemed as if all the women and children of Bermondsey were being spirited away by some pied piper of the hop fields. The station was boiling with families milling about, trying to keep together, desperate not to lose either children or luggage.

'Elsie, where's Elsie gone?' Their mother's eyes searched the jostling crowd. Milly, tall enough to see above the surrounding heads, spotted her sister standing before a poster advertising a seaside holiday in Ramsgate. Three beautiful young women in flowing summer dresses, with wide-brimmed hats and parasols, were perched frivolously on the promenade railing. Elsie was staring intently. Milly elbowed her way through the crush and caught her by the arm. 'What are you doing? Do you want to get left behind?'

'Milly, look, perhaps they're sisters, don't they look like us a bit? Wouldn't it be lovely to go to the seaside, instead of down hopping?' Her unfathomable, almond-shaped grey eyes stared up at the poster. Milly couldn't tell if she was being deliberately provocative. The beautiful girls in their expensive dresses didn't look anything like the 'set of jugs' from Arnold's Place.

'Don't be so ungrateful, you're lucky to be going at all! Just think of me staying home with him.'

Elsie grimaced and shuddered, as Milly hauled her back to her mother. Soon the smell of the stoking boiler and the shrill hoot of the train whistle pierced their goodbyes. Milly hoisted the hopping box up into the carriage, kissed her mother and waved as the train moved out with a final, mournful hoot. She stood on the smoke-wreathed platform till the last of the train's trail of steam had completely disappeared. Then, heavy with a sudden loneliness, she turned her feet towards the house in Arnold's Place, which, without her mother or her sisters, could never be called home.

4

Home Comforts

September 1923

'Where's the soap?' The old man's growled question wasn't entirely unexpected, but still it made Milly jump. She was in the kitchen, frying sausages on the range, and pretended not to hear him.

'Where's the soddin' soap?' he bellowed again from the scullery.

Her father had come home from work and gone straight to the sink to scrub himself clean, as he usually did. She'd carried in the required kettle of water, making sure it was tepid rather than boiling hot as he normally liked it. Then she left him to it, while she cooked his tea. She'd hidden the soap earlier.

'Comes to something a man can't get a wash in his own house!' She heard him banging around in the cupboard beneath the sink. She could imagine him, braces hanging down, long-john sleeves rolled up.

'What have you done with the soap? For chrissake, gel, can't you even make sure we've got a bit o' soap?' His voice was getting louder; she wasn't sure how long to leave it.

She poked her head into the scullery.

'No soap? Oh, Mrs Knight come to borrow some. I'll run and get it back. Tea's on the table.'

She lifted her coat from the peg in the passage and slipped out. She intended to be gone a while. Let him stew. She knew he would never eat until he'd scrubbed his hands. Let his dinner get cold. She couldn't be held to blame for his fastidiousness.

She'd been waging her own little war for almost three weeks now, ever since her mother and sisters had gone to Kent. It had occurred to her that she might as well make him regret his decision to keep her at home, and if she was persistent and brave enough, she might make his life so uncomfortable that he'd be forced to change his mind. She cooked him inedible meals, let the fire die down and hid the poker, made sure his long johns were left damp and his shirts unironed. One evening when he was late for the pub he'd grabbed the flat iron from the fire himself, brandishing the red-hot metal in her face. For a moment she feared he might brain her, but instead he'd spat on it and started smoothing his best shirt himself.

'What's that mother of yours thinking of, not teaching you how to use a flat iron! You're worse than useless, yer dozy mare.'

And this evening, she hoped the disappearing soap might tip him over the edge, perhaps even force him to concede that life would be much more pleasant without her around. With a small surge of satisfaction, she felt the bar of soap nestling inside her coat pocket. She decided to walk to Bermondsey Wall and back. By then he should have left for the pub and the inevitable consequences of her defiance would at least be postponed. Strolling to the end of Arnold's Place, she turned back past the Swan and Sugarloaf and down the stiflingly narrow Hickman's Folly, towards the river.

It had been one of those balmy September days that could have been high summer; pure hopping weather, she'd thought wistfully, every time she'd looked out of the high factory windows. Now, as she approached Bermondsey Wall, the narrow streets threading their way towards the river ended, here and there, in breaches between high-walled warehouses. Suddenly she saw the Thames. At least here was some space and a view of the sky.

By the time she reached the river wall, it felt as though she were struggling for breath. These last weeks with the old man had felt like a prison sentence and she longed to break out, to find some air. She went to the small wooden jetty, protruding between the wharves. Walking to the end of it, she leaned against the sturdy wooden railing, silvered with age. She had felt its sharp edge pressing into her back as Pat pinned her there, with the moonlit river behind her. Why, she wondered, did she submit to those kisses, which so often left her unmoved? Perhaps it had to do with that hollow pit of loneliness inside her, which had deepened since her mother and sisters had left. She didn't want to hurt Pat, but there was something she was meant to be feeling, which she was not. If she ever managed to join them down hopping, perhaps she would try to forget about Pat and let him drift away as softly as the tide now running beneath her feet. She scanned the green sweep of river, all the while taking great gulping breaths of sharp air. Downstream, towards Greenwich, she watched as huge, billowy white clouds sailed like floating ships above the water. Upstream was the long V-shaped inlet of St Saviour's Dock, after which Dockhead was named. Milly had learned in her history class that once, long ago, this whole stretch of riverside had been home to the Folly Gardens, a pleasant place on the banks of the Thames where fashionable city dwellers from across the water could exchange the stink of the city for sweet air and cooling river breezes. But that distant past was not in evidence now. The Folly had seen too much wretched life for that, and Milly thought it was unlikely ever to be a garden again.

The tooting of a lorry horn jolted her back to the present.

'Does your mother know you're out?'

'Pat!' She jerked round to see him, with that familiar cheeky smile, half leaning out of the cab window, and hoped he hadn't noticed her blushing at this interruption of her secret disloyal musings about him.

'Me mother's down hopping, as well you know!' she called back.

'How's the old man today?'

She shook her head, turning back to the river.

'No wonder you're looking sorry for yourself.' He jumped down from the cab and came to join her on the jetty. He had always

38

been a stocky young man but now, as he leaned his muscular arms next to hers on the wooden railing of the jetty, it was obvious how the lorry driving was filling out his physique. When Pat wasn't moonlighting, his daytime job was to deliver to and from Butler's Wharf. He had a small lorry yard nearby in Shad Thames and was a familiar sight making deliveries around Dockhead.

'Ain't you going down at all this year?' he asked, offering her a cigarette.

She shook her head. 'Not for the want of trying. I've been making his life a misery this week. But he's not budging,' she said, pulling a face.

'I'm going down meself at the weekend,' he said, drawing deeply. 'Taking a few of the husbands down in the lorry. Why don't you come with us?'

'What, in the lorry with the men?'

'You'll be in the cab with me. You won't come to no harm!' He laughed and flicked ash into the fast-flowing tide below.

Many working husbands visited their wives in the hop fields at weekends, but the journey there usually turned into a drunken beano.

'I'm not worried about that, I can take care of myself!' Milly pulled herself up to her full height. At seventeen she was already a little taller than Pat, and lugging around seven-pound jam jars had given her arm muscles a docker would envy. Sometimes she found her strong frame an embarrassment and now, suddenly self-conscious, she wrapped her arms tightly around herself.

'Thanks for the offer, Pat, but I'd have to work on the old man, and you know what he's like.'

Pat chuckled. 'Oh, I know! There's a good reason why Wilf pissed off at sixteen to join the army!' Her youngest brother had volunteered during the last year of the war, lying about his age, but Pat had no such patriotic tendencies. Instead he'd stayed home and done pretty well from his black-market dealings. He threw his cigarette end into the river. 'I expect he'll drive you out too, one of these days.'

He squeezed her shoulder sympathetically, giving her a quick kiss on the cheek, before jumping back up into the lorry. 'Just let me know before the weekend. We're leaving Saturday morning, meet outside the Swan at eight.'

'Thanks, Pat, I'll let you know.'

When the lorry was out of sight she turned for home and smiled. Pat's offer of a lift had given her a glimmer of hope. She'd been wishing for wings to fly away, but if escape came in the form of Pat's lorry instead, who was she to argue? Perhaps Pat wouldn't be drifting away from her on the tide after all.

Back in Arnold's Place, the old man was gone and the sausages were congealing on the plate. She inspected them gingerly. She was hungry herself, but even her normally healthy appetite couldn't face them; she'd burned them black. They went into the dustbin and she went up to bed to wait for the old man to come home, hoping that when he did roll in, he'd be too drunk to drag her out of bed for the hiding she knew would be coming. When the front door finally opened and he stumbled upstairs, she was gratified to hear him tumble all the way back down again.

'Good, hope you break your bloody neck!' she muttered silently and turned over.

Next morning, she made sure she was up and out of the house before him, but he caught her that evening as she walked through the door. His fist hit the side of her head, spinning her round across the kitchen before she even had time to register his presence. He must have been waiting behind the kitchen door. Normally she was home first and if she'd had some warning at least she could have run, but now he had her.

She tumbled over one of the chairs and now lay sprawled in front of the fire, face down on the rag rug. She felt his boot in her side, lifting her over on to her back. He leaned over her, his face red with rage, poker in hand. She rubbed the side of her head. She might have taken this without complaint if her mother had been home because it was always her mother who ultimately paid the price for any rebellion on Milly's part. But now some demon of defiance rose up.

'I see you found the poker.' She grimaced. She had hidden it in the scullery, knowing how addicted he was to his ritual of poking and prodding at the fire when he came in. Nothing annoyed him more than not being able to find the poker.

'Think you're effin' clever, think I don't know what you're trying to do?' he said, swiping the iron down towards her. But before it could smash into her ribs, she shot out a hand, twisting the poker from his grasp. Jumping to her feet, still dizzy from the blow to her head, she tried to judge which way to run. He stood facing her, his taut frame trembling with anger. She was as tall as him now and somehow that realization gave her the strength to stand her ground. She pushed him even further.

'Southwell's said I can have next week off—'

The back of his hand struck her cheekbone with a crack, and sent her stumbling back towards the fire. Catching at the mantelpiece with her hand, she steadied herself. She could feel the warm trickle of blood on her cheek, where his ring had broken the skin.

'I'm sick o' the sight of you! Go an' eff off down hoppin' if you want, but see how you like walking all the way because you won't get a penny train fare from me!'

Milly wiped the blood from her cheek, smiling behind her hand. She had won the war.

Milly was the only woman there. A group of men were already clustered round the doors of the Swan and Sugarloaf when she arrived that Saturday morning. She stood, awkward and unnoticed, on the edge of the group, wishing Pat was here to meet her. His lorry was parked outside the pub, but he was nowhere to be seen. She recognized many of the men, some were drinking pals of her father's, others from Southwell's or neighbours. At first she hung back, clasping a battered cardboard box to her chest. As well as her clothes, it contained tins of food, filched from the supply her mother had left for the old man. She hadn't told her father how she'd be getting to Kent; in fact she'd said no more about going. She liked the idea of him waking up to find her bed empty and no breakfast on the table – he had told her to eff off down hoppin' after all.

She was relieved when Pat and his friend emerged from the pub, carrying crates of beer. Pat nodded at her with a smile as he slid the crate on to the back board.

'Fuel for the journey!' He winked and came over to take her box. 'This can go in the back too, but you're coming in the cab with me. This lot'll be pissed as puddin's before we get to Seven Mile Lane and I did say I'd look after you!'

She didn't remember him saying that, but was grateful she wouldn't be bouncing around on the back board all the way to Horsmonden. Soon she was settled in the cab and the back was loaded up, crammed with men, boxes of supplies and gifts for their families, which, along with the beer crates, made it a tight squeeze. But they were all in high spirits and as soon as they were on the road Milly heard them start up the hopping songs, accompanied by someone on an accordion.

'*When you go down 'oppin, 'oppin down in Kent, you try to earn a bob or two, to pay the bloomin' rent, with an ee ay oh, ee ay oh, eeay, eeay, oh!*'

Pat was right. By the time they'd made their slow way through heavy traffic in Old Kent Road and left the smoke behind, the songs grew bawdier. Pat grinned at her sheepishly, but Milly wasn't shocked – she'd heard them all before. She was content to drink in the increasingly fresh air, leaning her arm on the open window of the cab, watching for the first green field to replace the suburbs.

After an hour on the road they stopped at a roadside café, and the men insisted she join them in a drink. She sat with her legs swinging over the back board, sipping from a beer bottle, beginning to relax in their company.

'How'd you persuade old man Colman to let you come, Milly?' Sid, one of her father's work pals, asked, eyeing the cut still visible on her cheek. 'He's a stubborn old git, never changes his mind.'

'I made his life a bloody misery, Sid, that's what I did. Burned his dinners and hid the poker!' Sid and the other men gathered round laughing. 'That's the spirit, love, you got to stand up to the mean old bully!'

She drained the beer bottle with a sense of triumph and Sid handed her another. As she sipped at her beer she reflected that Sid was right, it *was* time to stand up to the old man. His bullying had been going on far too long. He'd always been a strict disciplinarian and she'd feared him as long as she could remember, but she clearly recollected the day when the cane on the table had been replaced by his fists. It was during the war, and she could see her family now, gathered in the kitchen of Arnold's Place. Even after all these years she could remember the sound of her father's laugh. A staccato burst that bounced off the kitchen walls. Amy, a toddler, had said something quick and clever and he'd swiped her up from the floor with something like affection. When the knock came on the door, he'd handed Amy to her mother. Milly saw her ten-year-old self, sitting on the kitchen floor, showing Elsie how to whip a wooden top till it spun in a blur over the lino. Absorbed in keeping the spin going for the longest of times, Milly barely registered her father opening the front door, letting in the cold and dark. And when he came back with the telegram, the top was still spinning. But as the words emerged dully from his mouth, 'Jimmy's dead', the top wobbled crazily, bouncing across the lino to her mother's feet. Milly scrabbled to grab it, just as her mother let out an agonized cry and let Amy fall from her arms. Some instinct made Milly dive. She caught her sister and held her close, as she'd seen boys dive to save a goal, while her mother's moaning filled the kitchen. 'Not my Jimmy too, not both my boys!' Over and over. The old man didn't utter a word, but pulled his jacket off the peg and walked out. She remembered the feel of his steel-capped boot in her ribs as he kicked her out of the way. Milly had put her mother to bed that night, along with Elsie and Amy, and she had looked after all of them till her father staggered home drunk three days later. That day the beatings began, almost as if he blamed his wife and daughters for being alive when his two sons were dead. Not long after that, Wilf signed up too and Milly never heard the old man laugh again. But now she was old enough and strong enough, and it was time to fight back, for all their sakes.

Back on the road, hedgerows began to appear, fields of cows and sheep, stands of trees, and the gently swelling Kent hills, dipping to sweet-scented valleys. She felt heady with beer and pride in her hard-won victory over the old man. She'd done it, she was free! She let the wind take her carefully waved hair, feeling it whip about her face. Leaning back as the warm September sun splashed through the windshield, she sighed with pure happiness.

'You look different.'

She hadn't been aware Pat was watching her.

'This is my happy face.' She gave him an exaggerated smile. He laughed, but then seemed to grow serious.

'No, I mean, you look more grown-up, you're looking . . . very pretty today.'

Pretty! She didn't think he'd ever paid her such a romantic compliment before, unless he was mocking her.

'You taking the piss?'

He shook his head, giggling.

'What's so bloody funny?' She felt uncomfortable now; perhaps the men hadn't been laughing with her, but at her.

'Nothing, it's just you're as prickly as one of those hop bines you're off to strip . . .'

She gave him a sidelong glance, keeping her face straight until he winked at her and they both burst out laughing. She would give him the benefit of the doubt; she was enjoying herself far too much to pick a fight today. Nearing the top of Wrotham Hill, the lorry juddered to a halt, then slowly but surely began to roll back down again. Pat groaned, pulled hard on the handbrake and leaned out of his window.

'Everyone off!'

The men all tumbled off the back and began pushing the lorry up the hill. By the time they'd struggled, panting, to the top, they were all thirsty and another beer stop was called. This time, when they started singing, Milly joined in with the strong, tuneful voice she'd inherited from her mother.

'*Oh me lousy 'ops, oh me lousy 'ops! When the measurer comes around, pick 'em up, pick 'em up off the ground. When 'e starts a-measurin' 'e never knows when to stop. Aye, aye get in the bin and take the effin lot!*'

When Pat started up the engine again, she went to jump off the back board, but Sid and the others refused to let her return to the cab.

'Stay and have another drink, Mill, don't get back in there with him!' Sid pleaded.

She liked being the centre of all this good-natured banter, and banging her fist on the back of the cab, shouted, 'Drive on, Patrick! Milady's staying back here for more refreshments!'

She ignored Pat's complaints and soon the lorry chugged into life, before hurtling down the other side of Wrotham Hill. Beer and joy had eroded their decorum, and she spent the rest of the journey sitting on a crate of beer on the back board, surrounded by hollering, swearing, joking men who seemed happy to accept her as one of the gang. She felt freer than she had in all her life. She scanned the countryside, looking out for the first oast house, and when she spotted a group of red-tiled conical roofs, topped with brilliant white cowls, she stood up for a better view.

'Careful, gel!' Sid grabbed her arm. 'You've had a drop too much, don't want you falling arse end over the side!'

Milly turned to him with a smile, bracing herself against the lorry's back board.

'Thanks, Sid, but I think I'm stone-cold sober.'

45

'Good gawd,' Sid called to his mates, 'look at her, steady as rock! She can drink us lot under the table!'

As they coasted to the bottom of the valley and slowed down through the village of Horsmonden, Milly smelled the tangy aroma of wood fires. Turning into the field where the hopping huts were situated, tantalizing smells wafted over to them from hopping pots, suspended over fires.

Sid breathed in deeply. 'Mmm, smell that, Milly, just in time for dinner!'

Excited children came running across the field as soon as the lorry came into view. Mothers left the cooking fires and ran with babies in their arms. This was the highlight of their week – the men were sure to have brought treats. Milly was the last to jump off the lorry, pulling her box down after her.

'Bloody deserter! You left me driving all on me own!' Pat joked, jumping down from the cab.

'Sorry, Pat, they just wouldn't let me off!'

'Well, I don't know what your mother'll say about you turning up blind drunk!'

She shrugged. 'You never seemed bothered before whether I got drunk or not. Anyway, I'm not tipsy!'

Eager to be away, she scanned the field for her mother and sisters. She was looking forward to surprising them. About two dozen hop huts were ranged in long lines round the edge of the field. Built of wood, they were topped with corrugated-iron roofs and looked little more than stable blocks, with only a door for light and ventilation. She wandered along the row of huts, dodging round cooking fires, greeting women she knew. Finally, at the very end, she saw her mother sitting on a wooden chair, stirring the hopping pot. Elsie sat with Amy on the grass; both held huge hunks of bread and balanced tin plates on their knees. Milly tried to creep up unnoticed, but Amy had spotted her, and she saw her sister's face fall.

'Oh no, what's she doing here? Now we'll have to squash up in the bed!'

Milly was anxious not to begin on a bad note, so said nothing. She dropped her box and dashed up behind her mother before she could turn round. Putting both hands over Mrs Colman's eyes, Milly whispered, 'Guess who?'

'Oh Gawd, *Jesus*, Mary and Joseph, you frightened the life out of me!' Her mother twisted round with a delighted smile on her face. She cupped Milly's face with her black, hop-stained fingers and kissed her noisily. 'How did you get here?'

Elsie hadn't said a word; she was looking at Milly without a trace of surprise.

'I had a dream about you last night,' she said solemnly. 'I knew you'd be coming.'

'Well, you're just an old Polly Witch!' Milly blurted out her normal response to Elsie's flashes of intuition and had to duck quickly as Elsie spun her tin plate through the air, narrowly missing Milly's head.

'Sod me if you've not started already!' Mrs Colman snatched the plate from the ground and Milly glared at Elsie, but was determined not to let her sisters ruin her arrival. She dug into the cardboard box, drawing out a paper bag of humbugs and another of cough candies. Her sisters accepted the peace offerings with bemused looks on their faces. Milly had learned during the past weeks with her father that there was more than one way to win a fight, and as she thought again of her musings on the journey down, she realized that once, long ago, her sisters had not been her enemies. The war between them had crept in, insidiously, with the cold and dark, the day her father had turned into 'the old man'.

Her mother's face relaxed as she saw Milly making an effort to be friends.

'I'll just go and put my things in the hut,' Milly said, 'then I'll tell you all about it!'

Ducking into the dark interior, the familiar smell of damp earth and sweet straw mattresses hit her. As always her mother had made their hut a home from home. The roll of wallpaper had been pinned over bare wooden walls, lino rolled out on the earth floor and, on a deep wooden platform at the back where they would all sleep together, the straw-ticking mattresses had been laid out, neatly covered with blankets. Milly stowed the box in the only spare corner and sat on the bed platform. Patting the springy straw-filled ticking, she sighed and lay back. Tonight would be spent at the village pub and tomorrow feeding the men at a great communal Sunday roast. She would have to wait till Monday for what she really longed for: to be among the wide hop fields, with blue sky breaking through green tunnels of bines, her nose assaulted by a thousand citrus explosions as she crushed papery hop flowers between her fingers.

The Snares of Paradise

September 1923

On Sunday morning Milly poked her head out of the warm nest of bodies curled up, top to tail, on the straw mattresses at the back of the hut. The others were still sleeping. Amy's small, grimy foot prodded her in the face as Milly pulled herself up gently. The wooden hut was freezing cold and damp from the morning mist, which seeped through every crack in the ill-fitting weather boards. She tucked the blanket firmly around Amy's legs and, wriggling to the edge of the sleeping shelf, slid off, trying not to wake the others. Slipping on her coat, she shoved her feet into her shoes and eased open the hut door. A mist-wreathed world of grey-green and pearl greeted her. Through the mist came the sounds of other hoppers already stirring, the splashing of water as buckets were filled from the standpipe, and the subdued murmurs of the early risers collecting faggots for fires. Sharp woodsmoke began to fill the air, and the crackle of kindling catching fire shot through the muffled sounds of their voices. She went to fetch a bundle of faggots from a nearby pile the farmer had provided. Carefully arranging the twigs, she made up their own fire and put the kettle on to boil. Once a good blaze had started and the kettle was billowing steam, she called her mother and sisters, who emerged from the hut, groggy and grateful for the hot strong tea and slices of bread and jam she offered them. These early morning hopping rituals were something she'd always loved, and in spite of the chilly start and the spartan hut, there was deep comfort in waking to the sounds of other pickers and the smells from dew-damp earth and dripping trees, all seasoned with woodsmoke.

'Hurry up and get ready, you two,' she urged her sisters after breakfast. They both looked as if they hadn't washed all week. 'I'm not walking up to the green with you looking like scruff bags.'

Her mother always seemed more lenient with them when they were hop-picking. Her sisters were allowed to roam wild over the countryside all day, with the other youngsters in the camp, so long as they first picked a bushel or two of hops. But today there would be no picking. As more and more hoppers gathered round the fires there was already an air of gaiety pervading the huts. People were dressing up in their Sunday best, ready for a walk up to the village green, where Bermondsey traders would be setting up their stalls. They followed their customers to the hop fields each year, and the pickers were grateful. Signs on many village shops warned *No hoppers!* And even those who did serve 'the foreigners' from London kept a suspicious eye on them. For however much their labour was valued, often, their presence was not.

The family took it in turns to wash in a bucket of cold water that Milly had already filled. But Amy's brief dip in the bucket with one hand didn't go unnoticed by Mrs Colman, who yanked her back as she tried to escape.

'Get here, you soap dodger. Nine years old and still can't give yourself a proper wash. Look at the tidemark round your neck! It's not had a drop of water on it.' After giving Amy's neck a vigorous scrubbing, she passed her over to Milly.

'Here, let me do your hair.' Milly reached for Amy, who ducked out of her grasp.

'I can do it meself!'

Milly caught her, marching her to the mirror.

'Look at this, it looks like that straw mattress we slept on!' And ignoring Amy's complaints, Milly began teasing out her sister's tangles. As she squirmed, Milly tapped her head with the brush. 'Stand still and be made respectable, you little scarecrow!'

She'd forgotten this side of hopping, the fractiousness of Amy and the dreaminess of Elsie, who was still mooning about outside, gathering wildflowers into a posy to brighten the hut. Their annoying traits intensified once they were freed from their everyday lives. They all seemed to become more vivid versions of themselves, and that was not always comfortable, especially when living together in a tiny hut.

Once she was satisfied that her sisters looked respectable, she got ready herself, putting on her second-best dress, a pale green shift with long sleeves. In the tiny mirror tacked to the hut door, she made the best of her dark wavy hair and put on a straw cloche hat. She slipped on her shoes and they strolled over to the gate. There had been little rain this season and the grass, though wet with dew, wasn't muddy. From every hut, families emerged, until the whole field of hoppers formed a straggling procession down the lane between the high hedgerows. Amy and Elsie ran ahead with the other children, while Milly ambled with her mother and neighbours, past oast houses and farm buildings. The mist had burned off to a bright morning, washing the wide village green in a golden warmth. Stalls decked with bunting made the green look like a fairground as groups of hop-pickers wandered from stall to stall, beginning to haggle with familiar tradesmen just as if they were back in Bermondsey.

Milly linked arms with her mother. The night before, after the usual walk home from the pub in pitch dark, followed by a sing-song round the camp fire, her mother had taken her aside and made her explain exactly how she'd managed to persuade the old man to let her come. Mrs Colman hadn't commented much, merely nodded and sometimes sighed. But today she resumed the conversation.

'Milly, love, are you sure you should stay for the week? He only said yes 'cause you pushed him. But you know how he stews, there'll be hell to pay when you get back. Why don't you go home with Pat on the lorry today, eh?'

'No, Mum! I'm not creeping back. I'm not scared of him.'

Her mother's face creased into lines of worry and she drew Milly in closer.

'No, darlin', but I am.'

'I'll make sure he doesn't hurt you, Mum.'

Her mother gave her a sad smile and shook her head. 'Brave words, love, brave words.' There was a melancholy resignation in her tone that seemed to surface when she was down here. At home, Mrs Colman held herself taut, ready for a blow, ready to stand between the old man and one of her children. But once away from him, she seemed to allow herself the luxury of regret and Milly's instinct was to resist it. But she hated to be at odds with her mother; instead she preferred to brighten her mood with a distraction, and she pointed across the field.

'Look, there's Hughes' stall, let's see if he's got any paraffin oil for the lamp, that hut's black as Newgate's knocker at night.'

'Mrs Colman, Milly!' It was Hughes' nephew Bertie, manning the stall. He gave them a friendly smile as they walked over to look at the oil cans. 'Nice to see some familiar faces. You and half of Dockhead seem to be down here.'

'Nice to have a friendly face serving us too,' her mother said warmly. 'Some of the shops down here only let us in one at a time, in case we 'alf-inch the stuff! Snooty buggers, as if our money's not good enough.'

Milly thought that Bertie looked a little uncomfortable at that; perhaps he was thinking about his uncle's not dissimilar treatment of Dockhead customers.

'Your uncle not down?' she asked Bertie.

'No, he's handed over the Dockhead shop to me. You won't be seeing so much of him.'

'Good . . . I mean, that's good . . . for you!' she stuttered, covering her blushes by pretending to inspect the tinned goods piled up on the stall. When she looked up, he'd raised one of those winged eyebrows and a smile was playing on his lips. She thought he'd got her meaning exactly.

They quickly bought their oil and moved on to the old clothes stall, where Mrs Colman found a replacement for Amy's everyday dress. Amy had ripped it to shreds on some barbed wire the previous week.

'That child's getting like a little savage down here,' she confided to Milly. 'Still, the fresh air's good for her, and at least she can let off steam without upsetting everyone the way she does at home.'

Milly privately thought Amy capable of upsetting everyone *whatever* her surroundings. She was the most wilful child she'd ever met. 'Yeah, shame she can't stay here.'

'Milly! Don't talk like that about your sister, one day you might be glad you've got her . . . and Elsie.' Her mother nodded sagely as if she knew something Milly didn't.

'Sorry, Mum, but I reckon that day'll be a long time coming.'

Seeing her mother's hurt expression, Milly softened. 'I am *trying* to be friends, Mum, but I wish you'd talk to them. They provoke me on purpose, you know!'

'Mary, Mother of God, give me strength,' Mrs Colman said, raising her eyes to heaven. 'And another thing I was thinking,' she went off at a tangent, barely pausing for breath, 'I heard from Sid you was on the back of that lorry on the way down, knocking 'em back like a good 'un.'

'It was only a bit of fun, we had a good old sing-song and I never got drunk at all!'

'Don't make no difference! Now you're getting older, Milly, you've got to be careful. You can't be drinking with men on your own, specially not on the back of a bleedin' lorry . . . you'll get a bad reputation, love, d'you know what I mean?'

Milly knew what she meant. But the accepted rules of behaviour of her mother's generation sometimes mystified her. To be seen drinking with men was one of the things that set the women talking, but a group of women her mother's age, sitting in the corner of the snug, singing the old songs and getting slowly sozzled, was perfectly acceptable.

'And don't let that Pat get too familiar either.'

Milly was startled, wanting nothing more than to wriggle out of her mother's grasp. 'Why not, he's a nice feller, I thought you liked him.' She blushed.

'Nice enough as a friend of your brother's, but he's had a girl in the family way before now, and I don't want you bringing no trouble home to my door!'

Her mother had never given her such a pointed warning before and as well as feeling deeply embarrassed, Milly resented the tone, which made her feel guilty without knowing why.

'Mum! He offered me a lift in the lorry – he was being kind, that's all!'

Her mother tucked in her chin and pursed her lips in such a way that Milly blushed to the roots of her hair. 'I'm just warning you, that's all,' her mother went on. 'Once the boys get down here, they think all the girls are easy, that's why you get so many babies born in June – we don't want no hopping babies! So if he asks you to walk up the field with him, you just say no!'

Milly sighed. 'All right, Mum, I'll say no,' she said obediently, and then desperate to change the subject she pulled her mother off in the direction of the baker's stall. But as bad luck would have it, the stall was pitched near the Gun Inn, outside which Pat and a group of men stood drinking.

'Milly!' Pat called and then the others joined in. 'Here comes our drinking pal, come on, Mill, give us a song!'

Her mother's grip tightened on her elbow. 'See what I mean!' she hissed, pulling Milly away, so that she barely had time to wave before being dragged to the other end of the green.

'What d'you do that for!' She felt hot with embarrassment. There was Pat telling her she looked grown-up and here was her mother, dragging her off like a naughty child. All her life she'd felt an unquestioning loyalty to her mother. But now that practised hard resistance she'd used to deal with the old man seemed to take over. She shook off her mother's restraining hand.

'Don't tell me you're turning into the old man, telling me what I can and can't do! I'll spend my time with whoever I want!'

Mrs Colman stood in shocked silence, and Milly felt her mother's gaze on her back as she hurried over towards the Gun Inn, yet she hadn't reached the end of the field before she regretted her harshness. Perhaps she'd spent too many weeks alone with the old man, and that had hardened her heart. Now she felt a tinge of fear, that she might have forgotten entirely how to soften it.

Most of the hoppers preferred to drink outside the pub. There were a few women drinking there, with their husbands and children, who had been treated to bottles of ginger beer.

'Here, Milly, hold on to your glass, that cost me an extra shilling!' Pat said as he handed her a pint of bitter. In spite of the good business the hoppers brought in, they were still charged a 'shilling on the glass' against breakages. It rankled, but not enough to interfere with their Sunday drink. She took the glass and went to sit with him on the green.

'Your mum didn't look too happy to see me.'

'Take no notice, Pat, someone told her I had a few drinks on the lorry. Says it'll ruin me reputation.'

He raised his eyes. 'She forgets you're grown up now, not one of her little set of jugs no more!'

Milly felt a pang of regret. A few years ago her mother had saved up the money to have that photograph taken of Milly and her sisters. They'd gone to the studio in Sunday best, brightly polished shoes, carefully brushed hair with bows tied neatly, Amy scrubbed clean of all the urchin dirt she so loved. And the photographer had positioned them, in height order. Milly first on the left, willowy and emerging from childhood, Elsie in the middle, skinny and gazing into the distance with a faraway look, and finally Amy, defiantly staring at the camera as though she were calculating what mischief she could get up to next. Her mother had loved it, exclaiming, 'Oh! Will you look at me set of three jugs, you're all so lovely!' Now she felt mean, to have turned on her mother as if she were an enemy, instead of her greatest ally.

She drained her glass. 'Better be getting back up the field. Mum'll want help with the dinner.'

Pat looked disappointed. 'I'll be down again next weekend, will you want a lift back home in the lorry?'

'You're a diamond, Pat. I can't afford the train, I'll need to save all me earnings to give the old man when I get back.'

'Right you are, I'll see you next week then.' He seemed to hesitate. 'Do you want me to walk up the field with you?'

She paused. 'All right, if you like.'

Halfway up the lane, he put his arm round her waist. She didn't look at him, but she could feel his slightly beery breath on her cheek as he bent to kiss her.

'I always liked you, Milly, even when I used to hang about with your brother, but now you're the prettiest girl down here, do you know that?'

Milly looked up at him, startled by her own power. She'd had childish boyfriends before, but Pat was older, a man. Now, with him standing so close, wanting something from her, she felt an echo of the power she'd had when standing her ground against the old man. But as he held her shoulders, pushing her up against the high hedge, panic caught in her throat and she remembered her mother's warning. Before he could steal another kiss, she had started away, sprinting up the lane, long legs flashing, shouting.

'See you next week!'

Without looking back, she flew along the hedgerow until she got to the five-bar gate. Stepping up on to the lower rail, she vaulted over without pause and ran full pelt across the field, arriving at the hut out of breath, with her hat in her hand. Her mother and the other women were in the centre of the field, tending a rudimentary brick oven, where a communal joint had been roasting all morning. Mrs Colman was forking baked potatoes out of the embers and now Milly kneeled to help her.

'Sorry, Mum.' She gave her mother a quick kiss on the cheek. 'It's just all that time on me own with the old man must have turned me grumpy as him.'

Her mother put a hand to Milly's face. 'I'm only thinking of you, love. Just don't want you to end up with a wrong 'un . . . like I did.'

Early next morning they made their way to the hop field and gathered round the empty hop bin. It was constructed like a huge manger, with crossed poles at each end and sacking suspended from two side poles. Elsie perched on one of the side poles and Amy stood on an upended bushel basket, while Milly and her mother placed themselves at each end. The pole-pullers were walking around on stilts, with their long-handled bill hooks, cutting down the strung bines, so that they fell with great green swooshes into the bins. Milly took up the first bine, pulling her fingers down its prickly length, stripping off her first hops. She waited for the sharp, acidic smell to be released and when it came, a bright green essence of the countryside, she inhaled deeply.

'Oh, Mum, the smell of them hops! It's like perfume!'

Her mother laughed, quickly stripping the flowers from her own bine. 'You couldn't bottle it, though, could you?'

Elsie and Amy were happy to pick a bushel or two, but soon grew restless. When the drone of an aeroplane caught their attention, they dropped the bines and stood looking up as it passed low over the fields. Milly could even see the pilot perched between the double silver wings; she waved. Soon Elsie and Amy were off down the high green tunnels of hop plants, running between the bins, their arms spread like aeroplanes as they headed for the wood at the edge of the field.

'That's their picking over for the day, we won't see them till they're hungry,' said Mrs Colman.

'It's up to us now then, better get cracking.' Milly wasn't sorry to see them leave. Most of the time they complained about the prickly bines or their legs aching. The truth was, she and her mother could get on much quicker without them. Soon their hands synchronized into a blur of speed, plucking hops so quickly from the bine that their individual movements were undetectable. Rosie Rockle, their neighbour from Arnold's Place, stood at the next bin and started up a song. All down the hop field women and children joined in, till the sound of their voices rang through the bines.

'They say that 'oppin's lousy, I don't believe it's true, we only go down 'oppin to earn a bob or two, with an eeay oh, eeay oh, eeay eeay ooohhh!'

The late September sun grew strong and Milly's pale skin had turned pink by the end of the morning. Already she felt as though her lungs had expanded to accommodate the richer, cleaner country air, and she knew that the struggle with the old man to get here had all been worth it.

At dinner time some of the women came back from the huts with buckets full of tea and they all sat together on the grass, eating large hunks of bread cut from the loaf, with hands already stained black from the hops.

'Should I call the girls?' Milly asked. She'd seen nothing of her sisters since they disappeared into the wood.

'No.' Her mother shook her head. 'They know where we are if they get hungry. Let 'em run free.'

They both leaned back against the bin, enjoying the brief respite from the morning's work.

'How's your back?' her mother asked, rubbing her own.

'Fine, this is nothing compared to Southwell's picking room!' Milly said with a grin.

After a couple of hours more picking, Ned, the measurer, came round. He was a man not much liked. His job was to scoop the hops out of the bins with a bushel basket, and then to weigh them. He could weigh them light or he could weigh them heavy. But Ned was notorious for tamping the hops down tight, so every last bit of air was expelled and the farmer got many more hops in a bushel for his tuppence. The pickers were always at his mercy.

Milly scooped up a handful of hops from the bin, they were good hops, fat and aromatic. 'I reckon we've done over twenty bushel,' she said to her mother.

But Mrs Colman shook her head, nodding in Ned's direction as he approached their bin.

'Not once he's finished pushing 'em down. I wish those girls would get back here, we need them to go round and pick 'em up.' Gleaning stray hops from the floor was child's work, but in their absence Milly did it, then waited in anticipation as Ned measured out their hops into the poke. Only seventeen bushels! They would have to speed up, or get the girls to help a bit more.

They settled down for an afternoon's work. The singing had stopped and people were picking in quiet earnestness, conscious of making up their day's pay, when suddenly a shrill scream pierced the serenity of the hop garden. Milly stiffened and shot her mother a fearful look. They dropped the bines and dashed in the direction of the scream.

'Where did it come from?' asked Rosie, puffing along beside them.

'From over there, in the trees!' Milly answered, beginning to outstrip the other women who'd followed them. Soon she was at the margin of the wood. A little way in, standing frozen under the green shade, was Amy. She was staring down at her hands, which were covered in a red sticky substance. At first Milly took it for the dark stain of blackberries, but as she caught hold of her sister by the arms, she saw the stain was not black but red. It was blood.

'What's happened, have you cut yourself?'

The young girl opened her mouth, but no sound emerged. She shook her head, seemingly mesmerized by the gory coating on her palms. Milly's mother kneeled down, frantically examining the child for a wound.

'Are you all right, love? Where've you hurt yourself?'

Amy's white face suddenly puckered. Then pointing back into the wood, she gasped, 'It's Elsie!'

Milly shot off, down the shadowed path that led into the heart of the small wood, tripping over roots and fallen branches. She sped on until she came to a small clearing and there, beneath a tree, was Elsie. Deathly pale, unconscious and very still, she lay on her side with one leg bent beneath her. As Milly drew closer, she saw blood pooled around her sister's skinny leg. It had been caught in the sharp jaws of a trap. For an instant Milly froze, then she screamed. 'Mum! She's over here!'

Her mother entered the clearing, with Rosie and a gaggle of white-faced children tumbling after. Milly was suddenly galvanized. She picked up a small branch and commandeered Ronnie, Rosie's grandson.

'All right, Ron, I'll open up the trap as far as I can, and when I tell you, wedge this stick in the jaws so it stays open, got me?'

Ronnie nodded and dropped to his knees beside Elsie, holding the branch at the ready. Milly grasped the jaws of the trap and heaved. Straining till her head felt it might burst with the pressure, she pulled with all her strength, but the jaws held fast.

'It's useless!' Then spotting Rosie's other grandson, a beefy boy nicknamed Barrel, she called out to him. 'Come and hold that side for me!'

Barrel held one half of the trap in his solid grasp while Milly strained on the other half, till it gradually opened a few inches. It would have to be now, before her strength ran out.

'Now, Ron! Shove in the stick!'

Ronnie rammed the stick between the two jaws, quickly removing his hands from danger, as Milly let the jaws ease off on to the stick and swiftly pulled Elsie's leg out of the trap.

'Oh, me poor baby!' Her mother was wailing and useless at Milly's side. The deep gash in her sister's leg ran the length of her shin, the flesh folding open like a meaty book, to reveal a pearl-white bone. Milly felt faint, but caught hold of the two halves of flesh and squeezed them tightly together. Vaguely aware of her mother's weeping, she looked up.

'Don't let go, Milly!' her mother said. 'Don't let go of your sister!'

'I won't let go, don't worry!'

Milly held tight to Elsie's leg while Ned and another man carried her across the field to the lane, where the farmer already had a lorry waiting. They laid the insensible Elsie on a blanket in the back of the lorry, then set off on a rackety, nightmarish ride through the narrow winding lanes of Kent, heading for the hoppers' hospital at Five Oak Green. Milly's hands were firmly clasped round her sister's leg the whole time, while her mother sat gripping the side of the lorry, moaning her low pleadings to Our Lady all the way.

The hoppers' hospital was no more than a large cottage, but the doctor there was efficient and gave his services free to the hop-pickers. Only when he assured her that she could release her vice-like grip did Milly let go of Elsie's leg. In an anteroom she washed her sister's blood from her hands. There was so much of it! What if she had lost too much? What if she never woke up? Milly's legs buckled and she held herself steady against the china basin. Suddenly a life without Elsie's odd presence seemed impossible; her thwarted grottos and derided dreams seemed brave now and sad, rather than stupid. Milly went back to the waiting room, and gripping her mother's hand, for once matched all her fervour and faith in praying for her sister's life to be spared.

6

The Hop Princess

September 1923

Amy stood defiantly at the hopping-hut door, still in the clothes she'd slept in, straw from the palliasse sticking out of her tangled nest of hair.

'I ain't having a wash today,' she said. She bore evidence of yesterday's drama, with streaks of mud and even some of Elsie's blood on her face.

Milly had been left to pick hops and watch Amy, while her mother was at the hospital. She'd spent an anxious night tossing and turning on the straw mattress, wondering what the next day would bring. Shaken at the prospect of losing one sister, she'd been unusually gentle with Amy, holding her during the night when she heard the young girl sobbing.

'Is Elsie going to die?' she'd whispered, her wet face close to Milly's in the darkness.

'No, 'course not, love. She'll be fine,' Milly soothed, hardly believing it herself.

But when the farm hand arrived early that morning to give Mrs Colman a lift, their mother hadn't been gone five minutes before Amy staged an outright rebellion. Milly was attempting to get her down to the hop field. She would need to pick like the wind, if she was to match her own wages and make up her mother's quota

'Amy, I've got no time for this. You look like a savage. Now go and wash some of that muck off, or else you're coming nowhere with me,' Milly ordered, desperate to get on.

'Don't care, I ain't coming picking with you today anyway! So you can stick your hops up your—'

Milly clamped her hand over the younger girl's mouth, and though Amy tried to bite her, Milly was too quick. She whipped Amy's arms behind her back and marched her to the bucket of cold water, which stood ready in front of the hut.

'I'll give you a bloody good wash, see if you like this!'

Milly flipped her sister upside down, and held her a few feet above the bucket before dunking her head in the water. Amy's scream came out in a gurgling choke as she kicked her legs in the air, squirming like an eel. Bringing her up for air, Milly shook her as effortlessly as if she were a wet mop.

'You listen to me, you selfish little mare.' She set the nine-year-old back on her feet, still holding fast to her arms. 'Mum's got enough on her plate without you making trouble, so do as you're bleedin' told for once. She's put me in charge and I say you're coming picking!'

But Amy's wet skin saved her and she managed to slip out of Milly's strong grasp, sprinting across the field, calling back to her sister, 'You can't boss me about!'

'Don't expect any dinner when you get back then!' Milly shouted after her.

Sometimes appealing to Amy's stomach did the trick, but not today, and Milly knew she would be wasting her time on a useless fight. She let her sister go and made her own way to the hop field, secretly glad to be rid of Amy. Rosie Rockle and the other hoppers had already left and she would have to hurry now to catch up. As she jogged down the lane, Milly began to feel guilty for letting her mother down. All she'd asked of Milly was to keep an eye on her sister. But, she reflected, with Amy it had been a battle of wills from the day she was born. Her mother had been so ill after her birth, and Elsie still so clingy, that it was left to eight-year-old Milly to care for the new baby. She'd been ill-prepared, but very willing to love her new sister. Perhaps she might have succeeded with a more docile child, but Amy turned out a red-faced, discontented infant, and Milly's burgeoning love had quickly changed to resentment. Whenever Milly wanted to run free or play with other children, Amy would have to be on her hip. And as she grew, so did her strong will. Awkward Amy they called her, and if Milly should ever suggest something was black, Amy would insist it was white. Milly reflected ruefully that she hadn't changed one bit.

With her mind far away from the hop garden, her hands were less swift than yesterday, but she noticed that the women around her had toned down their rough banter, and sent their children over to help pick up the hops that had fallen far from her bin. She spent the day in an agony of worry about Elsie. The doctor had said she'd lost far too much blood to be moved and when they'd left her the night before, she lay deathly pale and unwaking. When not worrying about Elsie, Milly scanned the field for Amy, who stayed out of sight all day. How could she be so selfish? But just as she'd convinced herself Amy had met a similar fate to Elsie, and was about to set off in search of her, the cry came to 'pull no more bines' and there Amy was, dead on cue, sauntering back from the wood with Barrel and Ronnie. Torn between relief and rage, Milly chose to ignore her. At least Milly wouldn't have to explain her absence when Mrs Colman came back from the hospital.

It was dark by the time the lorry pulled up in the lane. Milly rushed to the gate as the farm hand helped her mother down. She looked tired and pale.

'How is she?' Milly asked anxiously, helping her mother off with her coat and sitting her down outside the hut with a mug of tea.

'The doctor said she'll be fine!' Her mother smiled wearily.

'Oh, thank God, is she awake, did you speak to her?'

'She was sitting up, but she's got to stay in. The farmer's going to send the lorry every day to take me to the hospital. He's a good feller. The only thing is, love, you'll have to pick for me.'

'Oh, don't worry about that!' Milly smiled. She was so relieved, she felt she could pick for a hundred.

So, for the rest of the week, she was left in charge of Amy, but Milly decided to take the path of least resistance and let her run wild. Her priority now was to pick for two and make up for their lost earnings. And besides, she knew that Amy was far more capable of looking after herself than Elsie. She would never wander off deep into the wood, as it emerged Elsie had done, following a baby rabbit. Amy was more likely to be setting the trap than walking into one.

Milly didn't see her from dawn till dusk, but the slices of bread and jam she left wrapped in newspaper at the hut were always gone by the evening. At least she knew her sister was alive and fed, and she was always back by evening, just before their mother returned from visiting Elsie. Milly preferred to be free of Amy. Her deft fingers flew along the bines, all the day long, and now she began to enjoy herself as she joined in the hop songs and banter. By Friday evening she had high hopes of having out-picked the entire field of hoppers. It seemed that her hopping holiday might turn out to be a success after all.

On their last evening at the hop field, the September sun sat low over the field while Milly waited at her bin for Ned to measure out the last bushel into the poke. The poke, a long sack, stuffed with the hops she'd picked, tamped down hard, was so heavy it took two men to carry it to the waiting cart. After all the bins had been emptied, Ned added up the tallies for each family. He nodded approvingly at Milly. 'You done better'n all of 'em, girl!'

She smiled proudly, relieved that she had almost doubled her normal week's wage. The old man would have nothing to complain of.

Saturday dawned; only one brief morning left to pick and breathe in the country air, one last chance to look up at open skies, etched with bines instead of ugly chimneys and rooftops. She didn't want to go back to Arnold's Place. As the morning drew to a close, she slowed her picking, as did everyone else. They all wanted to be the one who picked the last hop. Tradition said it meant good luck all year. If it was her, perhaps the old man would get sober and her sisters turn sweet. But her swift fingers undid her, she could not hold back, and it was Rosie Rockle who picked the very last hop of the harvest.

There was one final ritual to be observed, though: the choosing of the hop princess, an honour reserved for the prettiest girl in the hop field. Before they left the hop gardens for the last time, a bushel went round and each picker cast their vote into the basket. Children jostled round one of the pole-pullers as he tipped out and painstakingly counted each vote. He stood up, calling for quiet, and as the hush descended, all the younger women looked eagerly towards him.

'Milly Colman, hop princess for nineteen-twenty-three!' came the shout, and as 'Hoorah for the hop princess' rang out, Milly felt she was floating on air.

Just then, she saw Elsie, seated on an old wooden chair, being carried on to the field by two pole-pullers. She ran, with the crown of hops wreathing her dark curls, straight to Elsie's side, and carefully avoiding her bandaged leg, hugged her tightly.

'Oh, I'm so glad you're better, love,' she said, pulling back to observe Elsie's pale, sharp features.

The young girl gave her a slow smile. 'I knew you'd be hop princess this year,' she said.

'Don't tell me, you had a dream!'

At lunchtime Pat arrived in his lorry, bringing the men for one last visit. There was a cheer when the lorry rolled up to the field and the men leaped down from the back board. Tonight, after the farmer had paid them all, there would be a party round the fire.

Pat came straight over to her.

'I see you're the hop princess!' He smiled, plucking at her hop crown. 'Didn't I say you were the best-looking girl here?'

She dipped her head, dark hair falling across her forehead, examining her blackened hands and muddy boots. 'I don't look much like a princess today!'

Pat laughed. 'Well, you're going in the bin all the same!'

He went to grab her, just as a group of men swooped down like a hoard of marauding Vikings. She had to make a show of running away – it was expected of her, an age-old demonstration of the hop princess's virtue. Her two sisters cheered the loudest as Milly sped along the strung lines, now empty of hops. Dodging between bins, leaping over the last pulled bines strewn across the field, her clumsy boots tripped her up; without them, she knew she could have outrun the whole pack of them. But finally, heart thudding, breath burning her chest, she shot down a row, only to be ambushed by a couple of boys blocking one end. Attempting to scramble away, she was finally captured when Pat came up from behind, bringing her down with a flying tackle. A loud cry went up among the pickers, as though she were a fox taken in the hunt. Then they were on her, four young men grabbing her arms and legs, running with her up to the hop bin. The children were jumping up and down, the men whistling and the women cheering.

'Be careful of my Milly, don't you break her back in that bin!' she heard her mother shout above the din.

But now they were tossing her up, once, twice, three times. They let go, she felt a rush in her stomach, then rising almost to the tops of the bines, she seemed to fly into the dizzying sky; suspended momentarily above the bins, it seemed that time stood still. All too soon, she came crashing down into an enveloping bath of green hops. She was drowning in them, swallowing them as they caught her hair and clothes. Struggling to surface, she was hoisted out and up into Pat's strong arms. Women came crowding round, draping her with hop garlands, till she had turned into a hop bine herself; tall, willowy, dripping in bitter-sweet hops.

She allowed herself to be carried on the men's shoulders down the lane, back to the hopping huts. Her mother followed, with Elsie still being carried, like a princess herself, in a sedan chair, looking for all the world like lesser royalty as she waved to the crowds. Milly waved back at her from her perch, grateful that her fanciful sister had come through her ordeal. Although the doctor had said Elsie would soon be well enough to walk, she would bear the lightning-like scar along her shin for the rest of her life, a constant reminder of the snares of paradise.

Amy scampered along in front, trying to deflect as much attention as possible from her sisters to herself. But today was Milly's day, and as the fields began to lose their warmth and dusk came on, she determined to savour the last moments of her brief country idyll, for who knew what realities she would have to face once it was over?

That evening a huge bonfire was set in front of the huts. The hop-pickers pooled the last of their food and the women stewed corned beef, potatoes and whatever leftovers could be put into the hopping pots. Everyone gathered round the fire to eat, and afterwards there was singing as Harry from the Swan and Sugarloaf started up on the piano, which had made its journey from Dockhead, lashed to the back of the lorry.

'Oh me lousy 'ops, oh me lousy 'ops,
When the measurer comes around,
Pick 'em up, pick 'em up off the ground,
When he starts a-measurin' he never knows when to stop.
Aye, aye get in the bin and take the bleedin' lot!'

The tea kettle went round and then the beer bottles. Milly's mother, who could now allow herself the luxury of indulging her sentimental side, struck up a song about wishing she was in Carrickfergus, a place Milly felt sure she'd never been to and never would. Lost in song and a few pints of stout, Mrs Colman was oblivious as Pat took her eldest daughter's hand and whispered, 'Come up the field with me.'

Milly shot one look over at her mother. Harry had progressed to 'When Irish Eyes are Smiling' and her mother was in full throat. Amy and Elsie had dozed off, curled up on the grass, warmed by the crackling fire.

'Come on, Milly,' Pat urged and, dreamily, Milly allowed herself to slip away with him. After all, what was a hop princess without her prince?

They found a place between a high hedge and the curving wall of an oast house. Warmth from the drying oven penetrated the brick, but she was still grateful for Pat's encircling arms to keep out the night chill. As his arms tightened round her, she let herself lean against him, and gazed up at the dizzying stars, spread like white smoke across a tar-black sky. But the night was so dark, moon and stars barely pierced its inkiness. This was the one thing that could frighten her; the utter darkness of the countryside. At home there was always light, from street lamps or pubs and houses, but now she held on tight to Pat, feeling small and vulnerable in all that vast blackness.

When he kissed her, he called her beautiful, and she thought of the old man, who only ever called her useless. His hands, when they had finished unbuttoning her dress, were unusually gentle, working man's hands but with a softness to them that she found irresistible. So different from the old man's hands, which were usually balled into a fist. And suddenly she didn't want to fight any more. So she let herself believe his choked, whispered words of love. She was his girl forever, he would never leave her, he needed her; it was all true and she melted into the fantasy of tenderness that he spun for her.

Next morning, the embers from last night's fire glowed feebly as pickers emerged from their huts, men coughing, bleary-eyed, and women bustling, conscious of so much still to do before leaving.

When her mother roused them, they were all grumpy.

'No use sweatin' in the bed, get up and pull out the mattresses!' she ordered, all the dewy-eyed sentimentality of the night before vanished, as the prospect of home loomed.

'Another five minutes!' pleaded Milly.

'Should have come to bed a bit sooner then!' Her mother hadn't missed as much as she'd hoped.

Milly rolled off the sleeping platform, dragging her straw pillow and pulling the mattress out from under her two sisters.

'Leave off!' snapped Elsie. 'I've got a bad leg.'

'Oh, we won't hear the last of this,' Milly said, lifting the injured leg to pull the mattress off the shelf. 'Come on, you!' She dug Amy in the ribs and was rewarded with a 'Sod off'.

'Get out the bed, you foul-mouthed little cow!' Milly pulled her youngest sister up, and together they dragged out mattresses, pillows, straw and old lino, dumping them on the fire, which spluttered to life, as other families began to burn all the evidence of their five weeks in the country. Even their hopping clothes were considered too verminous to be taken home and were added to the fire.

Milly stared at the conflagration, while flames flicked and sparks flew. How could she have let that happen, last night with Pat? Had becoming the hop princess stripped her of all her defences? She had entirely forgotten the girl from Rotherhithe, she had ignored all the warnings, she had suppressed her carefully practised instinct for survival. She was appalled at her own weakness. Now, in the grey mist of the morning, as she stared into the crumbling embers, she found him, unexpectedly, at her side.

'How's my hop princess?' He grabbed her, spinning her round to face him. He looked pleased with himself.

She looked at him uncertainly. He looked so different this morning, bleary-eyed and dishevelled. Her hop prince had changed back into plain old Pat Donovan.

'Ready to go home?' he asked, smiling broadly.

She turned back towards the fire, wondering if last night she could have confused deviousness with tenderness. If she had, she feared she might live to regret it.

'Yes, I'm ready to go home,' she said, letting her hop garlands fall into the fire.

7

A Bloody Good Hiding

Autumn 1923

Rosie Rockle was standing at her open front door. Even on this chilly, autumnal Saturday afternoon, many of the neighbours still stood outside their doors, gossiping and catching up on the life of the Place. But today Rosie was alone and as Milly returned from her Saturday morning shift, the woman beckoned to her.

'There's been murders this afternoon, Milly,' Rosie said in a hushed voice, though there was no one within earshot. She folded her arms across her faded pinafore, nodding towards the Colman house.

'Why, what's happened?' Milly followed Rosie's look and noticed, with alarm, that her own front door was ajar.

'I just wanted to warn you, love, before you go in. I did my best, but . . . well, you'd better go and see to your mother—'

Before Rosie could finish, Milly turned and shot across the alley into her own house. Inside it was too quiet. Normally at this time on a Saturday, with the old man's wages already handed over, there would be the bustle of preparing Saturday tea, groceries for the week dumped on the table, waiting to be packed away, the younger girls picking at the new bread, dipping fingers into the jam and generally getting in the way. The silence didn't seem that of an empty house. She made her way from the passage, cautiously now, into the kitchen.

Her mother was sitting by the cold grate, head bowed in her hands, crying softly. The two younger Colman girls sat at her feet, white-faced and subdued. If Amy and Elsie had nothing to say, then Milly dreaded to think what they had witnessed.

She ran to her mother, as her sisters shuffled aside to make room.

'What's he done to you?' Milly asked, her voice sounding distant to her own ears, drowned out by the drumbeat of her heart.

Her mother raised a puffy face. Milly let out a cry. Blood oozed through broken skin on her mother's cheek, an angry bruise already blooming. Ellen Colman held her hand to the side of her head, and as Milly gently removed it, making her mother wince, she uncovered a bloody patch of pink scalp just above the temple. Elsie tugged at Milly's skirt, silently holding up a handful of long pale hair. It was her mother's.

'I asked him for his wages, same as always, and he just turned on me,' her mother said, almost as though this had never happened before. 'Then he's done no more than dragged me round the kitchen by me hair. Calling me all sorts. I thought he was going to kill me.' Her mother's voice cracked as she tried to control the trembling that ran through her body. 'I must've screamed,' she went on, gripping her hands tightly together, ''cause all the neighbours come running.' She sank back, looking despairingly at Milly. 'I'm so ashamed, what must they think of me?'

'Oh, Mum, why should *you* be ashamed? It's him!' she said, as rage began to burn like ice, detached and slow. It was not the normal hot-tempered flare-up she usually felt with Elsie or Amy. It was an anger born of many similar incidents, conceived on those nights when Milly and her sisters would lie awake listening to the thuds and crashes as the old man kicked their mother round the kitchen like a football. It had been nurtured every time he'd lashed out with a careless blow, when something annoyed him. But now the feeling was coming of age.

She disentangled herself from her mother. Turning to her sisters, she said, 'Amy, can you get a clean cloth and wash Mum's cuts? Elsie, make up a fire, will you?'

The sisters jumped to their tasks, with no arguments, while Milly went to the corner cupboard where her father kept his brandy.

'No, Milly, don't take that!' Her mother's face was suddenly alert with fear. 'He'll miss it.'

'Sod him, here, you have a drop.' She poured a little into a cup and put it carefully into her mother's shaking hands.

'Where's he gone?' she asked, watching while her mother sipped slowly.

'Down the pub, I expect, I don't suppose we'll see him till late.'

'Maybe *you* won't, Mum, but I will.'

'No, Milly!' She grasped Milly's arm. 'Don't cross him! You'll only make it worse for all of us. Just let him have his bellyful and we'll forget it.'

But Milly shook her hand off and walked out of the kitchen, aware of Elsie's fear-filled eyes following her. She hadn't taken her coat off and she was glad of it, once out in the misty chill of the late afternoon. She stepped over some children sprawled across the paving, playing alley gobs, and set off up Arnold's Place, towards Dockhead, vaguely aware of Ronnie Rockle and Barrel falling in behind her. She registered Rosie and Mrs Knight poking their heads out from their doors as she passed, and thought she heard them call a warning, but nothing could distract her from the slow burning rage which had begun to rise from the pit of her stomach and was now grabbing at her chest. Her breath came in shorter gasps and by the time she passed Holy Trinity Church, the rage had reached her throat. She glanced at people going in for confession; she would not be joining them today. A couple of nuns from the convent came towards her, habits flapping in the sharp breeze, like two black-winged crows. They smiled at her. They'd once been her teachers, the ones she'd made nightgowns for in sewing lessons. But she looked through them without acknowledgement, darting suddenly across the road, narrowly missing a tram, then turning right towards the Swan and Sugarloaf.

There was a pub on every corner at Dockhead; the old man had plenty of choice, but the Swan was his favourite. The pub was now heavily cloaked in river mist. Milly blinked, but her eyes wouldn't clear. It was as if the mist had seeped behind her eyes and, almost unseeing, she gripped the brass handle, flinging open the pub door.

It was a smoke-filled, beery cavern, packed with men in flat caps, who were already well into the Saturday ritual of drinking away their week's wages. None of them interrupted their drinking to turn round. She stood in the doorway, letting the freezing wind that whipped up from the river blast its way into the warm fug.

'Put some wood in the bloody 'ole!' a young man barked, glaring at her.

When she continued to hold the door open, more and more faces turned towards her. She recognized some of the men she'd travelled to Kent with, on Pat's lorry. There was Sid, and Harry, reaching up for the pint on top of his piano. Then she spotted the old man, his back towards her, holding a pint of bitter. He was loudly recounting some joke, surrounded by mates from the tannery. She was struck by how jovial and carefree he seemed. None of her mother's pain had touched him. His features, though bloodshot and drink-befuddled, lacked their domestic scowl; he could almost be taken for an amiable man. It was his laughter, the laughter she never heard at home, that finally caused her building rage to burst free.

'You bastard, get out here!' she roared at him. Now every head snapped round. Pints halted mid-sip, conversations stopped and mouths opened. He was almost the last to turn. A look of bewilderment changed, chameleon-like, to embarrassment, as a purple blush suffused his face.

'What the fuck d'you want?' he slurred, turning unsteadily to face her.

She didn't answer. Instead, using his drunken surprise to her advantage, she charged, barrelling through the crowd. Men jumped out of her path, beer spilled over her, as, head down, she launched herself straight for his midriff. She had grown taller than he was in the last year and was much quicker on her feet. His glass crashed to the floor as he doubled over, winded, gasping for breath. She bent her knees, bringing up her fist as she did so, to connect with his jaw in a satisfying crack that sent him spinning.

'You ever . . .' she grabbed his jacket, spun herself round like a discus thrower and using muscles built up hauling seven-pound jam jars, flung him towards the door, 'hit my mother . . .' and he sprawled flat on the beery sawdust as she aimed a kick at his backside, 'again . . .' His head cracked the edge of the door. 'An' I'll kill you!'

She brought her booted foot up under his midriff, sending him clean through the door and out into the street. Her breath came like a serrated blade, in jagged bursts, as she bent forward, hands on thighs. Almost spent, she became aware of the crowd surrounding her on the pavement, some cheering her on, others jeering and laughing at the old man.

'Go on, Mill,' she heard a friend of her mother's shouting, 'give the bastard some of his own treatment!'

She heard a piano, playing incongruously, and realized that Harry was still pounding away, almost as though he was providing musical accompaniment to the drama. She straightened up. Her father was still lying on the pavement, seemingly unable to get up. Remembering all the times her mother had been his football, she ran forward, aiming one last punishing kick into the old man's kidneys as he struggled to rise. He slumped back, curled into a ball and covered his head. She leaned over him, whispering hoarsely into his ear, 'Don't you *ever* touch my mother again.'

Spent now, panting and trembling, she felt the world around her coming back into focus. She recognized individual faces in the crowd, saw Ronnie and Barrel among the hooting children attracted by the brawl. She even noticed the passengers on the top deck of a passing tram, staring down curiously at father and daughter trapped like two prizefighters, in a ring of bodies outside the Swan.

Pushing her way through the crush, it struck her like the blow that he hadn't landed: her father was a coward. It seemed so obvious now, but how had it taken her a lifetime to discover it? All those years they'd suffered under his tyranny and she had left him back there, a cowering bundle on the pavement. But coward or not, she knew there would be consequences and, realizing what she'd done, a tremor of fear, not for herself but for her mother, seized her. She ran towards home.

The day Milly Colman called her old man out of the Swan and Sugarloaf was talked of for many years in Arnold's Place. It was embellished so much that one version even had her ending up killing him and swinging for it. But for Milly, it was the day her life changed forever. The word had quickly got back to Arnold's Place, and she was confronted by a huddle of neighbours outside her front door.

'Good on yer, Milly,' Rosie Rockle nodded approvingly, 'he won't hit her no more, not after that pasting. Our Ronnie said you give him a bloody good hiding!'

'I did, Rosie,' said Milly, as the other women moved aside, murmuring their admiration. 'I'd better tell me mum.'

'I think she already knows, love,' said Mrs Knight, but her look was pitying rather than admiring, perhaps not so convinced that Milly had helped her mother at all.

Elsie and Amy had been part of the welcoming committee on the doorstep and now followed her inside. The kitchen looked just as it normally did, the furniture had been straightened, the fire lit and the groceries put away. Her mother was sitting at the kitchen table, hands flat on the white scrubbed boards. Other than the bloody patch, which she had tried to hide by combing over her hair, she looked her normal tidy self, face washed, and a clean pinafore wrapped around her skinny body. She raised hopeless eyes as Milly entered.

'It won't do no good, Mill. You've only made it worse.' She shook her head. 'He'll end up killing you. I know him. You've shown him up in front of his mates and he won't let it be.'

'I had to, Mum—'

'We've still got to live with him!' her mother interrupted. 'I need his wages for their sakes.' She nodded towards the girls. 'But I'm scared what he'll do now. He'll kill you in your bed and I'll never be able to sleep quiet again. I think you'll have to go, love, keep out of his way for a bit.'

Milly sat down heavily on the chair opposite her mother. She was right. There would be no peace in the house for her mother or sisters, not while Milly was there. Even if she'd scared the old man enough not to beat her mother, there were other ways he could make all their lives miserable.

'It's all right, Mum,' she said, moving round the table to grasp her mother's hand. 'I'd made up me mind to go, but now he knows what I can do, he'll leave you alone . . . at least for a while.'

'Oh, Jesus,' her mother sobbed. 'Me poor girl, you've got nowhere to go. But you can't be here when he gets home—'

Just then they heard the front door banging open and the old man stumbled into the kitchen. He had lost his cap and his choker was askew. Milly's mother jumped up to stand in front of Milly. Her father staggered, holding one hand to his ribs. He didn't look at Milly; his eyes slid past her to Mrs Colman.

'Get me the liniment, she's broke me fuckin' ribs.' He slumped down into his chair by the fire, wincing. Her mother went to the sideboard and the old man stared at the fire, speaking almost to himself. 'Keep her out of my sight. I don't want to see her.'

'Go on . . .' Her mother was pushing Milly out into the passage. 'Make yourself scarce.' She lowered her voice to a whisper. 'Come back when he's in bed!'

Milly stepped out into the street, where by now the excitement had already died down. Domestic disputes came and went with great regularity in Arnold's Place and they were always conducted in public. The houses faced each other with only nine or ten feet of paving between them and the front windows were positioned opposite each other, so that any degree of privacy was minimal. But the neighbours had retreated inside for Saturday tea and Milly found herself contemplating a long evening alone. She looked for regret in her heart, but couldn't find any. The remembered sensation of her fist connecting with his jaw was so sweet it was worth a lifetime's exile, and she had the deeper satisfaction of knowing she'd saved her mother from any more abuse, at the very least until his ribs healed. She absent-mindedly rubbed her grazed knuckles, then made up her mind.

Saturday night was dance night at Bermondsey Baths and she'd arranged to meet some of the other jam girls there. Why should she change her plans? If her own home was denied her, she would find another, on the streets of Bermondsey.

She headed for the two-up two-down in Hickman's Folly, where Kitty Bunclerk lived with her parents, five sisters and little brother Percy. After six girls, Mr Bunclerk had wanted to name him Perseverance, but Mrs Bunclerk, being more merciful, had suggested they compromise with Percy.

When she arrived they were sitting down to Saturday tea. As one of the older Bunclerk girls ushered her through the narrow passage, Milly smiled at the three youngest children, who were seated on the stairs, plates balanced on their laps. The tiny kitchen wasn't big enough for them all to sit round the table at once and Milly could barely fit herself into the room. Mrs Bunclerk welcomed her in, just as Kitty came out of the scullery.

'You're early! We heard you give your old man a good hiding! Has he chucked you out?' Kitty asked, wide-eyed.

'Not yet, but I'm steering clear of him for a bit.'

'You'd better keep your head down, love,' a toothless Mrs Bunclerk smiled cheerily, 'and lock the bedroom door an'all, he's the sort'd kill you in your bed!'

'Mum! Stop it, you'll frighten the life out of her. Come in the scullery, Mill.'

The others looked disappointed as Milly squeezed round the table and out into the back scullery.

'What are you going to do now?' Kitty turned her bright, concerned eyes on Milly.

'I'm going to the dance, what else?'

Kitty burst into giggles. 'Milly Colman, only you could pay your dad in front of the whole world and then go dancing as if nothing had happened.'

'Well, I'll need to tidy myself up a bit first, look at the state of me.'

She peered into the small mirror hanging on a nail above the sink and pulled at her hair. Looking down at her coat, she noticed it had lost a couple of buttons in the scuffle. 'And look at me dancing shoes!' Milly lifted her foot, to show her friend the old work boots she was still wearing.

'Come upstairs with me, there ought to be *something* we can find for you to wear, with six girls in the house!'

Squeezing back through the kitchen and stepping over the children still seated on the stairs, they made their way up to the bedroom where each night Kitty and her five sisters squeezed into the one bed, while Percy still slept in their parents' room. After a little rummaging around in a narrow wardrobe, Kitty emerged with a pair of strapped shoes and a blue shift dress.

'This is our Ada's best dress, she's more your size, and try these shoes on, her plates are bigger than mine.'

Milly took the shoes. 'Shouldn't you ask her first?'

'She's not going to need them. She's doing overtime tonight. You try 'em on, I'll go and talk her round!'

Kitty disappeared downstairs while Milly slipped into the dress and shoes. Soon Kitty reappeared with Ada, who was younger than Milly and not quite as tall. She worked at Southwell's too, but in the candied-peel department. Ada always held her large hands under her armpits, as though she were nursing them. They were permanently red and swollen with inflamed cuts, from peeling citrus fruit.

'Ohhh, you cow,' she said enviously, as Milly turned round, 'you look better in that dress than I do!'

'D'you mind, Ada, just this once?'

'No, you go out and enjoy yourself, Milly. You deserve it after the show you give us all today!'

Ada told her that the crowd outside the pub had included many of the jam girls, and they'd all enjoyed themselves afterwards, retelling the fight blow by blow. Milly felt like one of the celebrated boxers from the Thomas A Becket. Conscious of the irony of moving from hop princess to prizefighter in a few short weeks, she gave Ada a wry smile. 'Well, I'm glad I brightened up someone's day!'

When they arrived at the Bermondsey Baths, there was already a crowd of young men and girls in their Saturday night finery queuing outside. There had been no time for Milly to give her mother her pay packet, so she still had it with her, and when their turn came to pay the entrance, she dug around in the envelope for a sixpence.

'Are you meeting Pat?' Kitty asked her.

Milly turned up her nose. 'I don't know, Kit, he's getting a bit of a handful. I might fancy a change!' She sounded more unconcerned than she felt, for that one night when she'd given in to Pat, down hopping, had never been repeated, much to his frustration, and she was getting tired of fending him off.

'Well, make up your mind quick, here he comes.'

Pat came up to her, smiling. His sandy hair had resisted the oil he'd plastered it with, but she could tell he'd made an effort to look smart, in his best suit and shiny two-tone shoes.

'Fancy a dance?' he asked eagerly.

'Let me take my coat off first!'

He took the coat from her shoulders and stood back admiringly. 'You don't look bad for an old bruiser!'

Kitty laughed and Milly shot her a look. Obviously there wasn't anyone who hadn't heard. The piano and little band struck up a foxtrot and Milly let herself be whirled away. She was a good dancer and could match Pat's long strides with ease. She loved the newer dances and the jazzier tunes, and before long she was abandoning herself to the rhythm of the music, swinging arms and legs and matching Pat, move for move, in a whirl of gaiety that banished for a time all the violence of the day.

Although officially there were no drinks for sale on dance nights, there was always a fair amount of illicit alcohol being surreptitiously consumed. Pat had smuggled in half a bottle of gin, and before too long she felt tipsy and numb. By the end of the evening, a cocktail of gin and natural optimism had conspired to mask her anxieties about the war at home. But when the dance was over, and they left the Baths, Pat began pulling her towards the river stairs at Southwell's Wharf. His hand grasped her wrist.

'Come on, Mill,' he slurred, 'give us a kiss.' But she didn't want to kiss him. She wanted to creep home and hide herself in some corner till her bruised knuckles stopped aching and her head stopped thumping.

'Goodnight, Pat,' she said, but as she turned away he reached out, catching her by the hair. Remembering the pale skein of hair the old man had ripped from her mother's head, bitter anger rose like bile in her throat. She spun round and said, with cold fierceness, 'Don't touch me, Pat. Just go home.'

She'd already fought one man today, and she'd rather not have to take on another.

8

The Sewing Circle

December 1923

Milly walked through the freezing December streets, coat collar up, chin buried in her scarf. Warm breath plumed up around her cheeks, but she was shivering. After an evening at the Bermondsey Settlement girls' club, it had been too early to go home and she'd been walking for over an hour, wasting time until she could be certain that her father had gone to bed.

It was over a month since she'd given her father a beating and from that day on, Milly had been forced to live a fugitive life. It had been an uncomfortable limbo. She couldn't move out, her wages simply wouldn't cover rent and board in a lodging house, yet neither could she feel part of the old life in Arnold's Place. Instead she haunted her home like a ghost caught between this world and the next. The only way to keep any semblance of peace in the house was to make sure she stayed out whenever the old man was at home. It was a game of cat and mouse, which meant she found herself thinking about the old man far more than she would have liked.

She usually ate her dinner in the Southwell's mess room, and after work, instead of going home, she took to meeting up with the other jam girls in the Folly or at the Settlement. She only ever returned home to fall into bed and sleep, but even then she made sure to wedge a chair against the bedroom door, to prevent any drunken intrusions from the old man. She often wondered if the hiding she'd given him had been worth it. Sometimes she thought her mother would have welcomed his regular beatings, in return for the old semblance of family life.

When Milly finally crept into the house, she found her mother sitting by the fire in her nightgown.

'Oh, Mum, you shouldn't have waited up,' Milly said to her softly. Careful to keep her arrival quiet, she tiptoed over to sit on the floor beside her mother, entwining her arms round Ellen Colman's skinny legs.

'Well, it's the only time I get to see you these days, love.'

Milly looked up into her face. 'You look sad.'

She allowed her mother to stroke her hair as if she were a child again.

'It's enough to make me sad,' her mother sighed. 'It's like being in the middle of a battlefield in this house, what with you and him at each other's throats and then you can't even be friends with your sisters. This house . . . there's never any peace in it.' She shook her head sadly. Milly felt so helpless. She'd done her best to free her mother, but with two children and no income of her own, Mrs Colman was in the same economic prison as all the other wives in Arnold's Place. And now Milly feared she'd only succeeded in making that prison a more unpleasant place.

'I wish I'd done a proper job and killed him, *then* we'd have had some peace,' she said fiercely.

'Milly Colman!' her mother said in a shocked whisper. 'You don't mean that! Whatever he's done, he's still your father!'

A long creaking came from the staircase and they both froze, holding their breaths, until it was clear the sound was only the wind finding its path through the ill-fitting front door. Milly snuggled in closer to her mother's legs, trying to catch some warmth from the fire.

Looking up at her mother now, she felt truly sorry that she'd robbed her of all those illusions that they were a real family. It had always been a stretch. Perhaps if she'd succeeded in her attempt to forge a stronger bond with her sisters, Milly would have tried harder to submit to the old man's tyranny, for the sake of a quiet life for all of them. But, even before her great rebellion, there seemed very little glue holding them all together. Her mother simply hadn't the strength to be the lynchpin in the family, and Milly, try as she might, had failed to be one either.

'I only ever wanted the family to stick together,' Mrs Colman said, 'but sometimes I truly wonder how we can all be the same blood. It's only that I know for a fact those girls are your sisters and he's your father!'

She gave Milly a searching look, as though she were answering some unasked question.

'Oh, I don't doubt we're the same blood, Mum. It's just we're all stubborn and selfish . . . except you.'

She got up and planted a kiss on her mother's cheek.

'You could at least try to get on with your sisters, they need you, now more than ever.'

'Oh, I've tried, Mum, but sometimes I wonder if they really do need me,' Milly said wistfully, catching her mother's melancholy. 'But Elsie's always off in a world of her own, and Amy's sharp as a box of knives . . . even when I offer to help her, she just pushes me away.'

Her mother shook her head in denial. 'You was the one looked after her when she was a baby, she thinks the world of you!'

Perhaps it had been true once, but now? She found it hard to believe. Amy had been a war baby. Charlie was dead before she reached her first birthday, and Jimmy before her second. When their brothers were killed, Mrs Colman seemed to fade away, hardly able to keep herself alive, let alone a baby, so Milly had become Amy's surrogate mother. She had a distinct memory of her ten-year-old self, just after hearing of Jimmy's death. Her mother had left Amy screaming, unchanged and unfed, and so Milly had taken it upon herself to look after her.

She remembered singing 'Rock a Bye Baby on the Treetop', with tears streaming down her face, as she bounced Amy along in her pram. Amy had laughed in delight, enjoying the rough bouncing, demanding more, yet Milly's own misery went unsoothed. She was little more than a child herself, her mother vanished in grief, her two brothers dead and her father, a brutal drunk, wreaking vengeance in all the wrong places. She had poured out all her tender feelings on the baby, but Amy seemed to sense she'd been born in a war zone, and from an early age had learned to survive on her own. Milly remembered picking her up that day, wanting to hold her softness against her wet cheek, but Amy had wriggled like a fury.

'Come on.' She pulled her mother up. 'Let's creep upstairs, before he hears us.'

They followed each other up, avoiding the treads that creaked, and Milly slipped quietly into her room, feeling like a burglar in the night. Amy lay with her head to the foot of the bed, and Elsie stirred as Milly rolled her over. She slipped into the warm spot her sister had vacated and reached down for Amy.

'Come up this end,' she whispered to the sleeping child.

Still half asleep, Amy obeyed. 'Are you cold?' she asked thickly.

'Yes,' Milly lied, putting her arms round Amy, so that they were spooned in the bed.

She lay awake for a long time, remembering that week in the hop gardens. Only two months had passed, but it felt like a lifetime ago. Two months? A sudden anxiety gripped her, with the dawning realization that those golden, early autumn days might have marked far more than the end of summer.

At the factory next day Milly took more than her allowed quota of toilet breaks – after the fifth time, the foreman told her he'd dock her half an hour if she went again.

'What's the matter with you?' Kitty said under her breath, when she returned. 'You never have weak bladder trouble when you're drinking in the Folly!'

Milly smiled weakly, but her stomach was churning. Her frequent checking only made her more anxious. She told herself to be patient, it could well be a false alarm.

At the end of the day she walked out of the gates, still lost in her own anxiety, and was waylaid by the last person she wanted to see. He was lounging against his lorry outside Southwell's, obviously waiting for her.

'Hello, stranger,' he called to her, 'I ain't seen you in days. Fancy coming for a drink?'

She shook her head. 'Sorry, can't, I'm going to the sewing circle at the Settlement.'

The girls' club at the Bermondsey Settlement had been a lifesaver for Milly. The rambling, soot-stained Victorian building was home to a group of young Methodist missionaries, called to live among the poor of Bermondsey. They were often doctors or solicitors, who visited the overcrowded terraces and tenements surrounding the Settlement, offering their services free of charge. They ran children's clubs and country holidays, put on lectures, and encouraged working girls and boys to better themselves.

Clubs were held on most nights of the week. Milly would go straight from Southwell's to the local coffee shop, have something to eat, then go on to the Settlement, where she could change out of her work clothes and spend the evening in the warm with her friends.

She was even beginning to prefer the sewing circle to a night in the Folly. And now, barely looking up, she attempted to hurry past Pat. Milly's interest in him had waned soon after their chase through the hop fields, and as she'd feared, once back in Bermondsey, she bitterly regretted those fumbles among the green hops of Kent. Out from under the spell of the hop gardens, she could no longer fool herself he was any sort of 'hop prince', any more than she was a princess. He'd quickly reverted to being Pat from Dockhead, familiar, predictable and somehow confining. She was sure she ought to feel something a little stronger for someone she was courting and had tried her best to rebuff him.

'Sewing circle! Makes you sound like some old gel.' Pat's scornful expression irritated her. She stopped and faced him.

'What's wrong with sewing? I'm good at it, and anyway, I can't afford to buy new dresses.'

'You only have to say and I'll get you a new dress any time,' Pat boasted, and it was true, he seemed always to have money in his pocket these days. Though Milly knew the majority of his business was conducted by moonlight and out of the back of the lorry, she hoped he was still trying to make a legitimate living during the daylight hours.

Milly shook her head. 'I wouldn't let you buy a dress for me.'

'Well, can I interest you in something else?' Pat said enigmatically, drawing her in. He whispered, 'I'm getting a load of tinned stuff tonight. Wondered if your mum could do with some?'

'Knocked off?' Milly whispered back.

''Course, knocked off, straight out of Crosse & Blackwell's!'

Milly hesitated. The old man seemed less and less willing to hand over the housekeeping each week, and she knew her mother would welcome the food.

'But if you're not interested . . .' Pat shrugged.

'No, I am interested, only I promised to meet Kitty at the Settlement after tea.'

'Well, I ain't getting it till after dark!' He winked at her. 'Tell you what, I'll pick you up from the Settlement, after your club.'

'Oh, all right then.'

'So what about that drink first?'

The warmth and life of the pub suddenly seemed preferable to a lonely tea in Reeny's coffee shop, and Milly agreed. 'So long as it's not the Swan.'

''Course not, we'll go to the Folly, same as always.'

'All right, anywhere the old man doesn't go's fine with me.'

It would be quicker to walk through the narrow courts and alleys than to drive in the lorry, so Pat left it parked outside Southwell's and they set off briskly through a freezing fog that was settling low over the rooftops. Milly jammed her hands into her coat pockets. They were chapped and bleeding from peeling a barge load of early Seville oranges, and the bitter cold of the unheated fruit-picking room hadn't helped. She hated marmalade season, for on bad days it ruined her fingers and robbed her of one of the few things in life that lifted her heart, her sewing. Still, tonight she was determined to finish the new dress she was making for her mother, sore fingers or not. Cutting down Farthing Alley, they skirted a few empty prams left outside front doors, then crossed a close huddled court of dilapidated houses, leading into Hickman's Folly.

'Shall we knock for Kitty?' Milly asked as they passed her door.

Pat looked a little crestfallen. No doubt he was hoping for an hour alone with Milly, but he nodded. The Bunclerks had apparently finished their tea and Percy opened the door with his face still covered in a good portion of it.

He screamed into the dark interior, 'Kitty, it's yer mate!' and dashed back down the passage.

Kitty came to the door and seeing Pat, her face hardened, 'Ain't you going to the club tonight?' she asked Milly.

'Yes, but we're going for a drink first, can you come?' Milly's expression was a mute appeal. Kitty knew that she was tiring of Pat and gave her an accusing look, which Milly knew she deserved. It was no good complaining about him to Kitty, if she encouraged him the very next time she saw him. Kitty threw on her coat, glad to get out of the cramped hubbub of her home, and they soon came to the Folly.

A weak golden glow from the gas lamp on the wall opposite cut through the fog and lit up the door. They hustled inside and were immediately hit by a pall of cigarette smoke, thick as the fog outside. But the gaslight and chatter and warmth of the packed bodies was welcoming, none the less. Some of Pat's friends spotted them and beckoned him over to a table in the corner, where seats were found for Milly and Kitty. Freddie Clark was there already, and Milly noticed a slight blush colour Kitty's face. Clara and Ivy, a couple of jam girls Milly knew, were sitting at the same table and the girls immediately fell into the latest factory gossip, eager to find out what each knew about the current round of lay-offs. Preserve making was always dependent upon the season and in winter, when the summer fruits disappeared, so did many of the women's jobs.

'The Seville oranges are early, they're rolling in off the docks,' Pat added helpfully. 'At least you'll have plenty of peeling and pulping to keep you busy on the marmalade. Matter of fact, I've got a couple of barrels round the yard if anyone's interested?'

Milly groaned. 'Talk about coals to Newcastle, don't you think we can 'alf-inch as many as we like? But I'm sick of the smell of oranges this time of year, look at the state of my hands! To think I used to look forward to getting an orange in me stocking every Christmas!'

Milly held out her raw hands for inspection as the other girls agreed with her. Working in the finishing room, their hands were at least saved from all but the irritating effects of the glue used to label the jam jars.

Pat suddenly took one of her hands.

'You should give that up,' he said suddenly. 'You're too good for that work.'

A round of 'ooohs!' from the other girls followed and Milly snatched her hand away.

'Chance'd be a fine thing,' she said, picking up the pint of bitter Pat had bought her. 'What else would I do? Make biscuits instead of jam?'

Pat was silenced. But Milly remembered how she'd once dreamed of being something else, a seamstress. The nuns at school had taught her needlework and had always praised her skills – except when she let her desire for beauty outweigh their instructions to make plain, serviceable garments. As schoolgirls they were set the task of making the nuns' nightgowns and once Milly, tiring of plain tucks, had set about inserting some fancy smocking on Sister Clare's nightdress. This particular nun was a gentle, sweet-tempered teaching sister, and Milly had simply wanted to do something nice for her. But her generous impulse was ill-judged, as it was Sister Mary Paul who was collecting in their work that day.

'Girl Colman,' had come the shrill voice of Sister Mary Paul, when the sewing class was over. 'You will unpick this frivolous frill immediately!'

This was all the thanks Milly got, along with a sharp rap of the ruler over her knuckles. She had wanted to ask, what was the harm? Was it so wrong to have something that looked lovely, as long as it did the job? But not wanting another rap or worse, she'd held her tongue and undid all her work. But the idea of becoming a seamstress, making beautiful dresses in expensive velvets and silks, had lodged in her child's imagination, and when the time came to leave school Sister Clare had found her an apprenticeship with a West End seamstress. For a few days Milly knew the joy of a dream come true, until it was squashed firmly by the old man.

'There's no money for bus fares over the West End, and anyway, she'll make better money in the jam factory. They're crying out for girls, God knows, they don't want the men any more since the war,' he'd told her mother. So she had gone to Southwell's and her dream had, if not died, at least gone into a long hibernation. Kitty suddenly interrupted her daydreaming.

'What you smiling to yourself for?' she'd asked, and suddenly Milly remembered where she was meant to be. She got up abruptly, pushing the chair back, so that it fell to the floor.

'Come on, Kit, for chrissake, get yourself moving or we'll miss the sewing circle!' she said in real panic, scrabbling to pick up the chair.

Pat had been very generous with the drinks, round had followed round, and by now both Milly and Kitty were far too tipsy to walk straight. Pat and Freddie were about to walk out with them.

'No, we're going on our own!' Milly protested, trying to push Pat's hand away as he steadied her. She missed him and toppled forward on to Kitty, who bumped back on to the table, rocking the glasses precariously.

'Mind the drinks!' Freddie lunged for the slopping beer glasses.

'All right, but I don't think you'll be getting much sewing done tonight!' Pat eyed them both uncertainly. 'I'll come and pick you up later, Mill, come and get the stuff, all right?'

But Milly and Kitty were already stumbling out of the door. Milly started to trot, her friend lagging behind her, as they weaved their way along Hickman's Folly. There was only one gas lamp in the street, so they stumbled several times in the soupy gloom of the foggy night. A figure came out at them suddenly, but it was only Quackers, a white-faced wraith of a man who never walked but only skipped and jumped across each paving stone, as though avoiding the unexploded bombs of no-man's-land. The poor man had been ruined by shell shock and was mercilessly taunted by the local children as he crouched at loud noises, earning his nickname by shouting 'Duck! Duck!' Milly usually stopped to talk to him; he reminded her of Charlie, and couldn't have been much older. But tonight they hurried on and had passed him long before he'd had time to warn them to duck.

When they finally arrived, breathless and giggling, at the Settlement, the doors were closed and the lights burning in every room. The lectures and clubs were obviously well under way. From inside came the strains of piano and violin, and a quavering soprano singing an old English folk song, a jaunty, country air, which seemed totally at odds with the soot-wreathed maze of crumbling courts surrounding the Settlement.

Milly caught Kitty round the waist and began to whirl her in a drunken country dance, which one of the missionaries at the Guild of Play had taught them when they were children. They ended by tumbling back down the curving flight of stone steps leading up to the Settlement door and were both on their backsides, laughing so loudly that Milly didn't hear the door open. Backlit by the warm light from the hall, Miss Florence Green stood, waiting for their laughter to subside. Sweet of face and nature, Miss Green was Milly's favourite at the Settlement. She ran the sewing circle and had encouraged Milly's talent for needlework. She loved Miss Green because she was always totally impartial. She'd come to help the poor of Bermondsey, and neither cared nor enquired what religion they were. Catholics and Protestants alike were all welcome to whatever charity was on offer, in the way of free country holidays, clothes, food or medical care.

Milly spotted her at the door and waved in drunken gaiety. 'Hello, Flo, me old cocker!'

As she pulled Kitty up, the two girls stumbled up the steps and Miss Green swung open the door to admit them. The young missionary stood facing the two girls, and Milly thought she read disappointment in her face.

'Milly, I believe you're inebriated,' she said sadly.

If it had been anyone else, Milly would have given her a cheeky answer, but instead she breathed deeply and tried to focus her eyes on the plain, pleasant features of Miss Green.

'Ever so shorry, Mishh Green,' she mumbled, as she passed into the hall, 'have we missed the sewing?'

She turned to Kitty for help. But her friend had unaccountably slumped to the floor and was now clinging to Milly's ankles like a drowning woman. 'Ohhh, I do feel bad, Mill. Can I just stay here and go to sleep?'

Miss Green sighed. 'No, you can't stay there, Kitty,' she said firmly, and bent to grasp Kitty's arms. 'Quickly, Milly, you take her legs. Help me get her into the dining room.'

Though she had twice the strength of Miss Green, Milly was less help than she would normally have been, and while they were struggling with Kitty a man poked his head out of one of the lecture rooms.

'Can I help?' he said to Miss Green, who nodded gratefully. As he lifted Kitty in his arms, Milly's unfocused eyes thought she recognized him. She followed him as he carried her friend to a chair in the empty, oak-panelled dining room where, slumped and insensible, she immediately began to snore.

'Thanks ever sho much . . .' Milly couldn't remember his name.

'Bertie . . . Hughes, and you're very welcome.' He smiled

and, as he left, laid a hand on Miss Green's shoulder, whispering something Milly could not hear.

'You sit down too, Milly dear,' Miss Green said, bringing up another chair. 'You're not fit for sewing tonight, I'm afraid.'

'Oh, that's not fair, I want to finish Mum's dress!' Milly protested.

Miss Green pulled up a chair close to the two girls. 'Milly, if you can't walk a straight line, I doubt you'll be able to sew one tonight. You don't want to spoil all your hard work, do you?'

The woman's good sense penetrated Milly's foggy, drunken haze and she began to feel ashamed of herself. What must Miss Green think of her, turning up here, of all places, blind drunk? But whatever she thought, her voice remained calm and gentle. Milly's home life was no secret and the woman had gone out of her way to make her feel comfortable in this wood-panelled imitation of a country house, amidst the slums.

'There's plenty of time to finish it before Christmas. You two can sleep it off in here, till we lock up. No one will disturb you.'

And with that, Miss Green glided out and back to her more sober pupils in the sewing circle.

Milly called a beery thank you after her and addressed an oblivious Kitty. 'God love her, Kit, that woman may be a proddywack, but I'll give a shilling for a pinch o' sugar she'll end up in heaven.'

Soon Milly had joined Kitty in her beer-fuelled slumber and it wasn't until almost eleven o'clock that Miss Green came to rouse them.

Pat was waiting outside, with his engine running. She said a quick goodnight to Kitty, then jumped up a little shakily on to the running board and into the cab. Soon they were rattling down Shad Thames, the long, narrow canyon of warehouses running parallel to the river. A group of noisy dockers, working night shift at Butler's Wharf, swore as they were forced to jump out of the path of the lorry. During the day the street was packed with lorries and carts, but was now largely deserted. Iron gantries criss-crossed above them at crazy angles, linking warehouses on either side of the road, blocking out the stars and adding to the claustrophobic feel of the narrow street. Milly was glad when they arrived at Pat's small lorry yard. Halfway down Shad Thames, it was little more than a space between two warehouses, bricked in at the back and with wooden double gates added at the front. Pat edged the lorry into the yard and jumped out. Milly went to follow, but he put out a hand to stop her.

'Stay there and shut your eyes. What you don't see can't hurt you!' he said, grinning. 'Can't have you witnessing a crime, can we?'

Ignoring his advice, she kept her eyes open. In the wing mirror she could see him lounging at the open gate, smoking. Soon she heard another lorry pull up and, slumping down in the greasy seat, she reached through the open window to angle the mirror for a better view. She was now quite sober, but the lorry smelled strongly of cigarette smoke and petrol fumes and she was feeling queasy. She craned her neck and saw Pat giving the driver of the other lorry a wad of pound notes. The other driver was well built with fair hair and although her view was obscured, she felt sure it was Freddie Clark. Soon there came a thumping and scraping as the two men transferred box after box of tinned food on to the back of Pat's lorry. The whole transaction took less than half an hour, and once the other lorry had driven off, Milly heard Pat pulling tarpaulin over the contraband.

'Let's have a look then,' she said, joining him at the tail board.

He started piling tins into a sack, then presented them to her. 'Your mother's going to love me!' he said.

The words were hardly out of his mouth when they heard a loud whistling and the sound of many booted feet, ringing along Shad Thames.

'Shit! Coppers! Quick, under there!' Pat shoved her towards the back of the yard, hastily covering her with a pile of old oily sacks. 'Don't come out till they're gone!' he ordered.

The first policeman was already at the gates. She heard him shout. 'Donovan, get out here!'

Milly was trembling beneath the sacks and feeling sicker than ever. Stifling her retches, she strained to hear what was going on at the yard gate. As more police arrived, there was a great deal of scuffling. It sounded as if they were removing the tarpaulin from the lorry.

'Going into the wholesale business, Pat?' she heard a policeman say.

'What about it? That's not illegal,' Pat replied calmly. 'They're seconds, dented.'

'Whether they're dented or not, I couldn't say, Patsy, but I'm bloody sure they're bent.'

She heard the coppers laugh loudly, and one said, 'You got any more stashed away? What you got down the end there?'

Milly held her breath, silently repeating Hail Marys as she waited to be discovered under the sacks. Stray bits of dust and sacking were getting down her throat and she gagged on her prayers.

Then another policeman, obviously in charge, called out. 'All right, lads, we haven't got all night, let's escort the gentleman back to Tower Bridge nick for a nice cuppa! Oh, and we'll be confiscating your lorry, Donovan.'

'I could do with a cuppa, strong, two sugars!' she heard Pat say cheekily, and wondered if he'd be less cooperative if she hadn't been bundled under a load of sacks at the back of the yard. She heard the lorry reversing out, but waited for another ten minutes before emerging from her hiding place. She shoved at the gates and groaned as they resisted. 'Oh, Pat Donovan, I don't think my mother's going to love you after all, and neither am I!'

She was locked in.

9

When the Bough Breaks

December 1923

Milly looked around the yard for a means of escape. She soon realized Pat had landed her in a prison every bit as secure as Tower Bridge nick. On either side were the sheer, brick walls of two warehouses; at the back was another unscalable wall. The gate was the only way out. She gave it a good kick, but the outer padlock held fast. If she couldn't go through, she'd have to go over it.

She began searching for something to stand on. Though the fog had lifted a little, the crescent moon gave scant light, and as she stumbled around the yard her foot caught on a hard metal box and she fell heavily on to the oily cobbles. She swore silently, *sod you, Pat Donovan, and your bloody tins of soup!*

The box wasn't large enough to help her over the gates, but thinking it might contain tools that could break the padlock, she lifted the lid. She drew in a sharp breath. Pale moonlight traced the unmistakable outline of a gun. She stroked her finger lightly along the barrel, feeling it slick and icy from the night fog. Her legs trembled as she got to her feet. Whatever Pat was involved in, it was far more dangerous than a few tins of stolen soup. With a thumping heart, she carefully closed the box, shoving it deep under the pile of sacks. She had to get away. What if the police came back?

Trying not to panic, she felt around the rest of the yard till she found some empty tea crates. Dragging them one by one to the gate, she piled them up like steps. Then clambering up to the top crate, she let the sack of tins fall to the ground, before swinging over the gate and dropping surefootedly to the other side. She checked each direction quickly, then grabbing the sack of tins, sprinted off down the dimly lit Shad Thames. She hurtled round Dockhead and didn't stop till she arrived, sweating and heaving for breath, at her front door.

Since Milly's exile, her mother always left the key on a string inside the letterbox, so she could come and go at all hours. She crept into the passage. No one was stirring, but as she let herself into the bedroom, Elsie roused.

'What time is it?' she murmured as Milly turned her over and slipped into bed.

'Not late, go back to sleep.'

'Phew, you stink of oil, you've been in Pat's lorry!' Elsie pushed herself up on to her elbow, peering at Milly in the darkness. 'And what's in that sack you put under the bed?'

'Mind your own business.'

'I'm telling Mum,' Elsie threatened.

Milly dug her sister in the ribs. 'Don't you say nothing, hear me?'

Elsie might be a daydreamer, but it sometimes surprised Milly how much she took in. Everyone in Arnold's Place called her 'Polly Witch' because sometimes her oft-ridiculed dreams came true. She'd recount a dream about someone visiting them, and sure enough that person would turn up. At other times the effect was more sensational. Only last year she'd gone around telling everyone that she'd dreamed of twins being born and the next week, Mrs Williams, who didn't even know she was pregnant, gave birth to two identical tiny boys. This had sealed Elsie's reputation as the prophetess of Arnold's Place. It unsettled Milly intensely, especially when there were things she'd rather keep secret, for Elsie had a way of looking sideways at her before revealing just the very thing that Milly had been hoping to keep to herself. Like tonight's escapade.

Still trembling with fright and the exertion of her escape, she tucked her feet under Amy, who lay like a warm lapdog at the foot of the bed, and eventually fell into a fitful sleep.

The following morning, Milly's mother woke her with a whispered, 'Did you hear about the shenanigans last night? Pat Donovan's been nicked with a lorryload of stolen tins down at his yard!'

How she'd found out so quickly was a mystery, but it seemed Pat's arrest was already known to everyone in Arnold's Place. Pat's mother, old Ma Donovan, who lived in a cramped court of six houses just off Hickman's Folly, was apparently already being visited as though she were in mourning.

'I'll have to go and see that poor mother of his!' Ellen Colman shook her head sympathetically, though Milly hardly felt the woman deserved any. She'd lived off Pat's thieving for years, had even encouraged it.

Milly was relieved that at least her mother didn't know about her own narrow escape. While she'd gratefully accept any goods 'off the back of a lorry', Mrs Colman wouldn't want her own daughter to risk arrest. She'd brought them up to be good Catholic girls and clung to the illusion that her family was 'respectable'. Milly thought her father had put paid to that fantasy years before.

'The old man's on earlies. While he's out of the way, come and have a bit of breakfast with us,' her mother urged. 'At least I'll know you've had something to eat.'

Milly didn't need much persuasion. She got ready quickly. The times when she could eat at her own table with her mother were few enough. But when she came downstairs and sat at the table, there was Elsie's pale pixie face opposite her, with those slightly upturned grey eyes, like clear accusing pools. She gave her a fierce glare while their mother's back was turned and mimed a strangling motion. But her sister stared at her, unblinking.

'Mrs Knight told me, when I was scrubbing the step this morning,' her mother turned towards her, while slicing a loaf held against her flat chest, 'that her old man said you was drinking in the Folly with Pat last night.'

She dumped a slice in front of Milly and pushed the dripping basin towards her. As Milly helped herself, Elsie piped up.

'She was in ever so late, Mum, she woke me up, *and* she hid this big sack under the bed.'

Mrs Colman looked sharply at Milly. '*Jesus*, Mary and Joseph, don't tell me you had anything to do with it, Milly!'

'Stop stirring it, you!' Milly gave Elsie a sharp kick in the shins and turned an innocent face to her mother.

'He just gave me a few tins of stuff, but I wasn't there when he got nicked!' she lied. 'I was at the Settlement last night, you can ask Kitty if you like!'

Her mother's face fell. 'Oh, Mill, don't you bring no trouble home to my door! If I haven't got enough of it, with the old man, I don't want you turning out like . . .'

Her mother left the words unspoken, but still they stung Milly. There were so many unspoken words between them these days, and so few opportunities for talking. But her mother's implied criticisms and disappointments smarted more than the Seville orange juice trickling into the myriad unseen tiny cuts on Milly's hands, at work.

'Oh, don't start jawing me, Mum. I see little enough of you, without you starting on me!'

Her mother pursed her lips and handed Elsie the knife and loaf. 'Here, cut yourself and Amy a slice, no more'n one each!'

Undoing her apron, she announced, 'I'm going to church.'

It was a weekday, but Mrs Colman had taken to going to early morning Mass whenever her home life felt particularly precarious.

As soon as she was gone, Milly launched herself out of her seat. 'You little nark!' She lunged for Elsie, but before she could reach her, the bread knife flashed between them and Milly rocked back, only inches from the blade.

Elsie's temper could be as swift and terrible as the old man's. And though Milly didn't believe Elsie would harm her, knowing her sister's unpredictability, she opted for caution. She backed away, picked up her slice of bread, pulled her coat off the back of the chair and strolled out of the kitchen, chewing on the bread, just to show Elsie how unimpressed she was.

'Milly!' Elsie called after her. 'If you get put away with Pat, the old man'll start on us again!'

So that was why she'd snitched. Milly hesitated, she wanted to turn back now, to say she'd make sure he never hurt her again, but she knew it would be an empty promise. Instead, Milly slammed the front door behind her and set off at a trot for Southwell's. She was late, but running might just dislodge Elsie's accusing words; perhaps they would blow away, like early mist on the Thames. That sister of hers! How was it she always managed to have the last word? Elsie might just as well have stuck the knife in her stomach and twisted hard. It hurt so much, to know that she couldn't protect them forever.

Elsie and Amy were snow maidens. Along with a dozen other girls, all dressed in long white smocks and pointed bonnets, carrying garlands of ivy and berries, they were performing an intricate country dance, the aim of which was to weave garlands into a great wreath. Amy had gone under instead of over, several times, so the end result was a little lopsided, but everyone clapped and Mrs Colman commented how cleverly her daughters had managed.

Milly had gone to the Settlement with her mother to watch Elsie and Amy perform in a Christmas pageant organized by the Guild of Play. Her sister Elsie loved the Guild, which endeavoured to teach poor city children the folk songs and dances of an idealized rural idyll, but she was especially fond of the fanciful garments they dressed up in. Milly had spent weeks at the sewing circle, finishing the smocking on Elsie's dress, which she had to admit was the best in the room. Her sister was an exacting client. Everything had to be just right for the performance and, this year, Milly was glad of the distraction from her own worries and the tinderbox tensions of home. If she couldn't protect her sisters, at least she could sew for them.

The Christmas pageant was very popular with the audience and was always followed by tea and Christmas cake. Old Ma Donovan had no children left at home. Her thirteen had all flown the nest, all except Pat. Nevertheless she'd come along, as had many of the neighbours, for the free entertainment and food. Stuffing a slab of cake into her pocket, while tucking into another, Mrs Donovan turned to Milly's mother.

'Did you hear, my Pat's been put on remand till after Christmas. They're saying he might get two years!'

Milly choked on her own cake. 'Two years!'

'They said the judge might be lenient, but I can't see it meself, 'cause it's not his first offence, which truth be told, it weren't, not by a long chalk.' Mrs Donovan shook her head sadly. 'But he's been a good boy to me. I expect you'll miss him, won't yer?' She eyed Milly. 'Will you go and visit him if he goes inside?'

Before Milly had a chance to answer, her mother interrupted, 'My daughter's not going anywhere near no prison, Aggie, so don't you get the boy's hopes up.'

Old Ma Donovan took offence at this and turned her back. Getting up to leave, she brushed the crumbs off her coat. 'She's no better'n my son, and as for you, Ellen Colman, you never turned your nose up at the stuff, did you?'

Mrs Colman looked rather shamefaced at this, as they'd had several good dinners from the stolen tins. And her mother had particularly enjoyed the oxtail soups.

'You walked into that one, Mum.' Milly grinned.

'You're still not visiting him,' her mother said firmly, crossing her arms, as if she still had a say in what Milly did.

'All right, if you say so,' Milly agreed, for although she felt sorry for Pat, she was secretly relieved that he might be removed from her life. A few tins off the back of his lorry were one thing, but a gun spoke of the sort of violence she wanted nothing to do with. She had enough of that in her own home.

The Settlement wasn't the only institution to put on Christmas celebrations. In Bermondsey there was a pub on every corner and a mission on every other, and Christmas was the busiest time for both. Not to be outdone by the Methodists at the Settlement, the Catholic church held a children's party and nativity play in the church hall. Amy had been chosen to play the angel Gabriel: being tall for her age, the nuns thought she was the most imposing of the bunch of undersized volunteers. The day after the Settlement pageant, Milly had slipped home for tea, knowing her father would have already left for a night shift at the tannery. Walking down Arnold's Place, she saw her mother looking anxiously out of their front door.

'Amy's not come home from school,' her mother said, when she reached the house, 'and Elsie doesn't remember seeing her come out. Can you go round there and see what's happened to her?'

'What's the matter with Elsie? Why didn't she wait for Amy?' Milly was annoyed, she'd hoped to have a peaceful hour at home, getting ready, before going with Kitty and some of the other jam girls to the Southwell's Christmas dance.

'I'm sorry, love, but . . .'

'Oh, all right.' Milly turned on her heel and hurried back towards the convent school, adjacent to Dockhead Church. When she arrived, the main gates were closed, so she rang the bell of the side door and waited. After several minutes, one of the Sisters of Mercy answered. Milly recognized her as the nun who'd once taught her sewing, Sister Mary Paul. She well remembered her wicked aim with the cane. The old witch always managed to catch you right on the knuckles.

'I'm looking for Amy Colman, Sister, she never come home from school this afternoon.'

The nun's pinched face was unsmiling and her gimlet eyes stared like dark little coals. 'Ah yes, girl Colman has been kept back for misbehaving. She's a disgrace to your poor mother.'

'What's she done now, Sister?' Milly wasn't surprised. Amy was stubborn and always game for some mischief.

'She was barred from the pageant for berating the Virgin Mary in the most foul-mouthed manner. Poor Theresa Bunclerk was reduced to tears.'

Milly deduced that Kitty's younger sister Theresa was playing the Virgin Mary.

'Well, I know Amy's got a mouth on her, Sister, but I'm surprised it was enough to upset Theresa.' Knowing how the Bunclerk household often rang to the good-natured oaths of Mr and Mrs Bunclerk, Milly doubted that was the cause of Theresa's distress.

'Amy can be a most trying child,' the stony-faced nun continued. 'Let us just say that the foul language called into question the virgin state of our Lady and by implication the virgin state of Theresa, pure young soul that she is . . .'

Milly had to stifle a laugh, but she'd had enough and wanted to get home for her tea.

'Well, I'll take Amy home now and Mum'll be sure to give her a talking to.'

'I'm afraid you cannot take her home. Amy has been kept behind for an hour!'

Milly stared into the nun's ember eyes and remembered all the times she'd tried to whip her hand out of the way as the cane or ruler swiped down. She remembered the beautiful smocking she'd been forced to unpick on the nightgown she'd made for her favourite, Sister Clare. Sister Mary Paul was now a head shorter than Milly, but as a child, all the nun's puffed-up, ruffled energy had been intimidating and Milly, like most of her pupils, had been terrified of her. Milly took a step into the passageway.

'Her tea's on the table and she's coming home with me,' Milly said, in a tone which brooked no argument.

She gave the nun no time to reply. Dwarfed by Milly's height and insubstantial by comparison, the Sister hopped aside. She followed Milly down polished corridors leading to the classrooms. The smell of lavender beeswax, combined with chalk dust and incense, brought back sharp memories of her own rebellions here. In fact she'd been a much more obedient pupil than Amy, and now Milly's childhood defiance seemed pathetic, just a few extra beautiful stitches added to a plain garment. But she took some satisfaction in knowing that, today, she was the one doing the intimidating.

Milly strode on, till she came to the room where Amy had been left in disgrace. Her sister sat at a desk in the front row and had obviously been set to writing lines. Her face was puffy from crying and she held her pencil at an odd angle. Going over to the desk, Milly glanced down at the lines: *I am a wicked foul-mouthed girl*, written over and over again. She must have been at it all afternoon. Amy looked up, and dropping the pencil, held up both palms. They were criss-crossed with raised angry welts.

'That vicious mare whacked me with the cane, Mill!' she wailed, fresh tears beginning to fall.

Blood rushed to Milly's face as an upsurge of indignant protectiveness took her unawares. 'It's all right, Amy,' she said quietly, 'you're coming home with me.' She helped her up. 'Go and wait outside a minute.' Amy hesitated at first, but then walked out obediently. Milly, her face still burning, turned to Sister Mary Paul, who was standing by the door in disapproving silence.

'You listen here.' She pointed her finger, well aware she'd dropped the normal respectful tone reserved for the priests and nuns. 'If Amy's naughty, you send a note home to our mother, but don't you *ever* lay a hand on my sister again!'

Sister Mary Paul opened her mouth to speak, but was forced to stand aside as Milly swept past her and out of the classroom.

Amy had witnessed the encounter through the glass-panelled door and she was now gazing at Milly in undisguised admiration. 'Blimey, Mill, I never thought you'd stick up for me like that!'

Milly, wondering at how her sister could not know, found herself taking Amy's hands. She turned them over and kissed the raw stripes. 'Of course I stuck up for you,' she said fiercely, 'you're my sister.'

By the time they arrived home Milly was running late. At least the old man was out of the way tonight, so she didn't have to get ready at Kitty's. The Southwell's Christmas dance was the highlight of Milly's Christmas. She'd altered her last year's best dress to keep up with the changing hemlines. It was peacock-blue satin, and Milly had shortened it and lowered the waist, adding a contrasting wide sash. The new, straight shape suited her tall, slightly boyish figure, which she flattened even further with a tightly laced under-bodice. She wore her hair in a short, wavy bob, with a sequinned headband. The whole outfit had cost her very little, but she could see that she had dazzled Elsie. The unpredictable rage that sometimes punctuated her sister's dreaminess was usually short-lived. However acrimonious the argument, it was as if the bitterness could not long survive in Elsie's fantasy world. Milly often heard Elsie talking to herself, as to some imaginary member of the family. She was convinced that in poor Elsie's head there lived the perfect, happy family and any reality that conflicted with it was immediately banished from her imagination.

That evening, all earlier animosity forgotten, she sat on the bed, gawping at Milly as she checked herself in the wardrobe mirror.

'Oh, Milly, you look just like a film star!' she cooed.

Milly laughed. 'Good job the films are silent then, or they'd boo me off the screen when I opened me mouth! Come and help with this, Elsie.'

Her sister began buttoning the back of the dress. 'Milly, I'm sorry about the other week, you know . . .'

'You mean when you wanted to slice me like a loaf of bread?' Milly joked, slipping on her black T-bar shoes.

'I don't know what gets into me.' Elsie appeared to be genuinely contrite. 'It's just with the old man being so handy, you've got to be on your guard all the time, haven't you?'

Milly understood exactly what Elsie meant. They had all been, for as long as she could remember, living in a state of siege with her father as the enemy. She felt she wouldn't know how to behave in a peaceful family. No wonder Elsie fantasized about a home where they didn't have to jump every time the front door opened, or start up in bed when stairs creaked, fearful of a drunken invasion by their father. True, he had kept well clear of her since she'd shamed him, but she couldn't be unaware of the building tension in the little house in Arnold's Place. Sooner or later the old man was going to explode, and Milly would rather it didn't happen on Christmas Day.

But when Christmas Eve arrived, she was facing a Christmas with very little peace or goodwill about it. The knowledge that the Colmans hadn't spent a peaceful Christmas together since before the war hadn't dissuaded her mother from making a brave seasonal attempt. The old man usually spent most of Christmas Day in the Swan, and the fact that he normally staggered in drunk, long after the family had finished eating, was the reasoning she used to persuade Milly to sit round the dinner table with her family that year.

'It's better if I'm not here to aggravate him, Mum,' Milly protested. 'He's bad enough on Christmas Day as it is! Besides, Kitty's mum says I can go round their house.'

'Don't be a soppy 'apporth, Mill, what room have they got? No, I'm not having you at strangers' houses on Christmas Day! You'll be in your own home, at least for dinner. You can go out with your friends later, eh?'

Milly feared it was a mistake. She'd been so careful, tiptoeing about like a ghost, dodging his every move. But Christmas, for her mother, was a fantasy of home, every bit as strong as Elsie's, and Milly could not disappoint her.

On Christmas morning, she was surprised to be overtaken by an unexpected feeling of joy. Her sisters, still young enough to be excited about their orange and sixpence, must have infected her. Only when the old man had left for the pub did they leave their room, giggling and jostling on their way down the stairs. As they helped their mother prepare turkey and boil Christmas pudding, they all sang together, '*Oh, we all want figgy pudding, oh, we all want figgy pudding!*' The rare look of happiness on her mother's face made Milly glad she'd given in, and for a single, charmed day, it seemed that Elsie's dream really had come true.

But like Cinderella at the ball, Milly stayed too late. Just as she was putting on her shoes and coat, they heard the old man's roar. He could barely walk, but the sight of Milly counteracted the brandies he'd consumed. With surprising swiftness, he lunged, picked up the covered plate waiting for him on the table, and hurled it against the kitchen wall. They all leaped up, watching the turkey dinner first stick to, then slowly slide down the distempered wall. The old man collapsed in a heap on the floor, as Milly rushed to help her mother clean up the mess.

'I'm sorry, Mum,' she said, choking back tears and picking up pieces of china. 'Don't let it spoil your day.'

10

Hop Harvest

January 1924

The meat pudding was simmering in the pot, billowing clouds of steam into the kitchen. Milly lifted the saucepan lid to check that it hadn't run dry. She was watching the pot for her mother, who'd taken an egg-custard tart to the Bunclerks. Percy was recovering from scarlet fever and while Mrs Bunclerk nursed him, the rest of her brood were shifting for themselves. Milly hoped she would be quick. She wanted to be out before the old man got home. She was topping up the pan from the kettle when she felt a presence behind her. Startled, she looked round to see Elsie standing at the kitchen door, staring at the pudding pot.

'That's broke me dream!' she said.

Milly hoped it was a short dream; she didn't have time for one of Elsie's sagas. Sometimes Milly thought she made them up as she went along.

'What was it about?' she asked dutifully.

'I dreamed you brought a bloody great big meat pudding into the kitchen, dumped it on the table and then started cutting into it, and guess what, when you opened it up, instead of steak and kidney there was a tiny little baby inside, all covered in gravy!'

Milly's heart lurched. She tried to laugh off the dream, as usual, but her face muscles refused to move. How could Elsie possibly know? She'd only just confirmed it herself. But again,

Polly Witch was two steps ahead, for Milly was most certainly in the pudding club, and if she hadn't been so terrified she might have laughed at the accuracy of Elsie's dream. But her immobile features were not lost on her sister and Elsie moved slowly over to where she stood.

'I didn't know what me dream meant until now. Oh, Mill, when are you going to tell Mum?'

'Tell me what?' Her mother had dashed in, and was quickly unbuttoning her coat. 'You let that pan run dry?' she asked accusingly, and Milly wished more than anything that her guilty secret was about something so mundane.

Milly nudged Elsie, and she slipped out of the room, unnoticed by her mother. Balling her hands into fists, Millie tried to quell her sickening fear. This was her mother, yet she felt more scared than if it had been the old man. Sometimes it was easier to take a beating than to disappoint someone you loved.

'Mum, you'd better sit down.'

As Milly broke the news to her, Mrs Colman sat at the table, white-faced.

'We'll have to tell the old man,' she said, smoothing the tablecloth over and over with the palm of her hand. 'He'll have to know sooner or later.'

Milly felt sick. 'Can't it be later?' She wilted under Mrs Colman's disappointed stare. She could swear there were extra worry lines on her mother's face since she'd told her.

'Didn't I warn you about that Pat?' her mother said. 'Didn't I tell you about going up the field with him? I told you not to bring no trouble home to my door. What did you think I meant?'

Her voice broke and Milly looked away, not wanting to meet her mother's eye. She was more ashamed of letting her down than of any moral lapse, though she knew there would be plenty ready to point that out.

'I'm sorry, Mum,' was all she managed.

'Well, he'll have to marry you, though if it's born in June, they'll all know it's a hoppin' baby anyway.'

Milly shook her head. 'Pat's not marrying me. He says I should get rid of the baby.' Her lip trembled at that and though she'd told herself she wasn't going to cry, she did now.

As soon as she'd been sure herself, she'd written to Pat in prison. His reply shouldn't have shocked her, but it did. He knew a man, he'd said, who could do it; he'd send her the money. She wondered if he'd suggested the same thing to the girl from Rotherhithe. Her vanity had convinced her that Pat loved her, and she'd even resigned herself to marrying him. But he'd referred to the baby as 'it', a problem, not a tiny being who would forever be intertwined with her, whether born into the world or not.

Her mother crossed herself. '*Jesus*, Mary and Joseph, don't say such a wicked thing, you'll go straight to hell.'

'Not much different from here then,' Milly muttered. A burning smell reached her as the saucepan began to spit and crackle. 'The pan's boiling dry,' she said, and went to top it up with more boiling water.

As the steam rose, Milly imagined herself sitting in the old tin tub, hot water scalding her body, with a bottle of gin in hand. She'd often heard the other jam girls talking about such 'home remedies', and perhaps in her desperation she might have tried something like that, but the cold butchery Pat had in mind was something that filled her with dread. Perhaps she should just tell the old man and get it over with; she'd let him knock her to kingdom come and do the job for her. She groaned; she didn't know what she wanted.

'Do I have to tell him tonight? I'm meant to be going to the Settlement.'

Her mother looked at her sharply. 'Your Settlement days are over, love, a baby's a full-time job. You'll have no time for clubs. You've made your bed, you'll have to lie in it.'

She couldn't bear her mother's muted disappointment. Her father's rage, when it came, might well be easier to counter. She was about to throw on her coat and make her escape, when the door opened and he walked in.

'What's she doing here?' he addressed her mother.

The old man persisted in the fiction that she lived elsewhere. They rarely saw each other in the house, and, in her imagination, he had grown much larger and more forbidding. But now, his actual, beery presence steeled Milly. It was time to gather in the Kentish hop harvest; like it or not, a hopping baby was on the way and she would have to face the consequences of her own stupidity. She let the coat slip from her shoulders.

'I live here!' she said defiantly. 'And what's more I pay rent and board for the pleasure of sneaking about in me own home.'

'I said,' he spun round, swaying, 'what's *she* doing in my house?' Suddenly his foot slipped from under him, his bloodshot eyes widened and, grasping for a handhold, he crashed back into the range, toppling the panful of scalding water down his trousers. He screamed.

Milly leaped to shield her mother, who had been spattered with boiling water too, and now sat frozen in shock. The old man rolled on the floor, grabbing his burned leg, howling loud enough to bring the two younger girls running down from the bedroom.

Milly sped past them into the scullery, 'Out me way, you two!' She filled a jug with cold water, dipped a cloth in it and rushed back. Swiftly wrapping her mother's arm in the wet cloth, she doused the old man's leg with water. It pooled around her feet and as her mother still hadn't moved, Milly bent to help the old man up.

'Get off me!' He flailed his arms at her, as though she were the devil who'd sent him to a burning hell, instead of his own flesh and blood. She flung the enamel jug at him. 'Suit yourself, you ungrateful bastard. I'm only trying to help!'

Grabbing her coat, she fled out into the street, knowing that whatever happened now, she would never bring a baby into this house. She ran to the end of Arnold's Place, weaving her way through back alleys and courts towards the river – her haven. She passed Southwell's jetty where she used to meet Pat, but that was the last place she wanted to go. She ran along Bermondsey

Wall, between high warehouses, beneath gantries, glimpsing the river between the dark wings of cranes, eventually coming to the Fountain river stairs. She clattered down them two at a time, slipping on their coating of slimy green algae. Teetering to a halt on the very last step, she took a gulping breath of musty riverine air.

The tide was out. Olive-green sludge, studded with stones, spread out before her, but she dare not step on to the river mud here, where its sluggish-looking water masked a treacherous current that could turn in an instant and sweep her away. She scanned the river. To her left, the fortress-like turrets of Tower Bridge were visible, and all the way from the bridge to where she stood, strings of unmanned tethered barges bobbed and banged each other. The occasional tug chugged against the tide, but at this time in the evening the river traffic was beginning to diminish. Only when she knew she was completely alone did she let out a long, despairing howl.

'Oh, Milly, what have you done! It's all ruined!'

She screamed at the swooping gulls till she was hoarse, and raved at the deep, indifferent Thames. Mourning her life, which had only just begun, yet which already felt wasted. So often the wide, calm river had been enough to absorb her youthful rages, but this time there was no comfort in its slow-moving waters. On Tower Bridge, she could see the early evening traffic trundling across its outstretched arms and the tiny, unheeding pedestrians hurrying back home for their untroubled teas. She wished herself to be any one of that anonymous crowd. Dusk was draping a gentle, violet gauze between the solid towers of the bridge, and the top walkway stood out, a black filigree. A good place for a suicide, so they said, and for a moment, Milly's pain at the loss of her future seemed to call out for some equally drastic remedy. She sat down on the damp step, breathing in the musk of the ooze below her. Leaning her head on her arms, she wept.

When all her tears had been spent, and the cold damp had reached her bones, she stood up, brushed off the back of her coat and wrapped her arms tightly around herself. She wiped her face with her sleeve. Nobody was coming to save her, least of all Pat Donovan. The only person who could help her was herself. Perhaps the river had done its work after all, for as she started to walk slowly back towards the Bermondsey Settlement in Farncombe Street, she felt a grim calm enfold her, and she knew what she must do.

It was too early for the sewing circle, but people were already going into the Settlement building. It was a soot-stained Victorian Gothic mansion with two wings and a central tower, at the base of which was the pointed-arched entrance. Oriel windows protruded from its grimy facade and clusters of elongated, brick chimneys twisted into the smoky air. The interior had the polished, studious calm of a Cambridge College, with wood-panelled lecture rooms and a carpeted music room. There was a gym and a courtyard where, when she was younger, Milly had joined in the hearty drills, designed to strengthen rickety bones.

The place was as much a missionary endeavour as any of those in darkest Africa, and the Colmans, though Catholic, were, like many other poor Bermondsey families, not too proud to benefit from the free doctors, free meals or country outings provided by the Wesleyans. But for Milly, the main attraction had always been an indefinable sense of possibilities, not glimpsed anywhere else along Bermondsey Wall. At the Settlement, she was allowed to make a garment, simply because it was beautiful. Elsie could sing harmless country airs of harvests and hedgerows, just for the sheer fun of it, and each May Day, Amy could whirl round a maypole as if Bermondsey still had a village green. Yet on this particular cold January evening, as she approached the Settlement, that sense of possibilities had deserted Milly entirely.

She mounted the steps with head down, lost in her own thoughts, and therefore didn't see the man just in front of her. He pulled open the door, stepped back, and collided with her. Apologizing, he turned, raising his brown trilby hat to her. She saw recognition spark in his blue eyes and he raised an eyebrow.

'Milly? From Arnold's Place?'

Seeing him out of context had confused her, but now she realized it was Hughes the grocer's nephew. Usually she saw only the top half of him, wrapped in his white grocer's apron. Tonight he was dressed smartly in a brown tweed suit and polished brogues.

'Yes, that's right.' She smiled. 'Sorry, I was in a world of my own. I don't think I've seen you here before.'

He opened the door to let her through. 'Haven't you? I've been coming to lectures here ever since Uncle Alf put me in charge of the Dockhead shop. Actually, I've seen you here a few times, girls' club, isn't it?'

Milly gave him a non-committal nod. 'Sewing.'

She really didn't remember seeing him here, perhaps because their paths had only crossed when she'd turned up blind drunk and insensible. Suddenly she felt hot with embarrassment at the thought of him witnessing her in that state. She stood in the doorway, aware of his quizzical eyes upon her, unable to tell if he was judging her or laughing at her. She blushed.

'Well, don't let me keep you from your sewing. Give my regards to your mother.'

He strode off towards the lecture hall, brown brogues clicking on the parquet flooring. She stood for a moment, with a feeling that she had been let off, and walked thoughtfully towards the sewing room.

She was the first to arrive. Kitty wasn't coming as she was helping her mother to nurse Percy. 'Spoiling him rotten, she is,' Kitty had said, though Milly knew that she was the worst offender when it came to indulging her little brother.

Milly went to the cupboard, where their sewing materials were kept, and pulled out her latest project. It was a rather grown-up-looking shift dress for Elsie, who, at thirteen, had finally been persuaded by Milly to abandon the childish frilled pinafores and ribbons she favoured.

Miss Florence Green glided noiselessly into the sewing room.

'You're the early bird!' she announced and, startled, Milly dropped Elsie's half-finished dress, along with assorted bits of material. Miss Green helped her gather them up, and they spread them out on the central work table. Milly thanked her, letting out an unconscious sigh.

'Whatever's the matter, Milly? You don't seem your normal cheerful self.'

It was now or never, and Milly couldn't afford to be proud. 'Truth is, Miss Green, I came early so I could have a word with you, before the others got here. Only . . . I might not be able to come to the club for much longer.'

'Oh, Milly, why not? I thought you loved sewing!' She sounded genuinely disappointed.

'I do, I do, there's nothing I like better, but . . . well, I might be . . . getting married.' Milly was ashamed of her own cowardice.

Florence Green smiled. 'Well, that's not a problem, Milly!' She put her arm round Milly. 'You'll just have to join the mothers' meeting!'

'I never said anything about being a mother!' Perhaps Milly's protestation was too vehement, for comprehension suddenly dawned on Miss Green's mild features.

'Oh, my dear girl, this is not like you, not like you at all!'

Miserably, Milly picked up an oddment of material, wiping away a solitary tear. Not like her at all? No, she'd always been so proud of her ability to take care of herself, hadn't she? Strong enough to fight off any man, yet weak enough to be swayed by one tender kiss. She was as much a fool as any other girl who got herself into trouble, and she hated the look in Miss Green's eyes that confirmed it.

'Is it Pat Donovan you're going to marry?' Miss Green asked gently. She sat down next to Milly and took her hand.

Milly shook her head. 'It would be, if he weren't in the nick.'

'Yes, I heard about that from Mrs Donovan. Do you know for how long?'

'It doesn't matter, looks like I'll be on my own,' she said, wiping away another stray tear, 'and I've got to do what I think's best for me and . . . the baby.'

'And what do your parents think is best?' Miss Green asked.

'The old man doesn't know yet, not unless Mum's told him by now. He'll chuck me out once he knows, and I wouldn't want to stay there anyway, not the way he is.'

Florence Green, like everyone else in Dockhead, knew of the old man's violent temper. She said nothing about him, but uttered soothing sounds.

'But your mother's a good woman, surely she'd help you look after the baby?'

'Yes, she is a good woman, Miss Green, but she's a good Catholic too, and you know it's such a . . . disgrace.'

Milly's face betrayed all the despair she was desperately trying to hide. But just then, sounds from the corridor announced the arrival of other club members. Miss Green squeezed Milly's hand. 'Stay behind after and we'll talk about it . . .' She got up, turning sadly away from Milly's defeated figure, hunched over the table, and began to greet the other girls as they arrived in cheerful, noisy groups for their night at the sewing circle.

The single women helpers of the Settlement lived in small rooms high in the gables of the Settlement building. As Florence Green drew the floral curtains across the tiny window of her room, Milly had the chance to look around. She was struck by how small it was, not much bigger than their kitchen. She had expected something grander. It was cosy enough, with a side table and lamp, a little desk and two armchairs either side of a fireplace, which housed a small gas fire. The iron-framed bed had been covered in a beautiful, bright patchwork quilt, no doubt made by Miss Green. But something about the room made Milly's heart sink. She imagined the many evenings the young missionary might have spent alone here, quietly sewing, reading from the gold-edged, black Bible on the side table. Milly, with her longing to be free of their crowded home, had often imagined the luxury of having a room of her own, a room just like this one. But now, in the face of Miss Green's seclusion, she realized, perhaps for the first time,

116

the appeal of her own rowdy nights at the pub, and the crowded streets, which meant that she need never be alone if she didn't want to be. Even to be squashed into a bed with her two warring sisters was a comfort, when cold nights encouraged a closeness never there by day. But what did she know of Miss Green's life? Perhaps the woman had more friends than she did.

'Now, Milly, let me make us some cocoa.' Miss Green turned brightly to a small sideboard, on which stood a gas ring and some crockery.

Milly watched her silently as she made the cocoa, carefully making a paste in the pretty cups, then adding boiling water from the tiny kettle and finally adding condensed milk from a jar. She presented the cocoa on a tray with an embroidered cloth, making Milly feel as though she were a visiting duchess, rather than a jam girl from Jacob's Island. The cocoa was sweet and thick and Milly sipped it slowly, waiting for Miss Green to speak.

'Milly, tell me, what would *you* like to do about the baby?' she asked.

I'd like to wish it back to where it came from, Milly thought, but instead she said,

'It's not about my life any more.' She repeated the words she'd rehearsed coming back from the river tonight. 'Mine might be ruined, but I can still make sure my baby gets a good life. And that won't be in Arnold's Place, will it?' Milly swallowed salty tears, along with a mouthful of sweet cocoa.

'Oh, Milly, you're too young to be writing off your own life!' Miss Green was suddenly animated. 'No matter how dark it seems, life has a way of persisting.' She reached over to pat Milly's hand. 'I thought my life was over once, Milly . . . ' She paused, glancing up at a framed photograph on the mantelshelf, which Milly noticed for the first time. It was of a young army officer. 'My fiancé, he was killed in the war,' she said simply, reaching up for the photo and offering it to Milly. 'I thought I'd never feel joy again, and it was a very long time before I did. But . . . as I say, life has a way of persisting with us, Milly, so don't give up, not just yet.'

'He was very handsome.' Milly felt that her response was inadequate, yet it seemed to please the young woman sitting opposite.

Miss Green smiled, still proud of her dead soldier beau and Milly's heart ached for her and for herself. For she knew that if Pat was put away for a lifetime, she wouldn't grieve as this woman did. No, the loss of Pat wouldn't rob her of her joy.

'I'd like the baby to go to a good home, but I don't think I want it to go to the Sisters.'

She knew her mother would want her to go to the Sisters of Mercy at Dockhead. They had homes for 'fallen women'. But just as she didn't want to bring a baby into the old man's house, so her heart rebelled against handing over her child to Sister Mary Paul.

'But the Sisters do wonderful work, and if it would make things easier for your mother, mightn't it be best?'

'No!' Milly was adamant. If all the sisters could be as angelic as her beloved Sister Clare, it might be a different matter.

Miss Green nodded. 'As you wish, Milly. There is a country home we have contacts with. It's a very lovely old place, in Kent. Normally girls go there early on in their pregnancies, work at sewing or suchlike – which you'd be very good at!' She smiled encouragingly, as though this were a new job they were talking about. Milly nodded for her to go on. 'Then once the baby is born, the child is placed in a good home.'

'Yes, that's what I want to do.' Milly forced out the words through dry lips and constricted throat. 'It's for the best.'

'Sorry it's not better news, Milly,' said Freddie Clark. 'I feel bad for Pat, seeing as I got away scot free, it don't seem fair.'

'Two years seems a lot!' Milly looked from Freddie back to Kitty. They were sitting at a corner table in the Folly the day after Pat's sentencing. 'For a few tins?'

Freddie looked hesitant. 'Well, it was a bit more than a few. That wasn't my first delivery to Pat's yard, but it wasn't just that. Someone tipped 'em off he was involved in that Post Office job

118

in Jamaica Road, the one where the bloke got shot . . . couldn't prove nothing but . . .' Freddie sipped his beer awkwardly. 'I know it's none of my business, but if I was you, I'd take your chance to get clear of him. He's my mate, but he's no good.'

Kitty, sitting next to him, nodded in agreement.

'But, Mill, if there's anything I can do for you while he's away, you know, anything for you or the baby . . .' Freddie let out a yelp as Kitty kicked him under the table. Then, blushing, he apologized. 'Sorry, I'm not meant to know, am I?'

Kitty raised her eyes in disbelief. 'I told him *in confidence*!' she said, scowling at Freddie.

'Oh, don't worry, Fred, and thanks, but just keep it to yourself till I've gone,' Milly said. No doubt she would have to get used to people talking about her behind her back.

'Are you telling Pat where you're going?' Kitty asked.

'No, what's the point?' Milly looked thoughtfully into her empty glass, and Freddie lifted it from her hands. 'I'll get another round in,' he said quickly.

Milly studied Kitty, as her eyes followed Freddie. 'Fred's a decent feller. Are you two getting serious?'

'Not serious, but I do like him,' Kitty said, in a dreamy way that told far more than her words had. 'Oh, Milly, I'm going to miss you,' she said suddenly. 'When are you giving your notice in at Southwell's?'

'Next week, then I'm off to the home the following week. I'll miss you too, Kit, but I'll be glad to be out of Arnold's Place. I feel like a leper at home. The girls won't come near me now, not even to annoy me. I wish they would come and get in my way, or pick a fight . . . something! But no, they just look at me as though I should be in the nick, as well as Pat.'

Her mother had told the girls that Milly would be going to work as a domestic in a big country house. But her sisters' reaction had taken her completely by surprise. They'd turned sullen and accusing. Though Elsie had guessed the true reason, Amy didn't have a clue why she was leaving. One night after she'd lain tossing and turning for hours, debating the wisdom of her decision about the baby, she gave up thinking and nudged Elsie. The truth was, she felt lonely. She knew she was in this on her own, but sometimes, in the middle of the night, she wished she had someone to reassure her. Now, in her isolation, she risked rousing Elsie's slumbering temper, which could be dragon-like if she was woken suddenly. 'What you doin'?' Elsie mumbled, yanking the blanket over her shoulder. Milly nudged her again. 'Els, Elsie!' she whispered.

'What?' The young girl rolled over.

'Why are you blaming me for going away? You know why I've got to, don't you?

Elsie's unblinking, grey cat's eyes were all she could make out in the darkness.

'I know,' she said flatly.

'I thought you'd be glad to get rid of me, we're always arguing.'

Elsie rolled over, turning her back to Milly. 'There's worse things than arguing. I told you before, once you're gone, he'll start on us again.'

Milly had lain awake for a long time after that, her hand resting lightly on her swelling stomach, a tight knot in her chest and a stream of salt tears making their slow progress towards the corners of her mouth. Her poor sisters.

She left Southwell's with little fanfare. Tom Pelton, the foreman, had said she could have her job back if she didn't take to 'domestic service'. She doubted he, or anyone else at the factory, were taken in by the lie, but if it helped her mother get through the disgrace, then Milly would gladly play along. After work Kitty, Peggy and some of the other jam girls had met for a last night at the Folly, though her heart wasn't in it. Now it came to leaving the bounded enclave of docks and factories that had been her home, she found herself conjuring fears out of the river mist. She'd believed she had no love for the constricting place that had for too long felt like a cage to her, but now, all the unknown tomorrows made her want to stay. If she could only hide here, find a haven for herself and the baby, she wouldn't care if it were in the meanest court on Jacob's Island. She quailed at the thought of the country home, staffed by other Miss Greens, sad-eyed, sympathetic and unsurprised at her fallen state. The countryside of Kent, however lush with apple orchards and blossoms, no longer held any attraction for her. She didn't deserve its beauty. She would concentrate on having the baby, and steeling herself to give it away. And then she would leave Kent and never go back, not for all the hop harvests in the world.

11

A Home in the Country

June 1924

Milly lay in the narrow, iron-framed bed, staring up at the sloping ceiling. The long dormitory stretched from one gable end to the other, and ancient oak floorboards sloped down towards the door, giving the room a rakish tilt that made her nauseous. But that was nothing new. She'd spent most of her pregnancy feeling sick. She turned her head towards the oriel window; one of its five oak-framed panes was propped open. The edge of the curving terrace wall that fronted the house was just visible from her bed, nearest to the window. From the terrace, the grounds fell away towards a copse and a reed-fringed lake. Beyond, she could see the hazy green layers of the Weald of Kent, disappearing into a purple smudged horizon. A cool, early morning breeze came through the open window, bringing the scent of dew-wet grass into the low-beamed room.

She eased herself on to her elbow, wincing as the baby shifted, catching on some invisible nerve with a probing toe or finger. Milly pulled the white bedspread up over her arms and sat up, leaning back against the iron bedstead. None of the other girls were stirring, but Milly often tried to wake up early. It was the best time of day to enjoy the quiet beauty of the place before the high-pitched chatter of the nine other girls in the dormitory intruded. She liked to play an early morning game of make-believe, that this was her very own house. The other girls vanished, and their gentle snores and mutterings faded away. She let her eyes rest on the wood panelling and the dark old paintings of religious scenes, and lastly she turned to the magnetic view from the window. For a few minutes each day, she'd been able to forget that her residence here was a temporary penance; she'd even sometimes managed to blot out the life she'd left behind.

But beyond the copse was a cluster of oast houses, rising above the treeline, and sometimes their pointed wooden cowls spun round like accusing white fingers. Then all her daydreams would be shattered as she remembered why she was here. Anyway, the baby was getting too big to pretend away; no amount of daydreaming could make the huge bump beneath her nightgown vanish. Soon her child would emerge to take its first look at the world, and Milly was torn between wanting the day to arrive and wanting to stave it off forever. His arrival would mean her departure, and she dreaded having to leave a place that, against all odds, she'd become attached to. The house was called Edenvale, yet like all Edens, it had its viper and its share of shame.

'Oooh!' She started as a sharp scratching feeling in her stomach caught her unawares. The baby had a peculiar way of getting her attention; sometimes it felt as if its little finger was deliberately stroking her from the inside. It was an odd sensation, not painful, but insistent and impossible to ignore. She might as well get up.

Quietly, she got out of bed, but the old springs creaked so that Rita, the sixteen-year-old from Whitechapel, in the next bed, stirred. Rita had been terribly homesick, though Milly couldn't imagine why. She'd told Milly one of her own family was the father of her baby, though she would never dream of naming him.

'Morning, Mill,' the girl said, stretching. Her eyes, sticky with sleep, forced themselves open and her oval face emerged, white as the bedspread. She'd had an even worse pregnancy than Milly. 'Gawd, I do feel sick! What day is it?'

'Sunday,' Milly answered. 'I'm getting in the bathroom.'

'Ohhh, I hate Sundays,' Rita groaned. 'Twice as many effin' prayers today!'

Milly laughed. Rita had the face of an angel and the mouth of a stevedore.

'Too right,' Milly agreed.

Prayer times at the home came far too often for Milly's liking. Aimed at making the girls suitably ashamed of their fallen state, little homilies urged them to be grateful for the chance of giving their babies away to parents more deserving than themselves.

The matron led them in prayers of penitence every morning at breakfast, but on Sundays they paraded down to the village church in a crocodile, wearing their unmistakable Edenvale uniforms. On arrival, their own clothes had been taken away to be 'deloused'. Much to Milly's disgust, they were issued with shapeless, long grey shifts and gabardine mackintoshes. Milly and Rita defied the humiliation, insisting on hitching up the shifts with sashes and rolling up the mac sleeves, anything to make them less drab and institutional. Some girls cried themselves to sleep every night after the weekly public humiliation. Milly never once cried with shame, but as the birth drew nearer, she sometimes found her pillow wet with the tears of an undefined yearning. She worried that she was losing her resolve, terrified that when the time came to give up her baby, she wouldn't be strong enough. Talking to Rita didn't help. The young girl was the least emotional of all of them, and viewed her situation with an almost brutal practicality. She was an expert – she'd been through it all before, when she was fourteen.

'No good getting attached, is what I say, Mill, you just got to push the little bastard out and say cheerio, ain't ya?'

Milly envied her detachment. Her own pregnancy seemed to have leached away all her old bravado. She felt her once hard muscles softening into maternal folds of flesh, and her inner strength melting into a sentimental pulp that filled her with impotent anger at herself. Now, as she shuffled off towards the communal bathroom, she felt tears welling and told herself to toughen up. Yesterday, Ida, a big-boned girl from Peckham, had given away her baby to a well-to-do, middle-aged couple. The poor girl had come back to the dormitory howling and no matter how much Matron told her to control herself, that she was upsetting the others, Ida continued to sob all day. Soon that would be her, Milly reflected, but she was determined not to howl. She would put her baby first and be glad to sacrifice her own feelings on the altar of maternal love.

The bathroom was a long white-tiled room, with a row of sinks and two baths at the end. She could hear the other girls waking and chatting, and hurried to slip off her nightgown. The baths were used on a rota basis and it was her turn this morning. A proper bath, with taps and running hot water, was an unheard of luxury for Milly, but she still hadn't got used to bathing in front of strangers. At home they would get the grey tin tub in from the yard, fill it a pan full at a time from the copper, and then she and her sisters would share the bathwater, Milly first, then Elsie, then Amy. They would scrub each other's backs, but then her sisters were not strangers.

Easing herself gently into the hot water, she realized with a pang just how much she missed those infuriating sisters of hers. That was one thing amongst many that had changed during her stay in Edenvale, which Milly knew was a paradise compared to other unmarried mothers' homes. Yet the orderly routine of prayers, hymns and hard work, scrubbing floors or sewing sheets, had seemed at first like a prison sentence. Still, it was a penitentiary that allowed for time in the gardens or accompanied walks in the surrounding lanes, and it was at such times that Milly found time to think. This was another luxury, like proper baths, that was little known in Arnold's Place. She was surprised to find that she was not the same person who'd arrived there all those months before. The things she'd imagined she would miss – the dances, the drinking, her friends at the Folly – she'd hardly given a thought to, yet here she was, missing the two people who'd always given her the most trouble, her sisters.

It was as she hauled herself out of the bath that the first contraction caught her. She stumbled, but managed to grip the rolled bath edge. Her breath coming in quick gasps, she waited while the pain diminished, then stood up naked, dripping and trembling. All modesty forgotten, she screamed out, 'Me baby's coming!'

Immediately she found herself surrounded by a gaggle of girls, grabbing at her, eager to help her out of the bath. Rita waddled off to tell Matron and, as another contraction doubled her over, Milly wailed at Rita's retreating figure, 'Mum never told me it would be as bad as this!'

Rita shot back, entirely unsympathetic, 'Lot of good that would've done you!'

Milly's delivery was relatively quick and later Rita told her she'd had it easy. But though the time might have been short, it felt to Milly as though she were being ripped open. She privately thought the speed of her delivery was down to the midwife who'd decided to move things along with a strategically placed knee in her stomach.

Afterwards, when she'd been stitched up and the midwife handed her the tightly swaddled bundle, Milly looked down at the round, tiny face staring placidly up at her and wondered how she could feel such tenderness for the little demon who'd just put her through hell. He had a broad button nose and a small 'o' of a mouth, but his eyes were captivating, almost oriental in their shape, and they sparkled with what she could only describe as delight. He looked happy to have been born.

'You be happy while you can, me old son.' She pushed back the white swaddling cloth and kissed the silky, gold splash of hair that covered the crown of his head. And as she began to nurse him, she saw his little fist creep up to her breast, until slowly his uncurled index finger began that familiar, rhythmic stroking he had perfected inside her womb.

They were allowed to keep their babies with them, day and night, for almost six weeks. The nurses always referred to them by surnames. Their adoptive parents, they explained, would give the children their *real* names. But Milly couldn't be so detached. She gave her little boy a secret name: to her he was Jimmy, named after her beloved middle brother, who'd died in 1916 at the Somme when she was only ten. She had worshipped Jimmy from afar, the hero who would surely return, unlike her poor elder brother Charlie, killed at the Battle of Loos the year before. When Jimmy had marched away, her mother promised her he would come back. God, she said, would not be so cruel as to take a second of her sons. God, perhaps, had not taken him, but a German shell certainly had.

Groups of prospective parents came to Edenvale each week to meet the newborns and choose their babies. Three other girls had given birth at about the same time as Milly, followed by Rita, whose little girl was blonde and as beautiful as her mother. She was the first to be taken away. And Rita, hard as nails, seemed genuinely relieved.

'Well, that's her sorted out. It's a weight off me mind, Mill. I can't wait to get out of this place and have a bit of life. I should think yours'll be next, people want boys, don't they?'

Milly nodded. She could only put Rita's hard-heartedness down to the circumstances of her pregnancy, but she couldn't share her steely attitude. Each day she spent with Jimmy only made it harder to contemplate giving him up. As he nuzzled her breast, she would dip her head to breathe in the scent of him, and when his eyes locked on to hers, she found it almost impossible to look away. It was as if she were becoming addicted to her own child.

The next baby to be chosen was indeed a little boy, larger and more robust-looking than Jimmy, then another little girl was taken away. When Milly saw Matron bringing Jimmy back to her, unclaimed, her heart filled with such relief, she thought it would break through her chest. As Matron stood before her, still holding Jimmy, she explained that the only couple left had been disappointed not to get the little girl, but were going away to think about taking Jimmy.

'But, Milly, you shouldn't get your hopes up, they really weren't sure if they wanted him . . .'

At that, something in Milly's heart rebelled. 'If he's not good enough for first choice, then I don't want them to have him at all!' She took Jimmy from the matron, and held him tightly to her.

'You can't afford to pick and choose, young woman.' Matron's face was full of undisguised disapproval. 'If you must know, these are a respectable, wealthy couple, with a beautiful house in Canterbury. Your boy will want for nothing. He's not exactly a robust infant; this may be his only chance. Would you rob him of that and take him back to the slum he was conceived in?'

'He wasn't conceived in a slum,' Milly said, her voice rising with anger. 'He was got in a hop garden and he's not anyone's second best. I'm telling you they're not having my Jimmy!'

'Keep your rough factory voice for the streets! The parents are having tea on the lawn and if they hear your common screeches, they'll definitely reject the poor child!'

Milly stood up, brushing past the matron and, still holding Jimmy tightly to her breast, she poked her head out of the dormitory window. There below was a well-dressed middle-aged couple, drinking tea with Mr Dowell, the home's foremost benefactor.

'Oi, you two! My Jimmy's too good for you, you ain't havin' him!'

Their polite smiles turned to embarrassed disapproval at the sight of Milly shouting from the window. As Matron pulled her back into the room, she heard Mr Dowell mutter hastily, 'A jam girl from Bermondsey, I'm afraid, but it wouldn't be fair to penalize the child . . .'

Milly twisted out of Matron's grasp. Turning her back on her, she began to nurse Jimmy, who'd been woken by her shouting and was now grizzling in her arms.

'See, you've made the poor mite cry, give him to me!' Matron held out her arms, but Milly stubbornly shook her head, so that the woman was forced to come and sit down beside her.

128

'See sense, Milly, you really have no choice,' she said, altering her tone. 'If you take him back to Bermondsey, we'll recommend you as unfit and he'll have to go into an orphanage. Is that really what you want?' When Milly didn't reply, she pressed further. 'I'm told his grandfather is a violent man?'

Would they use that against her? Milly was astonished that the matron knew so much. Who had told her, Florence Green?

'I can look after him on my own. I'm not taking him back home.'

'Where would you take him?' The woman pushed on with her maddeningly sensible, inescapable practicalities. Where would she take Jimmy? How would she live? But these questions paled beside her utter determination not to allow her beloved little boy to go to a home where he could only ever be second best.

As she lay awake that night, she wondered how she could ever have considered giving away her baby. Yet there still seemed no other option. Perhaps if she could contact Miss Green, she'd send her the fare home. If she could only get back to Bermondsey, things would come clearer, she knew it. She would write to Florence Green tomorrow. Meanwhile she would just have to fend off any future adoptive parents, and on today's showing that wouldn't be too difficult. All she need do was open her mouth.

But the next day, Jimmy wasn't brought to her for his morning feed. She watched as each infant was carried up from the nursery and handed to its mother. Growing increasingly agitated, she waited patiently till all the other girls were contentedly settled with their babies. Perhaps this was Matron's idea of a punishment, Milly thought, leaving her till last.

'Nurse, aren't you bringing Jimmy? He's such a hungry little bugger, it's a wonder he's not screaming the nursery down by now!'

Nurse Prior was a kind-hearted soul, who never joined in Matron's shaming tactics. But now she blushed and, hesitating at the door, she came back over to Milly's bed.

'I'm sorry, dear,' she said, taking Milly's hand, 'but Matron says it's better for all concerned if baby Colman is bottle-fed from now on.' Before Milly could protest, she went on. 'You must realize that, in any case, your milk is not sufficient for baby, it's why he's always hungry.'

Nurse Prior was right, Milly thought miserably, her milk *was* drying up. She couldn't even feed him properly, let alone give him a proper future. It was almost as if her body knew she was preparing to give her baby away. Perhaps she should just give in and let him go. But as she watched the nurse leave, closing the door behind her, Milly was filled with a cold, rising panic. She leaped up and ran from the dormitory, following the nurse down the stairs.

'But I want to see him! I can bottle-feed him! She can't stop me seeing my own baby.'

The nurse barred her way. 'Milly, dear, you made your choice when you came here. I know it seems cruel, but you'll have to let him go sooner or later. Come on,' she coaxed, 'come back to the dormitory, and I'll ask Matron to let you say goodbye to baby Colman before you leave here.'

Say goodbye? It struck her, sharp as a knife between her ribs. This was the cold reality of her choice in coming to Edenvale. Now it had arrived, it felt as impossible as pulling her own heart out and watching while it bled over the highly polished wooden floors of the lovely old house. She'd been living in a stupid dream and now she had to wake up. But shouting and bawling would do no good. She stilled her thumping heart and bit her tongue.

'Yes, Nurse, I'd like to be able to say goodbye. Has he already been given to that couple in Canterbury?'

The nurse shook her head. 'We're still waiting for their decision. Matron's had baby moved to the sick nursery.' This was a little room, just off Matron's office, where the poorly babies were nursed. 'I'm sure she'll let you see him one more time.' The nurse put a comforting arm round her, before Milly nodded and turned away.

She waited all morning for word from Matron, but when none came she didn't ask after Jimmy again. She went to meals, said prayers, sang hymns, all the while trying to deaden her heart to the wrenching loss she must go through. She'd been set to light sewing tasks following Jimmy's birth, and had proved so adept that she'd been kept on in the laundry, doing all the household mending. She worked like the wind, fingers flying, heedless of the thumb pricks and blood spots that spattered the sheets. Anything to keep her mind distracted, anything to subdue the quiet desperation that threatened to break through into violent rebellion. All the while, she schooled herself in the many good reasons for giving Jimmy up to a life of privilege and comfort. In no time, she had finished patching the mound of sheets that should have taken her all day.

'Goodness, you've done well!' Mrs Jones, the laundress, nodded in approval when Milly presented her pile.

'I'll take these to the cupboards and fetch some of those nightgowns that need mending. You stay there,' she told Mrs Jones, who'd been about to get up.

'You're a good girl.' She smiled at Milly and handed her the set of keys. Milly set off up the central staircase for the linen cupboards on the top floor. But just as she reached the first landing she heard Matron's voice. Milly peered down the stairwell and saw Matron in the entrance hall below, talking to Nurse Prior.

'She's getting too attached. I'm afraid we'll only have another violent outburst if I allow it. No, Nurse, I'm convinced she's not a fit mother and in fact I've just had a telephone call from the Masons. Fortunately, they weren't put off by the mother's antics and they're coming to take baby home tomorrow.'

The two women passed through the hall, leaving Milly immobile on the landing. Slow minutes passed before she noticed the sheets weighing on her arms. She turned mechanically for the linen room. Jimmy was going tomorrow and she would never see her little boy again. She unlocked the door and shoved the sheets on to one shelf, pulling down a pile of nightgowns, in need of mending, from another. Cradling them in her arms, she sank to the ground. How could she think of mending nightgowns, when all that was precious to her was about to be ripped away? Would her life be like this forever, meaningless tasks masking the emptiness where Jimmy should have been? Is that what her mother's life had been since she'd lost her own boys to the war? No wonder she let the old man beat her black and blue and never seemed to care. Only now did Milly understand why her mother sometimes seemed so insubstantial. Half of her was indeed missing.

Swiftly, before she could change her mind, she moved to the back of the linen room where all the girls' own clothes were stored during their stay. The clothes were neatly folded inside calico bags, labelled alphabetically. She quickly sorted through till she found the bag marked *Colman*. It contained everything she'd come into the home with, except for her money, which was kept in the safe in Matron's office. There wasn't much. Her train fare had been paid by the Wesleyan Mission and she'd spent most of the few shillings she'd brought with her on clothes for her baby. The ones little Jimmy wore now – the ones he would be stripped of, no doubt, the minute he got to the beautiful house in Canterbury. They would never be considered good enough and, Milly was convinced, neither would he.

She picked up the calico bag and hid it inside the pile of nightgowns. Then, making her way to the empty dormitory, she stuffed it under her bed. Milly had learned her lesson. Sometimes stealth was more effective than bluster, and this time no one would know of her plan until it was too late.

Rita and the other girls in the dormitory tiptoed around her. They all knew what had happened and understood there were no words that could soothe Milly now. Even Rita, with an unaccustomed delicacy, made no mention of Jimmy's absence.

After lights out, Milly waited till she was certain all the girls had settled down to sleep. She lay very still, until the moon came into view through the oriel window. Then she eased herself out of bed and slid the bundled clothing carefully out from under it. She crept across the moon-striped oak boards and eased open the door leading to the bathroom, holding her breath till she was sure it wouldn't squeak. In the bathroom, she pulled on her clothes and headed for the back servants' stairs. These would be safer than the main staircase which was in full view of the nursery and the night nurse. Milly knew that Jimmy was the only baby in the sick ward, and with Matron asleep next door, she was gambling there would be no nurse on duty just for Jimmy. Moonlight illuminated the first cot in the sick ward. There was her baby, peacefully sleeping, breathing softly, unaware that his fate was being decided. She hurried to the cot, but a sudden cough from next door made her freeze. Matron was awake. She had no time to hesitate. Quickly she dipped to scoop him up, wrapping him tightly in the cot blanket as he protested softly, his eyelids fluttering open like the wings of a disturbed moth.

'Shhh, shhh, Jimmy boy,' she whispered. 'It's only your mummy, come to take you home.'

12

Goodbye to Eden

July 1924

The moon gave just enough light to see the road in front of her. But she could also find her way using the stars – a trick she'd learned on all those pitch-dark hopping nights when, as children, they would follow tipsy adults back from the pub to the hopping huts, along shadowy hedgerows and dark tree-tunnelled lanes. The impenetrable darkness had terrified her then, especially when the children lagged behind, scaring each other with ghost stories. But now Milly welcomed the night-draped countryside. The only terror she had tonight was that someone would discover her escape before she could get away.

The moonlit July night was kind to her, and with only the lightest of breezes and hardly any cloud cover, she carried her baby unhesitatingly towards the church. She followed the same route every Sunday, on their journey of shame, but at least this church visit would be doing her some good. She felt the place owed her something.

A candle was burning in one of the church windows, and when she tried the iron ring handle she found the door unlocked. She'd been prepared to break the back vestry window, but perhaps God didn't condemn her as much as Matron would have her believe. She was met by the smell of dusty hymn books and beeswax. Looking around for somewhere to lay Jimmy, she noticed moonlight splashing the old stone font at the back of the church. She remembered the vicar had called it 'the Wealden

Font', and said it was as old as the Saxons who'd built the first church here. She'd always liked the worn carvings around the sides. Now, as she kneeled to lay Jimmy down on its flat pedestal, she spotted the unmistakable figure of St Christopher carrying the Christ child upon his back. On an impulse she deliberately dipped her hand into the basin. Scooping up the few drops of water, still pooling in the bottom from the last christening, she dripped them on to her baby's head.

'James,' she whispered. 'There you are, Jimmy boy, don't matter if it's not a caddywack church, that's the name your mother give you and they can't take that away from you now, can they?'

Then, creeping to the table where the little church history books were stacked, she found the donations box, also unlocked. She was about to empty the contents when she heard a creak. It seemed to be coming from the vestry. She cursed her stupidity for ignoring the unlocked door. If the verger came out now, she'd be trapped. Long moments passed as Milly stood very still, holding the tin box. But nobody emerged, and finally she slipped the few shillings into her coat pocket. If it didn't get her all the way home, at least it would be a start.

Then a rustling came from the porch. This time she was not mistaken; someone was definitely there. Darting back to the font, she grabbed her baby and in a panic, put him inside the font. As the oak door creaked open she ducked behind a box pew. Weak moonlight illuminated the dull ochre floor tiles and from the doorway came a quavery voice. She recognized the ancient verger, half blind and deaf as a post, or so she'd thought.

'Whoever you are,' his tremulous voice called out, 'there's a bite to eat and a shilling for your journey in the porch. Shut the door on your way out.'

She heard his shuffling feet retreat. Holding her breath, she ran to the font. Jimmy was lying inside, contentedly staring up at the golden painted cherubs carved into the oak ceiling. 'Someone's on our side tonight, eh, Jimmy?'

She slipped out of the church, picking up the verger's shilling and a wrapped sandwich from the stone seat in the porch. Then, striking out across country to the oast houses at the edge of Edenvale's grounds, she began her journey home.

As soon as she reached the oast houses she knew where she was. One year, when they couldn't get a place at the Horsmonden farm, they'd spent a few weeks hop-picking nearby. If she followed the margin of the hop fields she should come to the lane leading to Marden, the next station down the line. If they were looking for her anywhere it would be at Staplehurst Station, nearest to Edenvale, and she hoped to throw them off her trail.

As dawn began to tinge the hop bines with a pink flush, she brushed the new plants with her hand. So young and fragile, nothing like the robust, crowding vines of September she was used to. It seemed fitting to be trailing through them now, with little Jimmy, and she sang to him softly as she hurried along the field edge.

'*They say that 'oppin's lousy, I don't believe it's true, for when I went down 'oppin, I come back home with you, with an eeayo, eeayo, eeay, eeay, oh . . .*'

As she changed the raucous original into a gentle lullaby, she felt keenly alone, yet driven on by a fierce protectiveness that had taken her totally by surprise. She had only ever been used to thumping her way through life, batting away obstacles and crashing in, heedless of consequences. But now she held a baby, and it had changed everything, even the way she moved. Her stride was more careful and she picked her way more cautiously as she made her way towards the Marden road.

One of her mother's survival mechanisms, in her running battle to cheat the old man of his beer money, had been to always have an emergency shilling sewn into the hem of her skirt. She had passed this on to her daughters. 'If you've got a shilling tucked away, you'll never starve and you can always get yourself home,' she'd advised.

Milly had done exactly that, when leaving Dockhead for Edenvale. When she arrived at the white weatherboard station building, she paused, feeling around the hem of her dress. She ripped her hem, and there it was! 'Thanks, Mum,' she said and kissed the emergency shilling, for this, with the verger's gift and her stolen church pennies, would give her just enough for a ticket to London Bridge.

Walking into the station, she checked the trains on the notice board. The first London train wasn't due for half an hour, but the ticket office was open. Taking her precious shillings in her hand, she approached the window.

'Third-class single to London Bridge, please.'

The drowsy-eyed ticket clerk jerked his head up at her broad cockney. 'Don't normally see your lot till September,' he said, pushing the ticket and a few pennies change towards her. 'What happened, fall for a local lad and come back to find him?' He grinned, eyeing the stirring bundle she held in her arms.

'Mind yer own soddin' business,' she said, grabbing the ticket. She walked, very straight-backed, on to the platform, angry that she was so obviously a girl who'd fallen for a hopping baby. The narrow platform was filling up quickly, with bowler-hatted city gents at the first-class end and labourers at the other, waiting to board third-class carriages. There was also a large woman, trying to control three excited children, and Milly hoped she would be able to get into their carriage. She didn't fancy the attentions of a group of navvies today. She nipped into the waiting room to feed Jimmy. She'd had no chance to filch any bottles from the home, so he'd have to last on whatever she could provide herself. She only hoped she'd have enough milk to keep him satisfied. But soon a shrill whistle announced the approaching train.

'Sorry, love, I know you're hungry, but grub's got to wait.' She bundled Jimmy securely in one arm, with her small bag over the other, and dashed back out.

Peering anxiously down the platform, she saw the steam-shrouded engine clattering into the station. It flashed by her so fast she was afraid it wouldn't stop, but with another deafening scream, it came to a halt, puffing steam. Doors banged open the length of the train and she followed the little family to the third-class carriages. She was about to board, when she was grabbed from behind. Spinning round, she was confronted by a man in a well-cut, dark suit and trilby, who looked familiar. Confused, she wondered if he was pointing out that this was a first-class carriage, and she was about to apologize for her mistake when he spoke.

'Miss Colman, I think you should come with me.'

'Let go of me, I've paid me ticket!' She searched around for help, but the large lady had already settled her children into the carriage and the labourers were bundling into the next one.

'I'm not coming nowhere with you!' She shook off his hand as he tightened his grip and pulled at her arm. Then she remembered where she'd seen him. He was Mr Dowell, the benefactor she'd seen talking to the Canterbury couple. Now he faced her with stern disapproval.

'We can't allow you to just walk out of our care with your child. You're a selfish, ungrateful girl. Now be sensible and come back to Edenvale.'

'Get your hands off!' She shoved him away with her free hand, just as the station master raised his flag. She had to board now or not at all. The shrill whistle blew and a cloud of steam engulfed them. It was then that the man in the trilby hat made the mistake of making a grab for little Jimmy. Half blinded by the smoke, he never saw Milly's fist coming, not until it had hit him squarely on the jaw. He staggered back, his hat flew off, the train pulled out and she felt strong hands hoisting her and Jimmy into the carriage.

'Up you come, miss, we're off!' a gruff voice said, as she was planted firmly inside the moving carriage.

The navvy slammed the carriage door shut with a grin. Milly dodged round him and stuck her head out of the window. Mr Dowell was brushing off his hat, staring at the disappearing train. She wasn't sure if he could still see her, but nevertheless, stuck two fingers out of the window for good measure and waved goodbye to Eden.

Milly blew up a strand of dark hair from her forehead and looked around the carriage for a seat. By this time, Jimmy was screaming and the group of navvies were staring. She hoped she wasn't in for more trouble.

'You've got a decent right hook on you!' the navvy who'd hoisted her in said, as she attempted to settle Jimmy.

'Well, he was trying to take my baby!' she retorted. Perhaps she hadn't changed as much as she'd thought. Her fist had connected with Mr Dowell's jaw before she'd time to think about it.

The navvy stuck out his hand. 'My name's Davey. Me and my mates would be honoured if you would join us. Shove up, lads.'

Milly smiled with relief, gratefully slumping on to the nearest seat. The men were dressed in rough working clothes and boots, and a couple of the younger ones looked shyly away as she glanced in their direction.

'Well, I'm pleased to meet you, Davey. You're a real gentleman, thanks for the helping hand.' She smiled.

Davey sat opposite her as the train picked up speed. 'You looked like you needed it. Why was he trying to take the littl'un, if you don't mind me asking?'

Milly blushed. 'I've been staying over at Edenvale.'

Davey nodded. 'Changed your mind, did you?' he said gently. 'I don't blame you, duck, I've got kids of me own. It'd break my heart to give any of 'em up.'

Tears pricked Milly's eyes at his unexpected kindness, but Jimmy's need was pressing and now his screams had become ear-splitting.

'Sorry, Davey, but I need to feed him, otherwise he'll deafen you all the way to London Bridge.'

Davey motioned to the other men, who each with great delicacy turned their backs, until Jimmy's contented nuzzling ceased and he fell into a milky sleep.

Milly would love to have joined him in a doze, but although the eventful night had sapped her energy, she couldn't allow herself to be rocked to sleep by the swaying carriage. Every atom of her being seemed to vibrate with an alert watchfulness. She wouldn't rest till she knew Jimmy was safe. Davey and his mates had no such compunction. After a little conversation about their families and the tunnelling job they were doing at Moorgate, they each fell to snoring and slumbering. She spent the journey watching fields disappear, replaced by suburban tiled roofs, and it wasn't until they had reached the dense smog of south London that she shook Davey awake.

'London Bridge next stop,' she said and he jumped up, lifting her bag down from the rack.

'You got anywhere to stay?' he asked as he handed it to her.

'Oh yes. I can walk it from London Bridge. I'm going home.'

In fact she had no idea where she was going. The extent of her plan had been to get Jimmy as far away from Edenvale as possible, but now she was within half an hour of the only home she'd ever known, she felt as barred from it as if she'd been Eve returning to the gates of paradise.

Davey helped her down and bade her farewell. He and his mates were soon lost in the crowds of workers leaving London Bridge Station and Milly found her way to the stairs leading to Tooley Street. She started walking towards Dockhead, following the railway viaduct, packed with trains spewing steam, which descended in clouds to the street below. By the time she reached the narrow inlet of St Saviour's Dock, Jimmy's white blanket was covered in black smuts, and as she approached Dockhead everything struck her as dingier and more cramped than she remembered. It reminded her of the times when she'd come home from hopping, sorely missing open skies and the uncluttered horizons of Kent. But now she welcomed the warren of streets and courts. At least she knew how to lose herself in their suffocating closeness, and if Edenvale reported her as an unfit mother she might have to hide here for a very long time.

She waited in a small courtyard off Arnold's Place, until she was sure her father would have gone to work, and then she walked with faltering steps to her house. At first there was no answer and she'd begun to think Mrs Colman was out, when she heard scuffling and the door was opened.

'Hello, Mum,' she said, lifting Jimmy like a shield against her mother's refusal. 'I couldn't give him up.'

Ellen Colman's hand flew to her face. 'Oh Gawd, *Jesus*, Mary and Joseph, bless us'n spare us'n save us'n keep us!'

It was as she took her hand away that Milly saw mottled red and blue bruises on her mother's face, and her right eye as bloodshot as her father's usually were after a night at the Swan and Sugarloaf. Before she could say anything, her mother reached out for the baby.

'Look at him, he's a little angel!' she said, cradling him in her arms, immediately entranced. Milly smiled at her unfeigned delight. It was clear that in Ellen Colman's eyes Jimmy would never be second best.

Milly followed her mother down the passage into the old familiar kitchen. While her mother sat with the baby, examining every toe and finger, Milly made tea and answered her questions about Edenvale and her change of mind.

'I can understand why you couldn't give him up, love,' her mother said, looking up after a while. 'You've got some gumption, standing up to them. But if you don't want them taking the baby away, you'll have to prove you've got a home and how will you feel . . . coming back to live with the old man?' She frowned and shook her head. 'He's been ten times worse since you left.'

'I can see that.'

'Oh, this.' Her mother's hand touched the bruise on her face. 'I got between him and Elsie. Poor little cow's been taking the brunt of it lately. And don't think you can give him another pasting and make it any better because you can't. You've got to live with the man, same as all of us.'

'No, I haven't, Mum. I'm not stopping here.'

'But where else can you go? You've got your baby to think of now, Milly,' she said, looking down at Jimmy as he lay contentedly in her arms. 'You've just got to swallow your pride for his sake.'

'Don't you worry about me. I'll get me job back and I'll find somewhere to live.'

'Worry? I don't do nothing else *but* worry about you. I'm sorry, love, I wish I could do something to help, but he keeps me so short.' Her mother reached down to the hem of her skirt, and began to unpick the hem. 'Here, have this.'

'No, Mum! That's your emergency shilling. I'm not taking that.'

But her mother shoved it into her hand. 'Take it, I'll get another to put in its place.' Milly swallowed her pride, just as her mother had said she must, and took the money.

'One thing you *can* do for me is look after him while I go over to Southwell's, to see if I can get a job.'

'Of course I will, love. Just be back before the old man gets home. I can't afford any more rows, he's broken nearly every stick of furniture in the place.'

Milly looked round. There were indeed a couple of chairs missing and the old sideboard door was hanging off.

'Don't worry, Mum. I'll be out of the way long before he's back.'

As she turned to leave, her mother caught her by the hand and Milly saw her eyes filling with tears. 'I'm pleased you're home, darlin', and . . . I'm glad you brought us back another Jimmy.'

13

Her Solitary Way

July 1924

'Milly Colman! What are you doing back?' Tom Pelton, sitting behind an old roll-top desk in a cubbyhole next to the clocking-on machine, looked surprised to see her. In charge of hiring and firing for all the departments, she would get nowhere without his say-so. Fortunately, ever since she'd first joined Southwell's, he'd taken a shine to her and she was confident he'd give her a job.

'I thought you were going into service?' he said diplomatically, and she decided to play along for the time being: if he knew she'd come back with a child, she'd have far less chance of getting a job.

'I didn't take to it,' she said. 'Cleaning up after other people! I think I'd be happier back here.'

Tom Pelton was a decent foreman and he'd always treated her fairly, but now he shook his head. 'I'm sorry, Milly, but the days of walking back into your old job are gone.'

This was the last thing Milly expected and he must have seen her disappointment.

'You could try Lipton's or Hartley's,' he offered, 'but I'm pretty sure they've taken on all their summer workers by now. Best thing I can suggest is come back tomorrow, in case any of the casuals don't turn up. There might be a month in the picking room for you, while the strawberries are coming in.'

She was stunned. Things really were changing. How often had she come back from hopping on one day and started at her old place the next? Now, when she desperately needed a job, it seemed she would have to go begging.

'I'd be grateful for the chance of that, Mr Pelton,' she said, trying not to show how crushed she felt. But she really needed to be sure of a job today. She'd have no chance of renting a room if she couldn't say she had a job, even a casual one. As she walked out of the gates and back down Jacob's Street, puzzling over where to go next, she decided she might as well try at Hartley's. It was a much bigger factory than Southwell's, and covered a vast area just off Tower Bridge Road. They had a reputation for treating their employees well, so it was unusual for someone to give up their job there. But they did employ huge numbers of casuals in the summer months. It was worth a try.

She walked back through Dockhead towards Tower Bridge Road, and at Hickman's Folly hurried past a group of women scrubbing pavements outside their doors. One of them carried a bucket of whitewash, and was painting the edge of the kerb. Milly stepped carefully over the still wet paint, but was stopped by a familiar voice.

'Good gawd, look who's turned up!' It was Mrs Bunclerk. She put the bucket down and suddenly Milly was being embraced by whitewashed hands. 'My Kitty'll be so pleased to see you! But we didn't expect you back yet, love.' She dropped her voice. 'Did the baby go to a nice home?'

Milly nodded. 'I think he did, Mrs Bunclerk – he's come home with me.'

The woman gave her a sympathetic smile. 'Well, at least you won't be on your own. Your mum'll help out, and even with a baby, you'll still have a darn site more room in Arnold's Place than us lot in ours!'

'Oh, I'm not going back home! I couldn't live with him, so I'm looking for a room.'

Mrs Bunclerk nodded doubtfully. 'It's just a matter of finding one that'll be better'n what you've got at home. You'll be lucky there, love.'

Milly knew there were plenty of rooms for rent all over Bermondsey. Often families of five or six would squeeze into one room and let out the spare room to a lodger, for the income. She hoped to do better than that, even if she had to go further afield than Dockhead. Still, her first priority was a job.

'Got to go, Mrs Bunclerk, let Kitty know I'm back!' she said, hastily kissing the woman goodbye.

'I'll keep an eye out for you, love, see if there's anywhere decent round here,' Kitty's mother called after her.

It was only after she walked away that Milly realized why Mrs Bunclerk was painting the kerb. Tomorrow was a festival day for the Catholic churches. The whole area was spruced up, ready for the children's parade. Crowds six deep lined the way and children, dressed in Sunday best, marched through riverside streets, carrying flowers and banners. There was a band and afterwards a tea at the church hall. In the evening, if it was fine, someone would trundle a piano into the street and there'd be an impromptu party.

How could she have forgotten the date? It had always been one of the highlights of their year, a day when beauty flooded the dour terraces and colour burst into the unrelieved drabness of slate roofs and brick walls. No doubt Elsie and Amy had been excitedly preparing their clothes for weeks, and once Milly would have been at the heart of it too. How different her life would be now! She might be home, but she was still in a sort of exile and festivals were not for her. She set her mind to the task at hand.

When she reached Tower Bridge Road, she turned into Green Walk and marched up to Hartley's gates, all the while praying there would be a job for her. The bandy-legged porter rolled out of his little sentry box and, without even asking what she wanted, pointed to a board. *No job vacancies.*

Not to be put off, she asked, 'I was wondering if you needed any summer casuals?'

'Can't you read?'

'No need to be so rude, I'm only asking.'

The porter growled and coughed. 'You try answering the same question umpteen times a day and see how you like it.'

'Miserable old git,' Milly said none too quietly. As she walked away, she gave the board a deliberate kick.

Hopping from one bandy leg to another, he shouted after her: 'And don't come back here expecting a job any time soon, you won't get through the gates!'

All her old bravado rising, she flung back, 'Wouldn't work in this dump if you paid me!'

She knew she'd just scuppered her chances of a job at Hartley's, at least as long as he was porter, but after so many weeks of being ordered about she'd felt compelled to strike a blow for her own dignity. She was beginning to realize that running away from Edenvale had been the easy part. But not to be deterred, she decided her next stop would be Feaver's, the tin bashers at the other end of Tower Bridge Road. She traipsed all the way back down the stall-lined street, with costermongers enticing her to buy fruit and veg she couldn't afford, and the bustle of women with baskets and purses making her feel even more of an outsider from her own life.

She was still wearing the winter clothes she'd travelled to Edenvale in, and now, as the sun broke through, she shed her woollen overcoat. The old clothes market was in full swing as she passed and Milly couldn't resist weaving her way through the stalls. Her eye caught flashes of good material or dresses that she knew she could improve upon, if only she'd had an extra bob or two in her pocket. There was a light knitted two-piece, perfect for summer, that she lingered over. *Your dress-buying days are over*, she told herself sternly and hurried on. But at Feaver's she was met with the same answer as at Hartley's. There were no extra workers needed.

By this time Milly's mouth felt like sandpaper and her stomach was cramping with hunger. She'd had nothing to drink since the cup of tea with her mother, and nothing to eat since finishing the verger's sandwich on the train that morning. Realizing that if she felt hungry, then poor little Jimmy must be as well, she made quickly for home. As she walked, the practicalities of keeping him began to hit home. She'd brought Jimmy back with nothing but the clothes he slept in and a handful of nappies filched from the nursery. How much would it cost to feed and clothe him? She'd have to buy bottles and tins of milk as her own wasn't enough for him. Where would the money come from? Now that Jimmy had cast his spell over Mrs Colman, Milly knew her mother would help however she could, but she'd have no money to spare. Anxiety knotted in her stomach. Perhaps bringing Jimmy away had just been selfishness? She'd told herself she was doing the right thing for him, but had she just done it for herself?

Along the way she passed more factories. First Sarson's, where she gagged at the acid, malty aroma coming from the huge wooden vinegar vats. She'd always avoided the more foul-smelling industries that clustered in Bermondsey, yet now she'd welcome a job in the bottling room. But again she was turned away. Hurrying under Tanner Street railway arch, just as several trains rattled over it on their way up to London Bridge, she felt the shuddering in her bones. The dank cool of the wide tunnel made her shiver after the bright sunlight of the morning and she longed to be home.

Home? What's that? she asked herself as she scuttled out into the bright glare of day and came to the tannery. Most tanning was men's work, the old man's work. Dipping heavy wet hides in and out of lime pits all day was beyond the strength of the majority of women. But girls were employed for the fine leather dressing and she stopped at the yard, still hopeful that she might find a job before she reached Dockhead. When the foreman shook his head, Milly felt a lump form in her throat and tears prick her eyes. Once too proud to even consider working in such a smelly, filthy place, now his refusal seemed to her like the end of the world. Having a baby changed everything.

When she arrived back in Dockhead she could hear Jimmy's screams from the end of Arnold's Place. A couple of women were standing at their doors, babies on their hips. One of them turned away without meeting her gaze, but the other was Mrs Knight's granddaughter, and she smiled at Milly.

'You've got a hungry one there, gel!' she ventured, then lowering her voice, said, 'I've dropped a few bits off at your mum's, stuff he's grown out of.' She nodded towards the child she was bouncing on her hip.

So now they all knew she was home with her baby; it hadn't taken long. Blushing, Milly thanked the woman, glad to know that she would find kindness as well as the inevitable condemnation at her homecoming.

As soon as she entered the kitchen, her mother thrust Jimmy into her arms. 'Here, take him quick. He's turned into a little devil!'

'You're the one who said he was an angel!' Milly managed a laugh. 'Oh, Mum, I'm gasping. Make us a cup of tea while I feed him.'

Soon the noise of Jimmy's contented sucking filled the kitchen. Reaching for the tea her mother handed her, Milly carefully sipped it over Jimmy's urgent nuzzling form.

'Oh, that's better, and my feet are falling off me.' She kicked off her shoes and wiggled her toes.

'Any luck?'

Milly shook her head. 'Not yet.'

'Jobs are getting terrible. The old man said it would all change.'

'I remember.'

She hated admitting that he had been right about anything, but he'd warned her the days of plentiful jobs would one day fade. She'd never believed him, not with so many factories and breweries, tanneries, warehouses and docks. How could there ever be a job shortage in Bermondsey? It wasn't called London's Larder for nothing. Half the country's food came in through the docks and it all had to be unloaded, sorted, packed and reloaded.

'Perhaps I could try up Hay's Wharf?' she mused.

'You always used to turn your nose up at the wharves.'

'Well, things have changed. And to be honest, Mum, I think I'd do anything now.'

Milly sighed and shoved her swollen feet back into her shoes, which she noticed were scuffed and looking down at heel. She lay Jimmy back down in the bottom sideboard drawer that her mother had lined with a blanket, just as the front door banged open. Her sisters' shrill voices, excited and tumbling over each other, preceded them as they burst into the kitchen. They stopped short in the doorway.

'What you doing home?' Elsie addressed her sullenly, all trace of excitement vanishing in an instant.

'Good gawd, you've not been in two minutes!' Their mother slapped her own knees for effect.

Milly shook her head. 'I can't do anything right, can I? Last time I saw you, you was begging me to stay!'

'Well, you didn't take no notice, and me and Amy's not sharing our bed with you. Are we, Ame?'

Amy ignored Elsie. She was walking softly to the open drawer. Little Jimmy's fists were just visible as he punched the air. Amy regarded him steadily.

'He looks a bit like a Chinaman off the docks,' she said, darting a look at Milly to see the effect of her words. Milly was pretty sure her sister knew who Jimmy's father was, but she hadn't come home to fight.

'When did you ever see a Chinaman with golden hair?' her mother countered.

'I suppose his eyes do look a bit oriental,' Milly said. But in truth, Jimmy's almond eyes, though darker in colour, reminded her of Elsie's.

Jimmy had grown still and was staring fixedly at Amy, who'd knelt beside the drawer. The three sisters gathered round him. Jimmy seemed to radiate a contented calm. Milly had noticed right from birth that he was a happy baby, except when he was hungry, and that was her fault, not his. His serene, unblinking eyes rested on Amy and then he smiled, lifting a hand to her hair.

Milly could see Amy's determination to be unimpressed weaken, and the merest hint of a smile answered Jimmy's own.

Then Elsie stretched her finger out, to be grasped by Jimmy's fist. As she did so, the sleeve of her dress rode up, revealing a deep, purple weal, striped across her arm. It had festered and a scab was trying to form over its angry centre.

'What's that?' Milly said, reaching for her arm. But Elsie twisted away and darting a look at her mother, said defiantly, 'The old bastard's been at me with the hot poker.'

'What did you do to upset him?' Milly's mouth had gone dry. Elsie's face was impassive, but still, Milly felt accused.

'She didn't do anything,' her mother said, with a face revealing as much guilt as Milly felt for not being there. 'It was my fault. He will keep poking at the fire when he gets in and all the smuts and soot cover everything. I hid the soddin' poker, didn't I? But she got the blame.'

'Oh! Mum. It's not your fault.'

There was silence in the kitchen, just the clock ticking and the unasked question in the faces of her sisters and mother. Would Milly stay to protect them? She looked over at Jimmy who was beginning to doze, blowing bubbles out of his tiny 'o' of a mouth with each breath. She straightened up.

'I need to go and find a job. Will you be all right with him, Mum?'

'Yes, love, he's good as gold except when he's hungry.'

'I know, it's me. My milk's drying up, but I'll put him on bottles . . . as soon as I get paid.'

Her mother nodded. 'No wonder he's been screaming, poor little bugger. Still, he's all right for now. You go, but make sure you're back before—'

'I will be!' Milly said, throwing on her coat and flying out into the street, as though she could escape all their expectations.

Hay's Wharf was abuzz with dockers, wearing uniform flat caps and tied cotton scarves. They were scurrying to and from the dense cluster of lighters moored near the dock edge. Some pushed hand trolleys piled with bulging sacks of coffee beans, others gathered in groups round the large vessel discharging its cargo. Platform cranes swung bales out of the hold and dockers guided them to dolly carts waiting below. Milly asked a boy in a too-tight waistcoat, standing guard over some tea crates, how far it was to the dried goods warehouse. When he pointed further along the wharf, nearer to London Bridge, she hurried along, hugging the warehouse walls so as not to collide with any barrows or swinging loads. The smell of coffee in this part of the wharf was pungent and inviting, and she inhaled deeply. But she was looking for beans of a different kind. The company employed hundreds of women to sort dried haricot beans, in a cavernous shed directly on the wharf side. But if the ship hadn't docked, the jobs wouldn't be there. She scrutinized each vessel as she passed, but was unable to guess their cargo.

Searching out the company office above the sorting shed, she leaped the stairs two at a time, and as she did, collided with an acne-faced youth holding an armful of shipping documents. The papers fluttered down towards the river.

'Shit, me bills of lading!' he cried out, vaulting the rest of the stairs. The wharfinger, a red-faced man with a carefully trimmed moustache, had witnessed the collision from the office, and as she approached he gave her an exasperated look, which told her she'd already made a bad impression.

'Can you tell me if there's any sorting jobs going?' she asked, fingers crossed behind her back.

'Well, you'll have to be a bit more careful sorting beans than you are climbing stairs.'

She swallowed her pride and her ready cheeky answer. 'Sorry, I was in a hurry. But I'm very quick-fingered. I'm used to sorting fruit at Southwell's.'

'Hmm,' he said, sounding unconvinced. He stuck his hands into his trouser pockets and peered out over the dock. 'Any rate, your luck's in, we've got two vessels docking tomorrow and I can use some extra girls. Come in early and you'll have a week's work.'

A week's work! He might as well have given her a thousand pounds. She felt so elated, she tripped almost lightly back down the stairs in spite of her growing weariness.

She knew full well it would be a horrible job, and the shed would be sweltering and airless. After the first hour her fingertips would start to burn, after a morning they would shred, by the end of the day her back and legs would be screaming and she'd probably be ready to throw herself into the Thames with boredom, but none of that mattered. With a job, she'd have the means to find a place for her and Jimmy to live.

But now she hardly knew where to begin looking for lodgings. Halfway down Tooley Street she came across a shop that advertised rooms to let, and took note of the addresses. She discounted those in the more respectable areas – Storks Road and Reverdy Road would be beyond her means. But a couple were cheap enough and close enough to visit this afternoon. The first was in Snowsfields, only a ten-minute walk, but when she left the traffic-filled bustle of Tooley Street and found the back court, her heart quailed. The narrow house bowed at the waist and seemed to have a broken pane in every window. The grime of ages smeared its walls and standing at the door, with a baby on her hip, was a greasy-haired woman surrounded by filthy children. Milly turned away without even enquiring. She would never take Jimmy there.

The next address was in Cherry Garden Street, a half-hour's walk away. Now the afternoon was wearing on and she knew she had to be back to collect Jimmy, before the old man came home. Still, she couldn't afford a tram, so she would just have to step out. *Come on, Milly, don't be such a feather legs!* she chided herself. *You can do better than this!* She lengthened her stride, ignoring the cramp that gripped her calves.

Cherry Garden Street hadn't seen a cherry tree for many a long year, not since men in knee breeches and women in high wigs were ferried over from the other side, to enjoy the pleasure gardens. Now, it was a down-at-heel terrace that led to Cherry

Garden Pier, jutting out into the Thames, and clustered about with tugs, lighters and steamers. The bowsprit of a large ship protruded right into the street, pointing its long finger at the door Milly was looking for. It wasn't as bad as Snowsfields. The window frames were peeling, but at least they had glass in them. A sign in one of the windows announced *Front room to let, share kitchen with respectable family.* She knocked hesitantly on the front door, which was opened almost immediately by a pale-faced young woman. She was hoisting a child up on to one hip and another clung about her skirt.

'I've come about the room.'

The young woman's face tightened with suspicion. 'Have you got a deposit?' she asked.

'Yes,' Milly answered, truthfully enough, but whether it was the amount the woman had in mind was another matter.

The toddler, a boy of about two, pulled at his mother's skirt and she reached into her apron pocket for a dummy which he shoved into his mouth.

'Are you in work?' she asked and when Milly nodded, the woman moved aside.

'You want to see the room? It's at the front.'

Milly followed her into the passageway of just bare boards, then into the front room. Everything in there seemed to be missing some essential element. There was a bed, with one side propped up on a couple of bricks, a kitchen chair with only half the rungs, a washstand with a cracked china basin but no jug, and a chest of drawers minus one drawer. Milly noted with relief that it wasn't too dirty.

The woman waited, hungry-faced and wary. Milly knew she represented income.

'I've got a baby,' she said bluntly. She might as well get that out in the open.

The woman sniffed, unconcerned. 'Join the club, love. One more in this house won't make no difference. I've got two more upstairs.'

And as if to corroborate this, Milly heard the sound of children's screams, and then feet thudding from one side of the ceiling to the other.

'They're good as gold really,' the woman said apologetically.

'I'll take it,' she said quickly. She was simply too tired to go on looking for a better place. Besides, she was running out of time. Her father would be home soon and although it wasn't ideal, at least it would save her from a night spent under the old man's roof.

Milly explained that she would be back in a little while with her things and her baby, and when she offered two shillings as a deposit the woman paused doubtfully, but just then a man appeared in the passage. He must have been listening from the back kitchen. His face was paler than his wife's, pockmarked and gaunt, and Milly could smell the beer on him.

'That'll do,' he said, pocketing the money and turning back to the kitchen.

Back in the street, Milly felt her legs trembling. Irritated as the unaccustomed weakness washed over her, she summoned up a last reserve of energy and headed towards Arnold's Place.

The old man stood with one foot braced on the bottom sideboard drawer. He was holding the poker, glowing still from the fire, in one hand and waving it like some aimless wizard's wand above the sleeping head of her baby. She stood very still, grasping the edge of the kitchen table. She was vaguely aware that Amy was crouched underneath the table and that Elsie was hiding in a shadowy corner of the kitchen. Her mother looked nervously from husband to daughter and made a move, which only resulted in a more energetic sweep of the poker in the air above the drawer. Milly's gaze fixed on the old man's bloodshot eyes, then moved to his leathery hand, his drunken, numb fingers loosely gripping the poker handle. Now he dangled it like a fiery sword above Jimmy. He swayed, then steadying himself, brought his booted foot down heavily on the edge of the drawer. Jimmy stirred, and she saw her

154

child's eyes open in calm wonder. It was his first glimpse of his grandfather. She edged towards the drawer.

'Ha!' the old man slurred, brandishing the poker. 'Not so brave now, are you, you little slut? And what makes you think you and your bastard are welcome in my house?'

She didn't answer, but halted, calculating just how drunk he was and how slow his reactions might be. Images of what might happen if his grip loosened on the hot poker paralysed her. But before she could decide what to do, she glimpsed a swift movement at her feet. Like a darting mouse, Amy was out of her hiding place and across the kitchen, before the old man had time to react. Grabbing Jimmy in one arm, she scampered back and threw him into Milly's arms. Milly clasped him tight, picked up her bag and flew down the passage out into the street. Heedless of Mrs Knight's greeting or the curious stares of other neighbours who had gathered to gossip on their doorsteps, she ran as fast as her burdens would allow, all the way back to the house in Cherry Garden Street.

14

Turning Tide

July 1924

The landlady showed her into the sparse room that was to be their home, with the offer of a cup of tea. Milly only wished there was some food to go with it. She hadn't stopped to eat all day and now she swayed with hunger and fatigue. She laid Jimmy on the bed and sat on the rickety chair, waiting for the woman to come back. Milly looked around the room, devoid of any warm, homely touches, and had to fend off the tears. She closed her eyes for a moment, but was soon jolted awake by a hand on her shoulder.

'Oh, sorry, I must have dropped right off,' she said and gulped the tea, sweetened with condensed milk, which the landlady handed her. Milly picked Jimmy up and began to feed him, while the woman looked on.

'Ain't he got no father?' the woman asked, already knowing the answer, for she carried on. 'Still, husbands ain't much cop 'alf the time.' She jerked her head back towards the kitchen. 'My useless lump's sleeping it off in there.' She sighed, then hearing her own baby crying, she said, 'I've got to see to mine.'

Milly could have wished for a more private lodging. There was no lock on the door but she shoved the chair up against it, and too exhausted to even undress, lay down on the bed, wrapping herself and Jimmy in her overcoat. But now sleep eluded her. Overwhelmed by her own solitary state, her thoughts flew to her mother and sisters, only half an hour distant, but feeling half a world away. The plum-blushed evening sky still gave light enough to pick out the sad testaments of her banishment: her pathetically small bag of belongings; this bare cell; and her baby, her only consolation.

Eventually she surrendered to a sleep, disturbed by Jimmy's stirrings and odd dreams full of angels falling from heaven, holding fiery flaming swords, and each with the livid face of her father. The noise which finally roused her completely was not loud, but an insistent squeaking and scratching, which in her groggy state, Milly at first put down to mice under the floorboards. When she realized it was the door handle being turned and the chair rattling under pressure from outside, she shot up, listening intently. Leaving Jimmy on the bed, she stole to the door. She could hear snuffling breaths outside and felt the rickety old chair begin to give way as the door opened a crack. A waft of beery breath and a low, hoarse voice reached her.

'I know you're there! Your sort won't mind a bit of fun, eh?' He rattled the door and shoved. The chair broke and he stumbled in, sending Milly flying back on to the bed.

Before she could get up, he'd pinned her down with his drunken, beery weight. Milly's first thought was for Jimmy. She flung out her arm to protect him and at the same time jerked up her knee sharply, causing the landlord to yelp and roll over in pain. Suddenly the bed collapsed, sending the pile of bricks thundering across the lino, and toppling him on to the floor. Milly had only seconds to decide what to do as he was trying to push himself up. She lunged for the china basin on the washstand, smashing it over his head, but the impact wasn't as great as she'd hoped. Already cracked, it simply shattered into fragments.

Where was his wife? Surely she must have heard the commotion, but either she'd gone to bed as drunk as her husband, or she preferred to stay out of his nocturnal adventures. In any event, there was no help coming. While he was still recovering from the crack on the head, Milly took her chance. She shoved on her shoes, bundled Jimmy in her coat, grabbed her bag and fled the house, leaving the front door wide open behind her.

She ran, not stopping until she reached Cherry Garden Pier. When she looked back, the street was deserted. Thank God, he hadn't followed her, so pausing to catch her breath, she wrapped Jimmy more tightly before setting off, she hardly knew where. Following the dank river smell carried on the cool breeze, she stumbled into a jog, forcing herself to keep moving, scared that if she once stood still, she'd have to admit she had no idea where she was going, or what she was going to do.

These side streets, hard by the river, had a muted peace during the night that was never present in daylight hours, when wharves would bristle with swinging cranes, delivery vans and swarms of dockers. Turning along Bermondsey Wall, deserted warehouses closed in silently around her as she made her way instinctively to a breach in their massive bulks. At Fountain Stairs she found the river – wide, calm and moon-striped. Stopping for a few heaving breaths, her hand gripped the dank river wall, then something impelled her down the steps, towards the river's inky waters lapping at their base. Detritus bobbed rapidly past her and the water flowed swiftly, as did her memory, back to the day when she'd sat on these very steps, deciding to give up her child. She had come full circle. Life, forcing her to make the same choice again. What on earth had persuaded her she could ever manage alone with a baby? It was impossible. Jimmy, now awake in her arms, looked up at her with those peaceful, accepting eyes, devoid of condemnation. She rested her face, wet with tears, against his smooth cheek. The river tugged her irresistibly downward, one step at a time. Never before had she understood why someone would come to the water's edge to end all their pain, but tonight, she understood.

Letting the tide of her own past choices take her, lacking strength to resist the fierce current of events she'd set in motion, she found herself succumbing to the river – she would let it take her and her child, there was nothing else she could do.

Up swirled the black eddies, rippling with moonlight, the dripping steps swayed beneath her. She flung herself forward, eager for the icy, swirling water to swallow her. But instead of its numbing embrace, strong hands suddenly yanked her backwards. Stars whirled into her vision, an indigo sky replacing the inky water, and she felt encircling arms grasp her and Jimmy.

As if from a great distance, she heard a man saying, 'You're all right, Milly, I've got you.'

She felt a hand beneath her elbow as she was helped to her feet.

'Here, let me take the baby.' And when she hesitated, he went on, 'This damp air can't be good for him, can it?'

The man's face was still obscured in the shadows, but the voice was familiar. There was something in it that made her trust him. She placed Jimmy into his cradling arm, and let him help her up the river stairs. At the top, by the light of a nearby gas lamp, she looked into the face of the man who had saved her and Jimmy. Half in shadow, at first she didn't know him.

'It's Bertie Hughes, Milly.'

She stared at him, willing her numbed mind to work. It felt as if part of her really had been swept away by the tide and she was hauling it back, second by second. Then she recognized him.

'Bertie? The grocer?'

'Yes. I just came down to look at the river,' he said in explanation.

'Me too.' The lie hung in the air between them. Trembling uncontrollably, she waited for him to leave her, knowing that then she would have to face her impossible choices again.

'I think you might have lost your footing . . . if I hadn't come along,' he said gently.

She nodded, dumbly ashamed that despair could have so overcome her instinct to protect her child.

'I think I must have fainted.' Again she lied. 'Not had a bite to eat all day, and . . .' a sob caught in her throat, 'and I lost me lodgings . . . and . . .' She heaved in a shuddering breath which ended in tears.

'Here.' He gave her a handkerchief and began leading her away from the river, along Farncombe Street. As they passed the Bermondsey Settlement, her grip on his arm grew tighter.

'You're not taking me there, are you?'

'Well, I just thought . . . you know Miss Green, don't you? Perhaps she can help.'

She pulled away. 'No, Bertie, I can't go there. They'll want to take my baby. The home said I was unfit . . . that's why I've run away from there this morning.'

He seemed to require no further explanation and hurried them on past the Settlement. Looking up at the Gothic arched windows, spilling light across Farncombe Street, Milly knew that sooner or later she must face Florence Green's disappointment, but not tonight.

'Now, listen,' Bertie said, shifting Jimmy on his arm and looking at Milly, 'let me take you for a bite to eat. You'll be able to think straight once you've got some food inside you.'

They had reached the end of Farncombe Street and were about to cross Jamaica Road, where the late-night dining rooms were open all hours for night workers.

'You're very kind, Bertie, but I can't take charity . . .'

He raised an eyebrow, in that quietly amused way she remembered now, and she was forced to smile at the memory of the grocer's slate which her mother had made such good use of over the years.

'Thank you, Bertie,' she said, 'so long as you let me pay you back.'

The dining rooms were brightly lit and clean, filled with wooden tables and a few booths round the walls. It was half empty, waiting for the rush of the next shift changeover. They sat in a booth towards the back, and Milly was able to lay Jimmy in the corner of the bench, wrapped in her coat. While Bertie ordered their food, Milly sank back, feeling the safest she had all day. She still felt oddly between worlds, and as Jimmy stirred, she patted him gently, trying to dismiss from her mind how she had so nearly taken him with her from this world to the next.

She hoped Bertie wouldn't refer to it again. He seemed to sense her reticence and while they sipped tea and waited for their food,

160

he made conversation about his night at the Settlement. 'I was there for a lecture. It was Dr Salter.'

Milly nodded. 'The doctor on the bike', as he was known, was their MP and well liked all over Bermondsey. He'd helped found the Bermondsey Labour Party and was considered more saint than politician. Not only was he famous for not charging fees to poor families, but he'd also won many hard-fought battles for better health care and housing in the borough.

'And then after the lecture, well, matter of fact, I was talking to Miss Green. Milly, she's a kind woman. Why won't you let her help you?'

'No, no, no!' She let her knife and fork fall, feeling as ready for flight as a cornered, wounded animal.

'I'm a friend of Florence and I know she's not the sort of woman who would condemn,' he said, and Milly saw a flash of something in his eyes – admiration for the woman, or perhaps something more, she couldn't tell.

'She's helped me already, and I've chucked it in her face. I can't stay.'

She bent to pick up Jimmy and leave.

'All right, Milly, I'll say no more,' he said, gesturing for her to stay. 'Please, don't go, carry on with your supper.'

She sank back. She had to eat. She was sick with hunger and fatigue, and she knew she would need all her strength for the next day's work at Hay's Wharf. With a jolt, she realized she was planning for tomorrow, and a sudden wave of gratitude washed over her that she and Jimmy still had a future. Bertie filled the awkwardness with more talk about Dr Salter's lecture.

'He wants to build a solarium in Bermondsey, can you imagine?'

Milly could not, and she admitted to not knowing what a solarium was.

'It's like a sun clinic,' Bertie went on, in undisguised admiration. 'Bermondsey children needn't suffer from rickets ever again,' he said. 'They would just go to the solarium for an artificial dose of sunshine!'

She thought of the many bandy-legged toddlers in Dockhead and had to agree it would be a marvellous thing to see them straight-limbed, though she privately thought it would be far better if they could just have the chance to grow up in the country, where the real sun could do its job for free.

'I tell you what, Milly, he's someone worth voting for.'

'Well, I can't vote for no one. I'm nowhere near thirty, I've got no home of my own and I'm not married, am I?'

'Oh, of course.' She saw a faint blush rise from his neck, and regretted the devilry that had made her burst his enthusiasm. She wasn't sure if he was kicking himself for drawing attention to her homelessness or her unmarried state, or for the ultimate insult that at eighteen she looked ten years older, but he covered it well.

'Anyway, I think women should have the same rights to vote as men. But when you *can* vote, Dr Salter's your man. He's even going to make Bermondsey beautiful. Says he'll make the council plant trees in every street!'

'Oh, now that would be something to see!' Milly's eyes shone with genuine enthusiasm, and Bertie, tucking into his sausage and mash, seemed relieved to have made her smile.

When they'd both finished eating and were drinking second cups of tea, Bertie asked, 'So how did you come to lose your lodgings?'

'The landlord thought I was fair game, tried to break into my room.'

Bertie looked away, she supposed in embarrassment, and called for the bill. When he looked back at her, his expression was unreadable. He said simply, 'Do you want to stay with me tonight?'

Milly dropped the cup down on the saucer, causing the proprietor to fear for his china from the look he shot them. Was there no man she could take at face value?

'I knew it!' she said, despair swallowed up in indignation. 'You blokes are all the same. Just 'cause I was caught out,' she nodded towards Jimmy, 'don't mean I'm a whore that'll go with any old Tom, Dick or Harry, and I'll have you know, sausage and mash don't buy me!' She stood up, trying to shuffle past him out of the booth, when he infuriated her even more by shaking his head with a small chuckle.

'God in heaven, strike me dumb.'

'What does that mean?' She glared at him, still trying to push past him, out of the booth.

The smile faded and he became serious. 'You're right, you've not been given much reason to trust any feller, but the fact is I've got a spare room and you need somewhere to stay. I'm not after anything else.'

He moved aside, allowing her to leave if she wished. Weariness and some instinct made her pause. Could she trust him? His actions at the river had revealed a kind man, surely not one who would take advantage of her weakness? She nodded her head and he stood up to pay the bill, then she followed him out into the chilly summer's night.

They didn't have far to walk. Bertie lived only ten minutes away, in a small terraced house in Storks Road, one of the better streets in Bermondsey. Milly was surprised, but relieved, to find that he no longer lived over his uncle's grocery shop in Dockhead. It would be hard enough convincing her mother that going home with a man she hardly knew was a good idea, without the neighbours running to tell her first. They turned into Storks Road, on the corner of which stood the Stork Picture Palace, silent now, unlit and shuttered. His house was a little further down the street; it had a round-arched front door, and arched windows to match. As they stepped inside the dark entrance hall, Milly immediately calculated that Bertie had twice the living space of all the Bunclerks put together. He led her past the downstairs front parlour, and pointed out the back kitchen and scullery. After lighting the gas mantles on the stairs, he showed her up to one of the spare bedrooms. It was by now almost midnight and her legs could barely carry her any further. She staggered into the room. Though Bertie was thoughtfully pointing out the empty

163

wardrobe for her things, she only had eyes for the comfortable-looking double bed.

Seeing her stumble as she went to place Jimmy on the counterpane, Bertie said, 'You look done in. I'll let you get some sleep.'

She nodded, and with mumbled thanks closed the door behind him, falling back against it in relief that, soon, she could lie down. She waited till he closed the door of his own bedroom, then turned the lock firmly in her own. She trusted him, but she no longer trusted herself, her instincts having failed her so miserably before. Moving Jimmy to one side, she undressed and slipped into the deliciously clean sheets. It was a feather mattress! She let herself sink into the soft yielding pile; it was like nestling into a warm cloud. Banishing all thoughts of the future, Milly gave herself up to the balm of sleep.

She woke only once in the night, sitting bolt upright at Jimmy's cry. Eyes closed and still half asleep, she fed him, then fell again into an untroubled sleep. At five o'clock, she woke to a soft knocking on her door. She jumped up and opened it a crack, peering out at Bertie, already dressed in shirtsleeves and waistcoat.

'I've brought you some hot water,' he said, passing her a china jug and basin. 'Let me know if you need anything for the baby.' She thanked him and as he walked away, he said, without looking back, 'Bacon's on for breakfast. I leave at six.'

He didn't sound as jovial or relaxed as he had the previous night. She wondered if he might be regretting his offer of a room. After all, he was a middle-class respectable tradesman, friend of council men, friend of Florence Green. His reputation could only suffer by association with the likes of her, a factory girl with a bastard child. It wasn't something the local parish council would approve of. Still, she remembered his genuine concern last night, the way he had thought of Jimmy first, carrying him in the crook of his arm away from the river, away from the danger she had put him in. She decided that this morning he was just trying to strike the right note, neither too familiar nor too formal. The awkwardness of having her staying in his house must be as acute for him as it was for her. She would take her cue from him. She came down to the kitchen, and was touched that he'd laid her a place. He put a steaming cup of tea in front of her and a bacon sandwich. She imagined what her mother would have to say about the doorsteps he'd cut, but she wasn't complaining. She was ravenous and any attempt to be ladylike was confounded by the wedges of bread stuffed full of bacon.

'What time do you have to be at Hay's Wharf?' he asked, for she'd told him about her temporary employment.

'Eight o'clock,' she answered, with her mouth half full, 'but I'm taking Jimmy to Mum's first.'

'Do you want to walk down to Dockhead with me?'

Was he really that innocent? Didn't he realize it would be all round Arnold's Place before dinner time, that Milly Colman hadn't been back five minutes and she'd got herself a fancy man to keep her? But she had a good enough excuse.

'I can't turn up too early at Mum's. I don't want the old man knowing she's looking after my baby.' It was the truth. 'I don't know what he'd do to her, if he found out, but Jimmy needs to go somewhere while I'm working.'

Bertie stirred his tea thoughtfully. 'Doesn't the Settlement run a crèche?'

'I'll have to earn a bit before I can pay for that. But anyway, I can't go near that place with my baby – they'll put the welfare on me. And while we're at it, I know you're friends, but I'd rather you didn't talk about me to Miss Green.'

'No, I'm not going to do that.' His blue eyes clouded a little. 'I'm not the type to talk about people's business.' He stood up and started clearing the plates, but she took them from him. 'Here, let me do that.'

Milly hadn't got used to the sight of a man so at home in the kitchen, or the novelty of being served breakfast by one. As she

165

took the plates, she tried to remember if she'd ever seen the old man even make a cup of tea, let alone a bacon sandwich.

'I do feel ungrateful, Bertie. I know it wasn't Miss Green's fault the matron at Edenvale was such an old cow!' she mused as she filled the stone sink with hot water. 'And I really shouldn't have given Mr Dowell such a wallop at the station.' Bertie had followed her into the scullery, and she looked round just in time to see him raising one of those flyaway eyebrows.

'God strike me dumb, if I ever get on the wrong side of you!' he muttered as he turned to go.

Her mother answered the knock, her face grey and pinched, dark circles beneath her eyes. She crossed herself, 'Oh Jesus, Milly, I've been out of me mind with worry. Fancy running off like that. Where did you stay last night?'

Milly felt a pang of guilt. She'd barely given her mother a thought since rushing out of the house the previous night.

'At a friend's. I told you I'd find somewhere. You mustn't worry about me, Mum.'

Her mother took Jimmy and laid him in the blanket-lined drawer.

'Which friend? Not the Bunclerks, they can't swing a cat.' A look of suspicion crossed her mother's face. 'You've never been round Mrs Donovan's?'

Elsie had come in from washing in the scullery and was now making faces at Jimmy, trying to coax a smile. Amy sidled up to the drawer, and with a mischievous half-smile on her face, said, 'Old Ma Donovan wouldn't have her anyway. I heard her telling Mrs Knight she didn't want nothing to do with Pat's whore or her bastard.'

Milly plucked Amy by the back of her pinafore dress and held her up like a troublesome kitten. 'Who asked you to stick your nose in?'

But Amy was not to be intimidated. She thrust her face even closer to Milly's and shouted, 'It's true, that's what she said!'

'I don't care if it's true or not. Don't you ever talk like that in front of my Jimmy, d'you hear me?'

'Don't be stupid,' Amy said sulkily as Milly dropped her. 'He can't understand.'

'No, but one day he will, and there'll be plenty of people saying that sort of stuff, without his family joining in.'

Elsie had scarcely seemed aware of the confrontation, but now she looked up from Jimmy and said gravely, 'Of course babies can understand everything. I can remember Milly singing to me in my pram.'

Milly was taken aback that Elsie should have remembered the days when she had taught her adored little sister every nursery rhyme she knew. But of course, she reasoned, there were all sorts of family stories, repeated so often they seemed like real memories.

Amy was sniffling now and looking to her mother for support.

'Don't look at me for help. You should learn to keep your trap shut,' her mother said in exasperation. 'Just think before you open your mouth in future.'

Then with a look of pure adulation, she turned to gaze at her golden-haired grandchild. At least Jimmy had found another champion in the world, Milly thought. But still her mother pressed her.

'Well then, where *did* you stay?'

'I stayed with Bertie Hughes.'

Her mother's face took on a puzzled expression, then hardened. 'What, that toffee-nosed grocer? Well, that takes the cake.'

'He's not toffee-nosed! His uncle is, but Bertie's different.'

'Well, different or not, he's still moneyed, and you know what they'll be saying round here, don't you?'

'I do, and I couldn't give a monkey's, 'cause I'm staying at his house tonight as well.'

Before he'd left for the shop, Bertie had offered her another night's lodging. He'd made the offer so casually, as if it were the most natural thing in the world. But though it would be a lifeline for her, she knew it could send him into a social wilderness.

'Are you sure you want every vicious-tongued tart in Dockhead talking about you and your jam girl?' she'd challenged him. It was no good pretending they were on an equal footing. He'd simply shrugged and insisted he took no notice of gossip. Now, remembering his casual air, she thought him a braver man than his mildness suggested. He would have to face the women's whispering and sharp looks all day, as they came in and out of the shop.

She arranged for her mother to bring Jimmy to Hay's Wharf mid-morning so that she could feed him, and handed her the few clean nappies she had. The rest were steeping in a bucket of soda in Bertie's scullery. She could only imagine the bachelor's surprise, when he got home later that night. A bucket of dirty nappies would test his genuineness like nothing else she could imagine.

As she was about to close the front door behind her, she felt Amy tugging at her coat.

'Milly, take this.' Her sister held out a small, engraved gold cross on a fine chain. 'Mum says Jimmy's crying 'cause he needs bottles and milk. Pawn this and buy him some.'

'Amy, I can't, not your cross!'

'Please, Milly, take it . . . for Jimmy. I can't bear it when he cries.'

Her sister was offering her most prized possession, sent by Wilf from the Gold Coast for her first Communion. Overcome with gratitude, Milly took the peace offering and wrapped Amy in her arms. 'Thank you,' she whispered.

15

Safe Haven

July 1924

Milly hurried towards Hay's Wharf along Tooley Street, which was jammed with horse-drawn carts, trams and motor cars. She'd stopped off at the pawnshop and now she was late. She jogged past boys pushing handcarts and darted in and out of the traffic. London Bridge Station disgorged an endless stream of bowler-hatted clerks, funnelling them across the bridge into the City, and to avoid the crowds, Milly nipped down an alleyway leading to the wharf.

The sky was a pearl sheen, veiling the sun, and the opaque river churned like dirty milk in the wash of a steam tug, piloting a big ship to the dockside. Another vessel was already unloading, and the stamps on the sacks revealed that these were the expected cargo of haricot beans. At least Milly knew she'd have work today.

The acne-scarred office boy led her to a vast shed on the quayside, where dockers trundled trolleys, piled high with overstuffed sacks, from ship to shed. As deafening as waves crashing into a pebbled shore, sack after sack of beans were tipped into hoppers. Conveyer belts criss-crossed the vaulted space, carrying the beans past ranks of women sorters. Handing Milly a coarse, wrap-around apron, the forelady took her to the back of the shed, before explaining the simple task of sorting out the bad beans from the good. It wasn't long before Milly was up to speed with the women on either side, her fingers moving independently of her brain, picking and flicking bad beans into a basket, in a blur of motion. The women around her were already chatting to their neighbours and she allowed her thoughts to return to the night before.

Her memories of the riverbank were too searingly etched to linger over, and instead she thought about Bertie. He was a puzzle. Since coming to run his uncle's shop, he'd always been friendly towards her, but she'd taken no more notice of him than of any other shopkeeper in Dockhead. But last night his actions had seemed more than those of a concerned acquaintance. He'd acted as if he were a friend, as if he knew her. Perhaps he would have extended the same help to anyone in similar trouble, but the help had felt pointed and personal. As more and more dried beans cascaded into hoppers, then clicked and bounced along chugging belts, she remembered how she'd caught him looking at her that morning at breakfast, in his quietly amused way. Their eyes had met for just an instant, but she'd seen nothing more than the kindness of a charitable man. In any case, from the way he'd spoken about Florence, Milly had a suspicion the only torch Bertie held burned chastely, for the respectable Methodist missionary with the sad eyes and warm heart. Milly was glad of it. Florence Green deserved to find happiness again with a good man.

Milly was grateful that Jimmy hadn't cried this morning when she'd left him. Today would be their longest time apart since running away from Edenvale, and even though she trusted him with her mother she'd still felt invisible cords tugging at her all morning. At their mid-morning break, Milly found Mrs Colman waiting outside the shed with Jimmy. There were other women who'd had their babies brought to them, some by their older children, and she followed their lead in turning down a less-frequented side passage.

'Is he all right?' she asked, holding her arms out for Jimmy as he began to cry in anticipation.

'A bit grizzly. He needs to get used to me, poor little love.'

She held him to her breast, her back muscles rippling with fire and her fingers raw from the morning's work. She leaned against the clammy wall and remembered the weeks at Edenvale, which had left her fingertips petal soft. She'd been so happy when she'd lost the leather-like pads, built up over years of hop- and fruit-picking, for it meant that when she stroked Jimmy's cheek, the smoothness of her own skin matched his. But now she could feel her sore fingers burn as she rubbed a smut from his forehead. It struck her as ironic; she hadn't even wanted the tips of her fingers to scratch or harm him, yet last night she'd contemplated taking him under the water with her. She found herself shaking as she handed him to her mother.

'I've got to get back,' she said quietly and turned quickly to leave, before her mother could see how upset she was.

Returning to the shed, she resumed sorting, wishing she could flick away her own self-condemnation as easily as she did a bean. The woman next to her must have mistaken her pained expression.

'Fingers giving you gyp?' she asked. Producing a roll of plaster from her apron pocket, she carefully taped up Milly's fingertips. The plasters slowed her down, but better that than the agony of shredded fingers. She tried to lose herself in the work and when the noon hooter sounded, she flew back to Arnold's Place, drawing stares from dockers as her long, stockinged legs found their effortless loping stride. On the way, she stopped at the chemist to buy two banana-shaped bottles and a tin of milk, blessing her sister's fit of generosity. At least her mother wouldn't have to bring Jimmy out to be fed at the wharf every day.

She arrived home out of breath. 'How's he been?' she asked, taking him from her mother's arms. Jimmy's face screwed up, threatening a scream.

'Good as gold – not a murmur, not till you walked in, and now he's started!' her mother grunted.

Milly felt the accusation sting. 'It's only because he's hungry. He's happy as a sandboy usually,' she said defensively, and settled down to feed him. She indicated the bag she'd brought with her. 'There's bottles and milk in there. At least you can top him up now.'

In answer to her mother's enquiring look, Milly offered, 'Amy gave me her cross to pawn . . . she's a good kid really.'

Her mother nodded wearily and picked up the bag. 'I only wish I'd got more to give you, Mill.'

Milly shook her head. 'You're doing more than enough. But I can't stop long. I'm calling at Southwell's before I go back, to check if there's any openings.'

'Sorting beans is a horrible job,' her mother said. 'Did I ever tell you I did it meself years ago? Before I met the old man. Terrible in the winter cold! No heating in them big sheds. You won't want to be staying there long. While you're at Southwell's could you ask for our Elsie? I'm sure she thinks she can stay at school forever – she won't even talk about it.'

'She probably still thinks she can go on the stage, like Matty Gilbie!' Milly replied.

Matty Gilbie was Elsie's heroine, a Bermondsey girl who'd made a name for herself in the West End theatres.

'All right, I'll ask, but I hope I'm not around when you tell her she's got to be a jam girl instead!' Milly said, laying Jimmy down softly. Just as she did, Elsie and Amy came in for dinner. Amy skirted her shyly, noting the baby bottles on the table and sneaking a look into the drawer at Jimmy. Then, sitting at the table, she looked at Milly solemnly and said, 'I don't think he does look much like a Chinaman off the boats, after all.'

She smiled at Amy. 'No, you're right. He looks just like himself and no one else.'

There were no jobs at Southwell's for either herself or Elsie, but as she was leaving Milly bumped into Kitty Bunclerk at the factory gates. Throwing her arms round Milly, Kitty said, 'Oh, Mill, why didn't you let me know you were coming home? I could have put the feelers out for a job.'

'I didn't know myself till the last minute. I ran away!'

'No! I can't wait to hear all about it, and I want to see the baby! Can I come round after work?'

Milly shook her head. 'I'm not living in Arnold's Place.'

Kitty's eyes opened wide in astonishment as Milly explained.

'With Bertie Hughes? You're going up in the world all of a sudden! He'll have you keeping shop before you know it.' Her friend giggled, and Milly shushed her.

'He's not like that. He's just been really kind.'

She expected Kitty to scoff at her naivety, but something in her friend's face softened. 'You're right, we shouldn't tar all men with the same brush. There *are* some decent ones around,' she mused, a faraway look in her eyes.

'How's Freddie?' Milly asked and when Kitty's face reddened, Milly knew she'd guessed the source of her friend's newfound trust in men. 'Well, you've changed, Kitty Bunclerk. He's a right little villain!'

Kitty shook her head and mockingly repeated Milly's own words. 'He's not like that. He's just been really kind.'

Milly smiled as Kitty tried to convince her. 'He's helped out with stuff for the kids and all sorts . . . All right, it's mostly knocked off, but Freddie's very generous-hearted, Mill.'

The friends hugged and Milly promised to bring Jimmy to Hickman's Folly as soon as she could. 'And let me know if any of the casuals drop out!' Milly called back as they parted.

She had to trot all the way along Shad Thames in order to get back for the afternoon shift at Hay's Wharf, but she felt lighter of heart now that she'd seen her friend. It had made her feel more at home than anything else since she'd returned to Bermondsey.

Milly's working day at the sorting shed finished earlier than at the factory, so it was still afternoon when she returned home to collect Jimmy. She was only paid by the hour, and she could have wished for a few hours more work, but at least it meant there was little chance of the old man discovering the baby at Arnold's Place. As she was passing Hughes' grocery, Bertie came to the window and beckoned her in.

Rosie Rockle stood at the counter with a jug. She looked up as Milly came in.

'Hello, darlin'!' she said, surprised to see her. Milly had always been her favourite. Dropping her voice, Rosie mouthed, 'How's the little one?' as though it was indecent to refer to her bastard child in front of Hughes the grocer. Milly was aware of a stealthy sadness invading her. Poor Jimmy, innocent of everything except being born to Milly. Why should he be talked of in lowered tones?

'His name's Jimmy,' she answered boldly, 'and he's beautiful, Rosie, just beautiful. I'll have to bring him to see you and all the neighbours soon!'

In defiance, she turned brightly to Bertie. 'What did you want that can't wait till tonight?' When he blushed, she immediately regretted her selfishness. Refusing to be ashamed of Jimmy was one thing, but now she'd put Bertie in the very position she'd been so keen to save him from. He drew out a key.

'I won't be home till late and I forgot to give you this. Didn't want you hanging about on the doorstep with Jimmy.'

He slid the key across the counter, not looking at Rosie, but as she pocketed it, Milly was aware of Rosie Rockle's eyes glimmering with hungry glee. However fond Rosie was of Milly, in these long summer evenings, when neighbours lounged in their doorways or sat in the street on kitchen chairs, catching the evening breeze, it was always good to have something new to add to the day's gossip. Milly had just handed her a plum and at the same time shoved Bertie into the vipers' nest. Her brashness disappeared and she turned placatingly to Rosie Rockle.

'I'm his lodger.' She felt the heat rise from her throat to her cheeks. 'Ain't I?' Then, looking at Bertie, she was appalled to see that his face was as red as the bowl of cooked beetroots in the shop window.

Rosie looked from one to the other. 'Don't make no difference to me, love. Good luck to you, I say!' she said knowingly, and thrust the jug into Bertie's hands. 'Penn'orth o' mustard pickle, please.'

Milly escaped miserably to her mother's house. Mrs Colman immediately commented on her pale face and Milly made her tiredness the excuse. 'I'd better not hang about in case he comes home early, but I want to get some clothes first. Can I borrow the hopping box?'

'All right, but make sure I get it back. I've got me letter, I want to start filling it up soon.' If she ever had a spare shilling, which wasn't often, her mother would begin stocking the box with tinned food and staples.

'Surely the old man's not turned over a new leaf?' Milly said, shocked that there should be spare money floating around in Arnold's Place.

'With the corner up he has! No, it's that Freddie Clark. He's been getting so much stuff lately, we've been living the life of Riley on the tins of beans and soup and gawd knows what.'

It made Milly smile that her mother could be such a good Catholic and never once feel guilt at accepting stolen goods – in fact she saw them as a gift from God, and would cross herself when any came her way.

'Oh, he's muscling in on Pat's territory, is he?'

'Well, he might be, but Mrs Donovan says he's been very good to her too, drops her a quid every now an' again.' Her mother sniffed at the mention of the woman who had so slighted her grandchild, and then went on. 'Do you think you'd better talk to Pat, you know, about what he wants to do?'

'About what?'

Her mother raised her eyes. 'What do you think? Now you've kept the baby you two'll be getting married when he gets out, won't you?'

Milly folded another of her dresses and placed it in the box. For a long moment it seemed she wasn't going to answer.

'Mum, I made a mistake with Pat. I don't think I'll be marrying him. I just want it to be me and my Jimmy from now on, that's all I need.'

Her mother came and kneeled down beside her. Placing her hand over Milly's, she stopped her from packing. 'Oh, love, listen to me, you're still young and your life's not over just because you've saddled yourself with a baby. Believe me, there'll come a time when you get lonely and you'll be glad of someone.'

She answered her mother's touch with her own and looked into her face, etched with worry lines and anxious love.

'I don't think I *will* want someone. Marriage ain't the answer to all life's problems, is it?'

'No, I won't make you wrong there, but sometimes it's the difference between being on the streets or not.'

And Milly knew that by 'on the streets' her mother hadn't meant homeless, and she knew too that Ellen Colman shared every one of Rosie Rockle's suspicions about Bertie Hughes' motives. She stiffened and rose.

'I'll make sure you have the box back, once I've found some proper lodgings. I won't be at Bertie's for long.'

Her mother sniffed. 'Let's hope not, love.'

Milly quickly kissed her goodbye and hurried back to Bertie's. Clattering the hopping box along Storks Road, she was conscious that in this more respectable street, she might be considered a spectacle. The box was stuffed full of her belongings and her baby was tucked up snugly on the top. She was grateful to slip into the seclusion of Bertie's home, and though it was a stranger's house, it felt like a quiet haven. This house, though only an ordinary brick terrace, felt a world away from Arnold's Place. Milly reflected that it really took so little to make the difference between a pleasant, comfortable home and one where every domestic activity was a struggle. Although her mother made valiant efforts to keep her house clean, the grinding fight against bugs and damp in the walls had all but worn her out. In Bertie's scullery there was an ascot over the sink and a gas copper that could heat up enough water for baths and laundry. How different from the kettle after kettle that her mother had to boil on the range to fill their old tin tub. Ellen Colman had told her of the days when the whole street would share a single standpipe, and how she felt herself lucky to have a tap in the house at all. But Milly had been to Edenvale. She had seen what was possible, what others considered necessary to live a decent life, and now, even in this modest house in Bermondsey, she saw glimmerings of the better life she wanted for Jimmy.

She didn't feel shy about going into Bertie's larder and preparing tea. He'd told her this morning to help herself. But she would make sure he had a decent meal to come home to; it was the least she could do in lieu of rent. And when he came home, his face cheerful and unreproachful of her indiscreet blabbing in front of Rosie, she felt genuinely glad to see him.

For the rest of that week Milly worked at Hay's Wharf and went every morning to check for vacancies at Southwell's. On Friday, a frazzled-looking Tom Pelton met her as he was coming across the yard. Before she could even ask, he had all but pounced on her.

'Can you start Monday morning?'

''Course I can, I'm only sorting beans by the hour. Where do you want me?'

'I know you're good at picking, but I need someone I can trust in the boiling room – one of the girls had a cauldron of jam down her this morning!'

It wasn't her favourite job in the factory, but the money was better than the wharf and she couldn't afford to be choosy. Bertie had literally pulled her back from the brink, and now it felt to Milly that she must grasp her second chance, if not for her own sake, then for Jimmy's. She would willingly spend her days hauling boiling jam from copper to cart, if it meant she could pay back Bertie and carve out a life for Jimmy. The comforts of Edenvale were nothing compared to that.

At tea that evening, she was eager to tell Bertie her news.

'So I'll be able to pay you my week's rent as soon as I get my pay packet,' she said. 'And with the extra money I'll be earning, I can look for proper lodgings, then me and Jimmy'll be out of your hair.'

Bertie didn't respond immediately. He was a man who ate very slowly, unlike the old man who, ever eager to get to the pub, bolted his food, hardly tasting it even though he always made such a fuss if her mother cut corners with the meat. But Bertie often paused between mouthfuls, laying down his knife and fork, to talk about his day in the shop. She was unused to such behaviour at the table, but on the whole she liked it. She'd been so used to anticipating her father's rap on the knuckles for any tardiness that habit made her jump up to begin clearing away, before Bertie had finished his meal. He grabbed his plate, smiling.

'Strike me dumb, if you don't want to take the food out of my mouth! Sit down a minute.'

She did as she was told, waiting while he finished every last morsel.

'That was delicious, Milly, you're a good cook.'

She pulled a face of disagreement. Her cooking skills were mediocre at best, but perhaps a bachelor might be impressed with any hot meal.

'Don't do yourself down, and that sewing job you did on my frayed jacket was perfect. Milly . . .' He hesitated and fiddled with the knife and fork on his plate.

She resisted the urge to jump up and take out the dirty plate. 'What?'

'I know you'll probably want to find a place nearer your mother, but I was wondering, what do you think about staying here with me?'

She felt her heart lurch. Here it came, the proposal that her mother and Rosie Rockle assumed had already been made. The disappointment must have been clear to read in her face, for he hastily continued.

'As a lodger, I mean! But perhaps instead of paying full rent, you could housekeep for me. I don't keep up the place as well as I should . . . and as I said . . . you're a good cook,' he finished lamely.

She was stunned. She'd been dreaming of a cocoon for her and Jimmy, and on the face of it, Bertie's offer was the answer to her prayers. Yet she would certainly be adding fuel to the gossips' fire. Her own reputation was already ruined, but would it be fair to risk Bertie's?

'Well, no rush, you can think about it, eh?' he said, seeing her hesitate.

She thanked him and then began clearing away. It wasn't until much later that evening, as she sat in a chair beneath the gas lamp, sewing a frayed shirt cuff, that she made her decision. He hadn't repeated his offer, and now as he sat opposite her, tamping tobacco into his pipe, she realized he never would. He would leave it to her. Without preamble, she said, 'Thanks for the offer, Bertie. If you're really sure you can put up with the gossip, then I'd like to stay.'

During the following week, Milly began to realize that her new roles of mother, housekeeper and jam girl involved a delicate juggling act. The most difficult part was making sure she always reached Arnold's Place in time to pick up Jimmy before the old man came home. He'd been mercifully absent, and even when at home was usually in a drunken haze, so she didn't expect he'd pick up on any clues. Besides, she made sure to remove all evidence of nappies, bottles and baby clothes every evening, before she took Jimmy back to Storks Road. The biggest gamble was trusting her sisters with the secret; between Elsie's forgetfulness and Amy's mischievousness, she knew she was walking a fine line.

She was alarmed, therefore, one evening, when her shift changeover had been delayed, to find her mother's front door wide open and a man's voice coming from the kitchen. She didn't relish another battle with the old man but would give as good as she got, and she marched into the kitchen ready for a fight. The scene was not what she expected. Florence Green sat drinking tea and chatting amiably to her mother while a bespectacled man in a dark suit sat opposite, holding Jimmy in his arms. The memory of Elsie with her leg in the bloodied snare flashed before her, and now she felt equally trapped.

'What's he doing with my baby and who told you I was back?' she asked Miss Green frostily.

The woman raised her soft hazel eyes and Milly thought she'd identified the culprit. 'Was it Bertie?'

'Bertie?' Miss Green looked puzzled. 'Bertie Hughes? No, why on earth would he know? I heard it at the girls' club, from Amy.'

'Oh, I see,' Milly said, feeling foolish.

The man stood up and handed Jimmy to her. 'He's a lovely little chap,' he said, 'and seems to be in perfect health too.' Milly took Jimmy gratefully, noticing a look pass between the man and Miss Green. Was he from the welfare?

'Oh, Milly, I wish you'd contacted me,' Miss Green continued. 'I had no idea you were unhappy at Edenvale. Will you let me help you?'

Milly looked nervously towards the bespectacled man as Miss Green guessed her thoughts.

'Milly, your mother's told me there was some talk at the home of you being declared unfit. Of course that's nonsense! But once such a charge is made, there have to be investigations . . .'

Milly felt her chest tighten as she clenched her fists, digging her nails into the palms of her hands. 'You haven't come to take him away, have you?' she challenged the man. He was large, with broad features and a wide mouth. His expression, though serious, wasn't hard. He didn't look like the villain of her nightmares, the one who would seize her child and leave her bereft. Now he held up his hands, palms outward. They looked like practical hands, but they were soft, milk-white.

'No, no, please don't be alarmed. I'm just here at my friend Miss Green's invitation, to give my professional advice as a doctor, and I'm quite happy with what I've seen. Your child is healthy, well cared for and . . . obviously very much loved . . .'

'Yes, and now, Milly, we can make a favourable report back to the authorities,' Miss Green went on eagerly. 'Once they've been assured that all is well with this little man, I'm sure there'll be no more said about unfitness.' She smiled.

'After all, what better stamp of authority could you have than Dr Salter's?'

Now Milly knew why the man had looked familiar, and suddenly weak with relief, she sank down into a chair, grateful that their sainted doctor MP had indeed lived up to his reputation. Wait till she told Bertie!

16

'Then Like My Dreams'

September 1924

From somewhere came the smell of woodsmoke. Milly inhaled its bitter sweetness and looked up at the charcoal plume, smudging a dove-grey sky. Smoke snaked across the metallic halo of late summer sun, struggling to pierce the clouds. Someone was probably burning rubbish in a yard further down Storks Road, but the smell spirited Milly away to the hop fields and the early morning faggot fires, whose sweet signals would warn those still lying in bed that it was time for that first cup of tea, brewed and drunk steaming hot, outside in the damp, misty field. Her mind flew back to the previous September and she realized with sharp regret that she hadn't even thought of going hopping this year. She simply couldn't afford to give up her Southwell's job and risk it not being there when she returned.

Times were changing, just as her father had predicted last year, and maintaining her precarious existence as the sole provider for her child was paramount now. The hopping box, which had served as temporary suitcase and pram for Jimmy, had been returned long ago, and her mother had just about filled it to the brim, ready for her yearly departure to the hop farm at Horsmonden. Over the past few weeks, Milly had allowed herself the vicarious pleasure of examining the contents of the box, and every so often she was able to donate a jar of jam or bottle of sauce, smuggled out from Southwell's. Bertie, whose only experience of hopping had been taking his uncle's stall down last year, had entered into the spirit of things and given a gift of a new paraffin lamp and oil. Her mother had at first baulked at taking his 'charity', but it hadn't taken Milly long to convince her it would be good for his proddywack soul to build up a few stars in the heavenly record book.

Apart from evoking a sense of loss, the coming of the hopping season this year presented Milly with another problem. Who would look after Jimmy? It was a conundrum that the woodsmoke had brought to the forefront of her mind, and she was pondering it as she walked back from early morning Mass. She was pushing the pram, a second-hand offering from the Guardians of the Poor, which was serviceable but very squeaky, when, above the creaking of the springs, she became aware of footsteps behind her – light, clipped, rhythmic. Darting a look over her shoulder, she was surprised to see Elsie, skipping along behind her, seemingly attempting an eccentric tap dance.

'Don't skip!' Milly's response was involuntary.

Don't skip, don't dream, don't make yourself such an open target for the world. She wished, in that moment, that her reaction to Elsie wasn't habitually one of irritation. But always, the sight of her sister's carefree, childish delight made Milly want to shake her. She told herself she just wanted Elsie to wake up to the ways of the world and her own coming responsibilities. But she knew herself well enough to recognize an unattractive streak of jealousy at the heart of her feelings. Surely she was not so mean-spirited that she wished some of her own burdens on to her sister's shoulders? She blew out a sigh. It was complicated with Elsie, and with Amy too, for that matter. It had always been so complicated. In spite of everything, she was certain, if they were really in trouble she would do anything for them, yet some equally opposite certainty told her that so far in their lives, she had failed them.

'For gawd's sake, Elsie, you're fourteen! If you dance along the pavement like that when you start work, they'll rib you rotten.'

The young girl looked up at her, surprised, as though she'd hardly been aware that Milly was in front of her. But the sudden spark of anger that Milly was expecting never came.

'Anyway,' she went on, turning the pram to face her sister, 'what are you doing here? Have you followed me from church?'

Elsie didn't answer. Instead she leaned over the pram adoringly. Milly had been surprised at how easily both her sisters had fallen in love with Jimmy.

'I bet you'll never tell him not to skip,' Elsie said, tickling him to elicit the throaty little gurgle, which at three months was barely a laugh but never failed to delight her. 'I bet you'll let him skip till he's an old man.' And Elsie giggled, pleased with the image she'd conjured.

Milly knew what she meant. Wouldn't she want Jimmy to be happy enough to skip along the street, without a care in the world? Would she want to squash his dreams as she did Elsie's?

'I wanted to ask a favour,' Elsie said.

They had reached Bertie's house and Milly was conscious that she had a morning's work ahead of her, for usually it was on a Sunday that she caught up on her housekeeping duties and made sure there was a good Sunday dinner ready for Bertie when he came back from the Wesleyan chapel.

Milly led Elsie into the house, leaving Jimmy outside the front door in his pram to benefit from the late summer sun. She set about preparing vegetables in the scullery while Elsie leaned against the draining board.

'Here, make yourself useful.' Milly gave her a bowl full of peas to shell. 'What's the favour anyway?'

'I need a new dress.' Elsie hesitated. 'But Mum says there's no money. Can you lend me some?'

Milly laughed. 'Elsie! What makes you think I've got any money to spare?'

'Well, you live with Hughes, and grocers have always got money, haven't they?'

Milly sighed. 'I swear you're as silly as a sackload o' monkeys sometimes. Just because Bertie's got money doesn't mean he gives any to me!'

'But Barrel says he *does* give you money, he says you're kept.'

'Barrel should keep his big nose out of other people's business, and you shouldn't listen to him.' She felt herself flushing, then returned to the subject of the dress.

'Why do you need a new dress all of a sudden?'

Elsie looked crestfallen. She really had believed that Milly could come up with money out of some imaginary pot of gold. Her sister's earlier light-heartedness faded and she said dully, 'I'm going in for a singing competition at the Star and I've got nothing decent to wear.'

'Oh, you're not still hankering after the stage? Elsie, love, you're starting at Southwell's and that's that. The old man won't have it any other way, so just get used to it, for God's sake.'

This was the spark that ignited Elsie's precarious fuse. 'That old bastard can't boss me about no more. I sleep with the kitchen knife under me pillow like you used to, and I'll get out, just like you did.'

Milly hoped her sister wasn't contemplating the same escape route as her own. Even a shot at the stage, however fanciful, would be better than that.

'Well, if you really want to try again, then I tell you what, I'll get you a cheap dress from the Old Clo', and I'll alter it. I can put fringing on and tart it up – it'll be just like new!'

But Elsie flung down the bowl of peas, green beads cascading on to the wooden draining board.

'There's no time for that. The competition's Saturday! Anyway, I'm fed up of always having your cast-offs. I want something new! Just for me!' She was shouting so loudly, they didn't hear Bertie come in. He stood in the scullery doorway, looking from sister to sister, then ducked his head. 'Got some business to do . . . I'll leave you to it.' He turned on his heel, seemingly eager to be out of the line of fire.

'Don't bother, I'm going.' Elsie pushed passed him and from the front door flung back. 'Comes to something when you'll do more for a stranger than your own family!'

Bertie looked at Milly, eyebrow raised.

'She'll get over it.' She turned to retrieve the peas. 'You got in the firing line, that's all. She just needs to grow up and realize life doesn't deliver your dreams on a plate!' She was angry now, flinging shelled peas back into the enamel bowl, so that they rang like the death knell of all her own girlish fantasies. Bertie came over to help.

'Steady on, Milly, you're losing more than you're putting back in. And anyway, I think you're wrong. Life gives you exactly what you expect of it, so why not expect the best?'

Now she felt as irritated with his determined optimism as she had with Elsie's fantasies. 'Will you get out of me way!'

As he retreated down the passage, she heard him say softly to himself, 'Strike me dumb for opening my mouth!'

The following Saturday afternoon Milly, her mother and Amy sat in the darkness of the auditorium in the Star Cinema in Abbey Street. Elsie walked on to the stage for her last attempt at singing stardom, before the jam factory claimed her and she entered a life to which she was totally unsuited. They had already seen a dozen hopeful acts, but now they summoned all their enthusiasm to cheer on the nervous, gawky figure, clutching her sheet music. Milly noticed immediately that Elsie was wearing a new dress – a green velvet shift, with thin straps, that showed off her skinny arms and boyish figure. Three deep rows of green fringing swished as she walked across the stage to the pianist and handed him the sheet music.

Milly leaned over and whispered in her mother's ear. 'A new dress *and* sheet music? Where d'you get that sort of money?' Her mother shot her a puzzled look, then shushed her. Elsie was about to start. She gave a nod to the pianist, who launched into 'I'm Forever Blowing Bubbles'. It was a favourite of Elsie's and she looked confident, her dreamy eyes gazing into the far distance as she began the yearning verse:

'I'm dreaming dreams, I'm scheming schemes,
I'm building castles high. They're born anew,

Their days are few, just like a sweet butterfly.
And as the daylight is dawning,
They come again in the morning.'

But as she came to the end of the verse, Milly saw Elsie glance nervously at the pianist. She almost missed the cue for the chorus and while Milly was aware that her own palms had begun to sweat, a sheen was now clearly visible on Elsie's brow as she swallowed hard and began the chorus.

'I'm forever blowing bubbles, Pretty bubbles in the air,
They fly so high, nearly reach the sky,
Then like my dreams, they fade and die.'

Now Milly could feel her mother shifting in her seat. 'Gawd, *Jesus*, Mary and Joseph, he's playing it too high!' Mrs Colman hissed.

Now Milly understood what was wrong. Elsie had never sung with sheet music – she'd always pitched the song lower to suit her own contralto voice, invariably reaching the top note effortlessly. But now as it approached, in this unknown register, it was a much more daunting prospect. *'Fortune's always hiding,'* she ploughed gamely on, *'I've looked everywhere, I'm forever blowing bubbles . . .'* As the high note was upon her, poor Elsie looked despairingly at her mother's reassuring face. From the front row where they sat, Mrs Colman was mouthing 'You can do it!' But it was obvious to Milly that her sister certainly could *not* do it. *'Pretty bubbles . . .'* Milly could see disaster fast approaching and knew of only one way to avert it. She jumped to her feet and in the strong soprano that she'd inherited from their mother, she belted out the high note without fault, lingering over the last phrase ' . . . *in the air!'* Holding it for the longest time, she covered her sister's faltering, cracked voice with her own. It brought the house down. The applause was tumultuous and the crowd stamped their feet and bellowed for more as Mrs Colman, wrapped in her old brown woollen coat and squashed black hat, stood up to join her two daughters. The threesome sang together, all the way to the end, when Milly and her mother sat down, letting Elsie take the bows.

Elsie's idol, the locally beloved music hall performer, Matty Gilbie, was the judge of the competition, which explained to Milly why Elsie had so wanted to be wearing a new dress. The elegant young singer, after handing out the first three prizes, announced a special award for the artist with the best supporting act. And although Elsie hadn't won the competition, she certainly looked happy enough as Matty Gilbie called her up on to the stage to receive her consolation prize. While her sister stood there curtseying, Milly had to admit that perhaps Elsie had proved Bertie right. If life gives you what you expect, then why not expect the best?

Milly waited for her outside the Star with her mother and Amy, but when Elsie emerged from the stage door, all her smiles for Matty Gilbie had faded and she met Milly with a scowl.

'Trust you to steal me bloody thunder!' She grabbed Amy by the arm and swept past Milly, with her chin tilted defiantly.

'And there I was thinking I'd done her a favour!' Milly said to her mother.

'Well, shit's yer thanks, love.' Mrs Colman summed up her feelings exactly.

She linked arms with her mother as they made their way through the happy Saturday afternoon crowd and turned the corner of Abbey Street, back into Arnold's Place.

'What did you have to pawn to get her that dress and the sheet music?' Milly asked.

'Pawn? Nothing. I thought you'd given her the money?' said Mrs Colman, giving her a puzzled look. Milly shook her head. 'She asked me for it, Mum, but where would I get money for a dress like that?'

'Well, if she never got it from you, then where the bloody hell *did* she get it?'

*

On the following Monday, Milly dropped off Jimmy at Arnold's Place before work, as usual. She left him outside, tucked up asleep in his pram, and went into a house that looked as if a steam train had ploughed through it. She stood at the door, immobile, unable to take in the devastation. She forced her feet to move, picking her way over kitchen chairs, reduced to kindling. Her skirt caught against the upended kitchen table and her feet crunched on the shattered remains of a glass gas lampshade as she walked to the sideboard. Both sideboard doors had been ripped off, and all her mother's ill-assorted china plates and cups had been pulled out and smashed into pieces around it.

Finally, she found her voice. 'Mum!' she called tentatively, then with fear grabbing her throat, she shouted, 'Mum, where are you?'

From behind the upended table came a whimper. Milly looked over it, to discover her mother cowering there, with hair dishevelled and wearing a torn, dirty pinafore. In her lap she cradled protectively her set of willow-pattern china jugs, which she had somehow managed to save from the surrounding destruction. She looked as though she hadn't been to bed or changed since Milly had last seen her.

'What's happened?' Milly asked, dry-mouthed, kicking away broken plates to kneel beside her mother.

'Oh, we've had murders, I don't know how he hasn't killed her,' her mother said hoarsely. She handed each of the jugs to Milly, with trembling hands. 'Here, put 'em safe.' And Milly did as she was told, finding an unbroken shelf on the sideboard.

'Killed who, Mum?' She guessed this was the old man's handiwork, but who had been the target?

'Don't you go and do anything like last time! You've got a baby to think about now.'

As if in answer to Milly's question, Amy crept in from the scullery, dressed, after a fashion, for school, with a pale unwashed face, a bruise ripening on her cheek and hair sticking out at all angles.

'What did you do to upset him?' Milly asked her sister. But Ellen Colman shook her head. 'It's not her.' Her mother's

189

shoulders began to shake and, swallowing her sobs, her garbled words began to tumble out all at once.

'He's dragged Elsie down Tower Bridge nick, this morning. Oh, Milly, I can't let them put her away, you know what she's like. They'll make mincemeat of her in one of them places.'

'What place? Mum, slow down and tell me what's happened.' She took hold of her mother's hands, trying to focus her own mind as much as her mother's.

But Mrs Colman buried her head in her hands and began rocking back and forth. 'Oh, me poor baby, Mill, she's never been fitted for this world, has she? With her silly games and her grottos, don't seem fair she was born in a place like this.'

And her mother, so rarely angry, so perpetually stoical, picked up one of her broken china plates and smashed it into a hundred more pieces on the cold hearth. Milly put her arms round Mrs Colman's heaving shoulders and held her while she cried, as if Milly were the mother and she the child.

Eventually Milly coaxed the story from her. On Sunday evening when the old man rolled in from the pub, he'd attempted in vain to light the gas lamp. When he'd gone to investigate why the gas had run out, he'd found the meter empty and the lock broken. Dragging the family one by one from their beds to find the culprit, he'd proceeded to bounce each of them round the kitchen until eventually Elsie broke down and admitted her crime.

'He kept us up all night, Mill, making us watch him smash the place up. Then this morning, he's done no more than marched her out the house and up the station. Oh, me poor Elsie, what am I going to do?'

Milly couldn't believe that Elsie had the necessary criminal mind even to contemplate such a thing as robbing the gas meter. She *could* credit that she'd have no thought for the consequences, however.

'Mum, are you *sure* it was Elsie did it?' She took her mother by the shoulders and looked meaningfully in Amy's direction.

190

'She's admitted it. Blamed you, in fact! Said when you wouldn't give her the money, she decided to nick it.'

Milly felt a surge of anger at Elsie, but she still couldn't see her having the cunning to carry out the crime.

'Did you tell her to do it?' She shot an accusing look at Amy, whose face crumpled.

'Why are you always trying to blame me? All I did was tell her Barrel showed me how to get money out of the meter.'

'And you told her how to do it?'

Amy nodded, shamefaced. 'I didn't think she'd be stupid enough to do it, though!'

It all made more sense, now that Amy's anarchic mind was in the mix, but of course, with her usual quicksilver survival instinct, she'd escaped the punishment, or at least most of it, the bruise on her face a testament to her loss of immunity at the hands of the old man.

'Oh, Elsie, Elsie . . .' Milly addressed her absent sister. 'Mum, if I'd had the money, I would've given it to her!' she said, feeling guilt's stealthy hand grip her heart.

And her mother said, 'Of course you would have.'

By this time Amy was crying as much as her mother, then Jimmy, perhaps sensing the distress coming from inside the house, joined his wailing to theirs.

'All right, the pair of you, turn off the water taps!' Milly ordered, realizing that she would have to start thinking clearly. 'It'll be all right. We'll just have to make sure the police know it was a mistake. Amy, go and fetch Jimmy for me and, Mum, you'd better sweep up all this broken china.'

Her mother heaved herself up from the floor and shook her insubstantial frame, glad to be upbraided. 'You're right, love. No good crying over spilt milk, is it. You get yourself off, or you'll be late for work.'

'It's all right, I've got five minutes,' Milly said more gently.

After settling Jimmy and brushing Amy's hair, she promised her mother she'd be back at dinner time to sort everything out.

But, as she raced to clock in on time at Southwell's, she realized she hadn't a clue how she would manage to save Elsie from the jaws of this particular trap.

All morning she was distracted, several times splashing herself with boiling jam and once nearly tipping a whole cauldron full over the feet of the forelady, who sent Milly to do jar washing as punishment. When the dinner-time hooter sounded, she bolted like a horse from the stall and almost ran past her mother, waiting outside the gates with Jimmy.

'She's not come home and neither has he.' Anxiety scoured Ellen Colman's face, and she licked cracked, dry lips. She had obviously been chafing all morning, and Milly wished now she'd simply abandoned work and gone to the police station first thing. She stroked her mother's hand as it gripped the pram handle.

'You'll make yourself ill worrying. Come on, I'll take the afternoon off, just let me go and tell Tom Pelton, then we'll get her home, all right?'

'Thanks, love, I don't think I could stand to wait another hour.'

But in fact they had to wait much longer than an hour. The reception desk at Tower Bridge police station was busy, and there was a long queue to see the desk sergeant who, when they arrived, was interviewing a broken-toothed, bald-headed man, loudly declaring his innocence. They joined the back of the queue, but Jimmy was restive, struggling in her arms, catching her anxiety. The sergeant, noticing Milly trying to pacify her hungry, crying baby, interrupted the bald man.

'Young lady, why don't you take the baby into that empty interview room?' He indicated a door to the right of the desk. 'It'll be a while before I can get to you.'

So while Mrs Colman kept their place, Milly fed Jimmy in the clinical, airless interview room. It contained nothing more than a table and two chairs. Only a meagre light filtered in through the high barred window. As Jimmy nestled against her breast, Milly looked around, wondering if Elsie had been interviewed here. How frightened she must have been. Even at fourteen, she was still such a child. Milly tried not to think about the old man. What he'd done to Elsie had rekindled that old, slow burning hatred and if she allowed it to take over, she might very well end up in a cell beside her sister, on a far worse charge. As Jimmy suckled steadily, his dark almond-shaped eyes were like twin anchors, preventing her from whirling off in a torrent of anger which, deadly as a Thames current, threatened to suck her under.

'That's right, me little darlin',' she addressed him softly, 'you'll keep me out of trouble, won't you?'

She rejoined her mother and eventually they reached the front of the queue, where Milly explained, as calmly as she could, that they had come to take home her sister Elsie.

'There's been a mistake, and me dad's jumped the gun. She didn't rob the gas meter, did she, Mum?'

Her mother stepped hastily forward and in the voice she reserved for priests and policemen, backed Milly up. 'I should like to say, my daughter is innocent as the day is long, Sergeant, as her father well knows!' But, as she warmed to her subject, her mother's true voice betrayed her. 'Honestly, she ain't got a bad bone in 'er body, 'as she, Mill?'

And Milly nodded vigorously.

The sergeant looked at Milly, not unkindly; she *was* holding Jimmy after all. But his look was too tinged with pity for her liking, and Milly grew uneasy as he avoided her mother's gaze, and addressed her instead.

'Yes, madam, I know the girl in question.' He looked down at his pad and coughed. ''Fact I was at the desk when she was brought in by her father. But I'll have to ask one of the detectives to speak to you about it, miss. I can't just let her go.' Dropping his voice, he added, 'Though having seen her father . . . if it were up to me . . . well, I'll see what I can do.'

He got up and disappeared down the corridor. Mrs Colman was fidgeting at Milly's side. 'What's he mean, he can't let her go? You said if we explained we could get her out?'

'We *will* get her out!' But Milly had never been good at hiding things from her mother and her own anxious face was the mirror of Mrs Colman's.

Just then, the sergeant returned. He beckoned them to follow and Milly found herself in the same interview room where she'd fed Jimmy. After a few minutes, they were joined by the detective in charge. Milly jumped up, but he motioned her to sit down and perched himself on the edge of the desk. He addressed her mother.

'I understand from my sergeant that you've asked to take your daughter home and you say she's innocent of the theft her father accused her of?'

'Yes! And what's more, he's the one should be locked up, for assault!' Milly blurted out before her mother could answer.

The detective gave her the vexed look of a busy man, unwilling to invite complications. Ignoring her, he continued to speak to her mother.

'I'm afraid the charge is a little more serious than robbing the gas meter, Mrs Colman.' He leaned forward, spelling out the words as though her mother were an imbecile.

'Your daughter turned very violent. She attacked her father with a knife she had concealed upon her person and then she turned it on a policeman. We've had no choice but to detain her. There's no possibility of you taking her home today.'

'Mary, mother o' God, no!' Her mother's hand flew to her mouth.

Milly tried to explain. 'But you don't understand. He's a vicious man; she was just frightened. I'm sure if we could speak to someone in charge, we can explain. My sister doesn't belong here . . .'

His guilty expression told her she had no need to explain, and that even if she did, there was nothing she could say to get Elsie out of this fix.

'Well, can we at least see her, please?' she asked meekly, wanting no hint of her usual belligerence to turn the detective's sympathies against her. Jimmy chose just then to smile at him, and the detective hesitated. 'Very well, I'll have to check what state she's in,' he said.

As Milly heard his footsteps disappearing down the corridor leading to the cells, she whispered in Jimmy's ear, 'You're my secret weapon,' and was rewarded with a gurgling chuckle.

The detective was soon back. 'Well, she's calmed down a lot, could almost be a different child,' he said, puzzlement softening his previous severity.

So, thought Milly, you've met the two sides of Elsie Colman, part fairy, part demon, no wonder you're confused.

The detective led them along the brown walled corridor to the back of the building, and down a flight of stairs to the cells.

Elsie sat on the edge of an iron-framed bed that appeared to be attached to the cell wall. Her skinny legs were not quite long enough to reach the floor. She'd come out without socks or stockings and the jagged hopping scar branded her shin, reminding Milly of that other trap Elsie'd found herself in only last year. Her pointed toes rested like a ballerina's on the stone flags. Her eyes, which had been lowered to her lap, darted an eager look at them. She had obviously been warned by the detective, for Milly could see her check the impulse to run to her mother. Mrs Colman had no such compunction and immediately rushed to gather Elsie in her arms.

'Oh, me poor baby, have they hurt you?'

The constable's audible snigger was squashed by a look from the detective.

'I can assure you, Mrs Colman,' he said, without a trace of humour, 'the constable here came off worse in the exchange.'

And it was only then Milly noticed parallel scratch marks running down the constable's cheek. Though her sister couldn't land a punch, she made the best of her nails in a fight.

'Can I count on you to stay calm and quiet, Elsie?' he asked and she nodded, dumbly, the fire seemingly all gone out of her.

'The constable will be just outside.'

They left them together and only then did Elsie's strained, white face crease into sobs.

195

'Oh, Mum, take me home with you, I don't want to stay here!' Her long-fingered hands were plucking at her mother's old coat, but Mrs Colman was incoherent with her own grief. Milly, though she wanted nothing more than to sweep her sister out of this hole, had to keep her wits about her.

'Elsie, you've got to keep calm and tell 'em what happened. They said you brought in a knife.'

The young girl's face hardened as she turned to Milly. 'If you'd just give me the dress money when I asked, I wouldn't be in here. I'll never forgive you!'

Her voice was rising and Milly feared if she got any louder they'd certainly be turned out of the cell. Arguing with Elsie about blame would have to wait. She decided to hold her tongue and use her secret weapon. She thrust Jimmy into her sister's arms and waited for him to work his magic. He put up a translucent-nailed finger to prod Elsie's cheek and immediately she turned her lips to kiss its pink tip.

'I knew you'd come for me, though,' she said more calmly. 'I could hear him crying for his dinner all the way down here.' She looked at Jimmy, while addressing Milly.

'Oh, Elsie, of course we've come for you, but you're in bad trouble.' Milly spoke as gently as she could. 'The gas meter was bad enough, but attacking a policeman with a knife? What on earth possessed you?'

The girl shrugged. 'I only had the knife 'cause when he dragged me out of bed I thought he was going to kill me. I hid it up me sleeve. When they tried to lock me up, I got so scared, I panicked! I didn't cut anyone with it, well, only the old man, he got one right across his neck. But I mostly just waved it about!' she said, blowing the little boy's hair as though it were thistledown.

Milly groaned and at that moment the detective came back in. He held some papers in his hand.

'Now, Elsie, I'm going to speak to your mother. Has she explained that you're staying here tonight?'

196

'No! Mum, don't leave me here,' Elsie whimpered, and her unwashed face was soon tear-painted. It broke Milly's heart to see her cling to Jimmy as though he could save her. Milly lifted him gently out of her arms.

'Be a brave girl, Elsie. I know you can, for Mum's sake. We'll come and see you tomorrow. I'll get you out, I promise!'

As they were hustled out of the room by the constable, Milly looked over her shoulder at the forlorn figure, seated in the same position as when they'd entered, toes barely reaching the floor, eyes lowered, fat teardrops rolling down each cheek. Milly fished into her pocket for a handkerchief she'd made out of an old sheet; it was embroidered with her name.

'Give her this for me, will you?' she asked the constable, who took it between finger and thumb and tossed it into the cell behind him.

Mrs Colman stumbled up from the cells, with the detective and constable supporting her on either side.

They were left at the desk, where the kindly sergeant explained, 'Your daughter's up before the magistrate tomorrow. I'll just need you to sign some papers for me, Mrs Colman.'

Her mother signed them like an automaton. 'Get me home, Mill, get me home before I fall down.'

17

Withered and Flown

September 1924

Milly sat on an old kitchen chair in the back garden at Storks Road, a long narrow strip of ground, fenced on either side with a brick wall at the end. It was the sort of space her mother would have loved to grow a few flowers in, but the Arnold's Place yards could only accommodate a brick lavatory and a wall to hang the tin bath on. Bertie had made his garden into a little haven of tranquillity. He'd planted lavender and climbing roses, past their best now, but still bravely blooming as the last of summer faded into autumn. Milly breathed in the evening scent of the thornless pink rose, growing nearest the back door. Bertie's dinner was already prepared, cold meat from yesterday with bubble and squeak, and while waiting for him to come home from the shop, she'd been wandering around the garden, deadheading roses as Bertie had taught her to. Now she sat with a lapful of the faded blooms, absently picking off the bruised-looking petals. She was thinking of Elsie, the thorn in her side, whom she would gladly give a thousand thornless roses to have home once again, tormenting her. Since she'd left her mother, defeated and hopeless, that afternoon, she'd thought of nothing else but how she could free her sister. She was singing absently to herself 'The Last Rose of Summer', one of her mother's favourite old songs, when she heard a noise behind her.

'That's a sad old tune!' Bertie stood, with his quirky smile, observing her. For some reason she found all the emotion of the

198

day overflowing, and tears spattered the roses in her lap. Bertie was at her side immediately.

'Milly, what's the matter, is it the boy?'

She shook her head and let the day's events pour out, then immediately regretted it. The man had been kindness itself since the day he'd found her on Fountain Stairs and brought her home. She'd vowed to pay him back with her usefulness, and she was reluctant to involve him in any more of her troubles.

'But it's nothing I should be worrying you with, Bertie. My family's troubles could keep you occupied two lifetimes. I'll sort something out. Now let me get your tea, you must be starving.' She wiped her tears on her pinafore, and as she stood up the petals of the thornless rose scattered at her feet.

He bent to scoop them up and, as he stood up, she was surprised by the hurt expression on his face.

'I hoped you'd come to think of me as a friend, Milly. It's not a trouble to a friend, to help in time of need.'

It was a shock to see his usually amused features suddenly so serious. Evening sun honeyed the back wall of the house, and reflected in his eyes. For the first time she experienced a warmth of feeling towards him, slow as the sleepy bees bumbling among the lavender. She smiled, not wanting now to deflect him with a joke or a brisk comment.

'It's just I'm so grateful . . . for what you've done already. I didn't mean to . . .' She wasn't often speechless and noticing her discomfort, he was quick to save her.

'Habits of a lifetime, eh? You always were the independent one.' And then she realized that Bertie Hughes had probably been aware of her for a very long time, certainly much longer than she'd been aware of him.

He allowed her to busy herself, setting his tea things before him, but all the while asking questions about Elsie's crime and what the police had said. In the end he suggested she go to Florence Green for help. Immediately her guard was up. Did he merely see her as a worthy charity case for his lady friend at the

Settlement? But she dismissed the thought with a blush, wishing she'd been made of less prickly stuff.

'You should go now,' he said, unaware of the effect of Miss Green's name on her. 'You'll catch her before the clubs start, and if Elsie's up before the beak tomorrow, there's no time to lose.' He saw her hesitate and put down his fork. 'I'll watch the boy for you. Or do you want me to go and talk to Miss Green?' He'd already half risen.

'No! No . . . I'll go. If you think it'll do some good, it's worth a try.' And before she lost her courage, she'd flung on her coat and hurried from the house.

Milly hadn't set foot in the Settlement for almost a year, but now as she stood in its wood-panelled calm, smelling the familiar mix of chalk dust, wood polish and dinner coming from the dining hall, she realized she'd missed it. It had always been such a strange oasis in her world of poverty, an alien settlement from a foreign world, where the promise of beautiful ordered lives hung about the galleries and music-filled classrooms, where in a world surrounded by malnourishment and rickety children, the prospect of health and physical prowess permeated gyms and exercise yards. She'd forgotten that such promise existed. Now, standing outside the dining room, waiting for Miss Green to finish her supper, she found herself clasping and unclasping her hands. She felt as though she'd treated Florence Green shabbily, and now here she was, asking another favour of the woman. But this favour wasn't for herself. It was for Elsie, and for her mother. She knew that Miss Green had a soft spot for Elsie, the fey child who had taken to the folk songs and dances she taught, and had embraced the precepts of the Guild of Play with such gusto. Fragile Elsie, who would spend all day making fairy grottos, beautifying the pavements, only to have them scuffed away by so many hobnailed boots and careless feet by evening time.

'Ah, Milly.' Miss Green came out of the dining hall, her gentle smile already dispelling Milly's doubts and fears. She took both

Milly's hands in hers. 'I was visiting Arnold's Place and heard of your family's trouble. Our poor Elsie, she must be got out at all costs!'

Milly was thankful for once to the gossipy neighbours. At least she was spared the long, embarrassing explanations of her family's collapse.

'I'm sorry I'm asking another favour of you . . . and I threw the last one back in your face,' Milly said.

'Milly, you did nothing wrong in wanting to keep your child.' She held Milly's gaze for a long moment, as if despairing that she would be believed. 'In any event,' she went on, 'this is why we're here. You mustn't feel awkward about asking for help. Come upstairs.'

Milly found herself once more in the poignant little room and remembered with shame her judgement on the single Miss Green. For all she knew, she and Bertie had already been deep into a romance all those months ago. Milly realized she'd been very short-sighted and resolved to judge less and observe more in future.

'Now, Bertie was right to send you to me. He may have told you that we have a lawyer on our team of volunteers and I will consult him first thing tomorrow morning. With your mother's permission, I'll ask him to appear for Elsie at the magistrate's court.'

'That's very kind, Miss Green. I can't see Mum objecting, but the old man . . . well, you know it was him that took her to the police?'

The woman nodded, distaste clouding her features. She gave a little shake of her head and went on to explain the court procedure. If the lawyer was successful, they could have Elsie home by teatime.

Milly made a few hasty arrangements with Miss Green for the following day and then, impatient to be off, so she could tell her mother the good news, she launched herself down the wooden staircase and out into the street. She sped along Bermondsey

Wall, taking the shortest route back to Dockhead, intent on getting home as fast as she could. Careering round the corner of Hickman's Folly, buried in thought, she suddenly found herself colliding with a heavy-set figure. Rebounding with an audible smack, she was about to apologize when she realized she had just bounced off the solid bulk of her father, making his way to the Swan for his nightly drink. She was aware of an almost animal growl coming from deep in her throat.

'You bastard! How could you do that to your own daughter?' She fixed her eyes on him, almost willing him to come against her.

But instead, he rocked back on his heels, giving her a smug grin of satisfaction. 'She's where she belongs. I'm not having another nutter of a daughter trying to kill me, like you did. It's what I should'a done with you, and I will do, if you give me any more trouble! Then see what happens to your bastard, when you're locked up!'

She checked herself. Jimmy. She'd called him her secret weapon, but, with a stab of fear, she realized he was also her greatest weakness. The old man could hurt her through Jimmy, any time he wanted.

He nodded knowingly. 'Ahhh, not so quick with your fists now, are you?'

She had a vivid recollection of the first time she'd ever seen electric light, the wonder of the invisible current that flowed and resulted in such instant incandescence. Now she seemed the conduit for two opposing currents: shooting through her veins like lightning was the impulse to fight him, the red-hot desire to feel again the triumph of that day she'd called him out of the Swan, but there was also a slower, contradictory current, originating in her heart, pulsing only a warning about her child. She turned her back on the old man, and walked away.

Early next morning, when Milly and her mother arrived for Elsie's arraignment, Florence Green was waiting with the young solicitor outside Tower Bridge magistrate's court. The lawyer introduced himself as Francis Beaumont, a lanky young man who, with his round face and smooth complexion, seemed far too young to be a qualified lawyer. But who was she to look a gift horse in the mouth? Even if he was inexperienced, he knew more about the law than she ever would. He led them up the white stone steps of the court building into the wood-panelled interior. The waiting area was dimly lit and lined with doors leading to the courtrooms. Beside each courtroom door was a wooden bench and the young lawyer indicated they should sit at one.

'Elsie's due to appear in court number three,' he nodded towards the door nearest them, 'at ten thirty.' He gave Mrs Colman a reassuring look. 'Not long now.'

Milly squeezed her mother's bony hand, the paper-thin skin contoured with protruding veins. She absently rubbed the swollen red knuckles; they were the hands of a much older woman.

'We'll have her home today, won't we, sir?' Her mother looked appealingly at the young man in his well-cut black suit and tie, and Milly saw him blush.

He looked at Miss Green, as if for reassurance. 'I will certainly do my best, Mrs Colman.' He swallowed hard. 'But it may not be today . . . exactly.'

'Don't worry, Elsie is in good hands. Francis is an excellent lawyer.' Florence Green came to his aid. 'He has a very promising career ahead of him!'

Milly only wished his promising career was half behind him, or had, at the very least, actually begun. They waited in an awkward silence, while other people came to sit on the benches. Two cocky-looking boys, in cheap, fashionable suits, strolled in together, closely followed by a bloated woman with a red nose and a large bag, clinking with what sounded suspiciously like beer bottles. Milly could hardly believe she'd brought booze to court, but as the woman passed them, her mother muttered, 'Smells worse'n the Anchor Brewery.'

On the stroke of ten thirty they were called into the courtroom. A cry broke from her mother's lips when Elsie was brought in.

Milly held on to her arm, unsure what Mrs Colman might do. Her sister looked pitiful. Her eyes, red-rimmed with crying, stared out of her sharp-featured face and fixed on Milly's.

'Get me out!' she mouthed silently.

Milly nodded, hoping the contact made her feel less alone. Then the charges were read: robbery, concealing a weapon, threatening to kill her father, inflicting grievous bodily harm on a police officer. Only now did Milly understand how serious matters were, and she began to fear the worst.

The detective gave evidence of Elsie's 'unstable mental state'. And, as he described her behaviour – the sudden violent rage, followed by a trancelike, almost catatonic state, the unprompted laughter, the songs and pieces of verse that she addressed only to herself, the lack of any remorse – Milly realized he was indeed describing her sister. However much Milly had called her 'a nutter' in the past, she never really believed it. She wanted to shout out to the drawling, dismissive judge that it all meant nothing – it was just Elsie being Elsie!

Every time a new charge was read out, she saw her sister slump closer to the floor, until eventually she had to be held up by the officer standing next to her. The whole proceedings seemed to take place outside of time, for afterwards, Milly couldn't remember who had said what, or when. Overawed by the formality of the room, where all was laid out to demonstrate the guilt of one and the power of another, Milly struggled to keep track of the arguments over Elsie's fate. Eventually she heard her mother's name mentioned and Francis Beaumont extolling her motherly virtues, a good Catholic woman, he said, who kept her children fed and clothed, made sure Elsie attended the school and church regularly. While he spoke of her, Milly's mother sat up a little straighter and lifted her chin, eager to show that she was here in support of her daughter and that everything Francis Beaumont had said was true.

The judge looked their way, unsmiling, and asked if there were any other character witnesses. Miss Green rose, and spoke of Elsie in glowing terms, though Milly wondered how much sway she would have with the hard-faced judge. Still, she praised Elsie's abilities in song and dance and drawing, and said that she was an unusually imaginative child, with a few character quirks, quite normal in the sensitive personality and not at all evidence of mental instability. Milly, for so long her sister's sternest critic, now ached to be able to say something in Elsie's defence, but she knew, that as a woman with an illegitimate child herself, she could do no good as a character witness for anyone.

Then the judge asked, 'Is the father here?'

'No, your honour,' Francis Beaumont replied. 'But there are allegations against him of brutality, which I respectfully suggest as mitigating circumstance for the . . . ahmm, attack. The police have indicated they would take this into consideration . . .'

The young man's confident tone had dwindled, as it became evident the judge's stern expression was not melting. His mouth was a tight, thin line that had not once curled into anything resembling a smile.

'Nonsense,' he replied testily. 'These are very serious charges and they cannot be dropped at this point, and furthermore, if neither the father . . .' here he looked over his glasses at Mrs Colman, 'nor the mother can control this violent child, then she must be put into the hands of those who can. I believe I've heard enough. The juvenile is to be committed to Stonefield Asylum.'

The gavel struck, wood on wood, and Milly's heart flinched from the blow. Elsie was half carried out, looking over her shoulder, bewildered and disbelieving. She fixed her eyes on Milly once more and mouthed again, silently, as though robbed of speech.

'Get me out!'

Outside the courtroom they gathered in a little huddle of despair, Francis Beaumont shamefaced and apologetic, her mother inconsolable, Miss Green disbelieving. But as Milly felt herself being sucked into their defeat, she decided she must replace it with determination. Whatever it needed, however long it took, she would answer her sister's mute cry for help. She would get her out of Stonefield Asylum, or 'the nuthouse' as it was commonly called. Its very name was used to strike terror into the heart of any wayward child. It was the place where young delinquents and unfortunates were sent to improve their ways, in the company of the slow of mind, the truly mad and the only ever mildly bad.

Bertie had been looking out for them. Milly saw him first, in his long white apron, standing at the shop door looking eagerly in their direction. They slowed down as they approached the shop and she saw his expectant, hopeful face turn to disbelief as he read her expression.

'What happened?'

Milly's mother's tears returned and it was left to Milly to explain.

'The lawyer was a nice young chap,' she said, trying to put a positive slant on things. It had, after all, been Bertie's suggestion she go to the Settlement for help. 'He did his best, but well, to tell the truth, Bertie, he wasn't much older than me.'

Bertie's face fell. 'So where's Elsie?'

'Stonefield Asylum,' Milly said softly.

'What? But that's ridiculous. She's not an imbecile!' His face flushed red and with unusual vehemence he slammed his hand against the door jamb. Then seeing Mrs Colman's renewed sobbing, he softened his voice. 'Come into the shop, Mrs Colman. Let me get you a drop of brandy before you go any further.'

Together they helped her mother to the chair that always sat by the counter, for those customers with weak legs, or with time on their hands for chatting. Soon her mother was sipping brandy and Milly was able to give Bertie the details.

'It was the knife did it, Bertie. She attacked a copper. To be fair to Mr Beaumont, not many lawyers would have got her off. The old man's testimony just put the dairy on it, and the judge said, if her parents couldn't control her, then someone else would have to try.'

'But why the asylum?' Although he worked at Dockhead, as a member of the shopkeeping classes, Bertie hadn't the same first-hand experience of the law and its ways that Milly had. She, however, had seen playmates come and go from a whole host of institutions and in the end it didn't much matter what they were called, they were all forbidding old Victorian buildings, echoing repositories for those too young or feeble to be placed into prisons. She remembered poor Johnny Harper in the class above her. He'd scaled the walls of the meat factory in Spa Road and stolen sausages, dipped into the barrels of oranges at Lipton's and lifted pats of butter from Fogden's Dairy. It was no coincidence all his contraband was food, for in a family of fourteen he was continually hungry. He'd always said he wasn't scared of Stonefield, but as others before him had discovered, there, the mixture of bad and mad was so toxic that if you went inside as one, you would certainly come out as the other. She feared that her sister, who had always skipped so precariously along the margin of both, would certainly be tipped over the edge in such a place.

And she couldn't bear the thought Elsie might suffer the same fate as poor Johnny, who now roamed the streets of Bermondsey, collecting newspapers in an old pram. He'd been given the new cruel name of 'pissy pants' and the last time she'd seen him he was emaciated and still hungry, living in a lean-to in Wild's Rents.

'Why Stonefield?' She shuddered. 'Because there's nowhere else to put her.'

Soon the word seeped out that they were back and the neighbours, eager to know the verdict on Elsie, began to join them in the shop. The tiny square of black-and-white tiles in front of the counter was soon crowded. Mrs Knight claimed to be so overcome with shock that she needed a tipple of what Mrs Colman was drinking, and Rosie Rockle, who'd been minding Jimmy all morning, offered to keep him for the afternoon.

'That's kind, Rosie,' Milly said in thanks. 'I need to get back to work and I don't know if Mum's up to looking after him.'

'No trouble, love. I'll take your mother home with me.'

Milly left her mother in the care of the neighbours, including old Ma Donovan, who gave her a curt nod. Dashing out of the shop, she glanced back just in time to see her scrutinizing Jimmy, while he contentedly observed the drama from the billowing bosom of Rosie Rockle.

After clocking back on, Milly sought out Tom Pelton. He'd bent the rules for her, allowing her extra time off and tacitly agreeing to cover for her if any questions were asked. The least she could do was let him know the outcome.

'Oh, Milly, love, I'm sorry to hear that. She doesn't deserve it. I don't know what I'd do, if anything like that had happened to our Theresa.'

Tom Pelton's only child had been a schoolfriend of Milly's. Spoiled, bespectacled and always a little more refined than her classmates, she hadn't been popular at school but Milly had always fought her corner when the bullies wanted to gang up, which she suspected was the reason for Tom's favouritism towards her.

'How's your poor mother taking it?' he asked.

Milly shook her head. 'She's in a state, Tom. If we don't get our Elsie home, I think it'll kill her.'

Tom put a comforting arm on her shoulder. 'If you need any more time, let me know,' he said, tapping the side of his nose with a finger. Some foremen were firmly company men, but Tom had been born in Dockhead and he always put 'his own' first.

She made her way quickly to the picking room, where she'd been working for the past few weeks, stoning plums. Plum jam was Southwell's most popular brand and the fruit had been piling up on the wharfside for weeks. She and Kitty were once again working alongside each other, and as she weaved her way through conveyer belts and wicker baskets to her station, she saw Kitty look up expectantly.

'Well, did you bring her home?' Kitty asked, making a space for Milly next to her.

Milly picked up the razor-sharp stoning knife and stabbed it into a dusty purple fruit. She shook her head, biting her lip. 'No luck.'

'Oh, love, I'm so sorry. Where'd they send her?'

'Stonefield.'

'Oh no!' Kitty's shock was noticed by the other women, and soon Milly heard the Chinese whispers of Elsie's name, coupled with 'nuthouse', passing down the line.

Milly picked up a plum, sliced the fruit in half, twisted and deftly de-stoned it. She flicked the stone to a basket on one side and the fruit into a pan on the other side. She'd stoned a dozen more, before she could speak again.

'I'll get her out, Kit, if I die trying.'

And wreaking all her anger on the undeserving fruit, she sliced, slitted, chopped and twisted her way through pounds of plums. Each one, she named: the old man, she stabbed with the blade; the judge she sliced in half; the copper she twisted apart; the detective she gouged; the Sisters of Mercy, one by one, she tossed aside, discarding the stones and pulp of them, though Sister Clare she spared for her kind heart; on and on she went all afternoon; the matron at Edenvale; Mr Dowell; the couple who had dared to deem Jimmy second best; but most often the name she gave to the fruit she cut was Milly Colman, the older sister who had never really been worthy of the name.

18

Gardens for Everyone

September 1924

Bertie was adamant that she should go. It was surgery night at the Bermondsey Settlement, when philanthropic lawyers, doctors and councillors would come and give free advice to anyone who turned up between the hours of seven and ten.

'You've got to take it further, Milly, and your best hope is with Francis Beaumont. I know you thought he was too young, but just because he's a volunteer doesn't mean he's second-rate. He's in top chambers at Lincoln's Inn. You shouldn't go by appearances.'

Milly sighed. Perhaps he was right and she had been too harsh on the young man. 'Well, perhaps nothing would have got through to that judge. I tell you, Bertie, he'd already made up his mind about what sort of family we were. And that's what sticks in my gullet, to think he condemned my mother as unfit – *my* mother!'

Bertie pushed his chair back from the table. In the two months they had been living in the same household he had, she noticed, found ways to stem the flow of some of her more vehement emotions. He was not one to be swept along by anybody, and he quickly brought her back to the subject in hand.

'Ask Florence to go in with you. She might be able to give Beaumont a better idea of the family situation. After all, he only had one night to prepare. And Florence thinks highly of him . . .'

And from some of the looks Francis Beaumont had given Miss Green, Milly thought, the feeling was mutual, so if Bertie did have any ideas where the woman was concerned, he'd better get a move

on and do something about it. But all she said was '*Florence?*'
Then smiling mischievously at his blush, she felt immediately
guilty when he said, 'I'll stay in and look after the boy.'

'But it's your lecture night!'

'Oh, I can miss this one, it's Councillor Stevens on the new
dustcarts.' He paused. 'I expect it'll be a load of old rubbish.'
And he lifted his eyebrow in anticipation of her laughter. That
was the unexpected thing about Bertie – however silly the joke,
he could always make her laugh.

Back up in her room, Milly dressed carefully. She wanted
to give a better impression to Francis Beaumont than she had
on that heart-wrenching morning in court. She'd been too
distraught to care about what she wore then and she must have
looked a wild woman. But now, realizing that her family, as
well as Elsie, was being judged, she was determined to show
Mr Beaumont that they were respectable. She took out her best
outfit, a low-waisted, coffee-coloured dress, with a cream collar
and pearly buttons down the front. She'd bought the material
from her favourite stall in East Lane, the end of a bolt, which
most people could have made only a cushion cover from. But she
made her own patterns from old brown paper, and had a knack
of eking out the last square inch of material. The buttons had
come from a pair of long gloves picked up at the Old Clo'. She
loved the way the soft pleats of the skirt allowed her shapely
legs all the freedom they needed for that long stride of hers.
And when she had the impulse to break into a sprint, she knew
she wouldn't be hobbled by a too-tight skirt. But tonight there
would be no sprinting; she would be ladylike. She slipped on her
low-heeled, strapped shoes and tucked her dark waves beneath
a cream, close-fitting hat.

'What do you think?' she asked Bertie, offering herself to view.
'Could Mr Beaumont mistake me for a lady?'

Bertie sucked on his pipe and for a moment she thought she'd
made a mistake in her choice.

'Should I change it for something plainer?'

'Strike me dumb, no! You look lovely, Milly, every bit a lady, I should say, though you don't need to dress up to prove that to anyone,' he said emphatically, beginning to pick at his pipe.

She smiled uncertainly. Was that just a meaningless compliment? But no, as she set off for the Settlement, she decided that Bertie was simply a very kind man, one who was never blinded by the judgements of the world. Where others would only see a common factory girl with a bastard child, he could look at Milly Colman, and really see a lady.

But after half an hour with Miss Green and Francis Beaumont, Milly realized that she would need more than a smart outfit and a smattering of hope to get Elsie's conviction overturned.

'What if I could pay? You know, for a full-time lawyer?' she ended by asking.

Mr Beaumont shifted uneasily in his seat and glanced at Miss Green, who'd readily agreed to accompany Milly. The surgery was held in a small music room and they sat at a folding table, squeezed between an upright piano and a line of music stands. Chairs had been stacked against one wall and propped in a corner stood a cello. This was the room where Elsie had learned the quaint old folk songs of wandering country lasses, of springtime and harvest, and Milly understood for the first time why Elsie loved them. It was for the same reason she herself loved hopping – both provided an escape to a gentler world, softer on the eye and heart than Bermondsey's grimy brick and smoke.

'Miss Colman?' She hadn't heard a word Francis Beaumont was saying. She pulled her gaze away from the cello. 'I'm afraid the fees are ridiculously high, Miss Colman. I doubt they would be within your means.'

'But if I *could* find a way to make some extra money, would it make any difference if we got a proper . . . I mean a full-time lawyer?'

He shuffled some court papers and sighed. She noticed blue shadows beneath his eyes; tonight he looked older. 'I don't think

I should give you false hope about your sister, Miss Colman. You're welcome to hire someone and I could give you the name of a senior partner, but I fear you'd be wasting your money.'

'So I've got to sit by while my sister's stuck in an asylum, for God knows how long, and the old man – my father – can knock us all black and blue and never get had up for it? It don't seem fair to me.' She stood up, smoothing down the coffee-coloured dress and holding out a hand.

'I'm grateful for your help, Mr Beaumont, thank you.'

'I'm sorry I couldn't do more,' the young man said, and she saw him already pulling out papers for his next visitor.

Florence Green walked her out. The queue outside the music room had grown since she'd arrived, and each face seemed to reflect her own feeling of powerless resignation. She hoped they felt better than she did after their interviews, for Milly had felt hope drain so completely from her that now she felt weak, as though water ran through her veins instead of blood. She fixed a smile on her face and began to thank Florence Green, when the older woman suddenly hugged her.

'Don't be too downhearted, Milly. There's always hope, there is!'

They had reached the outside stone steps, and a dribble of people hurried past them, late arrivals for Councillor Stevens' lecture on new refuse practices in the borough. She knew Miss Green meant well, but even with all her experience of working in Bermondsey, what did she really know of being trapped by poverty in a life without choices, without power, without influence? She *chose* to live here; Milly and her family had no such choice.

She shook her head. 'Nothing changes. If I'd walked in there with a thousand pounds, would he've told me there was no hope? Look at it!'

Her voice trembled with emotion as she flung a hand in the direction of the surrounding streets, some of the worst hovels in Bermondsey, huddled, vermin-infested courts and crumbling back-to-backs, with families of nine or ten living in one room.

Light was locked out by hulking warehouses on one side and a mass of rooftops on the other. Its life-sapping, oppressive leaching of her spirit made her lightheaded, and suddenly she found her legs giving way beneath her.

Florence Green caught her before she slumped to the floor and, supporting her down the steps, led her to the back of the building where a little garden had been planted. They sat together on a wooden bench, as evening bleached the riverside sky to duck-egg blue and rose pink. Sounds of boys drilling in the exercise yard came to them on the wind.

'Breathe, Milly, breathe deeply,' Florence said, an encouraging hand on her back. 'You've had a hard time of it over the past year. It's no wonder you feel the strain of this, but it's not all on your shoulders, you know?'

Milly lifted her eyes enquiringly to Miss Green's.

'Sometimes the answer comes, from out of the blue.' Florence lifted her eyes to the pale green sky, just beginning to glow with gold. 'We don't deserve it, we may not have even worked for it, but sometimes, out of the blue, the answer to our prayers comes.'

Milly had never thought Miss Green a beautiful woman. She was too sad for beauty; too many tears for the dead fiancé lying in a Belgian grave had washed the glow from her cheeks. But tonight she looked beautiful.

'Francis wouldn't tell you this, but he is probably the best lawyer you could ever get, even if you *had* a thousand pounds. He's brilliant, Milly, absolutely brilliant.'

When Milly ventured a look into the woman's eyes, she realized that Bertie's hopes were all for nothing. Francis Beaumont had obviously been the answer to Florence Green's prayers, if not her own.

'Well, if the best the law can offer can't get Elsie out, then I suppose I'll have to rely on the Lord God himself. Better get down to Dockhead Church and say a few Hail Marys. That should please me mother!' Milly managed a smile, thinking of Mrs Colman's dogged faith and her determined belief that one day Milly would turn into the good Catholic she'd always wanted her daughter to be.

'Pray, yes, do that, Milly, but don't forget to dream. You told me to look at all this.' And again the woman lifted her eyes, this time taking in the soot-encrusted walls and endless roofs that surrounded the Settlement. 'But soon this whole place could be a garden!'

Milly snorted. 'Soon? What, when God lets Adam and Eve back into Paradise?'

'Sooner than you think, if our Dr Salter's dream comes true,' she said, more serious now. 'He wants to sweep all this away and build cottages, with gardens for everyone!'

The image captured Milly's imagination. The saintly doctor was campaigning for re-election as their Member of Parliament and his vision for a beautiful Bermondsey was beginning to take hold. For a moment she tried to imagine flowers where there were filthy courtyards, and trees breathing green amongst the surrounding factory chimneys. The image hovered like a mirage and then was gone.

'Our Elsie is a dreamer,' she said finally, 'and look where it's got her.'

She left Florence Green sitting in the little garden, but all its brave daisies kindling like yellow flames in the setting sun now seemed to Milly like fool's gold, hopeless cases. How on earth could they breathe in this soot-laden air? If she didn't get to the river soon, she felt that she too might die from lack of oxygen. Her breath was tight in her chest as she walked towards Fountain Stairs; she hadn't been there since the night Bertie found her. She hesitated, but couldn't stop there. Turning the other way, she walked towards Dockhead instead, thinking she might go to the jetty near Southwell's, but again memories of trysts with Pat barred her. She decided to go to see her mother in Arnold's Place. Immediately she heard her mother's voice, 'misery loves company', but nevertheless she set off briskly, stretching her legs against the soft pleats of her dress. And though she'd vowed not to run tonight, she broke into a slow lope, taking the back way along Bermondsey Wall, beneath cranes and loading bays, edging deeper into the canyon of purple shadows between warehouses, until, finally emerging near Dockhead, she slowed to a more sedate walk.

Arnold's Place was full of life, in the evening warmth. Women sat outside their houses on kitchen chairs, chatting to neighbours across the narrow paving, feeding their babies, calling out to the children playing round the gas lamp outside Mrs Knight's to keep their noise down and being ignored. As Milly approached, she realized she'd been spotted. Amy, playing in the crowd, animated, unaware, was obviously the leader of the little troop and was giving her orders, pushing her index finger into Barrel's chest.

'You're it! Everybody, run out!' But she was stopped by another girl, who pointed to Milly.

'It's your sister.' Milly heard her audible whisper. 'She looks like that film star Clara Bow, but taller!' The girls in the group turned their admiring eyes on Milly, who was suddenly aware that, at eighteen, she must seem to them like a grown-up woman. But even with a baby of her own, she seldom felt grown-up.

'My old man says she looks like a slut,' Amy said matter-of-factly. 'Come on, run out!'

And they were off, scattering like a hunted tribe, hiding from Barrel, whose task would be to find each one before they could return 'home' to the old tin can placed on the pavement beneath the gas lamp. Milly remembered playing the game herself not so many years ago; 'Tin tan tobbernopple, one two three, I see Amy coming to me!' If Barrel could intercept the others with those words, while furiously banging the tin on the ground, he would have 'captured' them, and if they reached the tin before he'd finished, then they had 'vanquished' him. It was a game that could last for hours, sometimes a whole day. Amy wheeled past, pretending not to see her, but Milly grabbed the girl's arm.

'Is the old man home?'

Amy snatched her arm away. 'Nah, he's out on the piss.' And she shot away like a whirlwind, leading with her chin as she always did when running, eager for the next moment, mind on nothing but the game, seemingly oblivious of the family tragedy playing out in the little house opposite.

Milly walked into the passage. Their front door wasn't locked – there was nothing worth stealing and whatever of value the house might once have held, the old man had either smashed or drunk away in the pub.

'Mum? It's only me!' She walked in to find her mother leaning over the hopping box. Milly could see she was emptying it. The new paraffin lamp donated by Bertie was standing on the floor, and she was now wrestling out some old enamel plates.

'Hello, love. Oh, don't you look beautiful!' Mrs Colman eased herself up, a soft grunt escaping her lips as she straightened her back. 'Here, take these for me, I've got no china left. He's smashed the bleedin' lot.'

'Why're you unpacking it all?' Milly asked, taking the plates.

'I can't go hopping, not with my Elsie in Stonefield, no.'

Milly took off her hat. 'Oh, Mum, you can't miss your hopping. You're not going to do Elsie any good stuck here with him for the next six weeks, are you?'

But her mother put her hand on the table, as though it were a holy relic. 'May I never move from this spot, till I get my Elsie home!' she said, rapping the wood to emphasize her vow.

Milly walked into the scullery to fill the kettle. Bringing it back to heat on the range, she began searching out some cups and, finding none in the broken sideboard, started rummaging in the hopping box herself.

'Mum,' she said gently, 'I've been to see that Francis Beaumont again tonight.'

'He's not worth the 'apporth o' coppers, useless!' Her mother rarely spoke ill of people, and though a few hours ago Milly had shared her opinion, after talking to Miss Green, she now believed that no lawyer could have helped them.

'It's not his fault. The judge was biased, Mum. We'll just have to wait till visiting day and see if there's any way we can speak to someone at Stonefield. Perhaps they'll see she shouldn't be in there. Either way, the rules are we can't visit for at least six weeks, so you may as well be out of it, earning a bit for some new crockery!'

Before her mother could object, Milly remembered her youngest sister, whirling like a dervish through the twilit streets. 'Anyway, don't you think it's best if you keep Amy out of his way too? You know that with me and Elsie gone, she'll be in the firing line?'

Her mother, who had been blowing the surface of the nut-brown brew Milly had handed her, paused. Surely Amy's vulnerability must have occurred to her? But there were odd blanks in her mother's understanding of the world, as if she had only enough energy to survive each day with the old man, with none left over to think about tomorrow. She lived from one day to the next, one Mass to the next, with no thought of changing anything in between.

'Why have you stayed with him all these years?' It was a question Milly had always wanted to ask her mother, since she'd been old enough to understand that there had once been an alternative.

Mrs Colman gave a bitter little laugh. 'I'll tell you a story,' she said. 'The first time he ever give me a wallop, we'd not been married six month and I was pregnant. He had to get up five o'clock of a morning to get to work and it was my job to wake him up with a cup of tea. Well, this particular morning, I overdid it, sleeping like a baby I was, when I feel him shaking me, shouting in me ear, "What's the fucking time? I'm gonna be late!" Well, before I had a chance to come to, look at the clock or anything, he gives me such a punch I thought he'd knocked me teeth out. "And that's for not waking me up in time!" he says. So I run crying to me mother with me split lip and she says to me, "You've made your bed, now you've got to lie in it." Not a bit of sympathy, nothing. So that's when I knew what my life would be, and it's the same for all us women, love. We might share the bed with the men, but when it comes down to it, seems it's *always* us that's made it!'

Milly hadn't heard the story before and she'd certainly never realized that her mother was pregnant when she married. It explained a little of the life of penance she'd allowed herself to live. 'But if Elsie gets out, she'll be working soon and if you went cleaning, don't you think you could manage without him then?'

Her mother shook her head. 'I know I get little enough of his wages, but it's still more than I could earn cleaning. No, love, my old mum was right.'

They sat in silence for a while, her mother thoughtfully sipping tea and Milly wishing there was some way she could increase her own income and support her mother. Ellen Colman drained her tea and put the enamel cup down decisively. 'But I tell you what, you've made me think twice about going hopping.'

Milly smiled, relieved that she'd at least been of some use today, even though it landed her with another huge problem. As if reading her mind, her mother said, 'You'll have no one to look after Jimmy, though . . . unless I take him with me?'

'Would you be able to manage with a baby down there?' Milly held her breath, pausing between relief at the answer to her problem and worry about letting Jimmy out of her sight.

'Of course I would! He's no trouble now he's getting his fill on the bottles. I'll have him in a bushel basket beside me while I'm picking, and it'll keep Amy from wandering off like a little savage all over the place. She'll stick to him like glue.'

When Milly looked doubtful, her mother said, 'You'd be surprised what a help she is with him in the afternoons. She turns into a right little mother.'

Milly had to take her word for it, but in truth, she didn't need that much convincing. If Jimmy didn't go hopping, then Milly couldn't work.

'I think he'll love it down hopping,' she said wistfully, wishing she could be going too.

'Hmm.' Her mother pulled a wry face. 'Well, he *was* made in a hop garden, wasn't he?'

But later that week, the pain of saying goodbye to Jimmy threatened to undo all her resolutions. How could she let him go that far from her, when she'd fought so hard to keep him? It felt like a betrayal, and yet what would he know of it? He would be with his grandmother, just as he was most days.

Yet images of Jimmy buried in hop bines or rolling into the cooking fire distracted her as she stood on the platform at London Bridge, waiting to wave off the hoppers' special. With Jimmy crooked in one arm, she waited while her mother and Amy settled themselves and the hopping box into the nearest carriage. She was being buffeted by the usual crowd of families rushing to find a seat and when the whistle blew, she still held him tight.

'Come on, love, hand him over, the train's going!' Her mother held out both hands.

'We'll look after him . . . promise!' said Amy. Before she could change her mind, Milly laid her cheek against Jimmy's and whispered, 'Don't forget me, I love you.' Then she thrust him into her mother's waiting arms.

'Bye, Milly!'

Her mother's voice was drowned by the shrill whistle, and soon she and Jimmy were hidden from sight, as steam billowed up around the moving carriage.

Milly was grateful for the veil of smoke which hid her from the departing train. She didn't want her mother to see the tears that had begun to fall. But she cried all the way back to Southwell's, not caring what people thought of her, lost in the utter misery of being parted from her child. Many times she sniffed and flicked the tears away, waiting for the grief to subside, but it was as persistent as her passionate devotion to Jimmy. She arrived at Southwell's early, and instead of going straight to the factory walked to Hickman's Folly in hopes of meeting Kitty on her way to work. She was almost at the Bunclerks' door, when Kitty emerged pulling on her coat while eating a slice of bread and dripping. A tangle of children tumbled out of the door after her.

'Mind me shoes! You're treading all over 'em!' Kitty shouted, when Percy trampled her in an attempt to be first out of the house. Kitty looked up in surprise when Milly called her name.

'Milly! What've you been crying for? You're all puffy, you look terrible.'

'That's nice. I'll know not to come to you in future when I need cheering up!'

'I didn't mean terrible. I just meant . . .'

'Terrible?'

Kitty laughed and together they walked arm in arm to Southwell's, while Milly poured out her heart.

'Well, listen here, you might as well make the most of it and come out with me and Freddie tonight. Anyway, he wants to talk to you about Elsie.'

'Freddie does?'

Kitty nodded, but wouldn't answer any of her questions. 'All I'll say is that it's worth hearing,' she said enigmatically, and Milly hadn't the energy to pursue it.

That evening, as she cleared away the tea things, Milly asked Bertie if he minded her going out to meet Kitty.

'Mind? 'Course I don't mind. Anyway, you need cheering up tonight.'

'Well, so long as you don't need me for anything here.' Milly felt awkward. The terms of their arrangement were so loose sometimes she felt like a lodger, at others an employee, and sometimes she felt like a friend.

'You don't have to ask my permission!' He chuckled, seeming genuinely surprised. 'Besides, I'm out myself tonight. I've had a rare invitation over to Dulwich!'

'Oooh, going over to see the rich relations?' she teased.

But he pulled a face. Bertie wasn't fond of his uncle, but

as his livelihood depended on him, he liked to keep on good terms.

'I'd rather be coming to the Folly with you, believe me!'

Kitty and Freddie were in their usual seats when Milly arrived at the Folly, but sitting with them was a young man Milly didn't recognize.

'What you drinking?' Freddie got up and while he was at the bar, Kitty introduced the young man.

'Milly, this is Bob Clark, Freddie's brother.'

Bob gave her a shy smile. He looked nothing like Freddie, who was big-boned and fair. His brother was of a slighter build, with soft brown hair, a gentle expression and eyes that seemed happy to be lowered, exactly the opposite of Freddie's sharp, darting looks.

'Pleased to meet you, Bob. I didn't even know Freddie had a brother!'

Bob Clark smiled and then looked down at the table. 'Well, I work away from home.'

Freddie was back with the drinks in time to overhear his brother.

'Go on, Bob, tell her where you work,' he urged, breaking into a grin.

'I work at Stonefield,' he said.

'Stonefield Asylum?'

He nodded. 'Yes, I'm the gardener.'

Milly looked from Bob to Kitty, whose face was triumphant. 'See, I told you it was worth hearing.'

'Have you seen our Elsie?' Milly whispered, leaning forward.

'You don't have to whisper, Mill, you can't get arrested for talking to the bloody gardener,' Freddie said.

'I'm sorry, no, not yet.' Bob shot an exasperated look at his elder brother; obviously he was used to being interrupted by Freddie.

'But that's one of the reasons we wanted to talk to you,' Freddie went on. 'Bob can help her, can't you, Bob?' But before his brother had time to answer, Freddie continued, 'You just write and tell her to volunteer for garden duty and Bob will keep an eye on her for you.' He sat back, basking in the adoring gaze of Kitty.

Finally, Bob lifted his eyes and managed to look directly at Milly. 'It'll be the best thing for her. If she gets on garden duty, she'll have some fresh air, she'll be away from . . . the others, and working with the plants, well, it'll keep her mind off things.'

Milly was overwhelmed. Florence Green had promised such help might appear out of the blue, and she'd scorned her optimism, but now she felt like hugging the two young men. 'Oh, that's so kind of you!' she said.

Kitty chimed in. 'It was Freddie's idea.' For once Milly didn't mind her trumpeting Freddie's virtues at all.

'I'll write tonight. But, Bob, is it really as bad in there as they say it is?'

He began drawing patterns in a small puddle of spilled beer. 'It's not *all* bad. They're well fed, we've even got our own farm. And clothes are all found, but she'll have to work hard, probably sewing or laundry. It's hard at first, getting used to people who're so . . . different, it can be scary.'

'He means the nutters,' Freddie interrupted.

'Don't call 'em that!' Bob said protectively. 'It's not their fault, and anyway, most of 'em are like Elsie. The courts just don't know where to put them!'

Milly liked Freddie's brother for that, and how could she not warm to someone who'd volunteered to help her sister? She asked him endless questions and came away with the impression that the asylum would be a harsher version of Edenvale, but with no prospect of reprieve and with the added anxiety of being surrounded by unstable, sometimes violent inmates. She wondered how on earth he'd come to work there.

'I used to work at St James's Vicarage, did odd jobs, then gardening. The vicar recommended me for the job. I was glad of it at the time – it was just after the war and with all the soldiers coming back, jobs were few and far between. And I love the gardening . . . it suits me.' He spoke half apologetically, perhaps feeling a little in the shadow of his more outgoing, entrepreneurial brother.

'I think Elsie will love the gardening too.' She smiled. 'Not that she's had much practice with flowers around Dockhead!'

Suddenly Freddie looked up. Although seemingly absorbed by Kitty, he'd obviously been keeping one ear on their conversation.

''Course, if worse comes to worst, we can always spring her, can't we, Bob?'

Kitty laughed nervously, but Milly saw Bob and Freddie exchange glances that looked entirely serious.

19

A Good Man is Hard to Find

September 1924

Bertie didn't answer her call and the house was in darkness when she got home from the pub. Assuming that he was still at his uncle's in Dulwich, she went upstairs to her bedroom. How empty it seemed without Jimmy; it was always his steady infant breath that gave the room its life and its welcome for her. She gravitated towards his cot, smoothing the blanket and then patting it gently, as though he were still there. Her mother had called Elsie 'her baby'. Perhaps children, whatever their age, were always their mother's babies. If she felt as hollow as this after Jimmy had only been gone a week, what anguish must her mother be feeling now. All down to the old man.

She went to the window overlooking the back garden and pulled aside the net curtain. A full, pinkish moon, riding high in an indigo sky, washed the garden with a pale blush. On the white climbing rose, a few late blooms glimmered, like fat candles. Suddenly her eye was caught by the orange glow of a match, and a face flared into life. Bertie was standing beneath the roses, trying to relight his pipe. His shadowy face, briefly defined by the flickering match, looked different. The flyaway eyebrows were drawn tight together and his normally amused mouth was set in a deep, unsmiling line.

She threw on a cardigan, hurrying downstairs and out through the scullery door. Picking her way along the moonlit path, she didn't speak until she stood beside him. 'Bertie? I thought you were still at your uncle's.'

Though he must have heard her, he didn't turn round, just continued to draw on his pipe.

'I've been home for a while,' he said in a low voice, finally turning to face her.

Now she could see that the sulphurous flare hadn't lied. He looked miserable.

'Are you all right? What are you standing out here in the dark for?'

He inhaled, lifting the rose nearest to him. 'Smell that, Milly, it's lovely.'

Rose scent vied with acrid pipe smoke and, normally, she would have made a joke about the smelly habit, but she instinctively knew he was in no mood for teasing.

'Yes, lovely,' she said, then shivered in the cool night air. 'Don't you want to come in? I'll make us a cup of tea.' She hugged her cardigan closer around her and he nodded, following her back along the path.

When the tea was made and they were sitting either side of the unlit kitchen fireplace, she ventured another question. 'How was Dulwich?'

He shifted in his seat and pulled at the neck of his shirt, from which he'd already removed the collar. Before answering, he took another deliberate swallow of the hot tea. Sometimes his slowness infuriated her, but now she held her tongue and waited.

'Not a pleasant evening. Uncle doesn't approve of me, says I'm a disgrace to the Hughes name.' His voice was dull and his face immobile.

Milly snorted with laughter. 'Do me a favour! You? You couldn't get a straighter feller! Uncle doesn't know his arse from his elbow, if you ask me.'

This brought a hint of a smile back to Bertie's lips. 'Well, as far as Uncle's concerned, anyone involved in the Labour Party has made a pact with the devil!'

But then something in his guarded look made her suspect this had nothing to do with Bertie's political activities, and everything to do with her. She preferred to have it out in the open.

'It's not you he disapproves of, is it? It's me.'

'Did I say that? Strike me dumb if you don't always want to be putting words in my mouth.'

'You didn't have to say it, Bertie. It's obvious. Your respectable uncle was never going to be pleased, once he heard I'm living here. Dockhead caddywack slut? Is that what he thinks I am?' And as he made to protest, she shook her head and got up. 'Don't worry, Bertie, I'll find somewhere else to live tomorrow. I don't want to cause trouble for you.'

He struggled to speak. When he was excited or animated, his words sometimes tripped over each other, and it was a while before he managed to say, 'You're doing no such thing! I'm a twenty-five-year-old man and I won't be told how to live my life. It's nothing to do with my uncle if I choose to campaign for Dr Salter – *nor* if I choose to have a live-in housekeeper!'

'But, Bertie, he's your livelihood, you can't afford to upset him. He's probably vindictive enough to sack you.'

'Well, he can stick his job up his arse!'

For the normally placid Bertie, this amounted to as violent a show of temper as she'd ever witnessed. Unlike her foul-mouthed father, he never swore, and rage was alien to him. She had grown so used to being in his even-tempered company, she sometimes wondered how he and the old man could even be of the same species. But she knew, however brave his words were, his heart was not that of a fighter.

'Don't be a fool, Bertie. You need that job as much as I need mine.'

'Well, there's other work I can do! Besides, it wouldn't come to that, we're family. He just made his disapproval plain, loves to preach a sermon, you must remember that.'

And she did. Hughes had always made sure to rub her mother's nose in the length of their tally slate, ever ready to point out the thriftiness of the proddywacks compared with the profligate habits of the drunkard caddywacks of Dockhead. It was absurd, as on any given night in Bermondsey, the religion of the drunks being kicked out at closing time was evenly balanced.

'I've probably got myself upset over nothing. I daresay it'll all blow over, Milly. You're not to worry, and there's to be no more talk of moving out. Hear me?'

Milly acquiesced because, for all her bold words, she knew very well there was nowhere else for her to go.

It had been almost a year since he was put away, but Milly, to her secret shame, had hardly given a thought to Pat Donovan in his prison cell. But her reaction to Elsie's incarceration had made her reconsider her indifference to Pat. In spite of all their antagonism, Milly had immediately wanted to move heaven and earth to free Elsie, and sometimes the imagined feeling of asylum walls closing round her would suffocate her, as though *she* were the one locked up in Stonefield. She doubted she could ever feel free, while Elsie was not, and realized, almost to her surprise, how much she loved her sister after all. But not Pat, which was no surprise. It seemed strange that, at one time, marrying him had even seemed an option. His sojourn at Her Majesty's pleasure had in fact set her free, and now she would rather face the disapproval of a thousand Hughes, or struggle with all the mountainous problems she faced in keeping Jimmy, than lock herself into a loveless marriage. Her talk with her mother had made that much clear to her. Milly was the child of such a marriage, and it was not what she wanted for her own son. If Bertie had never come along, that night on Fountain Stairs, if he'd not been so kind, had never given her the lifeline of a place to live, perhaps she might have ignored her misgivings about Pat and persuaded him to marry her when he got out. She would never know, but she felt as though she owed her freedom to Bertie, and just hoped he wouldn't be made to suffer for it.

So on this Saturday afternoon, the sight of old Ma Donovan on her doorstep hit her with the force of one of the old man's wallops. The woman, short and pugnacious, was done up in her best coat and hat. Milly waited for her to speak.

'Is your fancy man home?' she said, tucking in her many chins, so that they creased like a concertina above her coat collar.

Milly's instinct was to slam the door in her face, but traces of guilt about her own treatment of Pat stopped her.

'I'm Bertie's housekeeper, not that it's any of your business. Now if you've got something to say and can be civil about it, you can come in. If not, you can sling yer hook!'

Milly was quite proud of her restraint. She put it down to Bertie's example – she'd noticed that his slowness sometimes had a strategy behind it. It gave him time to think. And Milly was glad she'd not immediately told Ma Donovan to piss off as she would normally have done. For now the woman held out a letter.

'I don't need to come in. I haven't come to black my nose in your dirty business. I've just come from visiting my Pat in *prison*. That's where he is, in case you're interested.'

The woman paused to see if her sarcasm had any effect, but Milly breathed slowly, waiting for Mrs Donovan to talk herself into a corner.

When Milly didn't reply, Pat's mother said, 'I've told him that boy's not his, which you know full well he's not.' Sharp eyes, buried in her fleshy face, searched for a reaction, but Milly stood, expressionless, still holding the front door open.

'Anyway, it's a mystery to me, but he wants you to have this.' Mrs Donovan thrust a letter into her hand, turned and waddled off. Milly didn't move from the spot, but took the letter. She turned it over. Stamped on the back was *HM Prison, Brixton* and Pat's prison number. She walked through to the backyard and, seating herself on the old kitchen chair, opened the letter. *Dear Milly*, he'd written,

I've heard from Mum that you didn't get rid of the kid when I told you to. I think you could have let me know, instead of keeping it behind my back. She says he don't look nothing like me, but I reckon he's mine and so I'm willing to give him a name and marry you when I get out. I know we haven't had the best of starts, but I always did think a lot of you, Milly. Perhaps you could see your way to visiting me, as you're going to be my future wife.

Love, Pat

Milly crumpled up the letter. *Future wife!* Prison had certainly changed his tune. What was she going to do now?

Perhaps Kitty would have some words of wisdom to offer. If the smooth progression of her friend's romance with Freddie Clark was anything to go by, she seemed to know how to handle men. Since Jimmy's departure, Kitty had been badgering Milly to make the most of her freedom, and had suggested they resume their old Saturday afternoon outing to the pie-and-mash shop and the Old Clo' market. But Milly had declined. She needed to catch up with Bertie's laundry and besides, being a mother had tamed the wild side of her that used to bowl along Tower Bridge Road singing at the top of her voice. But she needed to see Kitty, so after she'd hung out Bertie's shirts in the backyard, she set off for Hickman's Folly. When Kitty ushered her in, the tiny house seemed almost spacious. She was the only one home.

'Mum's taken the lot of 'em down hopping, thank gawd! And Dad's gone down for the weekend with the husbands.'

Kitty explained that, as Pat was not there to do it, Freddie had offered to drive them all down in his lorry.

'Didn't you want to go with your dad and Freddie for a visit?' Milly asked.

'No fear! I hate the country, sleeping on straw with all them bugs.' Kitty gave a visible shudder. 'I'd rather be here. Look at me, I don't know what to do with all this space. I'm wandering from one room to the next, looking for someone to trip over!'

Milly chuckled, but as there were only four rooms in the house, she thought the novelty might soon wear off. Still, it was certainly nice to be able to sit in the Bunclerks' kitchen, stretching out her long legs, without kicking someone.

'Anyway, what brings you here?' Kitty asked. 'I thought you was doing his laundry today.'

Milly was never sure about Kitty's opinion of Bertie. She suspected that in her mind he was an outsider, a middle-class interloper in their closed tribe, to be politely tolerated rather than warmly welcomed. But Milly could no longer feel that way.

'Oh, he doesn't make a lot of laundry. You don't get dirty working in a shop, not like the filth the old man brings home on him from the tannery.' She fished out the letter from her handbag. 'This is what I wanted to ask you about.'

Milly waited while Kitty took in the contents of Pat's letter. When she'd finished, a small whistle escaped from her lips.

'Leopard's changed his spots! What are you going to do now?'

Milly let out a long groan. 'I don't know. That's what I've come to ask you!'

'Well, you'll have to make your mind up quick, love, won't you? Now he's getting out early.'

'What do you mean, early? You've got that wrong, Kit. He's got another year to do.'

'He's told Freddie they've taken time off for good behaviour.'

Milly's mouth went dry, and a fluttering in her chest signalled a rising panic as she insisted, 'But he's said nothing about it to me!'

Kitty shrugged. 'Perhaps he wanted to surprise you.'

'It's a bloody surprise, all right, but did Freddie say when he's getting out?'

'Let's put it this way, he might be hoping for a Christmas wedding!'

They spent the rest of the afternoon going through Milly's options, but of course, she should have known, this was a decision no one could help her with. Perhaps she should be grateful it had been forced upon her. Afterwards her way would be clear and

231

uncluttered, and all she'd have to worry about would be Jimmy . . . and Elsie, of course.

That evening she told Bertie she needed to write a letter, and asked if she could have some of his blue writing paper and borrow his fountain pen. She went to her room early and sat looking out of the sash window over the pretty garden, searching for words that were truthful, yet not unkind. Perhaps she should just tell him she'd fallen for someone else. It was true, in a way. It was just that the 'someone else' was her own child, and now the world revolved around him and his happiness. Pat Donovan would contribute nothing to that, she felt sure, and so Pat Donovan would have to go. She sighed in exasperation, crumpling the third attempt and throwing it into the grate. All Bertie's paper would be gone at this rate. She began again.

Dear Pat,
I heard from Kitty you are getting out at Christmas and
I'm really happy for you. Please don't think you have to
make any promises to me. It's decent of you, but truly, Pat,
I am doing very well now, with a job and a place to live, so
you've no need to worry about me. The boy is healthy and
contented and I've decided to bring him up on my own.
So I want you to feel free to get on with your life once you
come out and not to feel any obligation to me. I think it's
for the best, Pat, and if we see each other when you get out,
I hope we'll still be friends.
    Milly

It was, she supposed, a cowardly letter, but would it help to add that she feared a man who kept guns in his toolbox might not be the best person to bring up her beloved child? No, it was the best she could do.

Bertie looked a little surprised next morning by his much reduced stack of writing paper. But it wasn't his way to ask questions. He simply said, 'I've got a stamp, if you need one.'

The next week dragged by, each day punctuated by the twin anxieties of Elsie and Pat, both far away, and yet still insinuating themselves into her daily life, so that she found herself living more in the brooding halls of Stonefield or the claustrophobic cells of Brixton than in the picking room at Southwell's. She had heard nothing more about Elsie and the letter to Pat stayed stuffed in her bag all week. Once sent, there was no going back.

Each morning she registered the clocking-in machine, but after that, she hardly knew if she were sorting blackcurrants or filling jam jars. Yet her most persistent daydream was of her child, nestled in a hop pillow, tucked in a bushel basket, swinging from a bine, her little hop baby. After a couple of days, Kitty grew exasperated.

'For gawd's sake, Milly, you need to stop worrying about everyone else and start living again. There's no sense in mooning around all week. Why don't you come to the sewing circle at the Settlement tonight, take your mind off things?'

Milly was about to make an excuse, when Kitty interrupted, 'And you could sew Jimmy a little outfit . . .'

It was true, she was doing no one any good, least of all herself, with her constant obsessing. For the time being, she'd done what she could for Elsie, and as for Pat, she just had to be brave and follow her instincts. Jimmy, she would have to trust to her mother and the presiding goddess of the hop gardens.

'Oh, all right then,' she agreed finally.

Kitty beamed. 'We've all missed you, Mill. It's been dull as ditchwater there without you.'

They met up outside the Settlement later that night, Milly following Kitty into the sewing room a little shyly. It had been almost a year, after all. The room looked the same, apart from the addition of some sewing machines, but the faces had changed. Some girls had left; Peggy Dillon had married a butcher and was

233

now living above his shop down 'the Blue', one of Bermondsey's main shopping streets. Kitty had told her about the wedding, which had taken place while she was at Edenvale. Kitty was convinced that the attraction was more for the meat than the man, adding wickedly that he resembled a pork sausage squeezed in the middle, topped with a face like a pork chop. Other faces were new and Milly didn't recognize them, but she got the same warm welcome from Miss Green, who eagerly showed off the new Singer sewing machines that had been donated to the Settlement.

'Can I leave you girls to practise on your own with the machines? I need to pop out for a minute.' She smiled at the girls, who nodded, whilst others were already intent on their tasks, leaning over the wheels and setting the treadles whirring. Milly spent a half-hour getting to grips with bobbins and treadles, and had soon mastered the different stitching attachments.

'You make me sick,' said Kitty, who'd got her cotton entangled around the foot. 'I practised all last week and still make a pig's ear of it. You catch on first go!'

Milly laughed and got up to sort out Kitty's machine.

It was at that moment that she glanced through the glass-panelled door into the corridor and saw Bertie, deep in conversation with Florence. She paused in surprise. He hadn't told her he was coming to the Settlement this evening. His face was flushed, and excited-looking. Florence Green had her back to Milly, but when she rested her hand on Bertie's arm and leaned closer to kiss his cheek, his face brightened even more. Milly felt a sharp stab of pain in her chest, ice cold, yet searing. She swallowed hard, unable to look away. Feeling pinned, caught in an invisible net, she marvelled at how this feeling had crept up on her. She felt an overwhelming need to know what they were talking about.

She slumped back down at her machine, all the fun draining away from the task. Even when Florence Green returned and sorted out an offcut of beautiful white lawn for Jimmy's new outfit, Milly couldn't rekindle her enthusiasm. She was fiercely annoyed with herself, knowing immediately what the pain in her chest meant, knowing, too, the complications she couldn't accommodate in her life. She would be ruthless with her heart. There was no place for her in Bertie's affections, and certainly no place in her life for a man. She was about to rid herself of one; the last thing she wanted, she told herself sternly, was another!

As the class ended, she began vigorously wrapping the half-made baby suit in tissue paper, so she could take it home to embroider by hand.

'It hasn't done you much good, gel, has it?' She looked up sharply as Kitty came to her side.

'What hasn't?' Milly asked in a flush of guilt. Had Kitty somehow divined her jealousy?

'The sewing circle! You look even more miserable now than you did this morning! Want to come for a quick one at the Folly?'

'Yeah, why not?' She certainly wouldn't be rushing home to make Bertie Hughes his evening cocoa. Perhaps she'd allowed herself to get too cosy at Storks Road. It wasn't her home, not really. It was just fantasy to think that she belonged anywhere other than Arnold's Place.

'Come on, Kit!' She grabbed her friend's arm and pulled her out of the sewing room. 'Let's go, if we're going. I'm gasping.'

She trotted them along the riverside streets until they arrived, Kitty puffing for breath, outside the Folly. The pub, with its peeling paint and grimy windows, was a stark contrast to the trim, well-kept Settlement building. Milly pushed her way through the corner door and into the smoke-filled bar. Its small interior meant that benches and tables had to be pushed back against the walls, leaving only a small square space in front of the wooden bar. She squeezed round a group of young men, pints in hand, huddled shoulder to shoulder in front of the bar. They were laughing loudly at some joke, jostling each other playfully, and she had to be careful to skirt them without getting beer slopped all over her. Kitty spotted Freddie, sitting with a man who looked to Milly like a sausage squeezed in the middle with a face like a pork chop.

She whispered to Kitty, 'Is that Peggy's butcher?' and Kitty hissed, 'Yes!'

'Jesus, Kit, you were right, he looks like a grilled dinner!'

Kitty let out a raucous laugh that made heads turn, and the girls squashed round the table, desperately trying to control their giggles. The young butcher introduced himself to Milly, sticking out a meaty hand, fingers clustered like chipolatas. She bit her cheek and kicked the still giggling Kitty under the table. Fortunately, Peggy arrived just then and her unsuspecting new husband stood up to buy them all a round of drinks.

Freddie had, that same evening, taken an unofficial delivery from a meat refrigeration ship. Both he and the butcher were well pleased with the transaction they'd just concluded, so were liberally buying the girls drinks. Milly's capacity wasn't what it had once been and before long, she found herself standing on the table, shouting to Maisie at the piano. 'Come on, Maise, give us "A Good Man is Hard to Find"!'

Maisie could always be relied on to know the latest jazz songs and Milly joined in with her full-throated voice, becoming especially impassioned when she got to:

'My heart's sad and I am all forlorn, my man's treating me
   mean,
I regret the day that I was born and that man of mine I've
   ever seen.
Lord a good man is hard to find, you always get the other
   kind.
Just when you think that he's your pal, you look and find
   him foolin' round some other gal!'

'Sh'true, Kit, true's I shtand 'ere!' She swayed precariously as she descended from the table on to the bench. She pointed her finger at Freddie Clark. 'You hold on to 'im!' Maisie launched into the chorus:

'So if your man is nice, take my advice,
hug him in the morning, kiss him every night.
Give him plenty lovin', treat your good man right.
For a good man nowadays is hard to find!'

Though Milly's voice was still foghorn strong, her vision was weakened and her foot missed the edge of the bench, so that she found herself lying under the table. Kitty and the others ducked down, peering at Milly as she curled like a cat round the table legs.

'Ahhh,' said Kitty, trying to pat her friend's head but missing her mark, comforting the butcher's two-tone brogues instead. Milly banged her head against the edge of the table as she sat up. Looking round at all the other smiling bleary-eyed faces, Kitty explained, 'She's mishin'er Jimmy, turned out a good mum, ain't she?'

Milly mumbled: '*Then you rave, you even crave, to see him laying in his grave* . . . no, thash no' true, Kit, didn't mean it . . .'

When the publican rang the brass bell, Milly's legs, her pride and joy, failed her. She suffered the indignity of being carried between Freddie and the butcher all the way home to Storks Road. How she got upstairs to bed, she didn't know, but from a long way off, she heard Kitty's apologetic voice explaining, 'Shorry, she's just missin' Jimmy. Sh'don't usually get like this . . . She can drink anyone under the table!' And someone replied, 'Strike me dumb!'

20

The Right Place

October 1924

Her eyelids were stuck fast. She tried to open one eye, then closed it swiftly against the harsh light falling across the bed. She realized she was fully clothed under the covers. A wave of nausea broke over her as she rolled on to her back. Clutching the bedclothes as if they were a sinking boat in a storm, she forced her eyes open again, only to find that the room was spinning slowly round her. She let out a long groan as she remembered the night before. It had been Bertie's voice. *Strike me dumb* he'd said, but what must he have thought of her? Her face burned at the memory. She simply couldn't face him this morning.

Crawling to the edge of the bed, she swung her legs over the side, but just then a wave heaved and tossed the boat up into the air, launching her across the room to the washstand. Grabbing the china basin, she cuddled it, groaning into its rose-patterned bowl. She never heard the soft knocking on the door.

'You all right in there?' Bertie called. 'You'll be late for work . . .'

She froze. 'I'm ready!' she lied. 'I'll come and do your breakfast now.' But at the mere thought of food, her nausea returned.

'Soppy date,' he muttered, as though he could see her predicament through the closed bedroom door. 'I've brought you a cup of coffee. I'll leave it outside.'

She heard his footsteps retreating down the stairs and shortly afterwards the front door closing softly, as he left for work. Very carefully, she tried her legs, and with one hand grabbing the dado rail, edged her way to the door. Bending down gingerly, she retrieved the still hot coffee, and sipped it slowly, until the room began to feel less like the merry-go-round at Blackheath funfair.

'Oh, you silly mare, Milly Colman!'

But there was no time for self-recrimination and even the strong coffee was not enough to make her limbs work at their normal speed. Milly was so late clocking on, she knew she would be docked half a day's pay, which was bad enough, but as she dashed across the factory yard, she heard her name being called.

'Oi, Milly Colman! Hold up!' It was Tom Pelton, the head foreman. She stopped in her tracks and whirled round to see him approaching from Southwell's riverside wharf. 'Just my luck!' she thought. 'I'm in for a rollicking now.'

Tom had been more than lenient with her of late, but there was a limit and she feared she'd just reached it. He didn't look happy.

'What time d'ye call this? I went up to the picking room first thing and you're not there!'

'I'm sorry, Tom! I wasn't feeling well, but I've come in anyway.' She played the sympathy card.

'Don't give me that old bull, Milly. I didn't just sail up the Thames in a boat. I heard all about you – up on the table in the Folly last night, singing your lungs out, *and* I heard they had to carry you home!'

Milly dropped her eyes. There was a time she might have told him to stick his job and simply run off to Horsmonden for the rest of the season, but not now. Responsibilities constrained her, twining about her like a twisting bine. Still nauseous, she drew in a sickening breath.

'I thought you'd changed your ways since you come back with your baby, and I've been more than fair, Milly.'

She looked up. 'You're right, Tom, I'm grateful for what you've done for me. It's just that . . . truth is, my Jimmy's down hopping with Mum and it's been so long since I've been out with the old crowd . . . I just got carried away . . .' she finished lamely. 'I promise it won't happen again.'

She held her breath, praying he wouldn't sack her on the spot, but her remorse seemed to soften him a little.

'I know you're only young to have all that responsibility on your shoulders, Milly, and God knows, you don't get any help from that old man of yours.' He paused, as if weighing whether to tell her something. 'Come in the office a minute.' He led her to his cubbyhole on the ground floor of the factory building.

'Sit down, Milly, and let me give you some advice: you're normally a good worker, but now's not the time to be slacking off. There'll likely be changes round here in the next few years. New machinery's taking over from the hand filling, and we'll have to start laying women off sooner or later.'

He let that sink in. Milly had done her stint in the filling room, where a hundred-odd women stood for hours in pits round low tables, doing the back-breaking filling work. Their job was to scoop the still bubbling jam out of copper-bottomed trolleys into stone jars, using heavy silver-plated ladles. The pits were designed to ease the strain on their backs, but it was still gruelling work. She immediately saw the impact of a filling machine: a hundred women would be out of work at a stroke. All they'd need would be a couple of machine hands, and of course these would be men. Since the war, most of the mechanical jobs had reverted to men, in spite of the fact that the women had practically run the place during four years of war.

Tom continued her train of thought. 'I can only keep the best workers on, so some of the filling girls will be going into the picking room or the boiling room, and I'll be weeding out the time wasters. Up till now I've been impressed with you. You can do any job in the factory, you do it quick and you do it well. I've even thought you might make a forelady in time . . . but, Milly, I can't have you being late. I've got to be able to rely on you.'

Her heart had leaped into her mouth. If she'd put her job in danger with one stupid drunken night, she'd never forgive herself, and a forelady's job one day might mean she could help her mother out, get her away from the old man even.

'I'll make sure it doesn't happen again, Tom. I won't let you down.'

'All right, off you go now, and no more coming the old acid, you're on probation!'

When she finally got to the picking room, she felt near to tears. She slotted herself next to Kitty in the line of women, washing and sorting damsons. In answer to Kitty's enquiring look, she simply shook her head. If she spoke, the tears might fall. She felt as if she were being stretched taut as a leather hide on a frame, and one day soon she might tear clean apart. It was too much for her to hold together: Elsie; her mother; Pat; her child; Bertie, and now this. The one thing that was keeping it all from falling apart was her job, and now even that was under threat.

She sniffed and tried to pull herself together, and when Kitty hissed under her breath, 'Coming to the Folly again tonight?' she growled back, 'No!'

When she got home that afternoon, she made sure Bertie's tea was ready. She put the plate in front of him the minute he came in and then made herself scarce. She knew she couldn't avoid him forever, but she was too embarrassed and too confused by her own feelings to be around him now. He was too much of a gentleman to bring up her drunken return home, and if she didn't mention it, perhaps she could, in time, learn to be easy around him again.

As it was, the following days were busy ones for Bertie. He'd volunteered to help with Dr Salter's election campaign and often he would go straight from the shop to the Labour Institute, or he would pop home for a quick tea and then walk to the end of the street for a campaign meeting in the Salters' own home. Milly had learned, to her surprise, that Dr Salter lived in Storks Road, just a few houses from Bertie's. As an MP she had assumed he would live somewhere grander, but Bertie told her the man believed in living where his patients and constituents lived. No country house for him, Bertie had said. Even though he and his wife loved trees and flowers, they had devoted themselves to the brick wasteland of Bermondsey, with its single park, the only green haven in thirteen hundred acres.

Milly would have been glad of Bertie's absence, if she hadn't known that Florence Green was also a volunteer. Some evenings she had the insane impulse to follow Bertie, hoping to see him with Florence, as though she desired even more bitter confirmation of her suspicions. She knew she was being foolish, and when she felt like that, she pulled up all the rugs in the house, took them out into the twilit back garden and banged them till her arm seized up.

It wasn't until Sunday morning that she had any time alone with him. Before she left for Mass and he for the Wesleyan Mission, they both usually breakfasted together on bacon and eggs from his shop. This was a meal she couldn't avoid without making him question her. She was determined to act naturally and besides, it was a ritual she'd come to look forward to. It was still a novelty to have such an abundance of food coming into a house. Milly's mother had always eked out her housekeeping hand to mouth. Hers had been a diet of bread and jam or dripping, mutton stew and potatoes; with the old man getting the lion's share of the food. Eggs were a luxury and oranges were for Christmas, though sometimes a kindly docker would toss some pulpy fruit to the children hanging around the wharves, or they would sneak on to the barges and steal a net full of coconuts. Since coming to Bertie's, Milly had never felt so well fed. It was fortunate she went everywhere at a run, or else, she feared, she'd soon be challenging Ma Donovan's girth.

'Uncle wants me to take the stall to Horsmonden next weekend,' Bertie informed her, cutting into a slice of bacon. 'I know you've been miserable without the boy. How do you fancy a run out there with me?'

Milly paused, with a forkful of egg halfway to her mouth.

'Really, Bertie!'

'Yes, really, and if you don't put that in your mouth now you'll be turning up at Mass with half an egg yolk down your dress!'

*

The following Saturday afternoon she was looking out for him from behind the lace curtains in the front parlour. She'd been back and forth from the kitchen a dozen times since getting home from the factory. Excitement vied with apprehension. There was nothing she wanted more than to see Jimmy, but the journey to Kent with Bertie, which would otherwise have been a joyful prospect, was tainted by lingering shame and awkwardness at her own half-acknowledged feelings. When Bertie pulled up outside the house in his uncle's van, she snatched up her box, dropped it in her haste and had to hastily repack it, before dashing out to meet him.

'Ready for a spin?' He smiled proudly, then jumped out of the driver's seat, smart in tweed suit, driving gloves and cap.

Uncle's new delivery van was painted brown and cream, with *Hughes the Grocer* inscribed on the side. There were brown leather seats in the driver's cab and the front headlamps were of polished brass. When Bertie opened the back doors for her to look inside, she gasped. The van was packed to bursting with tins of food, large stone jars of jam and pickle, sacks of flour, sugar and a chest full of loose tea. There were drums of oil, pots, pans and any other hardware goods a hopping family might need. There wasn't an inch to spare.

'Looks like you've packed up the whole shop!'

'Well, Uncle's looking for a good profit this weekend. Takings are down, with everyone hop-picking. Arnold's Place is deserted!'

He helped her up into the cab, with her dented box of belongings, and she settled self-consciously into the seat next to him. Soon they were puttering along Jamaica Road on their way out to Kent. Compared to last year's trip in Pat's lorry, this was luxury, but she'd certainly felt more relaxed in the company of all the men, sitting up on the back board, singing the old hopping songs. This year, she was only a visitor, and felt a sense of loss that she wasn't at the heart of things. She felt nervously self-conscious, alone with Bertie in the close confines of the van, and painfully aware of how she'd let herself down. He hadn't said a word about that drunken night, but he must be thinking she'd reverted to type; perhaps he was even regretting getting into trouble with his uncle over her. But, as well as that, her unexpected reaction to the sight of him with Florence Green had startled her. It had been an illuminating moment, like walking out of a deeply shadowed wood into bright sunshine. One minute she was in the cool shade of an easy-growing friendship with Bertie, and the next, she was in the fierce glare of . . . what? Love? Milly hardly dared admit it to herself and she would struggle with all her being to return to that shady wood. Impulsively, she decided to tackle the awkwardness head on.

'Bertie, I've been meaning to say sorry, for coming home in such a two and eight the other night.'

She felt herself flush to the roots of her hair, grateful for the breeze streaming in through the open window. She shot a look at him, but his face was serious as he concentrated on the road ahead, where a horse-drawn cart was lumbering in front of them up Shooter's Hill. He shifted gear and she noticed, for the first time, the fine capable strength of his hands. He was a skilful driver. Once at the top of the hill, with the cart behind them, he turned to her, his flyaway eyebrows raised in amusement.

'It's nothing I've not seen before!' he chuckled. 'I watched you and Kitty Bunclerk rolling up blind drunk to the sewing circle. In fact I spent more time working out which of you would fall down first than I did listening to the lecture I was sitting in!'

She was mortified that he should have witnessed that particular episode, but she shouldn't be surprised he'd seen the funny side of it. Bertie never said what she expected him to. He was always a surprise.

'Don't look so embarrassed. I know why you had a drink too many the other night.'

I hope not! she thought silently. Bertie was nodding. 'Because you're missing Jimmy and there's all this going on with Elsie. Have you heard any more?' he asked.

'Nothing, except that we can visit in a few weeks. They say it's best to let her settle in first. Francis Beaumont and Florence Green

244

couldn't help us . . . but I don't blame them,' she added hastily.

'Florence said he did his best.'

'Oh, did she tell you that the other night?' She turned her face towards him and saw she'd taken him off-guard.

'When?'

'I saw you talking to her, when I was in sewing circle.'

Now it was his turn to blush. 'Oh, did you? Can't remember.' He turned his face back to the road. 'She got up Shooter's Hill all right, didn't she? Wonder how she'll manage Wrotham?' For a mad moment Milly thought he was still talking about Miss Green, and then realized he'd turned the conversation inexpertly to Uncle's new van.

'We normally have to get out and push,' she said.

As it was, the van took Wrotham Hill in its stride, and in fact the journey took half the time it had in Pat's old lorry. They had made such good time that, when the oast houses and hop farms came into view, Bertie suggested they stop to stretch their legs.

He turned off down a smaller country road, a green cathedral, arched with overhanging trees. Afternoon sun dappled the road ahead, which climbed steeply. Bertie changed gear and the van slowed as birds dipped across their path, stitching together the hedgerows on either side, seeming to beckon them on. Eventually Bertie pulled over.

'I wanted to show you this place. I used to come here as a boy with Mum and Dad.'

They jumped down, and Milly stretched gratefully.

Bertie said 'Follow me,' and led her down a narrow path to a clearing, where a little wooden bench had been hewn from a fallen tree.

Suddenly the view broke out before them and Milly let out a long sigh of delight. 'Oh, Bertie, it's like heaven!'

They were high up on a ridge, overlooking a patchwork of hop fields, corded with fresh green bines, and apple orchards folded between hedgerows. She could even make out the individual farms.

'Look, Bertie, I think that's our farm!'

And his eyes followed where her finger pointed, beyond the village.

'See if we can pick out Mum and Amy in the fields!'

But that was beyond either of their vision. Still, she was glad he'd given her this bird's-eye view of her beloved hop gardens. She might not be down there picking, but there were compensations to being a visitor. She had the time to take in the beauty of it all. Her mother would have no chance to look up from the papery hops; her eyes would be on the ever-filling bin. But Bertie had given Milly the opportunity to step back and gaze. He left her there, on the edge of the rise, with her hand shielding her eyes from the hazy sunshine. She was still lost in the scene before her when he came back, with a knapsack.

'How about a picnic lunch before we push on?'

'A picnic! Have you brought one?' She pulled herself away from the view and joined him on the bench, where he was opening up greaseproof paper parcels. She could see bread and cheese, half a pork pie and a stone bottle of ginger beer.

He handed her a hunk of bread. 'You're always surprising me, Bertie! I didn't know you'd planned this.'

Milly was so delighted with the secret, beautiful place that she forgot her awkwardness for a moment, her embarrassment faded and she began to be easy with him again. After they'd eaten, she slipped from the bench, contentedly stretching out her long legs on the grass.

'How old were you, when your mum and dad brought you here?' she asked.

'Oh, Dad was a great walker, he used to drag me and Mum out to Kent as often as he could. He discovered this place on one of his rambles. I must have seen it first in that scorcher of a summer, back in 1911, I think. You probably don't remember it, but I was about twelve, and I thought every summer would be like that.'

'I *do* remember that summer! I could only have been about five, but I remember following the ice-cream cart, singing "Hokey Pokey penny a lick", and the ice cream all melting, and me and

Wilf got underneath the cart, opened our mouths and just let the lemon ice pour in!'

They both laughed at the image.

'Just think, Bertie, you might have been up here, looking down on me, when I was hop-picking as a kid.'

'I might have been, but I lost Mum and Dad not long after, so that was the end of my country rambles.'

'Is that when you went to live with Uncle?'

Bertie pulled a face. 'I did, till the war, then I volunteered as soon as I could, lied about my age.'

'Like our Wilf, he was only sixteen.'

Bertie, like most of the men she'd known who'd been through the war, never spoke about it. She only knew he'd served and survived; the rest was easy to imagine.

'I was seventeen.' He turned clear blue eyes to her, the same colour as the wide sky above the fields. 'And this place,' he swept his arm to include the sky, the fields and farms, 'the thought of this place got me through it.'

She held the silence, not wanting a word of hers to stop him revealing the true heart of him.

'It was the place I remember being happiest, perhaps because I still had my parents, or because I thought the sun would go on shining forever and because, well, it's so beautiful. In a funny way this place is what I was fighting for, to keep it safe, just like this, forever. I didn't have anyone I loved to come back for, but I had this place and I knew I had to survive, and come back here one day.'

'And here you are.'

He turned to her and smiled. 'And here I am.'

Leaning back on to the warm silvered wood of the log bench, she smiled back at Bertie, and his eyes beneath the winged eyebrows met hers. Suddenly there it was again, blinding sunshine, drawing her out of the cool shaded wood that she'd thought would shield her from love forever. And whether it was the spell cast by the fairy-tale place or the generosity of his heart in bringing her here, to this beloved spot, when he leaned down to kiss her, she had no thought of ever returning to that cool shade. Her own heart leaped up to meet him in the full light of the sun, and once again Bertie Hughes surprised her, with the passion of his kisses and the strength of his embrace which had all the sureness of a man who knew exactly what he wanted.

As a child she had heard fairy tales of people falling into deep sleeps in such bowers as this, and being spirited away to marry the prince of the fairy folk. She squeezed her arms even tighter round Bertie and then braving the shattering of all her illusions, she pulled away, so that she could look him full in the eyes. They were shining, full of joyful surprise.

'Don't tell me I've surprised you too, Bertie Hughes?' she asked.

He opened his mouth to stutter, 'Y-yes! You have, but it's the best surprise I've ever had in my life! I didn't think you'd look twice at me, Milly.'

Turning to lean her head on his chest, she thought, *and neither did I!*

With his arm round her, they leaned back on the fallen tree trunk, while Milly let him ask all his questions about how and when she'd come to love him. It was hard for her to answer in ways that wouldn't disappoint him, for she hardly understood her feelings for him herself.

'So, a few months ago, you hadn't even thought of me?' he asked, a little crestfallen.

'A few weeks more like!' Seeing his face fall, she immediately wanted to soothe him. 'Well, I never imagined you'd want to hook up with someone like me, Bertie, not in a million years. Uncle said it all, didn't he? Besides,' she paused, 'I didn't think you were free.'

'What do you mean?' he said, with the eagerness of a new lover, anxious only to prolong that first conversation, endlessly fascinating to the two people whose lives were being bound together with every disclosure.

'I mean Florence Green,' she ventured, so softly that he had to ask her to repeat herself.

'What about her?' he asked.

'I thought you loved her!'

In answer he threw back his head and laughed, a little drunkenly, she thought.

'I like her, respect her, and we're friends, but no, I don't love her, Milly. And besides, she's engaged to Francis Beaumont!'

'But, I saw her kiss you on Thursday and then you looked so happy!' She ended with a sort of wail that sobbed into tears as the remembrance of her sudden, painful jealousy broke over her, mixing with her present heady happiness into a strong brew of emotions.

'You soppy date, I was happy because I'd just told her what I planned to do and she was congratulating me in advance.'

'What did you plan to do?'

Bertie took his arm from round her shoulders, and dug into his pocket. The ring was a single diamond on a claw clasp of platinum; the sun, now low in the sky, lifted warm glints from the facets.

'Milly Colman,' Bertie said, turning towards her, 'will you be my wife?'

She twined her arms round him, and forgetting how impossible it was, her answer was whispered softly against his cheek. 'Yes, Bertie, I will.'

It was hard afterwards for Bertie to drive them the short distance to the hop farm. He kept taking his eyes off the road, searching out Millie's gaze, almost as if he feared she would be spirited away. They talked all the rest of the way, about her confusion over Florence Green and his fear that she would refuse him. She learned that he'd loved her long before he found her on Fountain Stairs.

'Remember how everyone in Arnold's Place used to call you three sisters "the set of jugs"?'

She smiled at the memory.

'Well, I used to have eyes for only one. You would come into the shop, your poor beautiful face all screwed up with fear that you wouldn't get back home before your father, and all I wanted to do, even then, was say *Don't go home, stay here and let me look after you!*'

'Really, Bertie? Really?' But how hadn't she seen that? Where was her mind, where were her eyes? How could she have had this marvellous man so close, every day, and never have looked at him twice? How could she have ever considered anyone else?

'I'm sorry I didn't know,' she said gently.

He shrugged. 'It just wasn't the right time,' he said.

'I was a different person then,' she mused as he slowed the van and turned into the field of hopping huts, where she would stay with her mother and Amy. 'The best I could imagine for me was to escape the old man. I couldn't see further than that. I looked in the wrong place, I suppose.'

He turned to face her. 'Well, you've found the right place now, Milly.'

21

Stonefield

October–November 1924

For the rest of that hop season, every weekend saw Milly and Bertie making the trip to Horsmonden, in Uncle's brown and cream van. The weather was kind to them, the mild late summer easing gently into a mellow autumn, and on every trip it became their habit to stop on the high ridge above the garden of England, where Bertie had proposed. But for the forced separation from Jimmy, who was thriving in the country air, these were the happiest days Milly had ever known. Yet it wasn't until the last day of hop-picking that she was brave enough to tell her mother about her engagement to Bertie. She wasn't sure what had made her hesitate, but however good the match might seem, something made her fear her mother's reaction.

The cry from the pole-pullers – 'Pull no more bines!' – had gone up for the final time, the last hop had been picked, and this year's hop princess had been chased and garlanded. Milly had held Jimmy tight, hoping the princess's garland would protect the girl more than her own had. Afterwards the farmer paid them and they walked back to the huts, singing all the way, ready for a final evening of celebration in the village pub and then round the big bonfire.

Milly handed Jimmy over to Amy, who'd grown so close to him she could barely stand a few minutes' separation. The young girl swung him on to her hip and went to show him off to the other children playing in the centre of the field. Her mother sat heavily down on the chair outside the hopping hut, following Amy with a wistful gaze. Perhaps she was thinking of Elsie. Milly drew in a long breath; it would be now or never.

'Mum, I've got some really good news . . .'

Her mother's face brightened. 'Elsie?'

Milly shook her head and launched in. 'Me and Bertie's getting married!'

There was a long moment's silence.

'Bertie Hughes!' her mother said finally, shock written over with disbelief.

Milly had been right to hesitate, yet she was still surprised by her own sense of disappointment. God knows, they needed some happiness in the Colman family, and even if her mother only thought of practicalities, surely she must see that this marriage would secure her and Jimmy's future, to say nothing of making Milly respectable again?

Milly flushed with anger. 'Yes, Bertie Hughes! And what are you turning your nose up for?' She was seated opposite her mother, on an upended crate they used for a table.

Mrs Colman, still tight-lipped, ignored her question. 'Well, if you're sure he's what you want . . .'

'Mum! I thought you'd be pleased for me. He loves me and my Jimmy . . . and I love him!' she said defiantly.

'Do you?' Her mother's simple question was more painful than any words of condemnation. Besides, Milly didn't really understand her resistance. 'All right, just tell me what's wrong with him.'

Her mother sighed and then, as though explaining simplicities to an idiot, said, 'Well, he's not one of our own, is he?'

'Not one of our own! Mum, he was born in Dulwich, not Timbuktu! And you can't talk, your family's all from Ireland!'

Her mother sat with hands firmly planted on her knees. 'He's a Protestant.'

Milly groaned disbelievingly. 'So you'd rather I marry a Dockhead Catholic villain like Pat Donovan, who'll never be any good to me, *and* a man that I don't love, than see me marry Bertie Hughes!'

'Pat's the father of your child, Milly. Doesn't he deserve to give the boy his name if he's willing?'

'He deserves nothing,' Milly snapped, not wanting to let on that Pat had suggested the same. 'And in case you've forgotten, he wanted me to get rid of Jimmy! Anyway, he's banged up and it won't be the last time either.'

Her mother's list of excuses hadn't satisfied her and she pressed further, as Mrs Colman plucked at an invisible thread in her coarse, hop-stained apron.

'Tell me the real reason.' She looked at her mother's disappointed face, with its sad eyes and tight lines, formed by a thousand blows from the old man, and she knew this was more about her own disappointed hopes.

'Milly, love, don't marry Bertie Hughes just because you think life will be easier for you and the family with his money coming in. Don't do it. Money's not everything, gel.'

'You think I'm marrying him for his money?'

Milly shook her head in disbelief and walked away, before she said something she would regret. *Money's not everything!* Milly knew that, but every lesson she'd had from her mother's failed marriage had taught her not to undervalue its presence. *Money's not everything!* And this from the woman who had to pawn their clothes every week. Too proud to go herself, she would always pay Mrs Carney the extra coppers to do it for her. Sometimes her mother's contradictory reasoning infuriated her. She made her way along the lane, and, picking up a fallen branch, beat the long grass and the hedgerow as she went. And what was all that about her not marrying for love, when she'd already explained it was the very reason she didn't want Pat?

By the time she reached the village green, she had forgiven her mother. However much Mrs Colman got under her skin, Milly knew that all her muddled suggestions were only demonstrations of love. And knowing the life she'd had, how could Milly stay angry with her? Perhaps her mother had taken one too many blows to the head from the old man. Brain damage would certainly excuse her addled thinking.

Bertie and the other stallholders were packing away. She knew he'd spotted her across the green, though he carried on loading chests and jars into the van.

'What's the matter?' he asked as she came up to him. 'You're ruining that beautiful face with a scowl, you know.'

She growled. 'Ugh, my mother! I can't fathom her sometimes!' She and Bertie had talked about the best time to announce their engagement, and had both agreed her mother should be the first to know. Understanding dawned on his face.

'You told her. What did she think, that I'm too old for you?' he asked quickly.

'No, Bertie, love, that was the one thing she didn't complain about.'

'Strike me dumb, Milly, I thought at least she'd see it would be security for you and the boy. I almost don't want to ask.' He slammed both van doors shut and leaned his back against the van. Then, taking her elbow, he walked her to the edge of the green where they sat together on a little bench.

Milly thought he was taking her mother's disapproval very well, but then she was finding that Bertie had a resilient core, one that wouldn't bend to pressure, especially if he believed in something strongly. She thanked her stars that he had believed in her enough to see past the bad reputation, the illegitimate child and her boisterous ways.

She catalogued her mother's reservations, leaving out the accusation that had troubled her the most – that she'd agreed to marry Bertie only because of his position, his comfortable home and income. It had set up a ripple of self-doubt that made her feel uneasy.

As she reached the end of his shortcomings, he heaved a sigh and said, 'See that sign?' He pointed to one of the nearby village shops, which had been re-enforced with shutters and chicken wire.

A white-painted board read *No hop-pickers*. 'Well, Dockhead's no different when it comes to outsiders. She'll come round, once she gets to know me.'

Milly only hoped his faith in human nature would be proved right.

More than six weeks had passed since Elsie's admittance to the asylum. They had received a letter telling them visiting times, but Elsie hadn't written and they'd heard nothing about her. Freddie hadn't seen his brother, who lived in staff accommodation at the asylum, which by all accounts was like a small village. Self-sufficient, with its own farm, Bob had told her they owned a herd of cows for milk, pigs, sheep, chickens and vegetable allotments. They even had their own well and gasworks. The inmates formed the workforce, maintaining the buildings, running the farm and generating much of the income needed to run the place by selling shoes, sacks and ironwork made in the asylum workshops. There was no reason to call on the local towns and villages for anything; they were like a self-contained island in the low-lying Kent marshland that surrounded the asylum. There was a laundry, a carpentry shop, a chapel, and every need, physical and spiritual, was catered for, except the need for freedom.

Milly, her mother and Amy took the bus all the way from Tower Bridge Road. Hour after hour of jolting and stopping took its toll on them all. Amy had to be sick in a paper bag, which her mother tucked neatly under the seat, behind her polished tie-up shoes. They were all in Sunday best, Mrs Colman wearing the only hat she possessed, stuck firmly with pins, Milly in her coffee and cream outfit, and Amy in Elsie's old best dress.

'How do you think she's been?' her mother asked Milly pointlessly.

'Oh, you know Elsie. She's been in a world of her own, probably loves it there with all the gardens and trees. Bob Clark said they've even got a recreation hall, with a stage. She's probably been putting on shows!'

Her mother smiled wanly, unconvinced by Milly's forced optimism. But, as the bus descended to Stonefield's bleak approach, the picture she'd tried to paint of Elsie's idyllic life in the asylum was firmly shattered. The place sprawled over a vast area. Two long, darkly forbidding, Victorian buildings loomed up, with rows of sharp-toothed Gothic windows, and wings jutting out at either end. As they descended from the bus and passed through the massive, wooden-arched door, Milly felt she was entering a mixture of church, court and prison. All the comforting fantasies melted away.

'This place is horrible!' Amy's voice, echoing in the vaulted entrance hall, spoke for them all. 'I don't want to go in.' She stopped dead and refused to go any further, holding up the other visitors filing in behind them. Amy was cringing against her mother's side. If such a normally defiant creature had been cowed into submission already, Milly doubted there was any hope for Elsie.

'Don't show me up!' Her mother stood, self-consciously rigid, looking towards a white-capped, blue-skirted matron, who was bearing down upon them. The matron clapped her hands against the confused hubbub.

'Visiting families, please follow me!' she said, and set off briskly, leading them down a seemingly endless corridor.

Amy dragged on her mother's skirt so much that Ellen Colman was in danger of losing it. Seeing her mother's mounting distress, Milly grabbed Amy's hand, swinging her away. She wished they'd left her with Mrs Knight as they had done Jimmy, but the girl had insisted she wanted to see her sister – though Milly thought there might have been some ghoulish interest from Barrel and Ronnie, in 'the nuthouse', which Amy had promised to satisfy.

'Listen, you wanted to come, now stop acting the goat!' she scolded her. 'Mum's upset enough as it is.'

Amy's wriggling hand was no match for her own strength, and somehow they managed to keep up with Matron and the other scurrying visitors. The corridor ended in a vast recreation hall, which looked almost as big as Dockhead Church. At one end was a curtained-off stage and all round was a high gallery, filled with seats. The hall had been set out with tables and chairs, and each table was numbered. Matron came to each family in turn, giving them a number and ticking their names off a list. Once everyone was seated at a table, a bell rang and a single file of inmates was led in by an attendant in a brass-buttoned, blue serge uniform. The inmates were all female, but Milly was shocked to see some were white-haired and frail. She had somehow assumed that Elsie would just be with girls her own age. The parade of inmates included many children, some of whom had difficulty walking and had to be individually attended; some who made startling sounds, wails or barks, which had Amy jumping nervously in the chair. Now, instead of pulling away, she put out her hand and grabbed Milly's, who, feeling Amy trembling, squeezed hard in reassurance as a middle-aged woman came towards them asking, 'Where's my baby, has anyone brought my baby to visit?'

She was immediately swept off by a nurse, who crooned, 'Your baby's at home, Dotty, with his grandmother, don't you remember?' But the woman repeated the question, until eventually bursting into tears and yelling, 'I know you killed my baby.'

A well-dressed man in a dark suit rose from a table and came up to her gently. 'Now, Dot, don't be silly, the baby's fine.' But Milly could tell he was lying, and had a pretty good idea what had happened to Dot's baby all those years ago.

'Where's my Elsie?' her mother asked fretfully.

The line seemed endless; a hundred inmates must have passed them already. But then Milly spotted her, squashed behind an obese woman. Giving a huge, toothless grin as she spied her family, the woman waddled off to one side, leaving Elsie exposed and vulnerable, weak eyes searching every table until she saw them. She started to run, but was held back by the attendant.

'No running.'

Elsie checked herself. Her eyes were fixed on the three of them and Milly noted that they looked even larger and paler in her face, which had sharpened to a knife-like point, she had become so skinny. Her dress and white pinafore were two sizes too big, reaching almost to the floor. Her hair had grown and was tied back tightly so that all the bony edges of her face were visible beneath the pale skin. There was no pretty bow for Elsie in here. She came and sat down behind the table. And immediately her shoulders began to shake.

'Wh-why, wh-y,' she heaved in a sob and as she let go, cried, 'wh-why did you le-leave me here?'

Her mother ran round the table and squashed her tightly against her breast, crying herself now. 'Oh, love, we tried, we couldn't do nothing about it! Milly went and got a lawyer and everything.'

Elsie looked pitifully at Milly. 'But you're taking me home now, ain't you? I don't have to stay here any more?'

'Elsie, we can't take you home today, love, you've got to be brave,' Milly said.

But Elsie was inconsolable. She seemed unable to believe there was no hope of her going home, and Milly, who had known her own much milder form of incarceration at Edenvale, felt sure that if she were going to survive, her sister had to have some hope.

'Elsie, listen to me, did you do as I said, and ask for garden duty?' she asked urgently.

Elsie nodded, unpinned a handkerchief from the pinafore and blew her nose noisily.

Milly noticed it was the one embroidered with *Milly*, which she'd given her in the police station. It was somehow comforting to think that Elsie had managed to keep hold of this little piece of home.

'And did you meet Bob, the gardener?'

She nodded again and said weakly, 'He's my friend. He let me help him plant a tree and everything.' The young girl smiled to herself suddenly. 'It was such a pretty tree and he said it was called a Tree of Heaven. And I told him he'd got that wrong, cos it must be a tree of hell in this bleedin' place.' And they all laughed with relief, that some spark of Elsie's fire was still burning.

'Well, love, Bob promised us he'd look after you, so behave yourself and they'll let you stay working in the gardens,' Milly said.

'They've got me in the laundry too, sewing sheets and pinafores.'

She held up sore fingers for their inspection.

'And do you get enough to eat, love?' her mother asked. 'You're looking so thin.'

Elsie shifted on the chair. There was so little flesh on her, Milly knew that sitting on the hard wood must be uncomfortable.

'There's enough grub, I suppose. We've got real chicken's eggs and proper meat from pigs and we get milk. But it all makes me sick. Can you bring in some bread and dripping next time? And bring Jimmy to see me,' she added.

Her mother promised she would and then, after distracting Elsie with Dockhead gossip for another half-hour, came the moment they were all dreading. A brass bell sounded the end of visiting hours. Elsie jumped, her eyes widened and she began to cry again.

Ignoring all her mother's attempts to soothe her, she turned red-rimmed eyes towards Milly, and in a low, choked voice said, 'It was you got me in here, so you bloody well come back and get me out of it! You get me out, or I'll never forgive you!' Her voice was rising to a shrill scream and as she threw off her mother's encircling arms, she drew the attention of the attendant, who came over to see what the commotion was all about.

'That's my sister,' she shouted as her arms were grasped and she was dragged away. 'She'll come back for me!'

Milly's legs felt like water as she rose from the seat and trailed back down the long corridor. Outside, a mizzle of rain fell from a leaden sky, turning the hulking, many-winged building a dull black. It seemed to gather its wings above them, warding them off, barring any way back, guarding her sister like a black-scaled beast that Milly felt powerless to fight. Feeling utterly defeated by the unassailable authority hanging over the place, she got on to the bus home without looking back, leaving Elsie, and hope, far behind.

The days and weeks that followed twined about her like a many-coloured thread. The gold of her happiness in Bertie's love and their plans for a future together were inextricably bound to the black strand of sadness she felt whenever she thought of Elsie's life. She didn't believe it was her fault that Elsie was at Stonefield, but it was enough that her sister did. And then another colour wove itself in, the silver of her mother's hair, all turned grey now, with the struggle to protect Amy, and herself, from the old man's sustained violence.

So when Bertie suggested one day that they marry sooner, rather than later, she found herself hoping that somehow her marriage would be a solution, and that her own happiness would lessen the sadness of those she loved.

She wasn't sorry to miss the next visit to Stonefield. Jimmy came down with whooping cough and she couldn't leave him, so it was from her mother that she learned of Elsie's further decline.

'There's nothing of her, Milly, skin and bone. I don't like the look of her.'

Her mother had come straight from the bus stop after visiting Stonefield and still had Amy with her. Milly made them tea and toast, and they were now sitting in front of the fire, trying to get warm. The place seemed to have that effect, and last time Milly had taken days to get the chill out of her bones.

'And she's gone off in a world of her own, you know how she used to, only worse. I don't like the look of her,' she repeated, in a tone that Milly had heard the women of Dockhead use only of the dying. Milly could give no words of comfort. Instead she dug out a slab of cheese and some eggs from the larder, and parcelled them up.

260

'Here, take these home, and don't you dare give any to the old man. Hide it. You two look like you're fading away as well. Doesn't the bastard give you any housekeeping at all, these days?'

'I think he's got himself a fancy woman,' her mother mouthed under her breath so that Amy wouldn't hear, though her sister was bright enough to know when her mother was speaking 'deedee', as it was known in Arnold's Place, and looked up sharply.

'Don't be stupid, Mother, who'd have him?' Milly said tersely.

Her mother pursed her lips. 'They say he's very free with his money in the Swan and Sugarloaf, doling out drinks to gawd knows who, and the money goes somewhere, that's all I'll say.' Her mother bent to pick up the rusty-black handbag at her side. 'Say thank you to Bertie for the cheese and eggs,' she said, picking up the parcel from the table.

'I will!'

She saw them off and went back to the fire, musing over what she could do for her Elsie.

The next day as they left the factory for their dinner break, she took Kitty's arm.

'Are you seeing Freddie this week?' she asked.

'We're going to the Grange Picture Palace tomorrow, want to come? You could bring Bertie!'

She was grateful that her friend was making an effort to get to know Bertie now, but this was one time when she didn't want him to join them. She shook her head. 'No, not this week, Kit. I really wanted to have a word with Freddie about his brother Bob.'

'Oh, is it your Elsie? What's happened?'

And Milly told her about her mother's visit. 'I know Bob's been kind to her. I just wondered if he was coming home at all, or if Fred can get a message to him?'

'Leave it to me, love. Me and Fred . . .' Kitty waggled her little finger and smiled. 'I get anything I ask, love, anything I ask!'

Milly's wedding day was fixed for the week before Christmas. She and Bertie would be married in a Catholic ceremony at Dockhead

Church. 'There's no point in upsetting your mum any more than she already is,' Bertie had said when she broached the subject. 'It's all the same God,' he'd added lightly, putting aside his own Wesleyan affiliations to make life easier for her.

'Bertie, you're a diamond!' she'd said, hugging him, grateful for his easy-going ways. After a life spent under the shadow of the old man's tyranny, Milly still hadn't got used to a man who was happy to defer to her, a man who seemed to turn every stony path into a pleasant country lane. She'd slowly begun to understand how rare a person Bertie was; he seemed to carry within him his own happiness and so she never felt the burden of having to supply it.

She made her own wedding dress, glad that it couldn't be white and traditional. Instead, she bought from Petticoat Lane a bolt of brand-new ivory watermarked silk, the like of which she'd never been able to afford on factory wages alone. Copying from the latest fashions, she created a low-waisted, double-skirted dress, with three-quarter-length sleeves and a chiffon shawl. Sometimes the current shorter hems left her feeling like a leggy colt, so for her wedding dress, where she wanted to look and feel like a lady, she chose a soft handkerchief hem, which flowed and softened her legs. Though she'd wanted no bridesmaids, Amy had looked so disappointed that she'd relented.

During Amy's fitting one Saturday afternoon, Milly noticed a change in her sister. She kneeled in front of Amy with a mouthful of pins, adjusting the hem to the pale peach satin dress. She'd been so full of excitement at being a bridesmaid, but now Milly sensed that an unusual lethargy had crept over her, dulling all her quicksilver energy. As she sat back on her haunches, studying the hem, Milly lifted the material and noticed a row of dark purple bruises on the backs of her legs.

'What have you been up to, playing British Bulldog with Barrel again?' she asked, naming the roughest of the warlike games that Amy delighted in. The girl hastily tried to pull the dress down.

'The old man?'

'He kicked me upstairs, said I'd cheeked him, but I hadn't!' Amy's lower lip trembled.

The youngest Colman sister had always seemed to Milly the strongest, but since Elsie's departure, she'd noticed patches in her armour. Whereas once she would never give an inch in an argument with Milly, now she caved in, resorting to tears, and though she still ran with the gang of urchins around Dockhead, sometimes at the end of her working day, Milly would find her waiting watchfully outside Southwell's gates, with Jimmy in his pram. She had always been one of three, and now she was just one, a single vulnerable target.

Milly pulled her in close. 'Now listen to me, if he starts on you again, you run out the house and come round here to me and Bertie, d'ye hear? Don't matter what time it is, you come straight to me!'

'But you'll send me back, and then it'll be worse.'

That was true. Even though Bertie's uncle owned the shop, he still only received a salary – a good one compared to a docker, but there was still not enough coming in to support two families.

'I'd take you in if I could,' she said. But no doubt Amy, like Elsie, thought of Bertie as a rich man, and, compared with most of the residents of Arnold's Place, she supposed he was.

After Amy's fitting she sent her home with a jar of Southwell's jam and a basin of brawn: her mother had said the old man was increasingly absent and there was precious little coming in for food. She took Jimmy with her to the front door to wave Amy off, and saw Bertie turning the corner into Storks Road. As Amy skipped up to him, he stooped to listen to her. No doubt she was prattling on about the bridesmaid's dress. He ruffled her hair as she went on her way, clutching the parcel of food. He had a nice way with children, Milly mused. He was patient with Jimmy and was happy to give her son the Hughes name. One day, perhaps, she would give him a child of his own.

The thought made her smile dreamily to herself, and this was how he came upon her, standing in the doorway. Jimmy wriggled in her arms. At five months, his first tooth was coming through and he'd been unhappy all morning. Even Amy hadn't been able to pacify him. But now he began excitedly twirling his little fists as he saw Bertie approach with outstretched arms. It was Jimmy's favourite game of the moment and Bertie never disappointed him. He caught him from her arms, tossed him into the air and was rewarded with the baby's throaty chuckle.

'What were you smiling at?' He shot her a look as he caught the baby.

'Ohhh, I was just thinking, you'll make a good dad.'

As he held the little boy in the crook of his arm, Milly saw his face grow serious. He handed Jimmy back to her. 'There's something I need to talk to you about, Milly.'

'Gawd, don't tell me you've changed your mind. I've made me dress!' she said, laughing. But when he didn't laugh back a tightness caught at her chest and she steeled herself, immediately thinking the worst. What an idiot she'd been to believe that such an impossibly good man could ever be hers.

She was about to ask him to explain, when they heard a loud banging on the front door.

'I bet you a pound to a penny that's Amy back already! I told her to come to me if the old man started on her!' She marched back down the passage and flung open the door.

'Who is it?' called Bertie from the kitchen.

There was a long pause before she called back.

'It's Elsie!'

22

She Didn't Come for Me

November–December 1924

'Get in here!'

Milly yanked her sister into the passage and slammed the door shut behind them. Her breath came in shallow gasps, and she felt trapped in the narrow confines of the passage.

'What are you doing here?' she demanded.

'You didn't come for me,' said Elsie.

'*Jesus*, Mary and Joseph! What have you done?'

Elsie's emaciated face was streaked with dirt and sweat, and beneath the shapeless asylum dress, her concave chest was heaving. Surely she couldn't have run all the way from Kent? At that moment Bertie came out of the kitchen, paused for a beat and then whistled. 'Strike me dumb, that's crowned it,' he said. 'You'd better bring her in.'

As Elsie staggered forward, Bertie ran to catch her. He carried her into the kitchen, sitting her carefully in his chair, closest to the fire. She was trembling uncontrollably, little jerks visible as she tried to steady herself. He took off his cardigan and draped it round her bony shoulders.

Milly's impulse to fire questions at the girl was held in check by Bertie's small shake of the head. 'All in good time. Let's get her a drink, eh?'

Milly went silently to the kitchen, too shocked to even imagine how her sister had managed the twenty-mile journey from Stonefield on her own, when she'd only ever travelled outside of Bermondsey on the hoppers' special. All the while she made tea, she could hear the ticking of the kitchen clock, punctuated by a low sobbing from Elsie and Bertie's mumbled reassurances.

'It's all right, Elsie, you're home now,' he said, but Milly wanted to shout from the scullery that it was not all right, it was all wrong, and Elsie had a world of pain coming to her when they came to cart her back to the asylum again.

When she came in with the tea, Bertie was sitting opposite Elsie, her birdlike hand in his. 'Drink your tea, duck, and tell us what happened,' he coaxed as Elsie gripped his hand.

'She didn't come for me!' She looked accusingly at Milly. 'So I run away!'

Milly held her tongue and let Bertie prompt her sister.

'But how did you get out in the first place?'

She gulped the tea and then held the cup out to Milly for more.

'I was working in the garden with Bob. All day we was planting tulips and he was telling me about all the colours you can get: yellow and red, striped and even black. So we finished all the beds and I was hungry, 'cause I can't eat their grub and I didn't want to go back in there because there's a woman sleeps near me, keeps waking me up and saying I'm her baby and it upsets me. And I just sat down on the garden bench and I said to Bob, I think I'll just sleep here tonight, and he looks at me funny. But Bob's lovely, he never tells me off if I can't do the gardening. Sometimes I just sit and watch him and he tells me all about collecting the seeds, so you have something for next year.'

Milly was about to jump in and hurry Elsie along, her nerves stretched to breaking point. She didn't know how long they'd have before the police came knocking for her sister. But Bertie read her fidgets and gave her a look she'd come to understand. She sat back obediently, letting Elsie's story tumble out. The clock ticked as Elsie slurped more tea, and Milly noticed her lips were cracked. She got up and went to the scullery, coming back with yet more tea, a plate of sliced bread and a bowl of dripping.

Elsie looked on hungrily while Milly spooned out the yellow fat and dark jelly, spreading it over the bread. She fell upon it as though she hadn't eaten since she'd walked into Stonefield. After she'd wolfed it all down, she licked her fingers and stared into the fire.

'If you'd come for me, I wouldn't have had to run away,' she said to the fire as it flickered and crackled. 'Bob says to me, *You don't have to go back inside, Elsie.* And then he gives me a shilling and says, *You can get a forty-seven all the way to Tower Bridge, and you know your way home from there, don't you? Just follow the river.* And I said I did. Then he says, *I'm going home now, Elsie, but I'm going out by the side garden gate and you can come and see me off.* So I followed him to the little door in the wall, and he says goodnight and he goes . . . but he leaves the door open a crack. And after a bit I walked through it. I went to the first bus stop I could find and I asked the conductor if he was going to Tower Bridge and he said yes, so I give him the shilling, but he said it was too much and he didn't have no change, so to keep the shilling.' She dug into her apron pocket to produce the shilling. 'So I sat on the bus for hours and hours, and when I see Tower Bridge and the river, I knew I was home.'

Elsie yawned. Calmer now that she had told her story, her eyes began to droop. Bertie lifted her up as though she were no lighter than Jimmy, and Milly followed him upstairs, where she tucked Elsie into bed as though she were a child. As she fell into an immediate sleep, Bertie looked on while Milly undid her hair from its severe tie, letting it fall loose on the pillow. Then going to her chest of drawers, she brought out the prettiest bow she could find and fastened it in Elsie's hair.

'She loves a pretty ribbon,' she explained, looking up at Bertie with tears streaming down her face.

Bertie put his arms round her and they crept downstairs together. He quietly closed the kitchen door behind them, so that Elsie wouldn't be disturbed, and held Milly close.

'Don't cry, Milly. It's not your fault, you know,' he said, holding her away from him and looking intently into her eyes.

'I know, but it breaks my heart I couldn't keep her out of that place and sometimes I think, if only I'd given her the money for that bloody dress!'

'But you didn't *have* the money.'

It was the plain truth, and for an instant gave her relief from the punishing cycle of guilt she'd got herself into, since her first visit to Stonefield.

'But what are we going to do with her? How can we let them take her back there? It would kill her.'

Bertie sat down, pulling her into his lap. 'We'll think of something. She's safe here for a while.'

'But she can't stay here. What sort of a life can she live? She'll be forever looking over her shoulder, waiting for someone to report her. And besides, Bertie, you want to be a councillor one day. How's it going to look if you've been hiding a criminal?'

He shook his head dismissively. 'They'll go to Arnold's Place first. They might not even think to come here. How would they know that you live in my house?'

She hadn't thought of that. She jumped up. 'I'd better get round me mum's and warn her!'

But he caught her before she could dash out. 'Hold up, you're best to stay with Elsie and Jimmy. I'll go.'

He put on his jacket and trilby hat and she smoothed his collar, then let her hand rest gently on his cheek.

'You look tired, love,' she said, noticing the dark circles under his eyes, and suddenly remembering how serious he'd looked earlier when he'd arrived home.

'You never told me what we needed to talk about.'

He kissed her on the cheek. 'That can wait, duck, best get a move on!'

While he was gone, she sat beside the fire, making a little winter coat for Jimmy. Sewing usually calmed and distracted her, but tonight she was getting little done, and, more often than not, the material fell to her lap as she imagined how her mother would take the news. She would probably want to rush round to see Elsie, but Milly only hoped Bertie would be firm with her. Nothing went unnoticed in Arnold's Place and once the news of Elsie's return was common knowledge, it would soon filter down Tooley Street to Tower Bridge nick. And she should have told Bertie not to say a word if the old man was there . . . but he wasn't stupid. She sewed a button on to the wrong side of the coat and gave up in exasperation. Eventually she heard him open the front door.

'She wouldn't take no for an answer!' he said as she gave him a withering look.

'My child needs me!' Her mother began unbuttoning her coat. 'And may I not move from this spot till I've seen her! Now you take me to her.'

She'd come out dressed still in her old apron and slippers. Poor Bertie, Milly should have known he'd be no match for her mother, when it came to one of her set of jugs.

Milly led her upstairs and watched as her mother sat gently on the side of the bed, taking Elsie's hand and kissing it over and over. 'Oh, me poor baby,' was all she said. 'I swear, Milly, sometimes I've felt like murdering that old bastard for what he's done to her, and if he dropped down dead tomorrow, I wouldn't be sorry. No, as God's my judge, I wouldn't.'

Milly joined her mother at the bedside. Stroking her daughter's hair back from her head, Mrs Colman smiled. 'Did you put the bow in her hair?'

'Yes, it makes her look more herself.'

'You're a good sister, and don't let her tell you any different. She'll want to be blaming you for everything, but don't you listen to her.'

Their mother knew them all so well, knew them and loved them in spite of their faults. Milly only hoped that she would be as understanding to Jimmy as he grew up. Right now, he was perfect, but she had no illusions he would stay that way.

Elsie stirred, her eyes fluttered open and she saw her mother. For a moment, confusion clouded her face. Then realizing she was home, she sat up, threw her arms round her mother's neck and sobbed.

Ellen Colman couldn't be coaxed from Elsie's side, so she slept in the bed with her and next morning, very early, she left, so as to be home before Amy woke. Milly still wasn't sure what would happen to her, but Elsie seemed to have been restored by their mother's visit. It was an almost visible change, as if suddenly there was more flesh on her bones. There was certainly a brightness in her eyes that had been absent yesterday.

'I'm going to Mass, and Bertie's going to chapel. Will you be all right on your own?' she asked. 'Don't, whatever you do, go out and don't answer the door to no one, hear me?'

Elsie nodded, but asked if she could go into the garden. Milly doubted anyone would see her there. Bertie had planted so many climbing roses, which even when bare of blooms still formed a rambling screen round the narrow backyard.

'All right, love, but wrap up in one of my coats if you do. It's chilly this morning.' And when Milly came back from Mass, Elsie was still outside. Peeking through the scullery window, she saw her sister passing up and down the garden beds, collecting seed heads in her apron.

Milly made a point of leaving early for the factory the next day, so that she had time to talk to her mother. She felt like a convict on the run herself as she ran the gauntlet of Arnold's Place. Women were already up and about, banging carpets, coughing and flinching as dust rose, or standing at front doors gossiping, arms wrapped round themselves against the cold. Some were turning children out of the house, getting them from under their feet, and a few men emerged, slamming doors, ringing hobnailed boots on the paving as they went off to docks and factories.

Mrs Knight was scrubbing her front doorstep and wanted to talk, but Milly waved and hurried on, keen to avoid any of the normal questions about 'your poor sister'. Mrs Carney was already making her rounds, picking up bundles for the pawnshop, and she was just emerging from her mother's house. She was a small woman to be burdened with so many bundles.

'Hello, ducks, I've just been telling your poor mother, there's so many want me services these days, I have to start early, otherwise I'd never get it all done!' She clucked like a scratching hen. 'I'm thinking of getting meself a pram to carry it all!'

Milly didn't doubt the pawnshop was doing a trade. Southwell's had already started laying off women, and the crowds of unemployed casuals at the docks, hanging around on the off chance of half a day's work, were growing by the day. She dodged past the old woman.

'Can't stop, Mrs Carney, I'll be late myself!'

She went in, handing Jimmy over to her mother, before going to the front window. She checked up and down the street, but there was still nothing unusual going on. 'I reckon you'll have a copper knocking on your door today, Mum. So remember what I said, not a word about me or Bertie or Storks Road!'

'I know, I know! I'll just say I've not seen hide nor hair of her.'

'Yes, but can you act surprised?'

''Course I can act surprised. Don't think I've survived all these years with the old man without being able to swear black's blue and keep a straight face, gawd forgive me.' She crossed herself.

'Does Amy know?'

Mrs Colman raised her eyes. 'She spotted me coming in this morning, eventually got it out of me, didn't she?'

Milly groaned. 'That's it then. It'll be all over Dockhead by tonight, once she's told Barrel.'

'Well, I've give her the gypsy's warning.'

'And we know how much notice she takes of that!' said Milly, thinking of the times Amy had laughed in the face of her mother's threats. Perhaps she would have to administer her own brand of warning, which Amy usually took more notice of.

'I noticed bruises on her legs,' she ventured and then wished

271

she hadn't. Her mother's eyes filled with tears and her hand covered her mouth.

'I'm at my wits' end, trying to keep her out of his way. It comes to something when you can't even protect your own children.'

Milly knew, more than ever since giving birth to Jimmy, what agonies of remorse her mother must have gone through during all the years of their childhood.

'Don't worry, Mum. I've told her to come to me, if it happens again.'

Her mother gave her a long look, and then a brief nod. Milly took it as unspoken permission to kick her father from one end of Bermondsey Wall to the next, if he laid a hand on Amy again.

At dinner time she went with Kitty to the café in Tooley Street. It was impossible to talk to her in the factory without someone overhearing them. Once they'd found a table and been served with sandwiches and cups of tea, she leaned forward and whispered, 'I've got a bone to pick with your chap!'

'What's he done? Wasn't something wrong with them tins of fruit he give your mum, was there?'

Milly shook her head. 'Bob's sprung Elsie!'

Kitty's eyes widened and she choked on her bacon sandwich. She leaned forward.

'She's out?'

Milly nodded. 'She's in Bertie's house!'

'Oh, Milly, are you sure it was Bob?'

'He left the bloody gate open for her, Kit! I never told Freddie to do that. I just wanted him to find out from Bob how she was!'

'I don't think Freddie told him to do it. I'm sure he was just joking that time he mentioned it,' she said uncertainly. 'I wouldn't put it past Bob, though. He's such a soft 'apporth, he's likely felt sorry for her and done it on the spur of the moment. But I'll find out.'

'Well, either way, it's a bit late now, love, unless he knows some way of smuggling her back in before they notice she's gone!'

By the time she picked up Jimmy, it was too late to smuggle Elsie anywhere. Her mother told her she'd given a performance worthy of the films. When the policeman knocked, she'd been indignant, and Milly knew that her mother could do indignant very well. Stonefield, she'd said, was meant to be protecting her child and now she could be anywhere, with no money, no food. What were they going to do about it, she'd demanded, and the young policeman had spent a half-hour drinking dark brown tea and offering apologies, never once suggesting that Mrs Colman could know anything of her daughter's whereabouts.

For the rest of that week, Elsie stayed sequestered in Storks Road, seemingly happy to occupy herself helping with laundry and housework. It was almost as though she'd grown so used to being without her freedom that the idea of leaving the house never occurred to her. She seemed simply happy to be home, and happy as well to be in Milly's company. They sat in the evenings sewing contentedly together, and once her mother brought Amy to see Elsie. Not to be left out, Amy insisted on taking up a piece of sewing herself.

Mrs Colman looked on wonderingly. 'Jesus, Mary and Joseph, I never thought I'd see me matching set of jugs with not a cross word between 'em!'

It had been over a week since Elsie came to them, and Milly thought it odd when Bertie came home the following Saturday and suggested they go for a walk in Southwark Park. The weather had turned icy and grey skies threatened snow. It wasn't a day for a walk in the park. What's more, Elsie couldn't risk going out and it seemed mean to leave her alone at home. When Bertie suggested they leave Jimmy with her, Milly grew uneasy. This simply wasn't like him. Perhaps he was having second thoughts about sheltering Elsie? If he did, then Milly hadn't a clue what she would do with her sister.

On the way to the park, Milly slipped her arm through Bertie's, leaning in to steal some of his warmth, glad at least of some time alone with him. Since Elsie's arrival they'd hardly had a minute to themselves and even though she saw him every day, she'd missed him. There were plenty of hardy little gangs of children hurtling about when they arrived, but only a few brave couples, who, like themselves, had nowhere else more private to go. Bertie usually walked at an amble, and her long legs always outpaced his, but today he strode, almost at a run, as soon as they entered the park.

'What's the rush?' she asked, tugging his arm. 'Now we're out, we might as well enjoy the walk!'

But he didn't slow down, or even acknowledge her. His face looked set, almost as though he were walking into battle, rather than an afternoon stroll with his sweetheart.

'Bertie, what's the matter?' She drew in a breath. 'Look, if you've had enough of Elsie staying, I'd understand. I'll find somewhere else for her.'

He shook his head. 'It's not that. It's . . . Oh, Milly, I'm sorry but . . .' He stopped in the middle of the path, seemingly unable to finish his sentence. She'd never seen him so agitated.

'But what? Bertie, spit it out. You're making me worried now.'

'Milly, I can't marry you!' It came out in a rush, his tone harsher than she'd ever heard it. 'I'm sorry, I can't marry you.'

With one deft slice, he had cut the heart from her, as though she were nothing more than a damson, to be stoned and tossed into a basket. She seemed to be looking at herself, cut open, flesh gaping, jagged and torn, an empty cavity where her heart should have been. Desperately wanting the words unsaid, or to have at least misunderstood them, she forced herself to speak.

'I don't understand. What do you mean, you can't marry me?' she said, her voice high and thin, straining against the constriction of her throat.

He tried to get her to walk on, but stunned to the core, she found herself unable to move. Now she understood why he'd chosen to do it here. He'd probably hoped that in a public place she'd rein in her tears and not make a scene, but he didn't know her as well as he thought. Decorum had never been one of her strong points and no matter how much he urged her on, she wouldn't give in but stood stock-still in the path, blocking the way of a young couple, who looked on curiously then hurried round them.

He laid his hand on her elbow. 'Let's go to the flower garden – we can talk better there.'

She shrugged it off. 'Don't tell me I'm showing you up! You should have thought of that, Bertie Hughes, before you asked a common factory girl to marry you!'

His lips were white in his pale face, she could see him swallowing dryly and, as he spun her towards him, his bright blue eyes turned stormy grey.

'I'm *not* ashamed of you! And if you'd just let me explain my reason, you'll understand it's for the best!'

'For the best!' Exactly what she'd told Pat, an empty phrase from an empty heart.

She wished she could feel more anger; it would surely hurt less. But instead she felt utterly betrayed. She knew there was only one way out of her pain. She had to let him speak, let him explain himself, and then persuade him otherwise. She began walking ahead of him, fighting down panic and tears of incomprehension. She had been so sure of him, sure of his goodness, sure that they could overcome all the obstacles of class and temperament, but now all her certainty proved as insubstantial as the flurries of snow whipping around the bare trees, melting on her face like so many cold tears. At the flower garden, she headed for a secluded arbour. Hugging her long wrap-around coat tightly to her, she put up the collar against a sharp breeze cutting across the beds. Bertie sat beside her, leaning forward, hands clasped so tightly that she could see his knuckles whiten.

'Remember, just before Elsie turned up, I said I had something to tell you?'

'Yes,' she said, 'I've been so caught up with Elsie, I forgot all about it.' She found she was holding herself rigid against the cold and against the words that Bertie was speaking, so that she trembled with the effort to keep still. 'So you've been wanting to call it off ever since then?'

He shook his head. 'No! I don't *want* to call it off, but I *have* to!' he said in an agonized voice.

'But why? What's changed? Don't you love me any more?' she whispered, with a sob.

His hand found hers. Still looking straight ahead, his fingertips lightly brushed her own. 'I'll never stop loving you, Milly, but something's happened that means I can't offer you the life I thought I could, not any more . . .'

'What's happened?'

'My uncle's disowned me.'

She almost wanted to laugh, so relieved that he still loved her, that it wasn't something she'd done.

'Why's he disowned you?' He lowered his eyes, and she knew why. 'Because of me?'

He nodded miserably. 'He came to the shop, told me if I married you it would disgrace the family, said I had to choose. I could either have a common jam girl, or I could have his shops when he died, but I couldn't have both . . .'

'So you chose the shops,' she said, all her relief vanishing in the face of his stark choice. He'd promised to stay with her forever, but if he could break faith with her for money, then perhaps he wasn't the man she thought he was.

'Strike me dumb!' he said, angry with her now. 'Do you think I'd take a penny from that man again? Marry or not, I'm finished with him, with them all. Uncles, aunts, cousins, all of them too up their own arses to remember where the family's come from, a hovel in the sticks!' His face grew red, and his eyes blazed beneath winged eyebrows, drawn into a sharp frown. 'The brass of him, talking like that about my future wife. I told him he couldn't pay me enough to stay in his shop. So the upshot is, love, I'll be out of work from next week.'

'But, Bertie, you silly man, we can still get married! I don't care about the life you offered me, I care about you! Besides, if you *don't* marry me, you'll be giving your uncle just what he wants anyway!'

He got up, pacing agitatedly in front of her. Suddenly he was kneeling on the sleety path in front of the bench where she sat. He took both her hands in his. 'Milly, never doubt that I do love you, but you've got Jimmy to think of and you mustn't be saddled with someone who can't even support you, let alone give you a decent life.'

'Well, I've still got a job, and you won't be out of work for long. There's other things you can do.'

It seemed so obvious to her that it wasn't the insurmountable problem he thought it was. Perhaps because she'd grown up in poverty, it didn't hold the same terror that it did for him. She pulled him up off his knees and made him sit next to her, snuggling beneath his arm. She felt more hopeful, now that she realized it was a practical problem and not one of the heart.

Bertie sighed. 'You don't understand, Milly. I was my uncle's partner. I've been getting a share in the profits from all the shops. Being a grocer is all I know. But the way things are going, with shops closing down for lack of trade, I'd be lucky to get a job as a delivery boy!'

'What's wrong with that? It's better than nothing.'

He gave a short laugh. 'That's my bold, brave girl. I know you think you can take on the world, love, but it'll likely mean I can't keep on Storks Road, and I couldn't give you and the boy a decent life. In fact I'd just be a drain on you.' Then, looking into her eyes, he went on. 'I planned to take you both on holiday to Ramsgate after the wedding . . .' he said wistfully.

'Holiday? Who needs a holiday, when we can go hopping?' She smiled up at him, but he gave her no answering smile.

'Well, if I thought you didn't have a choice, I might ask you to risk it with me,' he said, and she felt his body go still as he went on. 'But I hear Pat Donovan's getting out at Christmas and I don't want to stand in the way of your chances there. He can always earn a bob or two.' He gave an uncharacteristically bitter little laugh and she disentangled herself from him.

'If you wanted to insult me, you've succeeded. What do you think I am? Some sort of whore who'll go for the highest bidder? You know very well I've finished with Pat, and you know why.'

She stood up. 'I'd better get back to Elsie,' she said flatly, but as she turned to leave, he called to her.

'Milly! Don't go like that!' But she didn't look back. She tucked her chin into the shawl collar of her coat and stuffed her hands into her pockets. Tiny balls of stinging sleet crusted the grass all around with a pale sheet and soon her coat was covered too. She broke into a run, feeling betrayed by her own ridiculous hopefulness, hot tears running freely, now that he couldn't see. She launched herself forward into the swirling ice and wind, sprinting now. Bertie Hughes might have been infatuated with her, but he could never have respected her. He was suggesting exactly what her mother had, that she was more interested in his money than in him. Perhaps Uncle had been right after all, and their two worlds should never try to mix. It simply wasn't worth the heartache.

23

Run Outs

December 1924

Bertie still went to the grocery on the following Monday. He'd told Milly he wouldn't leave the Dockhead customers without a local shop. Many of them bought tea and other staples in very small quantities, and those who were bad managers often came to him on Monday morning with an empty purse and an equally empty food cupboard after the weekend blowout. They would be counting on the slate, till they could get to the pawnshop. But his uncle had been ruthlessly efficient and by the end of the day a new shopkeeper was installed in Hughes' Dockhead grocery, an older, married cousin of Bertie's, a true-blue Tory, with three children and a respectable wife. Bertie had wished him luck, come home and started looking for another job the next day.

His plan was to find a shop manager job, or, he'd told Milly, even a sales assistant position – he couldn't afford to be choosy. After trying every shop in Tower Bridge Road, he went on to the Blue, and when he had no luck there started along the Old Kent Road. But as he'd predicted, wherever he went, shops were closing at an alarming rate. He'd even tried Peggy Dillon's butcher, who'd confided that the free flow of meat to the Dillon family might well be drying up, if takings didn't pick up soon.

Each jobless day dawned, with Bertie still stubbornly refusing to change his mind about the wedding, and after a few days of pleading Milly retreated into a punishing silence. She pointedly ignored Bertie's vigorous flicking through the job pages in the

South London Press as she dashed about the kitchen, hastily gathering Jimmy's things and making sure that Elsie had all she needed for another day in hiding. She and Bertie hadn't spoken to each other for a week and Milly certainly wasn't going to be the one who broke the ice. Bertie sighed and looked over at her with a hangdog expression that at any other time she would have found funny.

'Don't expect any sympathy from me!' she said finally, in exasperation at his pigheadedness. 'It doesn't have to be like this at all. I've said I'll marry you without a penny, and all you want to do is push me into the arms of Pat Donovan!'

He flung the paper away and stood up, jamming his pipe into his mouth. 'Strike me dumb, how many more times? I never said I didn't *want* to marry you, I just said I *couldn't*! When I get back on my feet, it'll be a different kettle of fish, but meanwhile, I'm not going to stand in your way if—'

'Oh, if, if, if! Stick your "ifs" in your effin pipe and smoke 'em!'

She was glad to see that Bertie got his oft-repeated wish, and was indeed struck dumb. He sat down again with the paper and miserably began turning the pages.

Elsie had witnessed all this while patiently holding Jimmy, who was flushed and grizzly, with teeth coming through. Now, as Milly scooped the little boy from her arms, Elsie said, 'Don't shout at Bertie like that. He's only thinking of you.'

Milly paused. 'You keep your nose out of it. You're not doing your precious Bertie any favours either. Fat chance he'll have getting elected on the council if he's caught harbouring a criminal!'

As soon as the words were out of her mouth, she saw Bertie's face tighten with disapproval. She let out a sigh of exasperation. 'You two have a lovely day. I know I won't!' As she banged the door, Jimmy began to cry. 'Don't you start, either,' she said sternly and Jimmy hiccoughed and started to gurgle. 'At least someone does as they're told,' she said softly, tucking him snugly into his pram. At six months, Jimmy still felt like the one thing in life that could never disappoint her. However much the compass of her own heart seem to waver, Jimmy was always true north.

Southwell's was beginning to seem like a pleasant relief from the strained atmosphere at home. She had kept her troubles to herself, hoping they would be resolved before anyone need know that her wedding was off. But that morning when Kitty came into the picking room, she knew the Arnold's Place bush telegraph had been at work.

'Milly! What's all this about the wedding being off?' Kitty, out of breath, had obviously taken the three flights of stairs at a run.

'That didn't take long to get round. Who told you?'

'Mrs Carney told Mum when she was collecting the pledges! And apparently Ma Donovan was full of it, telling whoever'd listen that her Pat wasn't coming home to Bertie Hughes' leftovers.'

Milly squeezed a pulpy Seville orange so that juice spurted up into her face. She flung it aside into the bin.

'Vicious old cow. But I'd like to know how it got out. I only told me mum yesterday!'

Kitty pulled up the corner of her apron to wipe Milly's face. 'Our Percy said Amy told all the kids, last night, that she wasn't going to be a bridesmaid any more. Oh, Mill, I bet you're choked. I really thought he was a decent feller.'

A tumbling mass of early Seville oranges was thundering along the conveyer belt. Shattered dreams were no excuse to hold up the line. Whatever dramas or heartaches might be uppermost in their minds, they picked and peeled, saving the spiralled skin for thick-cut marmalade, placing the pulp into the bin, turning back again to the conveyer belt, while Milly explained in a hushed voice what had happened.

Kitty's response surprised her. 'Well, it's his pride, Milly. What bloke wants to ponce off a woman? Unless, of course, he's like your old man!'

'You may be right, Kitty, but it feels like an insult to me, as if I only wanted him for his money! That's what I can't forgive.'

281

Talking about it didn't help; it only made the tightness in her throat worse. She'd choked back so many tears these past few days, she thought they must all be dammed up somewhere behind her chest. Her hands were growing red and sore, inflamed by the thousand little unavoidable cuts washed by the acidic juice, and Milly winced, though more from the memory of Bertie's decision than the physical discomfort in her fingers. In fact the pain was somehow a welcome distraction from her heartache.

'That's a load of old codswallop, Milly Colman, and you know it. If you really want him, you should remember your own advice to me, that time you got blind drunk.'

When Milly looked puzzled, Kitty began to sing under her breath: 'A good man nowadays is hard to find . . .'

She wished Kitty hadn't reminded her.

And it was a long day. The marmalade season was already upon them so there would be no let up until well into February. Day and night, the bitter-sweet smell of marmalade being turned over in Southwell's huge copper boiling pans filled Dockhead and beyond. This, combined with the cinnamon and nutmeg smells from the spice grinders in Shad Thames, was as much a herald of Christmas as the changing vestments of the priests at Dockhead Church. Milly only wished she could feel more in the festive spirit, but how could she, when each day only emphasized the absence of her Christmas wedding? The wedding dress and bridesmaid dress were in their covers, hanging from a hook on the back of her bedroom door. The wide-brimmed hat she'd chosen was in a box on top of the wardrobe. The miniature sailor suit she'd made for Jimmy was folded up in a drawer, along with her hopes and dreams.

Walking back to Storks Road with Jimmy that evening, she missed the feeling of warm anticipation she normally had when returning home. She braced herself for more tussles with Bertie, more worry over Elsie. After manoeuvring Jimmy's pram into the passage, she left him sleeping there and went to the scullery, expecting to find Elsie. She had to admit that her sister had made herself useful this week, preparing the tea before she came home. But tonight the scullery was empty.

When she stepped out of the back door into the garden, she could see straight away that Elsie was not in her favourite place. She wouldn't call out, for fear of waking Jimmy, so she went upstairs, looking first in the spare room where Elsie had been sleeping, then in her own. She couldn't imagine why Elsie would be in Bertie's room, but she went there nevertheless. The note had been carefully placed on his pillow. She picked it up and read it. *Dear Bertie, I don't want to get you into no trouble. Please tell my mum I'm sorry I couldn't say goodbye. Elsie.*

Milly sat heavily on Bertie's bed, holding the note in her trembling hand. A small but undeniable ripple of relief was followed by a chilling thought. What had her sister meant by *sorry I couldn't say goodbye*? She knew from her own desperate times that Elsie wouldn't be able to survive on the streets alone, and what if the river seemed the only way out, as it once had to her? She found herself stroking Bertie's pillow as she remembered her own rescue that night at Fountain Stairs. She looked around the room, neat and tidy, like Bertie himself, but so full of his absence it hurt her. It had been her jibe about Bertie harbouring a criminal that had pushed her sister out, she was sure of it. 'Oh, Bertie, why aren't you here now?' She spoke to the empty room, looking round it for some other evidence of her sister's intentions. It was no good; she would have to look for Elsie herself. She couldn't sit there, doing nothing. She hurried downstairs, threw on her coat, took hold of the pram and was about to dash out of the house with Jimmy, when she saw the front door opening.

'Dear Jesus, let it be her,' she prayed, in the dim light of the passage. She started forward, knocking the breath out of Bertie with the pram, just as he came through the door.

'Blimey, Milly!' he said, startled. 'I know you've got the hump with me, but no need to attack me with a deadly weapon!' He edged round the pram. 'What's happened?' he said, seeing her stricken face.

'Have you been out looking for her?' she asked.

'I've been to a job agency. Looking for who?'

Of course, Elsie would have waited for him to go out first. And the thought of her sister, making her sacrificial plan and carrying it out all on her own, suddenly moved her to tears. 'Oh, Bertie, Elsie's gone!' She covered her face with her hands in despair and he gathered her up like a child. 'I'll never learn to keep my trap shut, and if she's done anything stupid, it'll be my fault!'

He hushed her and held her tightly, then asking to see the note, read it slowly, shaking his head.

'I know what you're thinking, but I don't think she'd do anything as desperate as that. Come on, bring the pram, time to rally the troops.'

They went straight to Arnold's Place and after the initial shock, her mother agreed with Bertie, that Elsie couldn't have gone far. The important thing was to find her before the police did.

Milly was amazed at the change in Bertie, the affable, easy-going grocer transformed into a sergeant major in the blink of an eye. She'd never seen this military side of him. The little she'd been able to prise out of him about his war experiences only revealed that, after volunteering in a noble impulse of duty, he'd quickly discovered that without a belligerent bone in his body, he'd had to call on pure survival instinct in order to level a gun at another human being. Now, for once, she stood silently and took his orders.

'Milly, you go to the Settlement. Tell Florence what's happened, and that we need the girls' club to help us search. Ask her to drop the sewing, drop the dumbbells, drop everything and get the girls combing all the streets from Bermondsey Wall East to Jamaica Road. Mrs Colman, you take Jimmy and tell the neighbours to be on the lookout. I'll go and recruit Barrel and his merry band!'

They all left the house together, her mother pushing the pram to the opposite end of Arnold's Place, while Milly walked with

Bertie to the gas lamp, where Amy was playing alley gobs with a gang of children.

Bertie called out, 'Barrel! Job for you lot!'

Barrel looked up sharply. 'How much?'

'Nothing, you cheeky sod, you're doing it for one of your own, not me!'

Once he'd explained who it was they were searching for, Amy was quick to make herself Barrel's second in command and jumped to his side.

'Oi, button it, you gobby lot!' Barrel shouted above the children's clamorous condemnation of Stonefield. 'We'll do it like Run Outs. All scatter, and if anyone finds her, bring her back to the tin!' He banged the old rusty tin can, used as home base in their nightly game. 'Come on. Run Out!' he bellowed and set off at a surprisingly fast pace.

Every boy and girl leaped up, some shoeless or coatless, and scampered off into the chilly night, soon disappearing into the pearl mist beyond the comforting pool of gaslight.

Bertie declared he would walk towards Tower Bridge and recruit anyone he knew on the way, to help with the hunt. But before Milly darted off towards Bermondsey Wall, he caught her by the arm.

Drawing her close, he kissed her and whispered, 'Don't blame yourself and don't give up hope!' He paused, then looked at her solemnly. 'But, Milly, you know that if we can't find her tonight, we'll have to go to the police?'

Milly nodded. Better she was alive in Stonefield, than dead on the streets from cold, or worse. She kissed him back, all their estrangement forgotten for now. Then pulling away, she hurtled into the fog-laden night. On the way she stopped at Hickman's Folly, gathering together Kitty and as many Bunclerks as were home. They called in at the Folly, so that by the time they reached the Settlement, Florence Green was met by a dozen or more volunteers. She quickly mustered the girls' club and the boy scouts who were meeting that night, giving them each a section of streets to search. They appeared to Milly like the 'children's crusade' that Sister Clare had taught them about at school, a brave little army, clattering down the gaslit stone steps. Many of them were schoolfriends of Elsie's and gave Milly sympathetic looks as they passed, trooping off in twos and threes.

The girls scattered towards the river, the boys into the less savoury, crumbling back-to-backs of the notorious Salisbury Street. Milly and Kitty joined the riverside search, and Milly insisted they first check Fountain Stairs. Whatever Bertie had said about Elsie's intentions, Milly had to make sure she wasn't there. Standing at the top of the mossy-green steps, she peered down to the river, invisible beneath the rolling fog. Descending two steps, she called out, 'Elsie?' The sound of her own voice echoed off the damp-encrusted river walls. Taking another step down, she heard the river slap and suck at the muddy foreshore. Low tide; for that she was grateful. It would be so much harder to throw yourself into the river when the tide was out. She listened intently; only the clashing river, tossing forward over patches of shingle, followed by its long withdrawing sigh.

'She's not here!' Milly called up to Kitty.

''Course she's not!' Kitty replied. 'No one in their right mind would come here on a night like this!'

But Elsie might not be in her right mind, not if the terror of returning to Stonefield had taken hold of her. Reassured that Elsie wasn't here, Milly set herself to search all through the night, determined not to return home without her sister.

When she came up from the slimy steps, she was shivering and Kitty linked arms with her. 'Come on, Mill, this place puts the wind up me. Let's keep moving, for gawd's sake!'

Milly felt she was in the sort of nightmare where every step forward brought her two steps back. With fog hindering their search, they sometimes found they'd gone in a complete circle, covering the same streets twice. Shouts punctuated the opaque night as groups of searchers called to other groups, checking on their progress. Once Milly's hopes were raised by a shout of

'Here she is!' only to find some boy scouts had been chasing a girl who'd turned out to be one of their own searchers.

After almost two hours, Milly said, 'I don't think she's up this end, Kit. Let's go back down to Dockhead and start again.'

Kitty, who was much less robust than Milly, nodded, but Milly could see her friend was flagging, struggling to match her long stride. In the end Kitty was half running in order to keep up, but Milly couldn't slow her pace. Back at Arnold's Place they walked past the old tin can, which hadn't been moved.

'Looks like Barrel didn't find her either,' Kitty said, looking anxiously up and down Arnold's Place.

Almost every street door was open despite the cold weather, and her mother was surrounded by women in coats and hats. A quick conversation revealed that all their searches had been in vain.

'But Bertie's still out there. Perhaps he's heard something?' her mother said hopefully.

'I'll see if I can meet him coming back,' Milly offered, not wishing to stand around with the worrying neighbours. 'Kit, you go home, you're dead on your feet.' And when Kitty protested, she insisted. 'Go on, home! You'll never keep up with me!'

Kitty admitted defeat, giving Milly a hug. 'You be careful out there on your own in this pea-souper, it's getting worse!'

Milly picked her way towards the end of Arnold's Place and set off for Shad Thames. A few dockers, changing shifts, were walking her way and she gratefully followed the ringing of their boots on the cobbles. When she reached Butler's Wharf she heard the stamping of hooves, then passed the dark, hulking shape of a carthorse, waiting to for its driver to return. Steam plumed from the horse's nostrils and as she skirted round him, he tossed his heavy neck into her path, unbalancing her. Faltering forward across the cobbles, she found herself suddenly surrounded by a crowd of nightmarish creatures. Bright yellow figures advanced towards her through the dingy fog. A cry escaped from her mouth as the first lunged at her. The smell was overpowering – was it sulphur?

She recoiled as a steel-like hand gripped her, then a rough voice came out of the yellow creature's mouth. 'Steady on, gel, y'all right?'

Milly's shaking subsided, and her legs straightened.

'Y-yes, I'm all right, just the horse knocked me for six!' she said, feeling foolish that the fog should have spooked her so badly. The man patted her arm, wafts of strong, eye-watering powder emanating from his skin and clothes. She should have recognized them; they were only the 'yellow men', demons of her childhood. She'd joined in the games, running along behind them, baiting them, till the 'yellow men' obliged by turning round with a roar, raising clawlike hands, sending the children into squeals of delightful terror.

The yellow men's undeserved sense of menace was added to by the many ghost stories woven around their demonic-looking presence. But for all that, they were only working men from the spice grinders, skin and clothes stained yellow with turmeric, billowing up from grindstones night and day. Even as she hurried past the spice grinder's yard, the deep rumble of massive grindstones turning upon each other reached her in the street. However foolish her fear, she was desperate now for lamplight and crowds. She turned off from Shad Thames into Tooley Street, still busy with late-night traffic, crawling along in the fog. Scurrying from one milky pool of gaslight to the next, she collided with an unseen figure hastening in the opposite direction. Rebounding, she found herself staring up into a familiar face.

'Blimey, that's a bit of luck, I was just coming to find you!' he said.

'Jesus, you frightened the life out of me!' She had no time to wonder how Pat Donovan came to be here; she just knew she wished him a million miles away. She interrupted him as he was about to speak. 'I'm sorry, Pat, I can't stop. I'm looking for our Elsie.'

'I know,' he said to her surprise. 'I've just seen that Hughes bloke. He told me to keep an eye out for her.'

'He's not found her then?' she said, her last hope fading.

'Don't look like it. Listen, Milly, that letter you sent me—'

'Pat, I can't talk about that now!' she cut him off. 'I'm so worried about our Elsie. I'm going back to Arnold's Place.'

'I'm going that way.' He fell in beside her and made her tell the whole story on the way.

'Stonefield! Think I'd rather be in Brixton. At least you've got the chance of getting out, but once they bang you up in the nuthouse . . .' He gave a low whistle. 'No wonder she run away.'

'Pat, I'm sorry about the letter. But it was for the best.'

'Don't be a dozy mare, Milly. I told you I'd give the boy a name and I meant it!'

Prison hadn't appeared to squash Pat's natural confidence.

'I know and I'm grateful, Pat, but I really can't marry you.'

'Why not?' he demanded, shocked that there might be any other choice for a woman in her position.

'Because I'm going to marry someone else,' she blurted out, believing with all her heart that while it wasn't strictly true today, it *would* be – one day.

Her mother's kitchen was crammed so full that she and Pat had to elbow their way in. Milly scanned the faces: her mother looking hopeful for an instant; Amy, glancing up briefly from Jimmy who was cradled in her arms. Mercifully, the old man was absent. No doubt he was the only person in Dockhead who hadn't joined the hunt. Mrs Knight and even Barrel and Ronnie were still there. Her mother sat in one of the two chairs she possessed and, to Milly's surprise, in the other sat old Ma Donovan in a dirty wrap-over apron and what looked like her dead husband's boots. Elsie wasn't there.

Milly slumped down on the floor next to the range, while the hubbub of Pat's surprise arrival went on around her. She seemed to sink into a silent vortex, while mother and son were reunited and everyone exclaimed over his early release. She was the only one who heard the front door opening. She jumped up, but before she could get out of the crowded kitchen, Bertie was standing there. His eyes locked on to hers and then he shook his head sorrowfully. One by one, people stopped talking. Bertie, swallowing hard, announced, 'The police picked her up this afternoon in Tooley Street. They've taken her back to Stonefield.'

24

The Joy Slide

December 1924–February 1925

On the night of Elsie's recapture, the neighbours had drifted away, leaving Milly, Bertie and Pat in an awkward triad as they faced each other across Mrs Colman's small kitchen. Looking from one man to the other, and with her father due home from the pub any minute, Milly felt like a trapped animal. But she had to know how Elsie had been recaptured. She made Bertie sit down in the chair that Ma Donovan had vacated. The woman had gone home to get a bed ready for her son, but Pat hadn't left with her and now he seemed to be waiting for Bertie to go, before he said goodnight. Of course, Pat still didn't know where she was living. But she couldn't worry about him at the moment.

'Do you know where they found her?' she asked wearily.

'Apparently she was walking past Tower Bridge police station; just walking up and down. A constable had her description and that was that, almost as if she wanted to be picked up!'

There was nothing she could do for her mother, who sat staring into the fire, in quiet grief.

'We've got to go, Mum,' Milly said after a while, looking towards Bertie.

Confusion passed over Pat's face as he asked, 'Oh, are you in lodgings?' He put on his cap. 'I'll walk you home.'

She should have told him before, and now his ignorance only added to the awkwardness.

As Bertie reached for his hat, he put a proprietary hand on Milly's elbow. 'No need for that. Milly's lodging at my house.'

Pat's face flushed and she knew he'd guessed the identity of her fiancé. She quickly took Jimmy from Amy's arms. 'Look after Mum,' she told the young girl, who'd been largely ignored, though she'd cared for Jimmy half the night without complaint.

Pat followed them out and as she was putting Jimmy into his pram, he came up close to her. 'Is he your fancy man?' His lips were trembling with emotion. 'All that time in nick I thought you was waiting for me and you've been shacked up with him?'

'It's not like that, Pat. He took me in. I had nowhere to go!'

'What, and now it's playing happy families with my boy, is it?' He jabbed his finger towards the pram.

'Now, listen here,' she said, ire quickly replacing exhaustion. 'If it was up to you, "your boy" wouldn't even be here! I had to do what I thought best for my child, and if it hadn't been for Bertie, we would've been on the street. So don't you start laying down the law about what I should and shouldn't have done!'

Bertie stepped to her side. 'Perhaps you two should talk about this another time. We're all tired, don't want to say things we'll regret.'

She hated his reasonableness, and even more she hated his 'you two' as though he were coupling her off with Pat already. Why wasn't he fighting to keep her?

'What's it to you?' she said under her breath. 'As far as you're concerned, the wedding's off!'

Then leaving the two men behind her, she shoved the pram into motion.

Christmas passed largely uncelebrated in Arnold's Place that year, and if it hadn't been for Milly's desire to mark Jimmy's first Christmas, Storks Road would also have lacked any festive cheer. She, her mother and Amy made the dismal pilgrimage to Stonefield and found Elsie withdrawn and sullen, rather than desperate. Milly thought she'd simply given up hope of ever coming home.

Surrounded by women who'd spent half a lifetime at Stonefield, some for no other reason than having an illegitimate child, Milly thought that Elsie had good reason to despair.

Her own planned wedding day passed without comment as she and Bertie fell into an awkward stalemate. She had exhausted all her arguments in trying to persuade him out of his stubborn refusal to marry her while he was without a job. He'd insisted that they were still engaged, but it didn't feel like it to Milly. She felt a check on all their intimacy; she knew he was holding back, even limiting his endearments, and she noticed with a pang every time he failed to call her 'love', or 'his beautiful girl', or any of the other affectionate terms that had been woven into the fabric of their romance. Words of love, which once had come tumbling forth in precious detail – praise for her hair, her eyes, her figure, her spirit – were now rationed to generalities. She tried to explain to him that his sense of decency was turning their love into an unwatered garden; he wouldn't starve his roses as he had her heart. Perhaps he was cutting himself off in preparation for her final abandonment of him, but something in her believed the springs hadn't failed forever. So, like a desert flower waiting to bloom, she curled in on herself, preserving her resources, knowing that all she needed was one glorious day of rain.

Meanwhile the confusion of her relationship with Pat Donovan only added to her anxiety. Pat no longer owned a lorry, but Freddie Clark now had two, and was giving him work as a driver. She'd often see him driving slowly past Southwell's gates, just at the times when she was going in or coming out. But he never acknowledged her and she gave him no encouragement, so it was unsettling that he should keep up the pointless vigil.

Then one Saturday afternoon, he turned up at Storks Road. He took off his cap and began rolling it so nervously into a tight wad that she began to pity him, until she caught the beery stink of his breath. Perhaps he'd missed his pint while in prison, but he'd certainly started early today.

'Pat, I've told you—' she began.

'It's not about you,' he interrupted her. 'Whatever's going on with you and Hughes . . . well, I couldn't give a monkey's. But my boy's getting older and he don't know me. Now that's not fair and I want to see him.'

She agreed. It wasn't fair; none of it was fair. She had made a mistake and it had been compounded by inexperience and ignorance. Perhaps it was time, once and for all, for her to be honest with Pat.

'I should have a say in how he's brought up. I've come to take him round me mum's. She's his nan after all.'

'No!' she said, a little too vehemently. She would never let him go off alone with Jimmy in this state, let alone trust her son to Ma Donovan, or 'sooky' as she was sometimes called behind her back, for the grime covering her windows and her front step, not to mention her own person. Milly's mother's house might lack furniture, but it was a palace compared to the Donovans'. Slovenliness wasn't Ma Donovan's cardinal sin, though. She had called Jimmy a bastard, and Milly would rather die than let him anywhere near her. It was impossible to think of asking Pat into Bertie's house, so to placate him, she suggested they go for a walk with Jimmy. Better by far to be in an open public space as far away from the Donovan house as possible.

While Pat waited outside she dressed Jimmy warmly in the new coat she'd made him. At seven months he was filling out, though she thought he would always be a small boy. With his ready smile and placid ways, he was an easy baby to love. His neat little head was now covered in silky blond hair that curled at his neck, and his ever curious almond-shaped eyes seemed to radiate a contented calm. Now he was older it was easier for her to see that Jimmy had nothing of Pat in him, and she was glad of it.

It was an icy January day of clear, pale skies and she suggested they walk the short distance to St James's Churchyard. She was dressed for winter in her woollen wrap-around coat and close-fitting hat, while Pat, warmed, no doubt, by the amount of alcohol he'd consumed at the pub, wore just a jacket and white cotton scarf over a collarless shirt.

In St James's Churchyard stood an incongruously rustic structure known as 'the joy slide'. In the shadow of the impressive 'Waterloo' church, it looked a little like a country cottage on stilts, with its black-and-white wooden tower over the stairs and a sweeping gabled roof covering the slide. Swarms of children were lining up for a go on the slide, bunching up together, some shivering in shirtsleeves or thin frocks, shuffling forward eagerly to the deep wooden bin, where they could pick up a horsehair mat before clambering up the stairs. Some were so tiny they had to hoist themselves almost into the bin to hook out a mat, and Milly smiled as one almost disappeared inside it. But their wait in the cold was obviously worth it, for their faces shone with excitement as they were rewarded with an exhilarating few seconds, swirling down the polished wooden slide, and as each child tumbled off the end, their joyful smiles lit up the grey day.

The slide certainly deserved its name, Milly thought. She remembered when it had been built, donated by Peek Frean's philanthropist owner. It felt as if a fairground had landed on their doorstep. Previously, their only slide had been the wide sloping stones either side of the church steps, worn smooth by the backsides of generations of children. She'd been too old by the time the new slide was built, but had taken Amy and Elsie there often, waiting patiently as they rode the slide again and again, screaming with joy. One day, when he was old enough, she would take Jimmy too. But for now, he would have to be content just to watch. She parked the pram where he could see the children flying off the slide, and he laughed, excitedly jiggling about as each one bumped to the ground.

'Reckon he wants to join in!' Pat said, rubbing his hands together against the cold. 'It's a bit uncle willy for sitting outdoors! Why don't you let me take him to Mum's, don't you trust me?'

'Of course I trust you,' she lied, 'but . . . Jimmy needs a bit of fresh air.'

He shrugged and sat down beside her on the bench.

'So,' he leaned forward, letting Jimmy grip his finger, 'tell me about my son. He looks bright as a button, handsome chap like his dad!' He grinned and tussled against Jimmy's hold and Milly's throat went dry; she coughed and stuttered.

'Yes, he's a lovely-looking boy, everyone says so, but to be honest I can't see you in him at all, Pat. The thing is, sooner or later, me and Bertie are getting married and you've had nothing to do with Jimmy . . . and I want him to grow up as Bertie's son.'

He withdrew his hand from the pram and turned to her.

'What are you talking about, nothing of me in him? Are you trying to tell me he's not mine?' His voice was rising and he was leaning in closer, so that she could see the fine lines that prison had etched around his eyes. Up close, the change in him was more obvious. He was leaner, his skin tauter on his face, his eyes harder. Perhaps his superficial cheeriness was still there, but there was a new harshness to his features that she hadn't registered before. 'Or was my old mum right, and you're just a fucking slut who's been stringing me along!' His raised voice drew the attention of some of the youngsters at the slide.

'Shhh, Pat, you'll frighten Jimmy!' she said, all the while thinking how easy it would be to tell him what he wanted to hear. If she once said 'He's not yours,' Pat would walk away; she knew that.

'Who's the father if not me? Is it that Hughes?'

'No!' she said, steel in her voice. 'Believe me or not, you can please yourself, and now you can stop your hollering around my son and sod off!'

Suddenly he caught hold of her arm and twisted. She wondered when it had first occurred to her that one day Pat could easily turn into a man like her father. Perhaps all those times when she'd seen how drink changed him, perhaps the night she'd seen a gun gleaming in the moonlight, or perhaps it was the possessiveness which had nothing to do with love and everything to do with control. But today she saw the similarity clearly, and for the first time understood the real reason she'd resisted marrying Pat so fiercely. She would never allow Jimmy to grow up with an 'old man' like hers.

'You're just like the old man!' she hissed, as softly as she could, so that Jimmy wouldn't be alarmed. 'Get your hands off me, or I'll knock your bleedin' block off!'

He leaped up, readying himself for her to carry out her threat. 'Why did you let me believe you'd marry me?' His bloodshot eyes, bruised rings beneath them, were full of anger.

She knew she'd never actually agreed to marry Pat, but had she let him think she might? Perhaps, but at the time she'd already spent weeks too frightened to admit what was happening, and, once it became obvious she was pregnant, too terror-struck by the consequences to think clearly about what she should do. Her choices had been stark: marry Pat or give up her baby, or keep her baby and live with the stigma forever. In the end the latter had felt like the only thing to do, and she didn't regret it.

'I'm sorry, Pat, if I gave you the wrong idea, but the truth is, I was never going to marry you.'

He slammed his fist on to the pram handle, startling Jimmy with the jolt. 'That's what I thought. You never loved me.'

He turned abruptly and walked off towards the churchyard gates, head down, hands jammed into his pockets. Her eyes followed him till he disappeared under the railway arch and then she looked at her own hands. They were shaking. Jimmy began to whimper, his lower lip trembling, forehead furrowed.

'Shhh, he's gone now,' she soothed him, gently rocking the pram till he fell asleep and her own shaking subsided.

The bitter cold hadn't done anything to diminish the popularity of the slide and as yet more children arrived to join the queue, Milly couldn't help but notice how ill-suited their clothes were for the winter. She and her sisters had always worn hand-me-downs. It was nothing unusual, but even if second-hand, her mother had always somehow managed to get them a winter coat each. But times were getting harder, and many of these children would have docker fathers on casual wages, or no wages at all. She'd heard only last week about more lay-offs at Neckinger Mills, the tannery where the old man worked, and at Crosse & Blackwell's and Lipton's. In fact all the local factories seemed to be scaling down. The missions and churches were opening free soup kitchens, and in households where food and rent was the priority, there was precious little money left for kids' clothes. She sighed. It seemed that for all the valiant efforts of people like Florence Green and Dr Salter to improve their lives, in Bermondsey there was a perpetual tide of poverty washing through the borough, stronger than a whirling current in the Thames.

But why did they have to depend on charity? Why did she always have to depend on a man's wages? Even as a child she'd suffered the old man's abuse because without him they would be in the workhouse. She was fed up with it, but though she might rail against it, surviving on her Southwell earnings alone would be nigh on impossible. It was simply not a living wage and without Bertie's subsidized rent she didn't know how she would live.

She had just come to the conclusion that if she couldn't earn a living wage at one job, then she must get a second to supplement it, when a pitiful crying broke into her calculations. The sound was coming from the bottom of the slide, where a tiny red-haired girl had landed awkwardly and was now sitting on the tarmac, screaming pitifully. An older boy, who looked like a brother, was trying to comfort her. Milly ran to help, picking up the child and rubbing grazed knees before setting her on to her feet, which were bare. The child was blue with cold.

'Hasn't she got a coat or jumper?' she asked her ginger-haired brother, who'd taken his sister's hand.

'Nah, she don't feel the cold.' He sniffed up a trickle of snot from his nose and wiped it with his shirt cuff. He at least wore boots. 'Fanks, missis!' he said and pulled at his sister. 'Come on, let's have another go!'

Milly watched as they gleefully hurtled towards the wooden staircase, envying them their childlike ability to shrug off pain in an instant, to jump up and head unwaveringly for another go on the joy slide. She wished she could be like that. Bertie had given her a glimpse of joy she'd never before known, and she was determined that neither Pat nor Bertie himself would rob her of it. She'd just bloody well pick herself up and try for another go!

At that moment, looking at her own boy, dressed snugly in the coat she'd made him, she was struck by the contrast to the thin clothes of the children she'd been watching. The beginnings of a plan began to take shape. Jimmy's coat had cost her a fraction of the price of a second-hand one. Surely, if the price was the same, any mother would prefer a clean, new coat or dress for their child over a second-hand from the Old Clo' market? She knew she could make a child's coat or warm dress, sell them just above second-hand prices and still make a profit.

Once it had taken hold, the idea seemed to have a life of its own. She hurried back to Storks Road, impatient to begin. All the way there, she was imagining ways of cutting a child's coat pattern so she could get two from the least amount of cloth. She might go even further, if she could get the money for material, and make adults' clothes as well.

If Bertie's only objection to them marrying was lack of funds, then she had in her own nimble fingers the remedy; she would make enough money for the two of them!

As soon as she got home, she ran upstairs and fished out an old tin tea caddy. Her hands shaking with excitement, she tipped out the coins on to the bed. She didn't have a trousseau, but she'd been carefully saving the odd spare sixpence into what she thought of as her 'wedding tin', so that she could bring something to the household. It was little enough, but it was a matter of pride that she could contribute something. But with no wedding on the horizon, she didn't feel guilty about dipping into the battered old tea tin. She pocketed the money and, without even getting Jimmy out of his pram, set off for East Lane market. Walking all the way to the Old Kent Road to save on tram fares, she arrived at the bustling street market, where everything could be had, from cauliflowers to cups and saucers, just as it was closing.

Bernie's was her favourite material stall and she set about charming him.

'Bernie?' she called to the stallholder, after he'd finished with a customer. 'Got any remnants, good for a coat?'

Bernie hurried over, a quick-moving man with darting eyes, ever watchful for a creeping hand lifting his goods from the stall.

'Milly! Where you bin? Beautiful as ever, though.' He gave her a wide grin and quickly turned to a middle-aged woman who was screwing up a piece of cotton to see how it creased. 'Are you buying that?' he said sternly and the woman hastily dropped the cloth. 'I got a nice bit of navy stuff here, Mill, what d'ye reckon?'

She picked it up. It was good cloth but probably too expensive. 'Can you knock any off that?' she said, waiting for Bernie to raise his eyes to heaven.

'Not seen her for months and now she wants to rob me!' he addressed a passing shopper, who was not in the least interested. Milly smiled; she knew Bernie always added a margin for haggling. Eventually he knocked off a shilling and the buttons were thrown in.

All next week she spent every spare minute pattern-cutting and sewing, working secretly in her room, for if her enterprise failed, she certainly didn't want Bertie to know it. By the following Saturday she'd made two children's coats that were warm, fashionable and best of all, brand new.

She took Jimmy with her to the Old Clo' market in Tower Bridge Road, joining the hawkers' pitches, up behind the stalls. They sold from upturned tea crates or out of suitcases, and she manoeuvred the pram till she found a space. Behind her was a wooden fence on which she hung the two little coats, pinning price tags on to them. The crush of people surged around her with barely an inch of pavement visible. She waited eagerly, curious to see what reaction her garments would get. There were plenty of women with children, scouring the stalls, and Milly scrutinized each one expectantly, confident that her creations would soon attract some interest.

But after an hour her initial optimism began to wane. Her legs were aching, and her pride hurt. What if no one bought the coats? She'd have wasted her money and be no closer to marrying Bertie. She waited a further half-hour, and even the hawker next to her began to commiserate

'No luck, gel?' he asked, and when she blushed, shaking her head, he seemed to pity her. 'Sometimes trade just don't come yer way. You're best to call it a day!' he said, closing his suitcase. 'I'm packing it in meself.'

But still she wouldn't allow the possibility of failure. Why hadn't her coats attracted any interest? Jimmy had received more attention, with several passers-by smiling at him as they looked into his the pram. 'He's bonny!' one woman had exclaimed, setting Milly glowing with pride.

But now, as she studied the bargain hunters still clogging the street, she noticed that, without exception, their eyes were all lowered to stall level. They grazed the wares like sheep in a field and moved on. She looked up at the two coats hanging on the fence above her. They were positioned too high! She whipped them down, searching for another place to display them, and when Jimmy let out a laugh, she smiled to herself. 'Thanks, you little angel,' she gave him a noisy kiss, 'you can be the salesman!' And she hung the coats over the pram handle, which was just the right height. Within minutes a thin woman, with a shopping bag over her arm and a little girl in tow, made a beeline for the pram. The woman did a double take as she checked the price ticket.

'Is this new?' she said, holding up the smaller coat.

Milly nodded. 'I made it myself. I make all my Jimmy's clothes.' She could immediately see the woman soften at the sight of him.

'Oh, they're lovely when they're that age.' The woman looked down at her own child, who had on a well-darned jersey and skirt. She held up the coat against the little girl and Milly could immediately see it was a bit on the long side.

'She'll get a lot of wear out of it,' she said helpfully and the woman nodded.

'Do you like it, Iris?' she asked the little girl, who nodded vigorously.

'I'll take it.'

The woman started to dig into her purse and Milly wanted to run the length of Tower Bridge Road. She was so proud that her plan had actually worked. The woman then called across a stall to her friend, holding up her newly purchased coat. 'Sophe, look at this coat, there's a bigger one might do your Annie.'

Within minutes Sophe had bought the other coat, so that by teatime Milly had earned more than her entire week's wage. With no time left to cook Bertie's tea, she decided to splash out on pie and mash, and was making her way back home with the wrapped pies and a tub of green liquor nestled at the foot of Jimmy's pram, when she spotted Bertie's familiar figure strolling ahead of her. He whirled round at her call and waited for her to catch up.

'Where've you been?' she asked, coming up to him, slightly breathless. Putting up her cheek to be kissed, she was pleased when he obliged, in spite of his awkwardness about showing affection in public.

'Oh, I've been to Spa Road, someone told me they needed an assistant at Fogden's, he said, naming Bermondsey's largest grocery. But before she could ask how he'd got on, he shook his head. 'No luck,' he said disconsolately.

'What've you been up to?' he asked, prodding the parcels in the pram. 'Mmm, smells like you've been to Manzes!'

She nodded. 'Thought I'd give us a treat. We're celebrating.'

'I could do with something to celebrate. What's it all about?'

In the past few weeks Bertie's unsuccessful search for a job had begun to dull his normally bright spirits, and although he never complained, she could see his confidence ebbing.

'I know you're a bit down in the mouth with this job business.' She began to push the pram. 'But I've just earned a week's money in an afternoon!'

Her triumph was short-lived as she saw his face fall slightly.

'How d'you manage that?' he asked, a hint of suspicion in his voice.

'By using my noddle, and these!' She waggled her fingers in his face and when he still looked confused, she explained. Only then did his expression show admiration. 'Well, I'll give it to you, Milly, you've got more nous than lots of businessmen I know! The money'll come in handy for you.'

She looked at him with incomprehension. 'Do you want us to get married, or not?'

'More than anything in the world, Milly, you know I do.' He had the air of a naughty schoolboy who knew he'd done something wrong, but wasn't quite sure yet what it was.

'Well then, just accept that whatever money I earn from now on is not for *me*, it's for *us*! Bertie, I know you've got this idea you should provide for your wife. But if it's me you want, then you've got to take me as I am, and I want it to be a partnership. You've given me more than I can ever repay . . .' She stopped pushing the pram, so she could look him full in the face. 'You gave me my life back.'

Then in the middle of Jamaica Road, his sense of propriety all forgotten, he lifted her clear of the ground and kissed her, in full view of whoever cared to look.

'And you gave me a life I never had,' he whispered in her ear, crushing her close so that she struggled for breath. 'Let's get married, Milly. We'll have a pauper's wedding for all I care, or we'll just jump over the brush, but I don't want to wait a minute longer.'

She laughed and grabbed his arm, dragging him home, like a victor with her spoils. 'We'll have a proper wedding at Dockhead Church, or Mum will never forgive us!'

*

With the profit from the two coats, Milly bought grey flannel material from Bernie. She made two pairs of boys' trousers and two girls' skirts. The following week she sold them at the Old Clo' and the week after that she made two ladies' dresses from a bolt of black silk that Freddie Clark acquired at cost, or so he said, from a warehouse near London Bridge. In a single month she'd made more money than she could in six at Southwell's.

Bertie needed no more persuading to take his leap of faith and they were married in early February at Dockhead Church. For Milly, the day was perfect, like putting into harbour after years at sea. Her mother's face, finally proud of her, perpetual worry lines smoothed by the joy of the day, her sister Amy, for once demure and trying very hard not to spoil the photo as Barrel and the gang stood outside the churchyard, attempting to make her laugh. Afterwards, the neighbours in Arnold's Place, along with Kitty and her friends, were invited for sandwiches and a drink at the Folly.

Ma Donovan scandalized everyone by turning up for the free beer. But the woman had come with news that filled Milly with guilty relief. It seemed that Pat had bounced straight back into prison, this time for his part in the robbery of a wine merchant's near Tooley Street. He'd been caught stashing barrels of port into a railway arch lock-up. Mrs Donovan, who'd had more than a few free pints, seemed proud of his exploits and, sipping her stout, held court with the tale. 'There he is, with his head stuck in a barrel o' port wine, sampling the stuff. The coppers charge in, he does no more 'an he dives into the bleedin' barrel! Over he goes, in he goes, up he comes, pissed as a puddin, tells 'em the drinks is on him!' Ma Donovan cackled like a crow and slapped down the pint glass. 'Drinks is on him!'

Her laughter sounded forced and as Milly turned away, the woman fixed her with unsmiling eyes. 'Some might think they're too good for 'im, but you've got to give it to my Pat, he'll put his hands up, he will, for *anythink*!' she said, reaching for her glass.

Some of the guests had joined in the laughter, but Rosie Rockle and Milly's mother looked on with frosty expressions. Mrs Knight urged her to turf 'the mean old cow' out, but Milly couldn't bear to spoil the day with rancour.

The old man, when he heard about the wedding, said he wouldn't spend good money on a collar and tie for 'that slut', and her mother told her he'd taken himself off to stay at his fancy woman's, for which she thanked Our Lady as it meant she could look after Jimmy, while the newly-weds had the night to themselves. The only thing missing in her perfect day was Elsie. Milly had hoped that by some miracle she would be released in time for the wedding. But it was a fantasy based on nothing more than her need to keep her own guilt at bay. In the end, she decided that making herself miserable on this happiest of days would do Elsie no good, and would certainly spoil it for Bertie.

After the landlord called last orders and the guests had all rolled home, she took Bertie by the hand and, weaving in a tipsy, euphoric stroll, led him through the dark, riverside streets till they arrived at St James's Churchyard. She let go of his hand and with two loping strides was at the railings. Grasping the top, she vaulted clear over them. Her landing on the other side was a little wobbly, but she straightened up and beamed at him.

'Come on, Bertie!' she urged.

'Strike me dumb, what are you doing?'

'Come and see!'

Bertie climbed the fence in a more conventional way and when he jumped down beside her, grabbed her round the waist. 'What trouble are you getting me into now, you minx?' He spun her round and she escaped his grasp. 'I've never been on it before, but there's always a first time,' she said, breathless with happiness and excitement.

'First time for what?' he said, rushing now to keep up with her as she ran round the side of the church. Moonlight bounced off the tall wooden structure, as Milly called back.

'Follow me, Bertie, time to live a bit. We're going on the joy slide!'

25

'Turn 'em Over'

December 1925–May 1926

Ellen Colman was cradling her granddaughter in her arms. She had been waging a campaign to choose her name, ever since the baby's birth two weeks earlier on a misty December morning in 1925. 'It's a disgrace. The poor child still hasn't got a name!'

'Mum, we've got plenty of time to register her,' Milly said. 'Anyway, I want something a bit different. There's already too many Marys in Dockhead!'

Her mother looked shocked. 'If it's good enough for Our Lady, it's good enough for her! And she was born at Christmas time, what else can you call her? I hope you're not going for any of Bertie's proddywack names.'

Milly laughed. 'Don't worry about that. I've already told him she's not being named after any of his Welsh relations, so she won't be a Blodwen if that's what you mean!'

At that moment Bertie came in with Jimmy; they had been in the Storks Road garden.

'Eggsies!' Jimmy announced. 'Eggsies!'

'Yes, you clever boy, you've been collecting eggs!' Milly said, holding out her arms to hug him as he ran towards her. All her attention had been on the new baby and she'd missed her little boy. He pulled out of her arms, then sidled up shyly to his grandmother. With a gentle forefinger, he prodded the baby's cheek. 'Baby.' He looked round smiling.

'Yes, darlin',' said Mrs Colman, 'and we'll be calling her that till the cows come home if your mother's got anything to do with it!'

Bertie caught Milly's eye. She hoped he wasn't going to give in, but she'd noticed that he would fall over backwards when it came to her mother. Though Mrs Colman would never forgive him for not being Catholic, her early distrust had mellowed and she'd begun to show grudging respect, and even affection, for her son-in-law in the past year.

'Well, if Mary's too common,' he said, looking with undisguised adoration at his daughter, 'what about Marie?' He pronounced it in the Welsh way.

Jimmy looked up at Bertie, then pointed at the baby. 'Mahri!' he said, mimicking Bertie.

Her mother nodded. 'That'll do. Marie's Our Lady, whatever way you want to pronounce it.'

'Well, I'm glad you three are happy,' said Milly. 'Now give Marie to me. She's hungry.'

Milly may have been tired, but she was happy too. Marie was not proving such an easy baby as Jimmy. He'd been passive and largely contented, but Marie seemed born fidgety. She couldn't keep still and apparently needed very little sleep. But nonetheless, Milly was captivated by her alert little presence, large blue comprehending eyes taking in everything around her, as though she'd already been a long time in the world. As if reading her thoughts, Marie pushed away from her breast and began grizzling.

'Oh, you don't know what you want, do you?' she asked her restless child, then making the decision for her, she tucked her into the pram and began to bounce it vigorously. No gentle rocking would pacify her daughter. She had to believe the pram was really moving before she would be content.

'Bounce the baby!' said Jimmy, toddling over to join in the fun, a huge grin on his elfin little face.

Milly looked on, marvelling at how, from the day she'd married Bertie, everything had gone right, and not more than a month after the wedding he'd finally got a job. She'd suggested that instead of looking for shop work, he use his other skill, and try for a driving job. Many factories were supplementing horse-driven delivery carts with motors, and it was one of the few areas where skilled people were in demand. One afternoon, walking home from Southwell's along Wolseley Street, she'd seen a sign outside the Jacob's biscuit factory advertising for drivers, and the next day Bertie was taken on.

It was a good job and though he would never have the sort of income he'd once had from his uncle's business, at least his pride hadn't been tested for too long, so Milly's ingenuity had only been required to keep them afloat for a short while. Bertie hadn't wanted her to go back to Southwell's after Marie's birth, but however much she loved being at home with the children, his wage would never be enough to pay the rent on Storks Road and keep them all clothed and fed, so she'd carried on making and selling clothes at the Old Clo'. She'd done so well that Bertie had shown her how to do simple book-keeping to keep track of the profits.

One evening, about a month after Marie was born, Bertie came home from Jacob's to find Milly with Marie asleep over one shoulder, Jimmy curled in her lap, a table full of material and a mouthful of pins. She was desperately trying to finish another dress for the market.

'Sorry, Bertie, love, it's cold meat tonight. I've got to get this finished!' she said, through the pins, lifting her cheek to be kissed and smiling gratefully as Bertie lifted Marie from her shoulder.

'Shhhh,' he said, quickly rocking the baby when she threatened to wake.

Milly darted him a look that needed no translation.

'You've only just got her to sleep then?' Bertie said, as one-handed he scooped up Jimmy. 'You look like you've had a day of it. I'll put them to bed, while you clear up your sewing.'

After they'd eaten, Bertie sat reading the local Labour Party newspaper and Milly took out her sewing again. They were silent for a while and then Milly became conscious of him looking at her intently.

'What?' she asked, puzzled.

'You look tired.' He reached for her hand.

'Not the fresh young thing you married a year ago?'

'Strike me dumb, I didn't mean that. I just wish you didn't have to do all this sewing.'

'Don't start on that again. We need the extra money, and anyway, you know I love it.'

'But it's wearing you out.'

'It's the kids wearing me out!'

'Well, life shouldn't be all work and bed. Let's have a holiday.'

She looked up sharply. 'We haven't got the—'

'And don't say we haven't got the money. I'll find the money. It'll be good for you and the kids. We're having a holiday.'

And that was that. Bertie was the most easy-going person she'd ever met, but he could also be the most stubborn. In the end he'd sold his father's gold hunter without any regret and booked a week in a guest house in Ramsgate. She would never have admitted it, but her second pregnancy and the demands of two small children had proved more energy sapping than any triple shifts in the jam factory, and by the time they boarded the train at London Bridge, she was secretly glad she'd given in to Bertie's urgings.

Milly narrowed her eyes against bright discs of light which bounced off the rippling waves. The tide was coming in, but the sea was still separated from her by an expanse of ridged wet sand and a paler strip of dry sand. She could see Bertie, with his trousers rolled to the knee, the small curling waves foaming about his bare feet. Her toddler stood next to him, one hand firmly in Bertie's and the other holding a red tin bucket. Bertie squatted down, so he could help the little boy fill the bucket with water. They had been building a sandcastle all morning and were now in the process of filling the moat, making laborious treks from sea to castle with buckets full of water. They were on their fourth trip.

Milly sat in the deckchair, her hand gently resting on the pram where Marie slept. She'd moved their little encampment back into the narrow strip of shade cast by the high promenade wall, grateful for some relief from the heat radiating off fine white sand. It was an unusually warm day in late April, and Ramsgate beach was crowded with holidaymakers and day trippers, encouraged out by fine weather. There wasn't a patch of spare sand between the red-and-white striped deckchairs. All along the shoreline, children splashed and ran in and out of the sea, while men with suit trousers rolled and women holding up skirts paddled and strolled along the sea edge.

This was Milly's first trip to the seaside, and she had been every bit as excited as Jimmy by the novelty of it. Some of the families in Dockhead were able to afford seaside holidays if the fathers were foremen or dockmasters, but generally there was only one form of holiday: hop-picking in Kent. Much as Milly loved the hop fields, the seaside had been a revelation. It was the air that struck her. Sharp as salt on the tongue; clean as a blade with a honed edge. Compared to this sea air, Bermondsey's was thick as dirty cotton wool, clogged with soot and smoke. At home, it was hard work sometimes even to breathe, but here, each breath was as easy and natural as the daily incoming and outgoing of the tide. Each morning she threw up the bedroom window of their guest house and took in a gulping breath. No wonder people loved the sea. And then there was the uncluttered horizon, not a roof or a chimney stack, just sky meeting the straight edge of sea, broken here and there by a steamer or a sail.

Now, sitting on the beach, enjoying the unaccustomed freedom of doing nothing at all, she leaned her head back and glanced up at the couples and families strolling along the promenade above where she sat. Her attention was caught by a laughing group of three young women, in summer hats and flowing dresses, who sat on the promenade railing swinging their legs. Suddenly she was transported back to another lifetime. She saw her little sister Elsie gazing up at a poster of three young women. *Wouldn't it be lovely to go to the seaside instead of down hopping*, Elsie had said, and Milly, so angry because she couldn't go, had dragged her off, dismissing her sister's longing as selfishness. Now she understood what Elsie had longed for and wished she could spirit her here. She closed her eyes, tears pooling beneath the lids – tears of regret and tears of guilt, for she'd visited Elsie only once since her marriage last February. Her sister hadn't even commented when Milly showed her the wedding photo. After that, the truth was, Milly had simply found it too painful to visit again.

Suddenly she felt her face being sprinkled with cold water and opened her eyes with a start.

'Wake up, sleepyhead, come and see the castle!' Bertie stood over her with Jimmy's bucket, ready to douse her again. She made a dive for him, knocking him off his feet, while Jimmy, his city child's pale body browned with sun and crusted sand, stood stock-still, a worried look on his face.

'Mummy's cryin'!' he accused, until Milly pulled him down too, wrestling them both into submission.

'Who's the king of the castle?' she demanded, sitting on Bertie's chest and tickling Jimmy until they both laughingly capitulated. 'Mummy is!'

Their first seaside holiday had been every bit the success that Bertie had hoped. Milly had the spring in her long stride again and even the children seemed less fractious. But as soon as they returned from their week at Ramsgate there came news that worried Bertie and frightened Milly. While they'd been away, there had been talk in the newspapers of a miners' strike in response to the colliery owners demanding more work for less pay. Bertie said the word at the Labour Institute was that if the miners went out, there would be a national uprising in support of them, for if it could happen to the miners, then everyone would be under threat.

One Thursday evening, not long after their return, Bertie came home from a lecture given by Dr Salter at the Fort Road Labour Institute with the news that a general strike of all workers had been called.

'The doctor's right when he says we should stick together like glue, Milly, or else it'll be every wage that's cut next. We've got to stand with the miners if the working man in this country is going to have any chance of a decent life. Look at us last week. Just a few days away at the seaside, and see what a difference it's made to you – you've got back the roses in your cheeks!'

She smiled as he reached out to stroke her face. 'It certainly made me feel alive! I suppose it's right what you said. It shouldn't be all work and bed, should it? But what would it mean, if we did "stick together like glue"?'

Bertie threw up the back kitchen window as he lit his pipe. The spring night air was mild, and the sweetness of bluebells planted beneath the window came wafting through to her.

'Come into the garden with me.'

They walked outside and she waited while he drew on the glowing bowl of tobacco and puffed. He could never seem to gather his thoughts quickly, or perhaps, unlike her, he preferred not to put both feet into his mouth as soon as he opened it.

'What he means by "sticking together like glue" is that all working men, wherever they are in the country, should come out on strike . . . in sympathy.'

She certainly had sympathy for the miners and their families. She'd read enough in the newspapers about their lives lately – worse off than before the war, many faced seeing their children starve, and they had little to lose by going out on strike. But what good would a sympathy strike do, she asked him. Wouldn't it just mean their own families and children starving?

'Not if we organize it properly, with a strike fund, so no striker's family needs to go hungry. And imagine, Milly, what would happen if the railways came out and the docks and the print, all the heavy industries?'

'The country'd come to a standstill,' she answered.

'Exactly!' He poked the air with his pipe stem. 'And then the government'd be forced to give the miners a living wage.'

She put her hand through his arm and asked softly, 'Would you go on strike, Bertie?'

'I would!' he said. 'I'd be ashamed to do anything else, Milly.'

She could feel him tense a little and knew he was waiting for her to dissuade him. Though some of his decisions might seem to others fanciful and impractical, they had always turned out for the good. She only had to look at her own life. Good sense would have told Bertie to run like the wind from common Milly Colman, teetering on the edge of the Thames with a bastard on her hip, but instead he had run in the opposite direction, straight into her arms.

'Bertie, whatever you do, I know it'll be the right thing,' she said, and she meant it, for if joining a general strike was his latest foolish quest, then it was hers too, whatever the consequences might be for all of them.

And it appeared most trade union members agreed with Dr Salter and Bertie, for on the third of May, the General Strike was called. That evening, when the first workers downed tools, there was a meeting at the Bermondsey Town Hall, which Bertie attended. He came home almost glowing, as he described how the whole borough council had voluntarily disbanded itself and set up a Council of Action for the duration of the strike. Bertie, along with most of the other drivers at Jacob's, refused to cross the picket lines at the docks, and as most of the raw materials for the biscuits came from the river warehouses, work at the factory virtually ceased. The same was true of all Bermondsey food factories, including Southwell's, which although it had its own wharf, couldn't land fruit or sugar without the stevedores' cooperation. It wouldn't be long before there was an impact on the food cupboards of the capital – Bermondsey wasn't called London's Larder for nothing.

Bertie immediately volunteered for the Council of Action and was given the job of helping distribute the daily bulletin, produced by the Bermondsey Labour Party. In the absence of any newspapers it was essential that all the strikers knew exactly what was going on, so the daily mimeographed paper was snapped up within minutes of it being distributed. Every evening, Bertie collected stacks of the newly printed sheets from the Labour Institute and drove a commandeered council van around Bermondsey, delivering the bulletin to official distribution points along Tooley Street, Tower Bridge Road and the Old Kent Road. When he told Milly the job he'd been given, her heart sank. Police were said to be arresting anyone producing or even reading a strike bulletin. But when she asked him if he couldn't do another job, he'd shrugged it off, saying they'd have to get through the barricades to catch him and that wouldn't be easy as all the roads into Bermondsey were manned by strikers.

The Town Hall in Spa Road became the centre of operations, and on the second afternoon of the strike Milly joined other women there for a packed meeting. They crammed into the hall. Many, like Milly, had husbands who were strikers; some were striking themselves, or, like Florence Green, were willing volunteers. She'd been surprised to meet Florence on the way to the meeting. Somehow she'd expected her to be one of the middle-class volunteers on the opposite side of the barricades, but as they walked together along Southwark Park Road Florence had explained.

'Bermondsey's my home now, Milly. I could no more cross the barricades than I could return to my father's parsonage, not after all the hardship I've seen. Besides, the doctor would have my guts for garters if I did!'

Milly laughed. Dr Salter might be a saint, but when it came to commitment to Bermondsey, he was a hard taskmaster.

'Everything's so quiet, isn't it?' Florence said.

Milly had to agree. The familiar Bermondsey streets had an eerie, abandoned feel, with the normal rumble of carts and crush of traffic silenced. It felt to Milly as though they were under siege. Main roads in and out of the borough were barricaded by the Council of Action, with only authorized vehicles allowed through. Pickets were being posted at the docks, railway and bus stations. It felt as though the natural boundaries of the borough had been sealed: the river to the north; London Bridge to the west; Rotherhithe Tunnel to the east; and the Old Kent Road to the south. They were turning the tiny borough into an impregnable fortress within the very heart of London.

The town hall was abuzz with the ear-splitting, high-pitched chatter of women. Milly had left Jimmy and Marie with her mother, but many of the women had brought their children and the hall rang with shouts from toddlers and cries from babies. As they squeezed past the crush into the hall, Milly heard her name being called. It was Kitty, beckoning them over. Although there was not a seat to be had, Kitty elbowed out a space near her in the aisle. There was an almighty banging from the stage as a woman with a gavel tried to establish order.

'It's worse than club night at the Settlement!' Kitty said.

Florence pulled a face. 'Oh no, club night is much worse, especially when Milly Colman and Kitty Bunclerk turn up drunk!'

The three of them giggled as the exasperated chairwoman bellowed, 'Order, ladies, please, it's not Saturday night at the Dockhead Tavern!'

In spite of the apparent chaos, by the end of the meeting rotas had been organized for soup kitchens, and volunteers signed up for supplying tea and sandwiches to men on the picket lines. Women who were on strike, like Kitty, would join the picket lines themselves.

'I wish you were still at Southwell's,' Kitty said. 'We might need someone who can land a wallop on that picket line!'

'If I didn't have the kids, I'd be there!'

As it was, she signed up for a daily stint at the Labour Institute, preparing food parcels for strikers' families. She was surprised at how quickly she'd been caught up in the excitement of all the preparations. There were plenty of wives who complained and made their husbands' lives a misery, failing to see any benefit to themselves in an enterprise that might leave them for weeks without a wage coming in. But she found it easy to believe in the rightness of the cause, and talking to Bertie just confirmed that this was the only decent, unselfish course of action, for both of them.

But Milly had her first glimpse of the earnestness of the government's resistance to their cause when she went to Arnold's Place, a few days after the strike began. Her mother was against the strike – the Archbishop had after all pronounced it a sin against God – but nevertheless, she juggled her conscience as she always did, and agreed to look after Jimmy and Marie while Milly went with Florence Green to deliver sandwiches to the pickets at Butler's Wharf. Florence hadn't been the only middle-class volunteer at the Settlement to surprise her with their support. Many of them, like Francis Beaumont, were Oxbridge graduates, who'd come to Bermondsey on short-term missions. Having lived among the poor streets of the riverside, they now found it impossible to cross the line and join the students volunteering at Hay's Wharf to unload vessels in an attempt to break the strike. When Milly had expressed her surprise, Florence told her that 'her Francis' had been helping Bertie deliver the strike bulletins.

'We both agreed which side we'd be on, when we heard about Blaina.'

Milly hadn't heard of the place, but Florence told her it was a small village in Wales, where children were near to starving. 'If we call this a Christian country, then I don't see how our government can countenance cutting those men's wages even further. Francis and I believe it's our Christian duty to stand with them, Milly!'

So there it was, Milly thought, God, as usual, was on both sides, and in the end, the only thing to do was to make up your own mind.

Her mother's front door was wide open when they arrived. Florence waited patiently, while Milly persuaded Jimmy it would be more fun to stay with his grandmother than to come with her. With the front door still open, it wasn't hard to hear the familiar bellowing of Barrel as he came hallooing along the street.

'That boy's got a gate on him like the Blackwall Tunnel!' her mother said as he, Amy and all the usual crew of urchins clustered breathless round the front door.

'They've sent in the big guns, the navy's arrived!' Barrel leaned on the doorpost, chest heaving.

As no newspapers were being printed, it was useful to have a little band of spies roaming the docks, and the children had proved very effective at slipping through the lines of policemen and soldiers and ferreting out information. People started to come out of their houses, curious to hear the latest development. Many were strikers, home for dinner or a break from the picket lines, and Milly could see looks of alarm passing from one to the other. Fear seemed to ripple along the street as women ran to gather up children and men headed off towards the river.

Milly handed Jimmy to her mother and then broke into a trot, with Florence at her side, the two of them following the crowd down to the riverside. They arrived at Horsleydown Stairs just in time to see two huge ships steaming into the pool of London. They dwarfed the tiny tugs and lighters ranged along the dockside, and as the arms of Tower Bridge rose to greet them, their combined grey bulk blotted out the Tower of London on the far shore. Lines of sailors, in smart whites, lined the decks, and just as Barrel had said, the big guns seemed to be aimed directly at the riverside streets and docks of Bermondsey. It felt like wartime all over again.

'Destroyers!' one man explained to her. 'I was in the navy during the war. They could blow us all to smithereens if they wanted to.'

It made Milly wonder how many of the strikers who surrounded her were ex-servicemen, how many had risked their lives in the trenches, fighting for the very country which was now turning its navy upon them. If anything could make you bitter, it must be that. Yet there was no eruption of violence; there was no call to arms. Instead the men seemed to accept the navy's presence, as though it were simply the opposing side in a football match turning up on to the playing field.

The effect, though terrifying to Milly, seemed to steel the strikers, and that evening, when Bertie came home from distributing the strike bulletin, she asked him if he believed they had any chance of winning.

She was surprised when he said, 'Not a chance in hell, love. They've got volunteers driving trains and buses; they've got the army delivering petrol and breaking the picket lines at the docks. Now they've even got the navy, so if they can't reach the docks by land, they'll go in by river. No, our mistake was thinking that once the country knew what the miners were being asked to agree to, they'd see it wasn't fair. But unless you've tried to live on that wage, well . . . I suppose I might have been the same once, but I've seen the other side, haven't I?'

'Well then, what's the point in going on with it?'

'Because it's still the right thing to do.' His voice was firm, but she detected that the glow of his initial excitement had begun to fade. Then, on the following evening, hers vanished altogether.

She was upstairs, putting Marie into her cot, when she heard him come home. His usual call of 'Where's my beautiful girl?' didn't come. Running downstairs to greet him, Milly found the front door already wide open. She looked into the rather dirty face of Francis Beaumont, Elsie's one-time lawyer and Florence Green's fiancé. She stopped at the foot of the stairs, suddenly cold.

'Bertie?'

'He's fine,' Francis said, then turned quickly to help another man get Bertie into the house. The two men got beneath Bertie's arms, taking his weight as he hobbled into the passage. His head was lowered, and he held a handkerchief tight to his forehead, trying to staunch blood which was already turning the white cotton into a red pulpy ball. The man nodded at Milly. 'He's been in a scrape, missus. He's all right, though, ain't you, Bert?'

'Thanks, Sid, I'll be fine.'

'Don't 'spect we'll see you tomorrow. Have a blow,' Sid said, tipping his hat to Milly.

Francis hovered, concerned. 'I think it looks worse than it is, Mrs Hughes,' he said uncertainly, 'but if you'd like me to get a doctor . . .'

'No, no . . .' Bertie, pulling himself up straight, replied. 'No need for that. Thanks for driving me home, Francis, g'night.'

As soon as Francis had left, Bertie lurched heavily against the passage wall and Milly rushed to help him.

'Bertie! What's happened to you? Oh, love, look at the state of you! Here, let me see.'

'I daren't move,' he said, lifting the handkerchief. 'I'll get blood all over the show.'

She examined his forehead. A deep gash oozed blood, and he quickly stuffed the handkerchief back over the wound.

'Come on, let me get you to the sink.'

She helped him through to the scullery, where she turned the tap full on. Soon the stone sink ran full of pink swirling water, as ruby lozenges continued to pool and drip heavily from his forehead. Lifting his chin to examine the wound, she grabbed a clean tea towel from the dresser drawer. 'Keep this pressed hard on it, while I fetch the medicine tin.'

Fumbling through the small tin she kept in the dresser for emergencies, she found a few rolled-up bandages and some antiseptic cream, and placed them on the draining board. Then she gently began cleaning the wound.

'Looks like you've got a load of grit in it. How the bloody hell did it happen?' She tried to steady her hand, but the sight of so much blood scared her. It wasn't just a surface graze – that much was obvious.

He tried to give his usual wry smile, but the gash cut right through his raised eyebrow, and he winced.

'Ouch, it really does hurt to laugh!' he said.

'Well then, don't laugh!'

While she removed bits of grit and made a padded bandage, he told her how he'd come by the wound.

'It was our lot! Those stupid sods up by the barricade in Old

Kent Road. Sid and his mates tried to turn Dr Salter's car over and I went and got in the way!'

'Sid? What, the one who brought you home?'

Bertie grimaced as she attempted to fasten the bandage. 'Yes, the chump, I think he felt guilty.'

'But why would they do that? Surely they're not turning on their own now?'

'Idiots didn't recognize him, thought he was police, trying to break through the barricade. Mind you, the doctor should have had the *Council for Action* sticker on the windscreen and he didn't, but you'd think they'd recognize the most famous strike supporter in Bermondsey!'

'So how did you get the worst of it?' She leaned down to see what damage he'd done to his leg. The ankle was swollen and turning a deep shade of plum. 'This'll need a compress, looks sprained.'

She helped him back to the kitchen, stopping as he swayed and almost toppled over. Then, easing him into his chair, she kneeled to gently wrap his ankle in a wet cloth.

'I'd just finished delivering the bulletin along the Old Kent Road, and I hear this almighty row going on up by the Thomas A Becket. There's about a dozen men at the barricade, surrounding some poor chap in a car. All I can hear is "Turn 'em over, turn 'em over!" And they start rocking it backwards and forwards. The chap's still in there and I'm thinking, they'll have it over with him inside, they could kill the poor feller. So I jump out of the van, grab one of them and try to talk sense, and of course it's too late. Some bright spark picks up a bit of broken kerbing and lobs it at the windscreen. That's when I recognized him. I mean, you can't miss him, Milly, great bald head, round specs, always got the same mac on. I starts shouting at them, "It's Dr Salter!" I'm hollering, but they're so fired up they can't hear, so the only thing I could think to do was jump up on the bonnet!'

Milly groaned. 'Oh, Bertie, you soppy sod.' She felt a mixture of anger and pride, but she only let him see the anger. 'You could've got yourself killed, and not a thought for your family!'

'Sorry, duck, but you're always telling me I should be more impulsive,' he said, shamefaced.

She got up to kiss him. 'Not like that! Anyway, what happened next?'

'Well, I got between Dr Salter and another lump of kerbstone that Sid tossed over. That one got me straight between the eyes and I tumbled off the bonnet, that's when I did my ankle. But it gave the doctor a chance to get out and show the idiots who he was. He gave them a bit of a telling off, said we weren't to resort to violence, but really, he took it in his stride. Thanked me and looked at the wound, said I should watch out for concussion and that he would drive me home himself, but he had to get to Westminster, find out what was going on. He writes the bulletins himself, you know.'

Milly was less interested in Dr Salter's journalistic skills than in the concussion. 'Well, you can't go to bed yet, we'll have to wait and see if you get sleepy.'

He reached for her. 'Why can't I go to bed? I think that would be a very good idea.' He drew her on to his lap. 'And I'm not at all sleepy!'

She smiled into his kiss and said, 'No! You're a wounded soldier and I'm the matron!'

'Well, I quite like the sound of that!'

Beneath the bandage, she could imagine the raised eyebrow and she thumped him gently on the chest, laughing now with relief that he seemed fine and not, as she'd feared, about to collapse from loss of blood. Still, they sat up for a long time, with Milly unwilling to let Bertie sleep too soon. Eventually, with both their eyelids drooping, she helped him upstairs to bed.

She lay listening to his breathing, which seemed even and normal. But to his deep irritation, she insisted on waking him every other hour. The sight of him covered in blood had shocked her into the realization of how precious Bertie had become to her, and she would willingly suffer his barks of, 'Strike me dumb, leave me alone, woman, I'm all right!' if it meant keeping him safe.

But in spite of all her vigilance, by next morning his symptoms had worsened. She took him a cup of tea and his hand grasped her wrist instead.

'Looks like there are two cups to me, just a bit of double vision from the knock.'

'We'll have to get you to Guy's!' was her immediate response, but he refused. 'Don't fuss, it'll go away on its own.'

'Don't worry about the money, we'll find it.'

'Did I say anything about money?'

But he didn't have to. Unforeseen medical bills were not in their budget, and usually anything that couldn't be cured with home remedies had the 'wait and see if it gets better' treatment applied to it.

'If only we hadn't gone to Ramsgate . . .'

His face seemed to crumple and she wished she hadn't voiced her regret. He'd been so proud to be able to take them on a proper holiday.

'But anyway,' she added quickly, 'I've got a bit put by from the clothes.' That wasn't entirely true, but she hoped to God she would be earning a bit at the next market.

She only realized how ill he was feeling when he tried to get up to do the bulletin run. Trying to ease himself out of bed, he swayed and fell back on to the bolster. Splayed out, he could barely raise himself.

'All right, love, I give in. I'm staying here today.'

She did not dare leave him, and spent a frantically anxious day, running upstairs to check on him every five minutes, while still trying to keep Jimmy occupied. As his second birthday approached, her lovely boy had been transformed into a biting, spitting little monkey. She was at a loss to know how her angel had been replaced by this demon changeling. She found herself longing for a knock on the door. Now she understood the value of Arnold's Place. If she'd been living there, she could have popped

322

next door, knowing her neighbour would watch the children while she went for a doctor. But Storks Road wasn't like that. It was a respectable street and people were polite enough, but nothing like Arnold's Place where the neighbours were like family.

When long hours passed and Bertie's vision and balance still hadn't improved, she began to seriously consider leaving him to call a doctor, and was about to put on her coat when the longed-for knock on the door came. Perhaps it was Florence Green, come to see why she hadn't turned up for her stint at the Labour Institute today. She flew down the passage and flung open the door to be confronted by a large man wearing a long mac. He was striking to look at, with his domed bald head and round spectacles.

'How's the patient?' he asked, holding up his medical bag.

'Dr Salter! Oh I'm so glad you're here! How did you know where we lived?'

The doctor smiled and said, 'How could I not? I'm your neighbour!'

She couldn't imagine how he'd managed to find time to come – according to Florence, he was spending hours canvassing support at Westminster, dashing back to give speeches at crowded town hall meetings, then often repeating his speeches late into the night, on the town hall steps, addressing the thousands who hadn't been able to find a seat inside. Milly knew he'd been at the surgery less since he'd become an MP, but now he explained that he always had his medical bag in the boot of his car or strapped to his bicycle.

'I couldn't sleep easily in my bed till I'd checked on my gallant protector! I suppose he told you that the men were a little overzealous at the barricades yesterday evening?'

She nodded. 'He said he thought you could've been injured!' The doctor waved away her concern as he followed her into the front parlour.

'Well, it must have been a near thing. It's not like my Bertie to get involved in a fight . . . To be honest, Doctor, I'm more likely to get in a scrap than he is!'

323

The doctor threw back his head and gave a surprisingly loud laugh. 'Well, I have a similarly fierce wife, though her scraps normally happen during the council meetings!' He looked at Milly for a long moment. 'But how are you, my dear? The strike is harder on the wives than on the men.'

'Oh, I'm fine, Doctor. I'm doing what I can to help at the Labour Institute.' He seemed pleased, then suddenly looked up. 'And how's the little chap?'

Milly paused, comprehending why the man had the reputation of a saint. He'd remembered! Out of all the thousands of mothers and babies who must have passed through his care in the past two years, he remembered that brief visit to her mother's, and her own situation.

'Oh, Jimmy is an angel . . . well, he was, until he started to use his teeth on everything but his food!'

Again came the hearty laugh, and picking up his bag, he said, 'Ah, I'm afraid there's only one remedy for that, let him know what it feels like, just a nip. You'll cry longer than he does, but he'll never do it again!'

Her own mother's advice exactly, though she hadn't had the heart to carry it out.

'Now, let's see the patient. How has he been?'

The doctor followed Milly upstairs as she recited the symptoms. She saw him into the bedroom and waited as he stood at the bedside, gently rousing Bertie. But after a while the doctor turned to her, his face suddenly serious. Bertie could not be wakened.

26

Absent Husbands

May 1926

The hours following Dr Salter's arrival sped by in a gut-wrenching series of shocks. The doctor's diagnosis was speedy and terrifying.

'He has severe concussion. We must get him to hospital immediately.'

Milly's strength seemed to melt away. She put out her hand, grasping empty air to keep her upright, and the doctor moved swiftly to her side. 'Listen to me, Mrs Hughes, I am going home to telephone to Guy's. Don't leave Bertie for a minute. Talk to him – he may be able to hear you. I'll be back shortly.' He patted her hand. 'Speed is of the essence, but be strong and try not to worry. These cases often right themselves.'

And he was gone, ramming his trilby on to his head, clattering down the stairs two at a time. He'd said he wouldn't be long, but each silence between the ticks of the bedside clock stretched for an eternity. She pulled up a chair to Bertie's bedside and took his hand. His face was pasty-grey, a film of sweat coating his forehead, his breathing so faint it barely moved the sheet covering him.

She lifted his hand to her lips and kissed it. 'Bertie, love, can you hear me? You've got to wake up, darlin'. Dr Salter's here, he says you've got to wake up.'

Milly felt that somehow the mention of the great doctor's name would galvanize Bertie. He would want to get up, for pride's sake. But he never stirred. She tried to swallow, but her tongue stuck to the roof of her mouth. She had seen her mother unconscious like this once, after a kick in the head from the old man, and though they hadn't been able to rouse her at first, after a while she'd come round. But it had been almost two days since Bertie's injury and now she blamed herself for not doing something earlier.

'Oh, I should have made you go to Guy's. You always say I can wrap you round my little finger, but it's not true, is it, love? You're so stubborn and now look at you . . . Bertie, wake up . . . please . . .'

She squeezed his hand tighter. But the only thing stirring in the room was the second hand on the clock, tick, ticking. Now she began to panic. What if Bertie should die? The doctor had told her to be strong, but she would never be able to bear it.

'Bertie,' she whispered, her voice hoarse with tears, 'don't leave me now, don't die, my love.' Her tears fell on his hand and, kissing the salt away, she pleaded, desperate for some sign he could hear her. 'You always say I'm a tough old boot, don't you? But the secret is, I'm not tough, Bertie, not really, so you've got to come back . . . hear me?'

She didn't know if Bertie had heard her or not, but at that moment the doctor returned. When the ambulance arrived to take him away to Guy's Hospital, she took the doctor aside.

'Doctor, I'm sorry, but we haven't got . . . What I mean is, with the strike and I'm not working, I don't think we can pay for the hospital . . .'

But the doctor simply patted her hand and said, 'You're not to worry about that, Mrs Hughes. There will be no charge.'

Normally she would baulk at such obvious charity, but this time there wasn't a choice. She wouldn't put pride before Bertie's life and she accepted with a grateful resignation.

There was no question of sleep. Although she couldn't be there at his bedside, she sat in vigil at home, staring into the fire's fading embers all through the night, until, in the dawn light, came a gentle knocking on her front door. She opened it to find a middle-aged lady, dressed in wellington boots and mackintosh, with a fisherman's rain hat pulled low over her forehead. She stood in the drizzle-filled, half-light, holding a covered basin.

'Hello, my dear, my name is Ada Salter, Dr Salter's wife. I've brought you some soup.'

Milly was dumbfounded. 'Oh, that's very kind of you, Mrs Salter.' She stepped aside so the woman could come in out of the rain. She'd seen the MP's wife at strike meetings and knew of her council work, but she never imagined having a conversation with her, let alone receiving a dawn visit.

'It's the least I could do. Your husband may well have saved my Alfred's life.' Ada Salter had an earnest air about her, but there was a warmth there too. She wiped her feet vigorously on the doormat, before following Milly into the kitchen and putting the soup on the kitchen table.

'Is the doctor back from the hospital?' Milly asked, holding her breath.

'Yes, he is, my dear, but I've insisted he get at least a few hours' sleep.' She paused. 'I know you'll be desperate for news, but I'm afraid Alfred says there is nothing to report, other than that your husband is much the same.'

The disappointment was like a punch to the stomach, knocking all the breath from her. The hope that, once in hospital, Bertie would recover, was all that had got her through the previous night. Now, with that hope snatched away, she slumped against the table, while Mrs Salter hurried to bring her a chair.'

'You must get some sleep yourself, Milly. May I call you Milly? Else you'll be no good to your husband. Now, let me warm this soup for you.'

Too exhausted to resist, Milly hardly registered the presence of this rather cultured, eccentric-looking lady, bustling about her kitchen as though she owned it. Mrs Salter sat opposite her while Milly reluctantly spooned in the hot soup.

When she'd finished, the woman got briskly to her feet, as though, realizing she could do no more here, she must be up and on to the next task. Milly noticed she had the same fizzing energy as her husband, which quietened down as they gave you their full attention but once satisfied they could do no more, instantly roused them to action, as though a thousand pressing tasks were spurring them on. She knew couples often grew to resemble each other, and though she'd only been with Bertie such a short time, she hoped she had grown more like him, that she had taken on some of his slow, kind ways and his thoughtfulness. Poor Bertie, she doubted there was any trait of hers that could have improved him. But thinking of him only brought back tears to her eyes and seeing them roll down her cheek Mrs Salter gripped her shoulder with surprising firmness.

'There's some soup left for the little boy,' the woman said kindly, and then almost shyly reached into the depths of the mackintosh pocket. 'I brought him a present.' It was a knitted rabbit, with long floppy ears and a scarlet waistcoat. 'I make them for all my young friends,' she said almost sadly, and before Milly could thank her she went on hastily, 'Now, my husband says you mustn't give up hope, though things look bleak. Sometimes all that's required is rest. And the same could be said of you, try to get some sleep!' She squeezed Milly's hand. 'No need to see me out, my dear.'

Milly's despair and fear had been subtly shifted by Mrs Salter's visit, and she was sure that her returning strength was not just the effect of the warming soup. She knew that the doctor and his wife had experienced their own share of tragedy, losing their only daughter to one of the frequent outbreaks of scarlet fever in Bermondsey. That had been many years before, but whatever individual fire the woman had passed through, it had given her a steel-like strength which this morning she'd passed on to Milly. Going to the front-parlour window, Milly's gaze followed Ada Salter as she strode down Storks Road, hat dipped against the falling rain, looking the very embodiment of grit and determination, and Milly suddenly felt strong enough to face the coming day, whatever it might bring.

There was no sign that he knew she was there. The strike had been over for almost a week, ending in bitter defeat for the strikers, many of whom felt they had been betrayed by their own leaders. The miners were now battling on alone, slowly being starved into submission. Milly felt the defeat keenly. Had her Bertie sacrificed himself for nothing? Looking at his sunken, grey face, from which all trace of his whimsical spirit seemed to have been erased, it certainly felt like it.

Her mother and Amy had stepped in to look after Jimmy and Marie, while she made the daily journey to Guy's Hospital. Dr Salter had told her she must be patient, that Bertie could wake up at any time. But patience wasn't her strong point and she couldn't sit by, doing nothing, while he faded away before her eyes. She pushed back the chair, and, heedless of Matron's rules, lay down beside him on the hospital bed. To be so near him and feel so far away was unbearable. Pale green screens had been drawn round his bed, to give him the peace and rest the doctors said he needed, though how he could be guaranteed either in this packed ward, she didn't know. Besides, she dreaded him having so much peace that he simply drifted away. Determined to keep him firmly in this world, she put her arm across his chest and lay with her lips next to his ear. She began to remind him of all the reasons it was worth staying alive.

'Bertie, it's time to come back to me, love. You can't save a person and then just leave them high and dry, do you hear me? It's not fair and I'll be so bloody angry with you if you do, I'll knock yer bleedin' block off . . .'

She waited hopelessly for his laugh. It was something she often said, when she wanted to make him smile. Milly kissed his unresponsive mouth, not gently. She knew he loved her fierceness, he loved her fire; she would remind him of all the things he loved about her, and force him back.

'The doctors say you need peace and quiet, but you don't want that really, do you?' Sometimes in the midst of their domestic cacophony, Bertie would reminisce in mock despair about his single days, when he could get a bit of peace and quiet, but it was just another one of his teasing jokes. 'I know you'd miss my noisy ways, you'd miss our Jimmy's tantrums and you'd miss Madam Marie's cakehole at two o'clock in the morning, I know you would . . . You don't want no peace and quiet . . . Bertie, you don't.'

She gripped the sheet that covered him, clutching at its shallow movement, a drowning woman grasping at a piece of flotsam. Then there was a stillness, whether outside herself or in her heart, she couldn't tell, but it was the stillness at the centre of a storm and she felt the strength drain from her. She sobbed noisily into his neck, repeating over and over, 'Don't go, Bertie, don't go,' till she was hoarse and the tight white sheet was stained with her tears. But there was only silence. He hadn't heard her.

She knew she must leave. Drawing away from him, she wiped away tears with the back of her hand. She had her children to think about, and though her mother was looking after them for as many hours as she could, Mrs Colman had her own troubles at the moment. Shortly after Bertie's accident, the old man had gone missing. It wasn't the first time. Her mother suspected he was with 'his fancy woman', a pub landlady in Whitechapel, but his absence had never lasted longer than three days before.

'Then when she's had enough of him, she chucks him out and he turns up here like a bad penny,' her mother had said. But it had been over a week and now she was living on tick and what the pawnshop brought in.

Milly pushed herself up from the bed, searching Bertie's face once more.

'I'll give the kids a kiss from you,' she whispered. 'See you tomorrow, love.' Pulling aside the screen, she looked back over her shoulder, dreading another anxious night, wondering if the next day would take him from her. But there was nothing there to give her hope, and she turned away, praying, 'Please God he'll be better tomorrow.'

As she left the hospital, she resolved to ease at least one worry in the family. She knew she should have done it before now, but with all her energies focused on Bertie, she'd had no interest in the old man. But if Bertie could speak, he would tell her to do it, for her mother's sake. It wasn't so much that Mrs Colman was worried about the old man's welfare; it was the uncertainty of when and in what state he would eventually turn up. How her mother would survive if he never came back, she couldn't imagine. She'd have to apply to the Guardians of the Poor, in Tooley Street, and what they doled out would be pitiful.

It was late in the afternoon when she turned into the Neckinger and made her way to Bevington's. Over the tannery wall, she could see a vast grid of square stone pits, full of various stinking liquors, where hides were soaked, limed and tanned. Bermondsey had more than its fair share of smelly industries, but this had to be the vilest, giving off a pungent aroma of rotting flesh, stinging lime, rendered fat, noxious urine and faeces, all topped off with the earthy mouldering bark of the tanning liquid. Yet, as a child, Milly and her sisters had played along this wall, totally unaware of the stench, curious only to peek through at their father and the other men lifting and dipping the heavy soaking hides. The lime pits ran right along the wall, so their game was a dangerous one, for if they should slip, they would fall into one of the deep pits and never get out again.

She waited at the tannery gates. In a few minutes the shift would change and she'd be sure to catch the old man then, either coming on or going off. When the whistle blew, she stood aside, letting the crowd of leather workers jostle out of the gateway. They were mainly men, but in the sea of flat caps four or five deep were little groups of women, employed in the lighter dressing and finishing processes. Milly stood on tiptoe, searching for her father's familiar red complexion and dark moustache. When the crowd had dwindled to a few stragglers, she waited for the oncoming shift, again the same tide of workers, but going in the opposite direction. Still there was no sign of the old man. But she did spot Arthur Cook, a drinking friend of the old man.

'Arthur?' she called out to him as he went through the gateway.

He spun round. 'Oh hello, Milly, love, what are you doing here?' He had a red complexion and a blue bulbous nose that had fascinated Milly as a child. She'd been convinced Arthur was a born liar, for she believed the tales that God punished liars by adding all those extraneous, blue-tinged bumps to a nose. Now she knew that Arthur was probably as honest as the next man and had merely acquired the extra blooms after twenty years frequenting the Swan and Sugarloaf.

'I've come to see the old man,' she said simply.

Arthur drew her to one side. 'Well, love, you've come to the wrong place 'cause he ain't turned in all week and the manager's talking of sacking him. Don't yer mother know where he is?' Arthur said with a knowing look.

So the old man hadn't had the decency to spare her mother his boasting.

'Does everyone know about his fancy woman over in Whitechapel then?' Milly asked.

Arthur ducked his head, the rosy hue of his face deepening. 'No disrespect to your poor mother, Milly, but wouldn't it be a blessing to her if he did sling his hook?'

Milly shook her head. 'If I was her, I'd put my hands together if he went, but Arthur, you know Mum, she made her vows before God and that's that. But didn't he say anything to you?'

'I was with him in the Swan last week and he never said a word about pissing off and he never give no notice here, neither. But he's a secretive git your old man, always has been.' And with that, Arthur tipped his hat and went in for his shift.

Milly sighed. If he hadn't been at work all week, then she suspected the old man had finally abandoned her mother, at least until the Whitechapel landlady ran out of money or drink to keep him.

*

The little house in Arnold's Place was in disarray when she arrived. Her mother was literally pulling at her hair with frustration, as Amy kneeled with Jimmy locked in an embrace that had nothing to do with affection.

'He's been a little cow-son,' was her mother's greeting. 'Biting and scratching. I know his dad's poorly but, Mill, you've got to discipline that child!'

Jimmy was howling, legs drumming, as he kicked back at Amy.

'Jimmy! Why're you being so naughty for your nan?' But as soon as the little boy saw her, he stopped flailing and put out his arms. On his chubby hand she saw two tiny puncture marks. 'Oh, Mum, you didn't!' She gathered Jimmy up and rubbed at his hand. Perhaps she did spoil him, but only she knew how near she'd come to losing him – twice over, and her dealings with Jimmy would always be tinged with guilty memories of that night she'd held him above the Thames.

'He's bit Amy and drawn blood too! Anyway it's only what you should've done weeks ago, and sure as I stand here, he won't do it n'more!'

She couldn't be too angry with her mother. She'd had enough heartache bringing up her own children, without the burden of another lot.

'I'm sorry he's been such a sod, Mum, but he'll grow out of it. He's a good boy really.' And she was rewarded by an angelic smile from Jimmy and a pat on her cheek from his soft, clammy little hand.

Amy rubbed her arm absent-mindedly.

'I'm sorry he bit you,' Milly said. 'Show me.'

'Didn't hurt. Anyway, it's not his fault.' Amy pulled her arm away as she turned to pick up Marie.

'How did you leave poor Bertie?' her mother said, sitting down at the table, ready to relax, now Milly was there to control her child.

Milly shook her head.

'Oh, darlin', I'm sorry. I've been saying me prayers.'

'Me too.' And if her mother only knew just how fervently, she would have been proud of her. 'But listen, Mum, I've been to the Neckinger on the way here.'

Amy had stopped rocking Marie, her sharp eyes fixed on Milly, like a cornered cat calculating which way to leap. Milly sometimes wondered what went on in her sister's head; she was always so elusive, so mistrusting, yet sometimes a spark of fierce devotion would burst from her, leaving Milly certain that half their conflicts growing up had been down to the old man. Amy had protected herself by building a wall that excluded even her sisters. Now, when the girl needed shielding from him most, it was almost impossible for Milly to offer help. She wondered if the wall between them was too well built and too long-standing to ever come down. She turned back to her mother.

'He's not been at work all week.'

'How d'you know that?'

'Arthur Cook told me, said the manager might sack him too.'

Her mother frowned and she began to nervously pluck at her bottom lip.

'Mum, I reckon he's set himself up at that woman's pub over in Whitechapel. I think he'll be gone for a while.'

Her mother was silent. Surely she must have seen this day coming? But perhaps she'd got so used to living under his tyranny, she couldn't imagine any other life.

'Mum,' Milly persisted, 'we've got to work out how you're going to live.'

To her dismay, her mother's head dropped and she threw up her apron to cover her face. Milly heard her muffled wailing prayer.

'Oh Gawd, Jesus, Mary and Joseph, bless us'n spare us'n save us'n keep us, what am I going to do now?'

In spite of Milly's best efforts it took a couple of hours to dispel her mother's fears that she and Amy would end up in the workhouse. Milly stayed with her, until at last she calmed down enough to admit that the old man leaving might be a blessing in disguise. Back at Storks Road that night she decided she must spend an hour with Jimmy. His new favourite toy was Mrs Salter's gift and they played with the rabbit till she felt she had her child back again. Then she took him on her lap and sang him one of her mother's old favourites. '*Mother, I love you, I will work for two. You worked for me, a long, long time, and now I will work for you.*'

'Again!' the little boy said, contentedly sucking at the rabbit's ear. And she sang it again and again, till all traces of his earlier rage had left those calm, brown eyes. 'There's Mummy's boy.'

She kissed him gently on the forehead and took him up to her own bedroom, where she lay down next to him. Waiting for him to drift off to sleep, she began to walk every possible path ahead of her. She and her mother were facing the same future. Neither of their husbands might be returning, and if that happened, she must be the one to ensure they didn't all end up in St Olave's Workhouse. She lifted her hand above her head; moonlight coming through the window made shadow patterns on the wall. This was a favourite game of Bertie's to lull Jimmy at bedtime. Now she waggled her fingers, making for him a swan, a dog, a deer and a snake. If only those fingers could conjure enough money to keep them all safe. But perhaps they could! It would be her own nimble fingers – sorting fruit at Southwell's, picking hops in Kent, sewing clothes into the night – that would keep them all afloat.

Soon the shadow patterns soothed Jimmy into peaceful slumber. She herself slept only fitfully, fully clothed, curled up next to Jimmy, and in the early light woke with a start, stiff and frightened. She had been dreaming that Bertie was home. He'd come through the door, calling for his beautiful girl, but he was more vibrant, more glowing with health than she had ever seen his pale grocer's face in reality. His smile was radiant, but as she ran to embrace him, he turned, and still smiling over his shoulder, walked out of the house. The dream left her bereft, as if life had taunted her with wonderful possibilities, only to snatch them away.

She'd slept a few short hours and it was now just past dawn. Groaning at the stiffness in her limbs, she eased herself out of bed and went downstairs. She took out the dress she'd been working on before Bertie's accident, and began to sew.

It was a simple navy shift, with a nautical feel, long white collar over a straight bodice, the low waist emphasized by a white band. After two hours' work, Milly was satisfied. She wrapped the dress and put it with another she'd made, identical, but in a different size. She'd intended to wait till she had enough money to rent a stall, but there was no time for that. She'd have to hang the dresses from the pram, and hope for the best.

Later that day Milly came home from the market with enough money to pay the rent on Storks Road, and some to spare. Pleased with her morning's takings, she decided to buy her mother some groceries when she dropped the children at Arnold's Place. With two children in tow, she didn't want to cart the shopping all the way from Tower Bridge Road, but when she reached Hughes' shop she hesitated, embarrassed to go in. She hadn't set foot in the grocery since Bertie's dismissal. For a while she fiddled about with the pram, making sure Jimmy was well strapped in at one end and Marie contented at the other. Then, determined not to let the Hughes stop her from shopping in her own street, she pushed through the door, making certain the bell rang loud enough to ensure she couldn't be ignored. Short, with wispy hair and a pudgy face, the man behind the counter looked nothing like Bertie. He gave her a stony stare.

'We don't give tick.'

This was plainly untrue as she could see the familiar slate hanging at the end of the counter. He obviously knew who she was. She shouldn't have been shocked at the depth of the Hughes' disapproval of her, but perhaps she'd grown so used to being Mrs Hughes, she'd forgotten she was once Milly Colman. Still, she was determined not to disgrace Bertie by making a show of herself. She clenched her fists to control her temper and swallowed the tart reply that rose to her lips.

Pulling her purse from her bag, she said, 'I can pay.'

'Well, I don't want your custom here,' he said, placing his squat hands on to the counter. 'You're not welcome in my shop.'

She stared back at him, then, about to turn round and simply walk out, something in her snapped. She could swallow her own pride but this man was insulting her husband, and that she could not let him get away with. She turned swiftly, shooting out a hand to grasp the lapel of his white overall. His eyes widened with shock and he pulled away, but this only strengthened her grip. *Forgive me, Bertie*, she said silently, knowing this would only confirm the Hughes' opinion of her, but she didn't care.

'First of all, it's not *your* shop, it's yer uncle's. And in case you don't know it, I'm your cousin's wife and you should have more respect when the poor man's lying in Guy's at death's door!'

She shoved him away, sending him crashing into an oil can, but as she flung open the door, he recovered enough to shout after her. 'And he's only there because he's hooked up with the likes of you!'

She didn't look back. With trembling hands she pushed the pram down Arnold's Place, her breath coming in short gasps, grateful that she had her back to the shop and Hughes could not see the angry tears his words had caused to flow.

27

Tuppence for the Tram

May–September 1926

The confrontation in Hughes' shop had shaken Milly more than she liked to admit. Her marriage to Bertie had given her a place to hide, a place to play at being a normal wife and mother, but Bertie's absence, combined with his cousin's disdain, had ripped that protection from her and now she felt again like that vilified, unmarried mother who could be scorned and ignored and insulted at will. Her charmed time with Bertie had perhaps softened her too much and now she felt she must rebuild the calluses. She missed her old thick skin, and the cruel wit that could ward off an insult as easily as a thump from one of her strong arms. She needed to toughen up, but only until Bertie came home, she told herself, just until he was back by her side.

The other thing she needed to do was find a job. Who knew how long Bertie would be in Guy's, and though Dr Salter had waived all the fees, she still had to find two rents and feed two families. She would have to go back to Southwell's. Bertie wouldn't like it, but he wasn't here to object. She only hoped that her help on the picket lines had gone unnoticed.

Outside the factory gates, a large board had been erected: *Former strikers wishing to reapply for their jobs are to report to the works office.*

Obviously strikers weren't being allowed to walk back into work, not without the humiliating exercise of begging for their old jobs. She joined the queue of men and women that stretched back from the factory gates, all the way to Southwell's Wharf on the river. Almost at the end of the queue she came upon Kitty and a group of the other jam girls.

'How long have you been waiting?' she asked Kitty.

'I've been back every day since the strike ended. They keep you hanging about then send you home, say there's a backlog. But it's punishment really. They could open the gates and take us all back in a morning, but the buggers won't do it. But how's Bertie, love?'

'He's no better and money's getting tight. I've got to go back to work, Kit, that's why I'm here.' She peered anxiously down the queue.

'Oh, you'll be here all day! But it's only strikers have to go through all the rigmarole, and you weren't on strike! New applicants can walk straight in!'

'But that's not fair – I could be taking your job. I won't do that.'

Kitty put a hand on Milly's arm. 'Don't be a dozy mare. You need that job and I say good luck to you, if you can get it. Go on!' Kitty shooed her off and Milly reluctantly made her way back to the factory gates. She began searching for her old champion, Tom Pelton, and found him outside one of the warehouses.

'No, no, no, you silly sod, don't lift it like that!' he was shouting at a young boy, struggling to manoeuvre a seven-pound stone jar off a trolley. He was obviously unused to lifting heavy objects. Tom spotted Milly and raised his eyes.

'Come on, Milly, show him how it's done, will ya!' He threw up his hands. 'See her.' He drew the boy's attention to Milly. 'She could lift that and you at the same bleedin' time. Now put a bit of effort into it.' But the boy's attempts ended with the stone jar toppling off the trolley, strawberry jam oozing slowly through the cracked top.

Tom groaned and turned away. 'I give up.' He shook his head. 'There's a hundred men out there could do this blindfolded. I've asked the managers to let me get 'em back to work, but will they? It's ridiculous. The business is suffering. Anyway, what can I do

339

for you, love? Sorry to hear about your husband, how is he?'

Sometimes she wished people wouldn't ask. 'Not so good, Tom.' She took a deep breath. It seemed like she'd come at the wrong time to ask a favour. 'Thing is, I don't know when he'll be out of hospital and I need to work. Have you got anything for me, Tom?'

'Have I got anything for you?' He rubbed his chin, keeping her waiting, then broke into a large smile. 'Have I got anything for a girl who can actually do the job, 'stead of standing round waiting to be told what to do? You just made my day, love. I've got a picking room full of strawberries and all the new women I've taken on don't know their arse from their elbow. Start when you like.'

The young boy behind them had cleared up the mess and now hovered behind Tom, holding the remains of the sticky stone jar in a sack. 'Where should I put it, Mr Pelton?'

Tom pulled a face at Milly. 'I'd like to tell him, but I'll only have to repeat it in confession on Saturday!'

Milly felt elated and guilty at the same time. She looked for Kitty at the gates but she still hadn't reached the front of the queue. It felt awkward to have gained from the vindictive rehiring procedure, but she was sure Tom Pelton wouldn't rest till he'd got all his old girls back. With a family the size of the Bunclerks', Kitty needed a job just as quickly as Milly did.

Visiting hours were strictly enforced at the hospital, two hours in the afternoon and two in the evening. This would be the last afternoon she could visit Bertie because she'd told Tom she would start work the next day. Even though the next two hours would be agonizing, it gave her comfort just to be near Bertie, to be close enough to hear his breathing. For however shallow, each breath meant he was still alive, still able to return to her.

As she walked to Guy's Hospital, she saw the scene at the Southwell gates repeated outside all the factories she passed along the way. Crowds of dockers who'd been turned away from a day's work huddled about wharves, and files of factory workers waited outside gates, hoping to be rehired. But they all had a broken, defeated air about them, as though, like Oliver Twist, they had been foolish enough to ask for more and now were being soundly punished for it. She remembered her favourite nun, Sister Clare, reading that book to them. She'd told them Fagin's den was a ramshackle wooden building on Jacob's Island, by Folly Ditch, a long-lost incarnation of Hickman's Folly, before it had been paved over and 'improved' with brick houses.

But thinking of the Bunclerks all squashed into their damp, rundown couple of rooms, Milly realized that not much had changed. Brick terraces might have replaced the earlier dilapidated wooden buildings, but life was still as hard. It was no wonder people like Pat and Freddie kept turning to crime. Somehow it seemed much less of a struggle than earning an honest bob or two. They might have to spend a couple of years in prison, but at least they never went cap in hand to anyone. Her Bertie was so different. There wasn't a dishonest bone in his body, and yet the strike had broken him, just as much as it had these dispirited dockers.

It was almost as though she had conjured him up with her musings, for just as she turned into the railway arch leading to St Thomas's Street she spotted him ahead of her. That familiar stocky figure, with his bouncy, cocky walk, hands stuffed in pockets, sandy hair curling from under his cap. She slowed her steps, praying that the dim light beneath the arch had misled her, but some instinct must have alerted him and he whirled round. Now she was certain. Pat Donovan had done his time.

She halted, feeling trapped in the echoing tunnel, as the beating of her heart competed with the thundering of a train passing overhead. Seeing her momentary hesitation, he gave a bitter laugh.

'What's the matter? Brave Milly Colman, scared of me?' His voice rang harshly in the brick vault.

She began walking slowly towards him. 'Scared of you? Do me a favour, Pat, try living with my old man, then see how hard you are.' She brushed past, half expecting him to tag along as he had in those long-gone days when he would walk her home from the Folly. But instead he caught her arm, jerking her round.

'Hold up, gel! I'm not the same stupid little git who fell for you, Milly Colman. You don't survive in nick by being a Mary-Ann like that grocer of your'n.'

She tried to shrug him off, but his grip tightened.

'Oh, I heard all about it, one tap on the head and he's out sparko. Is that where you're goin'?' He shoved her aside. 'Go on then, off to see yer wounded soldier. But don't think I'll let the likes of him keep me from my own son.'

Quickly regaining her balance, she let herself look him full in the eyes.

'I haven't got time for this, Pat. All this old flannel about *your* son.' She shook her head. 'It won't wash with me. You've got kids from here to New Cross! You don't care tuppence about my Jimmy! You're just jealous I'm with Bertie. Now get out of my way. I'm going to see my husband.'

A flush crept up from his neck as he rammed his hands back into his pockets. 'Don't be too sure of yourself. You might still come running to me when Hughes don't wake up.'

As he moved to grab her again, she dodged out of his reach, walking swiftly towards the arc of daylight ahead, all the while wondering, what if he were right? What if Bertie never did come back to her? Only when she reached the end of the arch did she look back, but Pat was nowhere to be seen.

Shaken and weary, she turned into the courtyard at Guy's and mounted the stone stairs to Bertie's ward. She thought of all the things she couldn't tell him. Nothing about her money worries, not a word about going back to Southwell's; nor about the old man going missing, and certainly nothing about Pat Donovan.

Bertie looked exactly as he'd done when she'd left him yesterday. She kissed his pale face and took his hand, shuffling the chair up close to the bed.

'Hello, love, I'm back,' she said as brightly as she could. But like a breaking dam, her attempts to reconstruct her old toughness gave way, and out of her loneliness, she found herself whispering to him half the things she had vowed not to.

'I'm doing my best, my darlin', but it's so hard doing it all on my own. I've got too used to you being there with me. And then that git of a cousin of yours wouldn't even serve me, said it was all my fault you've ended up here. And I didn't give him a wallop, Bertie, 'cause I didn't want to give him the satisfaction, but oh, it knocked me for six and I don't know why it should matter . . .' She ended with a sob, glad after all that he couldn't hear her self-pity. She lifted his hand and rested it against her wet cheek. 'Take no notice, love.'

She kissed his palm and, getting up to leave, her eye was caught by a movement. She thought the unbandaged, winged eyebrow had moved. Holding her breath, she waited. Yes, there it was again. His eyelids flickered, then, gently as clouds parting to reveal a mild summer sky, the familiar blue eyes were open, still veiled with confusion, looking beyond her. She bent forward, placing herself in his line of sight.

'Bertie?'

He blinked, some comprehension seeming to flicker there, but just as suddenly, his eyes closed again and she couldn't bear the blankness.

'No, Bertie!' She caught his face between her palms. 'You're not going away again!' And as she breathed against his cheek, his face seemed to ripple like a still lake beneath a gentle breeze, and, softly, his eyes opened. Through his parched lips came a sound. Milly leaned closer, conscious of tears streaming down her cheeks.

'What, Bertie?' she choked. 'What are you saying, darlin'?'

'Strike me dumb, Milly,' Bertie whispered hoarsely, 'you don't half look a state, love.'

Though they hadn't been the words she'd imagined he might speak when he woke, they were the sweetest he'd ever uttered.

343

'Come here.' He held up weak arms and enfolded her in the longed-for embrace. She smothered him in kisses, stifling his questions. When finally she let him go, he asked how long he'd been there.

'A week! But how've you managed on your own – the coffers must be dry by now?'

'You're not to worry yourself. Mum's been helping me, and Amy. She's been a godsend too, though she wouldn't thank me for saying so! And I've managed to sell a few dresses.'

Bertie shifted uncomfortably in the bed. She knew it still rankled that he couldn't be the sole provider; now wasn't the time to tell him about going back to the factory.

'I'm tiring you out, darlin'.' She leaned over the bed and kissed him. 'I wish I could stay all night.' She clung to his hand. 'Oh, Bertie, I don't want to leave you now you've come back to me, but that matron's going to chase me off soon enough and I've got to tell her you're awake! She's such an old dragon, I'd like to see her crack a smile before I go!'

He returned her kiss with as much strength as he could muster, and it wasn't until she had left the ward that she realized she hadn't told him about the strike. There would be time later for disappointment. But for now Milly wanted to run home, and on the way she wanted everyone to ask 'How's Bertie?' just for the joy of hearing her own voice telling them: 'He's awake!'

Once out in St Thomas's Street, she broke into a run. Holding her hat firmly on her head, she dodged the traffic and sped along pavements. Not caring what stares she attracted, she darted across the junction at Tower Bridge and raced down Shad Thames. Halfway along she heard a voice calling, 'Where's the bleedin' fire?' Without stopping, she glanced up to see Freddie Clark, standing above her on the back of his lorry, covering a load with tarpaulin.

'Bertie's woken up!'

'Bloody marvellous, I'll tell Kitty!'

She waved her thanks and hurtled on, arriving in Arnold's Place flushed and out of breath. Mrs Carney was standing at her doorstep, and before she could ask, Milly said, 'He's woken up!' That would take care of the rest of the neighbours. She pushed open her mother's front door and ran into the kitchen.

'He's woken up!'

Amy jumped up and swung Jimmy round in an arc of celebration and Milly, touched by the genuine affection Bertie had stirred in her sister, picked her up and swung her round too.

'Oh, darlin', that's the best news we've had since that bloody evil strike started!' Her mother joined them in a little dance round the kitchen, then stopped, holding her side. She sat down heavily and banged the table. 'But I tell you, if, God forbid, he hadn't come back, I would've blamed the unions, as God's my judge I would.'

'Don't start about the unions, Mum, let's have a celebration. Where's the old man's tipple?' She reached into the corner cupboard for the bottle of brandy. Somehow its presence there cast a chill over her. Drink, for the old man, was as precious as gold. Why would he have gone off for good and left a full bottle of brandy behind?

It was another week before Bertie came home. Her mother and Amy were at Storks Road with the children, ready to greet him. Jimmy launched himself at Bertie as soon as he stepped through the door. Still weak, the impact of the toddler made him stagger, and when Jimmy put up his arms for Bertie to toss him into the air, Milly picked the little boy up, saying, 'Daddy's still poorly, Jimmy!'

'Give him here,' Bertie said. 'I'm not an invalid!'

But his ashen face, taut with the strain of his illness, told her otherwise, and she insisted he sit down with Jimmy on one knee and Marie crooked in his arm.

Amy, with uncharacteristic shyness, kissed Bertie on the cheek. 'I'm really glad you're better,' she said, adding quickly, 'Your kids are such bloody hard work!'

'Amy!' Her mother was ready to remonstrate, but Milly knew this was the nearest her sister would ever get to showing a chink in her emotional armour. Laughing it off, she said, 'Why do you think he got himself knocked over the head in the first place – he needed a rest!'

'And if you think my children are a nuisance, you should try living with my wife!' Bertie said.

When Amy replied sourly, 'I have!' even her mother had to laugh.

After an hour Mrs Colman insisted on leaving.

'We're tiring him out, look at him!' she said, and Milly was grateful.

But she was just seeing them off when Florence Green and Francis Beaumont arrived for a visit. Bertie was told all the details of the strike's failure, which Milly had tried so hard to shield him from. She saw his face fall as they recounted the sudden caving in by the TUC, even though most of the strikers had been willing to fight on.

'So it was all for nothing in the end?' he said disconsolately.

And Milly hated to see his usual optimism so battered.

'Well, Bermondsey's sticking by the miners. It's not over for them,' Florence said. 'In fact we've adopted a Welsh village called Blaina, and we're going to make sure at least *they're* not starved out.'

The little village had virtually every male inhabitant out of work, there was no poor relief and the hospital had closed when the miners' contributions to its upkeep dried up.

'There are children dying of starvation and lack of health care, and even if the miners go back, they'll still be on starvation wages! We're determined to raise enough money to keep them going for a year if necessary, aren't we, Francis?' Florence gripped her fiancé's hand.

'Indeed we are, my dear. In fact we're travelling to Wales on Saturday to present a donation from the Settlement.'

'We'll help out, won't we, Milly?' Bertie said, and she was glad to see a flame of eagerness gleaming in his tired eyes. She wasn't going to dampen it with the knowledge that they barely had enough to pay their own rent. She put off telling him that she was back making jam at Southwell's.

When they were finally alone and he'd eaten a child's meal of beef broth and bread, she sat opposite him. The excitement of coming home, and the visitors, had left him exhausted. He leaned his head against the chair and closed his eyes. She watched him, unobserved, grateful to the depths of her being to have him just sitting there.

She thought he had fallen asleep, and was happy to sit watching him all night, when he spoke, eyes still closed. 'I don't know if they were just dreams, but sometimes I thought I heard you, when I was sleeping . . . at the hospital. You sounded so far away, but I was sure I heard you telling me off, saying I couldn't leave you high and dry. It was you, wasn't it?'

'Yes,' she whispered, 'it was me.'

'You made me come back, Milly. I never realized just how much you loved me . . . and needed me.' His eyes opened and rested on her. 'But now I do, and I promise, I'll never leave you again.'

She dropped from the chair to her knees and laid her head on his lap as he gently stroked her hair, till the twilight faded to night and the room was quite dark.

Next morning, she was already in her hat and coat by seven o'clock.

'Going out?' he asked groggily.

She'd just popped back for her bag and the damn bedroom door had creaked. She'd been creeping about, hoping not to wake him, but now he'd caught her and she'd have to confess. She picked up the bag and bent to kiss him quickly.

'I meant to tell you, love, but everything happened so quickly . . . I've gone back to the factory.'

His face set hard and he attempted to push himself up. 'You know I didn't want you to do that. I'll be back at Jacob's in a few days. There's no need for you to be slaving away at Southwell's!'

She didn't have time to explain just how little money she'd been managing on since the strike started, but she had to be realistic for both of them.

'Bertie, you may not get taken back at Jacob's. Lots of strikers have been locked out, you know, especially the ringleaders, and don't forget the management know you were distributing the strike bulletin. I was lucky to get this job, love. Kitty's not even been taken back on.'

She hated to upset him, so soon after his return, but he was too weak to argue with her. 'Now all you've got to worry about is getting better! Mum's downstairs, and she'll be staying here with you and the kids during the day, just till you're up and about. I've got to rush.' And she kissed him again, before he could object.

At the factory, the atmosphere was uneasy. Strike breakers were being shunned, and strikers lucky enough to have work were equally resentful of the new hands replacing those still locked out. That morning Milly stopped to speak with Kitty, who was again queuing for her job. Milly thought she looked thinner and frailer than ever, shoulders slumped as she shuffled along, edging nearer to the works office.

'Oh, Kit, haven't they taken you back yet?' Milly put her arm round Kitty's small shoulders, wanting nothing more than to sweep her up to the picking room.

'I don't know why you're being penalized. I see they've taken your Ada back in the boiling room.'

Kitty shrugged. 'Suppose I spent too much time on the picket line shouting me mouth off! They know my face, simple as that. What's it like in the picking room?'

'Chaos, up to our ears in strawberries going rotten before we can sort them. There's just not enough of us. I heard that Hartley's were back up and running straight away. It won't be long, love, before our lot see sense and take you all back. They can't afford not to. Want me to have a word with Tom today, see if he can put a word in for you?'

'Oh, would you mind, Mill? Mum's been up to the Guardians

every day, but a loaf of bread's all you get and our Percy's such a gannet it's gone in no time!'

No wonder her friend looked half starved; she was probably giving all her share to Percy. 'Look, I've got to dash now, Kit, but I'll do me best with Tom!'

She hurried through the gates and across the yard. Half a dozen trolleys that would normally be transporting filled jars to the warehouses were standing idle, and as she passed the boiling room she could see that only half the copper pans were steaming away. The whole place, which normally ran like clockwork, had a ramshackle, untidy feel to it. Shipped-in labour was keeping the wharf running, but they took a day to unload what an experienced gang of dockers could do in an hour.

And it wasn't just the factory that felt this way. Milly sensed unease permeating the whole of Dockhead. The strike had felt like civil war at times, and now headlines of triumphant celebrations were a bitter pill for those left on the breadline. And all around her, those who laboured to keep London's Larder full, dockers and jam girls alike, were returning to work, feeling that they counted for nothing. A heaviness hung in the air, a stink of betrayal, more acrid than the coke and smoke from the hundred chimneys that forested Bermondsey. The noxious smell of their defeat fought with the sweet scent of strawberry jam boiling in Southwell's copper pans, and was equally inescapable.

She made her appeal for Kitty that dinner time. Tom was one of the more sympathetic foremen, but his response wasn't encouraging.

'My hands are tied, Milly. They don't listen to me.'

She was about to walk away, but thought better of it. 'Well, a friend of mine works in Hartley's order department, says they've started stealing all our business. Customers won't hang about out of loyalty these days, will they, Tom? Not when there's Lipton's, and Pink's as well, for them to choose from.'

Tom smiled. 'I always said you should be a forelady. Want to come and tell management that?'

'They wouldn't listen to the likes of me!'

'Maybe not, but it's a fair point and I'll be sure to pass it on.'

'What about Kitty Bunclerk?' she pressed.

He scratched his forehead and sighed. 'Oh, all right, you cheeky cow. I'll get her in somehow, just to get you off me back!'

Milly gave him her sweetest smile, wishing that she was on equally good terms with the foreman at Jacob's. Bertie thought it would be plain sailing to walk back into his old job, but the world had changed while he had been sleeping.

It was the middle of June before Bertie was strong enough to return to work, though it had been a constant battle for Milly to keep him at home. Her Southwell's wages and what she could make at the Old Clo' were not enough to support them, as well as her mother and sister, and eventually she had to give in.

She put out his work clothes, and it broke her heart when he had to call on her for help shaving. His hands were trembling so much with the effort that the cut-throat razor shook dangerously in his hand. She carefully finished the job, holding his head still, while she drew the razor through the thick soap he'd applied to his face.

'Bertie, love, if you can't even shave yourself, how could you possibly drive a van?' she asked him as she wiped away the last spots of soap.

He stood up and slipped on his waistcoat. 'I've got to show my face otherwise they'll think I'm not coming back! Once I've started moving about, I'll get stronger.'

He took the razor from her and began washing it carefully. 'Anyway,' he said softly, 'you know as well as I do that we're going under. Doesn't look like your father's coming back, and you can't keep them all on your own. We'll have to take in your mum and Amy.'

He'd obviously observed more from his sickbed than she'd realized. 'Who told you about the old man?'

'Amy's been keeping me company in the afternoons.'

'Typical, she's such a contrary mare. Tell her to keep quiet about something and of course she does the opposite. She knew I didn't want you worried!'

'Oh, don't blame her, Milly. She just wanted to talk to someone about it. You do know she's terrified of him coming back?'

She helped him on with his jacket. 'Of course I know, but why didn't she talk to me?'

She stood behind him as he checked himself in the wardrobe mirror and their eyes met in the glass. There was the old quizzical look, the one that always made her ask herself what she was missing.

'Because she didn't want to worry *you*.'

Milly guffawed. 'Oh, do me a favour, Bertie, Amy only does what she wants to do. I don't think she even realizes I exist half the time.'

'That's not true. She's been a good 'un looking after the kids, and who do you think she's doing that for?'

She didn't want to argue with him, not now. So she swallowed her retort.

'Well, thanks for suggesting we take them in, love, but I'm not sure if my mum could survive anywhere but Arnold's Place.'

'We'll talk about it tonight. Now, how do I look?'

Older than his twenty-seven years, was the answer, and his jacket swamped his weakened frame, but she tightened his tie and said, 'Very smart! Don't forget your hat!' She handed him the trilby and saw him out, with a silent prayer that Jacob's would be more forgiving than Southwell's when it came to ex-strikers.

So that evening when she came home with the children she was relieved to find that Bertie wasn't there – he must have been taken back on. They would have to celebrate somehow, though looking round the bleak little larder she had trouble imagining how. She sliced the remains of some boiled bacon and made a pease pudding. Then with the last of her flour, she made Bertie's favourite treat, Welsh cakes. Though he was London born, Bertie's grandmother was Welsh and she'd made them for him when he was a child. Milly put the children to bed and waited. She wished she had a bottle of beer for him, but there was some ginger wine which she'd kept for Christmas, and that would have to do.

An hour after his normal time for arriving home, she began to worry. She would have to heat up the dinners again and the pease pudding would undoubtedly spoil. Perhaps they were keeping him late as punishment for striking? She sat sewing in the light of the gas lamp, her mind circling the possibilities. What if he really had been too weak to drive the van and had crashed? *Come on, Bertie, where are you?* she chafed, putting her sewing away. It was no good, she'd attached the sleeves the wrong way round and would have to re-do them. This was torture. After another hour, she heard his key in the latch and ran to greet him.

'Oh, love, I'm sorry you've had such a long day! I've made you a lovely dinner to celebrate and the buggers have kept you late!'

She was pushing him towards the kitchen, plying him with questions.

'Strike me dumb, let's get me coat off first!'

She took his jacket. 'Sit down at the table. You've got Welsh cakes for afters!'

She put the dinners on the table and sat opposite him. 'There's only ginger wine, but we should celebrate. I really didn't think they'd take you back!' She lifted her glass to him.

'Well, this looks lovely!' he said, beginning to eat in his normal slow fashion.

'Have a drink with me then. You don't look too happy about getting your job back.'

He picked up the glass and sipped at the fiery wine, then put it down carefully.

'I didn't get the job back, Milly. They've locked me out. But there's no reason why we shouldn't be celebrating. I'm alive at least.' He gave a little laugh.

She slammed down her glass so that the wine spilled on the tablecloth. 'Why can't you be like a normal person and tell me straight away when there's bad news!' It was so typical of him, to not give her the most crucial piece of information as soon as he walked through the door.

He smiled at her again.

'But where've you been all day?'

'Looking for something else. I've been all over for driving jobs; Peek's, Pearce Duff's, Crosse & Blackwell's, everywhere, but I'm on some sort of blacklist.' He finished wearily. 'I'll try again tomorrow. But that was lovely,' he said as he finished his dinner. 'Now where are those Welsh cakes?'

'You must be worn out. Did you get trams?' she asked anxiously, putting the plate of cakes in front of him.

'Trams, what do I want with trams? I've got to build up my strength, otherwise I'll be useless whatever job I get!'

She'd expected him to lose his job, and she'd been right, but she'd also expected him to be crushed. She wasn't quite sure if his optimism was real, or simply put on for her benefit. Whatever the case, she suspected he would have to keep it up for a good long time if he'd been blacklisted by every firm in Bermondsey.

The heady sweetness of strawberry jam eventually faded from the riverside streets, giving way to the sharper notes of blackcurrants and gooseberries. When the delicate scent of raspberries seeded the air, Bertie began to look outside Bermondsey for a job. He walked all over south London, going back to his birthplace in Dulwich, calling in on the shopkeepers he knew from his grocer days. He refused to take trams and as his shoes slowly wore out, so did his poor feet. By damson season, when Milly was busy stoning fruit, Bertie had begun making cardboard soles for his shoes. Seemingly still optimistic, never complaining, he walked even further afield in his search for work. Milly worried that he'd never truly regained his strength after the accident and now he seemed to be surviving on sheer will power.

Late one August evening, after a day of torrential rain, he came hobbling through the front door and collapsed into his chair in the kitchen. As Milly eased off his shoes, what was left of the paper soles came away in a soaking, red-stained pulp. His feet were bleeding.

'Oh, my poor Bertie, why didn't you pay the tuppence for a bloody tram!'

She preferred anger to the alternative, which was to wet his feet with her tears. She turned up the legs of his trousers. 'Sit there and don't move!' she ordered and ran for a basin of water from the scullery. When she came back, she was surprised he'd obeyed her. He hadn't moved, but he had his head in his hands, and when she lifted his chin she was shocked to see his face wet with tears. She gathered him into her arms. She knew it wasn't for the pain in his feet that he wept, but for the anguish of not being able to provide for his family.

'Don't worry, Bertie, darlin'. We'll manage, love, don't get yourself so upset.' But he seemed inconsolable, trying to hide his tears yet unable to stop them flowing, as though all the months of pretending had caught up with him in this one day.

Eventually his shaking shoulders were still and he pulled out a handkerchief. 'Sorry, Mill, didn't mean to cry in front of you.'

'Don't be a soppy 'apporth, Bertie. I'm your wife.'

'Well, I wouldn't – not normally. But it's upset me today, and not just because of coming home with no job. It's that so-called family of mine!'

She'd never told him of his cousin's insulting behaviour towards her, at least not while he was awake, but for a moment she thought he might have found out.

'Why, what've they done now?' she asked fearfully.

'I thought I'd have another go in Dulwich, the rain come on and I got soaked through, and the damn boot soles melted. I must have walked around in it for another couple of hours, but my feet were killing me. So when I found myself back in Dulwich High Street I thought I'd have to get a tram home, but I didn't have a penny in my pocket. I shouldn't have done it, but I was so tired and I didn't think I could walk another step. I was passing Uncle's shop, so I went in and he gave me the cold shoulder, didn't expect much else. But then I said I didn't have the money to get home and could he lend me tuppence for the tram. He could see the state of my feet, and you know what? He wouldn't even give me tuppence out of the till! I've never felt so worthless in all my life. I just turned round and walked out. I wish now I had more of your fight in me, Milly. I would have liked to knock his block off. You would have done!'

Her heart bled for Bertie then, but she knew now was not the time to shower him with sympathy. His strength was in his principles, not his muscles, and to her way of thinking, that was a far superior strength than her own.

'Now listen to me, Bertie Hughes, you're not worthless. You're a better man than I'll ever be!'

He looked at her for a long minute, then lifted his eyebrow, a smile played around his mouth, and realizing what she'd said, she threw her head back and laughed. They both roared till they were breathless and their tears of sadness had been replaced by tears of laughter.

28

The Slut on the Stairs

September 1926

Milly suspected that Bertie's chances of finding another job were diminishing daily, and she decided there was nothing for it but to seek out another source of income herself. A full day at Southwell's and weekends taken up with sewing or selling her clothes meant that her options were limited, but she would think of something. She was preoccupied as she manoeuvred her way through the crowd of women arriving in the picking room and was almost at her station before she saw Kitty, already dressed in overall and mob cap, sharpening her stoning knife.

'You're back!' Milly wrapped her arms round her bird-boned friend.

'Thanks to you! Whatever you said to Tom finally worked. He came and got me himself!'

Milly picked up her own knife and began sharpening it on the long strop they kept by the conveyer belt. 'I just told him that we was losing orders to Hartley's! He did the rest. He's a good bloke, Tom.'

'Mum'll be jumping for joy when I get home. She was getting worried about the rent, but we'll be all right now.'

'Talking of your mum, can you ask her to do me a favour?'

'Course, what is it?'

'Bertie's having no luck . . . I think I'll have to go cleaning and I was wondering if your mum would put in a word for me?'

Kitty's mother worked as an office cleaner in the City, leaving home in the early hours to clean banks and offices before the hordes of city workers began filing across London Bridge. The pay was poor, but it was an ideal job to combine with bringing up a large family. Milly reckoned if she left at four in the morning, she'd have just enough time to do a couple of hours' cleaning before the morning shift at Southwell's.

Kitty agreed to ask her mother, and the following Monday Milly found herself, before dawn, walking at a brisk pace across London Bridge, with Mrs Bunclerk at her side. A full moon still rode above the skein of river mist, and a cold wind whipped down the Thames. Milly breathed into the scarf wrapped up around her ears, grateful for the brief warmth on her cheeks.

Mrs Bunclerk had found her a job at a large insurance office and had agreed to show her the ropes. Milly guessed there wouldn't be much to it, just lots of elbow grease and buckets of water, and she was confident she'd have the stamina for it. But she'd gone through hell with Bertie, trying to persuade him to let her do it. In the end she'd had to pretend it was as a favour to Mrs Bunclerk, who couldn't keep up with the workload. Milly was glad she wasn't alone. It would help to know what the supervisor liked, whether she checked every skirting board and door top, or if she was the sort who would let them skimp. Right now, she was just eager to get to Gracechurch Street and out of the biting wind.

The damp September mornings had begun to smell of woodsmoke, and this early rising in the chilly dark reminded her of hopping mornings. She could never think of those mornings without an aching longing, tinged with regret. So Mrs Bunclerk's homely chatter cheered her, and soon the stone-faced, many-windowed insurance office came into view.

'This is it, love, nothing special, though to hear some of them insurance brokers when they come in of a morning, you'd think it was Buckingham Palace. They let you know if you've not done the brass right, I'll tell you that for nothink! Though their own houses is probably shit'oles.'

As she'd never met an insurance broker in her life, she couldn't argue with Mrs Bunclerk's opinion of them. Her only experience of insurance was Mr Allcot, who collected her mother's penny policy money, and had always been a very polite man. Every week he'd taken the money, filled in the book and stayed for a cup of tea, if the old man wasn't at home. Sometimes as a child, Milly would sit under the table, listening to his sonorous voice as he sipped tea, discussing with her mother the goings on in Arnold's Place, and she would close her eyes and wish Mr Allcot was her father. She found herself wondering if any of the insurance brokers in this place would be like him, but from Mrs Bunclerk's repeated warnings to make sure all the cleaning was done before they arrived, she doubted it.

'They like to have it clean, but they don't want to know how it's done, you see, love. Bit like my husband, come to that!' And Mrs Bunclerk gave a barking laugh, which rattled in her chest.

The supervisor gave Milly the job of cleaning all the back stone staircases and when that was done, she was to finish up with the front steps leading to the brass-studded double entrance doors. She began at the top, with her bucket of soapy water and scrubbing brush, working her way laboriously down the six flights. Whenever she needed clean water she had to return to the basement to fill the bucket and, by the time she'd done two flights, her kneecaps were bruised and chafed. After an hour, Kitty's mother had finished her job and was going off to a large bank in Broad Street to do another hour there.

'I've got to get a move on, love. You be all right getting home on your own?'

Milly dropped the scrubbing brush into the soapy water and pushed back a strand of hair with her wet hands.

'Oh, I'll be fine, thanks, Mrs Bunclerk.'

'Just make sure you're finished before seven. That's when the early birds get in. Bye, love!'

And Milly was left alone in the echoing back staircase, with still another flight left to clean. She started on the front steps at quarter past six, but she was certain she'd be finished before half past six and back home by seven. She hadn't, however, counted on the white stone, which the supervisor said she would have to use on the front steps. Grinding the wet stone on to the steps until they were returned to their pristine whiteness proved a laborious, back-breaking task. The early sun was still low, and she was scouring away, head down, elbows out, backside up, when the elongated shadow of a man rippled over the sun-gilded steps. She didn't like to look up. She'd been told to be invisible, so perhaps if she just kept grinding the stone, the shadow would simply pretend she wasn't there. A long, pinstriped trousered leg, ending in a black patent shoe, arched over her head, quickly followed by a second leg. It was as if some gigantic spider had stepped carefully over an ant. It appeared she had been ignored, but as she glanced up at the retreating, suited figure, she saw him stop in the vestibule, and loudly address the porter who had just come on duty.

'Jones, I've just had to step over the slut on the stairs! Could you get rid of her before the chairman arrives?'

'Of course, sir,' the porter replied softly, and Milly flushed as she saw him approaching her.

She would have liked to take the bucket of dirty water and tip it over the broker's bowler hat. Instead she stood up and listened, cheeks flaming, as the porter told her, not unkindly, to finish up sharpish and be quicker tomorrow.

Walking back over London Bridge, she was dimly aware of the sky, enamelled in gold, turquoise and ruby red. Some retreating part of her recognized its beauty, but instead of enjoying the river's expansive skies as she once would, she found herself trapped on those stone stairs, frozen in time, while the broker insulted her over and over again, seeing not a wife, not a mother, not a daughter, seeing nothing but 'the slut on the stairs'.

She was still replaying the scene when she got home. Bertie had the children ready for her mother's and they set off together. She said nothing to him of her mortifying morning, but he knew her too well.

'You don't look so chirpy this morning. Was it hard work?'

She knew he'd be glad of any excuse to dissuade her from office cleaning, but much as she'd like to, she couldn't afford to give him one.

'No more than picking a dozen bushel of hops,' she lied.

As she pushed the pram, he carried Jimmy, but encircled her with his free arm. 'You've got to be the most beautiful char in the City,' he said softly, leaning in to kiss her cheek.

'Bertie, in the street!' she protested, but was secretly pleased.

In her old charring clothes or the hideous green Southwell's overalls, she felt plain, ugly even. Perhaps that was why she found such pleasure in the clothes she created. They might be made of cheap materials, but she had the means to make something lovely out of her imagination, and for Milly it was always like breathing fresh Kentish air when she took up her needle and thread.

'When did you start getting so respectable?' he asked, pretending to be rebuffed.

'When I married up.' She pulled a wry face and Bertie raised his eyebrows.

'Strike me dumb,' he said, chuckling, and gave her another squeeze.

When they reached Arnold's Place Bertie joined the stream of other casuals heading for Butler's Wharf, ready to try their luck in the daily scrum for a day's work. If Bertie could barge or elbow his way to the front, when the dock foreman threw the work tickets in the air, he might be lucky enough to catch one. But he had no sway with the gangers, no favours to call in; it would all be down to brute force and luck. She watched him as he disappeared round the corner, his familiar swinging walk, hand in one pocket, trilby hat slightly tipped, his three-piece suit, worn but still neat. He was a grocer, not a docker, she concluded, and she was his wife, not a slut on the stairs, but hard times bred hard choices and they simply could not be all that they would like to be. If she'd been seeing Jimmy off on his first day at school, she couldn't have been more anxious.

A cry from Marie drew her attention.

'All right, all right, don't fuss. We're nearly at your nanny's!'

'See Amy!' Jimmy joined in.

'Yes, we'll see Amy too,' she said, turning the pram towards her mother's house.

When they arrived, Amy threw open the front door. 'Hello, pickle!' She lifted Jimmy from the pram and waved a letter in front of Milly. 'We've got our letter!'

Milly felt her heart sink. Her mother and Amy would go to Horsmonden and that meant her children would have to go away with them.

'Oh, that's good!' She feigned enthusiasm, knowing how anxiously they'd been waiting for the farmer's letter. As Milly struggled to get Marie out of the pram, the disappointment on her face must have been obvious, for Amy gave her a rare hug.

'Sorry you can't come too, Mill,' she said.

Milly was stunned. Never, in all their years down hopping, had Amy shown the slightest pleasure at her presence. Hard times might breed hard choices, but sometimes they held surprises too. Maybe it was just that Amy was growing up. At almost thirteen, she'd be starting work soon, though she'd already told Milly she wouldn't go near Southwell's.

'I don't think I can stand smelling of strawberry jam and marmalade like you,' she'd said to Milly one day. 'When I start work, I'm going to Atkinson's!'

As far as Milly was concerned there wasn't much difference, but Atkinson's cosmetics factory was considered 'clean' work. She supposed it was better to smell of 'California Poppy' than strawberry jam, but either way it would be repetitive factory work.

'How did you get on, office cleaning?' her mother asked as soon as they were in the kitchen. 'Bet it was blowy, going over that bridge first thing!'

Milly forced a smile. 'It was all right.'

'Perhaps I should come too,' her mother said tentatively. 'I should be paying my way.'

'No! You've got enough to do looking after my kids all day. No!' she repeated sternly. After this morning's experience, this was something she wouldn't give in to. 'We're managing all right, and Bertie might get called on today.'

'Poor feller, he was made for better things, wasn't he?'

'He's the same as any man, Mum. He'll do anything to earn a bob or two. He can't be fussy; none of us can,' Milly said, remembering the long leg stepping over her on the office steps that morning.

Bertie stood at the dock gates all morning, but wasn't called on. In the afternoon he hung about with a crowd of other hopefuls, but when the light failed, he came home having earned not a penny. He did this every day for a week, each day returning a little more defeated, a little less buoyant, until finally Milly couldn't stand to see him diminishing in front of her eyes. In the early hours of Friday morning her mother had taken the children on the hoppers' special to Horsmonden, and when Bertie came home that evening the house felt empty. They sat together after tea, in silence, she sewing and Bertie flicking through the job section of the paper, each pretending to be busy, each silently occupied by their shared worries. As Milly pictured Jimmy, tucked up cosily on the straw pallet in the hopping hut, an idea occurred to her.

'Bertie, I'm thinking there is a way you can earn a bit of money. Why don't you go down hopping with Mum? You could help her pick, or you might get work as a pole-puller?'

He looked up from his paper, not answering for a while. Perhaps this was one step down too far. Only the poorest of the poor went hop-picking. He would be further than he'd ever been from his middle-class Dulwich relatives. He folded the paper.

'But you'd be all on your own here.'

She smiled. 'I'll come down at weekends, on the lorry – with the husbands!'

He simply raised an eyebrow and Milly knew that, without even a battle, it had been decided; Bertie would go to the hop fields. That weekend, Milly went with him in Freddie's lorry. Sitting together on the back board, crammed with visiting husbands, boxes and beer crates, Milly looked at Bertie for any sign of discontent.

'Bit different from Uncle's van,' she said searchingly. 'It'll seem strange, not to be bringing down the groceries.'

He gave her a knowing look. 'Surely you don't think I'm too proud? The only thing I'm ashamed of, Milly, is not being able to support my family. No, it's honest work.' He leaned back against the side board, looking genuinely happy. 'And at least I'll be earning something for us at last.'

When they passed the turn-off to their special place high above Horsmonden, where he'd proposed, he reached for her hand and smiled. 'I don't care whether I'm pole-pulling or selling sugar, I've got you, and that's all that matters to me.'

She put her arm through his and reached up to kiss him, drawing whistles from the men, but she didn't care.

Eventually they turned into the field of hopping huts, and searching the crowd of pickers surging towards the lorry, she spotted Jimmy trotting unsteadily towards her across the tussocky grass.

'Careful, darlin'!' she laughed as he toppled over in his eagerness. But the laughter caught in her throat like dust as she saw Pat Donovan getting down from the driver's cab of Freddie's other lorry. She lifted Jimmy into her arms, turning swiftly away, to be greeted by Amy, carrying Marie. The cloud of Pat's presence could not overshadow her joy at seeing the children, but as she gathered Marie into the crook of her other arm, she shot an anxious look back at Bertie. Thankfully, he was taken up with getting down their box and in the hubbub hadn't appeared to notice Pat's arrival.

For the rest of the day she saw no more of Pat. But later that night, after the bonfire had been lit, he found her. She was sitting alone, enjoying the smell of woodsmoke and the warmth of the flames, reaching into the dark night. Bertie had taken the children back to the hut, while her mother and Amy were at the end of the field collecting faggots. She felt his presence, smelled his breath before she heard him. He'd obviously been with the stragglers returning from the pub.

'How've you been?' he asked.

He was grinning beerily at her and she searched his face in the firelight, for any trace of the venom she'd last seen written there, but she saw nothing other than a seemingly tipsy benevolence.

'I'm all right, Pat, still at Southwell's,' she said politely, wondering what he was up to.

'The boy's getting on . . .' He paused, sipping from a bottle of beer. 'And I see you've got another nipper.'

She nodded. 'A girl. Jimmy loves her.'

He looked at her for a long moment. 'How's it working out with Hughes?' He jerked his head towards the huts, his smile fading.

'He's good to Jimmy,' she said carefully. It was the only information she felt comfortable giving Pat.

'Pole-pulling's a bit of a comedown. Still out of work then?'

'Him and a thousand others.'

'Me too.'

'What happened to the job at Freddie's? I thought I saw you in his lorry.'

'Just doing him a favour, bringing down the blokes. Didn't you hear? I did another six weeks inside. Nothing much, just receiving.'

She hadn't heard, but didn't respond.

'Freddie had to let me go. Can't blame him, there's hundreds queuing up for one job. I didn't expect him to hold it open. Anyway, there's other ways I can get money.' He hunkered down, lowering his voice. 'Went to see me bank manager last week. Tower Bridge Road.'

'Tower Bridge Road? That was you?' He nodded proudly in answer to her unspoken question and dug a wad of money out of his inside pocket.

A chill ran through her. She'd read in the *South London Press* about an armed raid at that branch.

'Pat, someone got hurt!'

'Shouldn't have tried to be a hero then, should he?' He shrugged. 'Anyway, I'm flush at the moment, and with Hughes out of work, if that boy needs anything, you let me know.'

She froze at the suggestion. She wouldn't let his money anywhere near Jimmy.

'Pat, don't start all that again. He doesn't need anything . . . I'm earning enough.' He had to know this wasn't true and she added quickly. 'I make a bit, selling clothes too.' She began to get up. 'I'd better go and find Bertie.'

'I hear he's working you like a fucking donkey!' A sneer replaced his smile, as he flicked the banknotes in front of her face. 'See this? I could use it to make your life easy . . . or hard.' He stuffed the money back into his pocket. 'Well, you run back to Bertie.' He got up abruptly. 'You've made your choice.'

Whatever Pat's motives were, she had a cold certainty that the welfare of her family was not uppermost in his mind. She stood up and walked away. She, who had never shied away from a fight, felt unnerved and frightened by his offer. He had seen their poverty as a way back into her life, and if she once opened that door, she was terrified that Bertie would walk out of it.

Milly made sure they kept out of Pat's way for the rest of that weekend, robbing him of any opportunity to wave taunting wads of money under Bertie's nose. But at least Bertie was lucky enough to be taken on as a pole-puller. He wrote to Milly after his first week, describing his early tumbles as he joined the other pole-pullers stalking the length of the hop field on unsteady stilts, unhooking bines from the strings. He gave her the details he knew she would love, the swoosh of the bines as they fell, the sharp smell rising as the pickers gathered them up and the songs echoing round as soon as they began stripping the hops. He sounded more light-hearted than he had for weeks, and she was convinced that the fresh air would do more for his recovery than any medicine.

For the tail end of summer and into early autumn Milly lived an almost solitary life. Pat had made no more trips down to the hop fields and she was glad that Bertie and the children had the chance to spend untroubled days in the country, but still she had to fight the unease that had dogged her ever since her encounter with Pat. His veiled threats had given her life an unpredictable edge, which was hard to ignore, especially when she bumped into him around Dockhead, and he would pass her without acknowledgement, deliberately staring through her. She became almost grateful for the distraction of all her jobs.

Early mornings, she kept her head bent low, hands flying across those stone stairs and tiled floors in the dawn light. Then after her windblown walk back over London Bridge, she spent the rest of the day boiling along with blackberry jam, as it bubbled away in steam-heated copper cauldrons. Her current job in the boiling room was to tip the swivel-mounted pans of simmering jam into copper-lined trolleys, ready for transporting to the filling room. She soon got used to being drenched in sweat from morning till night, and by the time she left work her arms were speckled with burns from scalding jam. In the evenings she sewed relentlessly, sometimes visited by Kitty.

One evening, not long after Bertie had gone to Kent, Kitty came to Storks Road for the final fitting of her wedding dress, which Milly had agreed to make. Afterwards they sat together talking about Kitty's plans for her impending marriage to Freddie, who had proved a faithful sweetheart. Freddie was doing well for himself – with three lorries now and a legitimate transport business, he no longer had to rely on his dodgy dealings to subsidize his income. Though there were still the odd clandestine sales of various goods under the table at the Folly, Kitty insisted it was more of a hobby these days and that after they were married she would put a curb on them. But for now, his shadier transactions were no embarrassment to Kitty and she talked about them as openly as Milly talked about Bertie's pole-pulling.

'It's all work . . . of a kind,' Kitty said. 'I'm just grateful he hasn't got Pat Donovan working with him any more. A bit of thieving's different from what he's involved in. Freddie says he's got in with a right hard lot over the Old Kent Road. Have you seen anything of him lately?'

Milly shook her head. 'Not to speak to, but that's no loss.'

'Well, just stay out of his way. Freddie says he's still going on about Bertie stealing you off him.'

But Milly needed no encouragement. 'Oh, I'll stay out of his way all right.' And eager to change the subject, she asked, 'Now tell me all about this honeymoon Freddie's got planned for you!'

But Kitty's visits were few, taken up as she was with the wedding, and most of Milly's evenings were spent industriously alone, so that by the end of Bertie's first fortnight away she'd made enough children's clothes and dresses to fill a stall at the Old Clo', if she'd only had the money for one. Instead she would have to sell them a few at a time from the pram in her old way.

When Florence Green asked Milly to come and pass on some of her sewing skills to the younger girls at the sewing circle, Milly jumped at the chance of a night out in the company of others. After the class, hearing of Milly's solitary state, Florence invited her for supper in her modest upstairs room. It brought back poignant memories for Milly. The last time she'd sat by that spitting gas fire, she'd made the worst choice of her life, to give up her child, but tonight Florence was full of questions about how she and Bertie were managing after the strike.

'To be honest, I can't see my Bertie ever getting another job. The pole-pulling only lasts till October, but what he'll do then I don't know. I'm doing three jobs as it is. I can't do no more.'

Florence handed her a slice of bread she'd toasted on the gas fire, and Milly spread it with damson jam. She held up the jar. 'Hartley's! That's treason for a Southwell's girl!'

Florence laughed. 'It's donated. We don't get a choice,' she said apologetically.

'Well, if it had been blackberry, I might have chucked it out the window. I'm boiling in it all day.'

As they ate their toast and jam, Florence pondered. 'The strike was more of a sacrifice than any of us had imagined. I just wish I could do something for Bertie.'

Florence poured tea into her pretty china cups with the rosebud pattern that Milly had always admired, and seemed to come to a decision. 'Milly, I may not be able to help Bertie, but I have been thinking about how you might make more of your sewing talents. I know if you could only hire a stall you'd sell many more of your lovely dresses. I'll speak to the committee – they may be willing to loan you the rent on a stall.'

She looked at Milly as though unsure of her response, but there was only one possible answer. 'Yes! Thank you!' Milly stuttered. 'But are you sure?'

'Quite sure. We have a fund set aside for this sort of thing and I can't think of anyone who'd make better use of it than you, Milly.'

Florence always had a slightly reserved air about her, which forbade overt shows of affection, but Milly was so overjoyed, she crossed the short distance between their two chairs and hugged the young woman.

'You don't know what this means to me, Florence.'

'Yes, Milly, I think I do,' she said, regarding Milly with her intelligent, compassionate eyes.

The following weekend, when she crammed on to the back of Freddie Clark's lorry with the husbands and the piano, Milly felt light-hearted enough to spend the journey entertaining them all the way down, singing the old Irish songs her mother had taught her. It would be her last visit to Kent that season, for the best day at the Old Clo' was undoubtedly Saturday, and if she was to repay Florence's faith in her, as well as the loan of the rent, next Saturday was the day she would have to set up her stall. The reunion with Bertie and the children was joyful, and before she'd even jumped off the lorry, Bertie came galloping over the field to meet her, a beast of burden for Jimmy, bouncing astride his shoulders. Marie astonished her with some remarkably word-like sounds, the most rewarding of which was *Umumy*. Her sister declared it was an attempt at *Amy*, but Milly knew better.

But in spite of her delight, the whole weekend seemed more like a long farewell. The family had all greeted her good news about the stall with congratulations; only Bertie's response had seemed muted. But that night as they rolled up tightly together on the floor at the far end of the hopping hut, she silenced his protests softly with her lips.

And on the last night, as they sat round the roaring bonfire, some of the husbands called again on Milly for a song. The piano had been de-mounted from the lorry and sat beneath an awning, outside the huts.

'Come on, Mill, give us an old Irish song!'

Beer and country air had made the hop-pickers maudlin, and with the children dropping off to sleep, curled up like dormice at their feet, Milly stood up in the flickering firelight. 'Give us "Two Sweethearts", Harry!' she called to the pianist, naming one of her mother's favourites. After singing the verse, about soldiers far from home seated round a campfire, she threw herself into the chorus, looking first at her mother and then at Bertie.

'One has hair of silvery grey, the other has hair of gold,
One is young and beautiful, the other is bent and old,
These are the two that are dearest to me,
From them I never will part,
For one is my mother, God bless her I love her,
And the other is my sweetheart.'

Towards the end of the chorus she lifted her hands to encourage the others, and all round the campfire voices joined in the sentimental song. Once, Milly glanced round to see her mother wiping her eyes with the corner of her apron and Amy, sitting behind her, exaggeratedly overcome by floods of sham tears.

*

The next week was as hard as the stone steps she cleaned every morning, her loneliness sharp as her stoning knife. The Storks Road house felt emptier still, now she knew there would be no more weekend interludes in the hop fields. But however alone Milly felt in the world, there was another member of her family she knew must feel lonelier, one she had guiltily avoided thinking about for many months but now was forced to remember. It was time to visit Elsie.

With her mother away, someone had to take on the monthly visit to Stonefield. Milly's excuses not to visit her sister had been accepted readily enough by her mother. With a new baby, a sick husband and the weight of all the family's needs on her shoulders, Milly felt she had ample reasons to stay away. Yet secretly she'd been glad of all those excuses. Her visits to her sister had been few and painful, for each time, she'd seen the Elsie she knew fading further away, her sister's dreamy nature overwritten with a blankness that was impossible to penetrate, and her flashes of fire all dulled. But she couldn't leave her with no visit at all and she steeled herself to go that Sunday.

But before that she had to face Saturday, her first full market day at the Old Clo'. She got up well before dawn, walking to Tower Bridge Road with her stock of handmade dresses and children's clothes on the pram. She couldn't afford to pay a boy to trundle her stall to the market, but the overseer seemed dubious as he gave her the key to the lock-up.

'You sure you can manage that?' he said, nodding towards the wheeled stall which she would have to pull the short distance to the market.

'Me? I'm built like a carthorse!' she said, demonstrating her muscles.

He left, still looking unconvinced, and she transferred her clothes to the stall, deciding to leave the pram in the lock-up. But when she tugged at the yoke of the stall, it stubbornly refused to budge. Looking round to make sure no one was watching she sat on the floor, put her back to the lock-up wall and shoved with her feet. It was unladylike, but very effective. The wheels started rolling and she had to scurry to grab the yoke before the barrow ran away from her. She yanked it to a halt, then straining forward, pulled the stall slowly to her pitch.

Once there, she hung dresses from the top rails and laid children's clothes at the front. She also had half a dozen shirts, a risky outlay, but she'd seen them at cost price on her way back from the City and couldn't resist. Surely there were some men left in Bermondsey who could afford a new shirt? She'd made sure to price them only just above what she'd paid, for she couldn't afford to have them left on her hands. Soon her voice was hoarse from trying to attract the attention of passing trade and she was sure she'd damaged her back, pulling the stall. After a few hours with not much to show for it, she began to suspect it had all been a waste of effort. But as the day wore on, a few of her faithful customers began to show up, and once a small crowd had formed, it aroused the interest of others in the bustling scrum. Soon she was taking money faster than she could give change and by the afternoon had almost run out of clothes to sell.

Arriving home exhausted and elated, she tipped out her takings on to the kitchen table. She was astounded. She'd earned almost a month's wages in a single day. She could pay back the loan on the stall, cover her materials and still come out with the equivalent of a fortnight's wages. She counted the money again, putting it into piles for rent and food and some to help out her mother, but as she swept the coins from the table into her housekeeping tin, they rang hollow in the empty house. If only Bertie were here to celebrate with her.

29

Escape Plans

September 1926–1927

The motor bus left the wide bowl of south London and chugged to the top of Shooters Hill. Behind lay the smog-filled basin and the silvered Thames, snaking down to the sea; ahead, wide streets, open skies and neat suburban houses with their bay fronts and red-tiled roofs. Milly was seated on the top deck, so as they reached the brow of the hill, she could see the Kentish plain dropping away before them. They were heading towards a band of hazy pewter light, sweeping the far horizon. There, where the Thames widened to its sluggish estuary, was Stonefield, its gloomy gables rising out of the low-lying marshland bordering the Thames. There was still a long way to go and Milly was already feeling sick with the jolting of the bus. Her nervousness at seeing Elsie again didn't help. It was only Elsie, for God's sake, yet she felt intimidated at the prospect of facing her own sister, a girl whose only crime was to dream too much and think too little.

Milly checked her bag. There were things visitors were allowed to bring and her mother had given her some moisturizer, a second from Atkinson's, though the price of it still made her head swim. But Elsie's skin was cracking in the dry atmosphere of the place and her mother had insisted she must have it. Milly knew that any spare money Mrs Colman possessed had all gone on treats for Elsie over the past two years, and she didn't begrudge her sister. She'd also brought photographs of Jimmy, and Marie at a few months old, for it saddened her that Elsie had never met her niece, considering how fond she'd become of Jimmy. Milly sat back, giving in to the jolting, contemplating the world of leafy privilege they were passing through. From her perch, she could see the expanse of Danson Park, guessing it must be four times the size of Southwark Park. She wondered how many of the well-wrapped families, out for a Sunday walk round the lake, realized how lucky they were. To be surrounded by such open, tree-filled space was just a dream in Bermondsey where, in the whole of the borough, there was only a single park. Of course they didn't know how lucky they were – not many people did.

When they finally turned into Stonefield's drive, she was feeling stiff and woolly-headed from her long confinement and grateful to escape the stuffy bus. She followed the other visitors as they crunched across gravel towards Stonefield's cheerless entrance. The bus had been running late, so the inmates were already seated at their numbered tables in the recreation hall. Milly's arrival, obscured in the surge of late visitors, was unseen by her sister, and she was able to observe Elsie. Her sister was sitting, hands folded, gazing up at the gallery windows; she looked like a nun. Milly was alarmed at her appearance. Elsie had matured – she was now a young woman, but a far cry from the woman she might have been, had she stayed in Bermondsey. Obviously she'd never acquired a taste for the food at Stonefield, for she was extremely thin, with her long neck accentuated by the bony face and sharp chin, and her long hair drawn back tight as a skullcap.

As Milly pulled out a chair, it scraped on tiles and Elsie turned, her face hardening with disapproval.

'Where's Mother?' she asked, and Milly noticed that her accent had changed. Less cockney, she had picked up the more refined vowels of the attendants and nurses who were her daily companions. It didn't sound like her sister; didn't look like her sister. For a moment, Milly was tongue-tied. The hubbub around them was overwhelming. Interspersed with normal chatter were inarticulate cries and whoops, expressions of excitement or

373

frustration. A young girl on the next table kept up a particularly distracting rhythmic clapping.

'Mum's down hopping,' Milly said finally.

'Oh, of course. I forgot.'

'Forgot! How could you forget?'

But Milly saw, suddenly, that this wasn't one of Elsie games, where she pretended to be more ignorant than she actually was, just to enrage Milly. No, the girl had actually forgotten something that had once been the highlight of her year.

Milly hastily delved into her bag and handed over her gifts, the moisturizer and her offering of a bar of Fry's Five Boys chocolate. Elsie regarded them impassively as Milly pushed them across the table.

'I brought you some of your favourite chocolate. The cream's from Mum. She said your skin's cracking.'

'It's not the only thing cracking in here.' Elsie's mouth twisted into a smile and Milly wanted to run out of the place. She swallowed hard.

'I've got a photograph of Jimmy and Marie . . . Want to see?'

Elsie's hands slowly unclasped and her bony fingers gripped the edge of the table. She stretched out her hand and, with silent relief, Milly handed her the photograph.

'Oh, she's beautiful.' The stone-like planes of Elsie's face softened and her upright posture relaxed as she leaned forward for a closer look. 'Jimmy's getting so big.' She looked up sharply. 'Have I really been here that long?'

Milly nodded. 'But me and Bertie went to see Francis Beaumont again.'

Elsie pushed the photograph back to her. 'Don't talk to me about him.'

'No, listen, he says when you're eighteen they'll have to reconsider, and he thinks they're bound to let you out then.'

'Eighteen! This place'll have killed me by then.' She stood up abruptly. 'I haven't got the patience. None of you understand what it's like in here. I might as well forget the lot of you, there's people been mouldering away in here for twenty years, Milly! Nobody gets out.'

Milly reached out, catching at the sleeve of the sack-like frock. 'You can't forget us and the kids. We're your family and do you think we forget you?'

'Yes, I think you do,' Elsie said, sitting down again because, Milly guessed, the alternative of returning to her dormitory was even worse. 'If you remembered me, you would have come to see me before now.'

Again she lifted her gaze to the high window in the gallery above. Milly thought she knew why. *She* would have wanted to look at the sky too, if she were locked in here every day. Perhaps it gave her sister the illusion of freedom.

'I know it's been hard for you in here, Elsie, but I've had a baby to look after and Mum must have told you about Bertie being so ill . . . I nearly lost him.'

'She told me, and I did pray for him, Milly.'

'Thanks, love, no good being a caddywack and not calling in the favours, is it?'

This brought a small laugh from Elsie and made Milly wish she'd made herself visit before now. Perhaps if she'd come, Elsie would still be more herself instead of this strange, straight-backed, rigid pale thing. But her sister's face tightened again in an instant.

'I like Bertie, but whatever excuses you make, you're not telling me you didn't have one spare day when you could come and see me.' She shook her head. 'I'll never forgive you for that, Milly, never.'

And she pushed back her chair, picked up the cream and walked, in an unhurried, almost stately, manner out of the hall. She left the chocolate sitting on the table. *Why did she leave the chocolate?* Milly asked herself. She would have bit my hand off for it before. It hurt her more than she'd ever admit, to think Elsie would rather deny herself her favourite treat than take it from Milly's hand. For some reason, that was the one thing that stayed with her all the way home on the bus. It was the one thing that convinced her that Elsie really never would forgive her.

The New Year of 1927 came roaring in with gales that blew tiles off roofs in Storks Road and rattled broken catchments in Arnold's Place. Bertie was on the dole. His money from pole-pulling at the hop farm had helped them through Christmas, as had Milly's profit from her sales at the Old Clo', but with rent hikes and price rises, whatever money they made seemed to buy less and less. Bertie had resisted the dole, until one bitter day, with shoes flapping like Charlie Chaplin's tramp, he was finally too ashamed to go out of doors.

Milly went to the St Olave's Board of Guardians and was given a second-hand pair of boots. She felt apologetic as she handed them over – they were brown, and as labourers only ever wore black, brown boots were instantly obvious as hand-me-downs.

'It's all right, Bertie, love, I'll put black boot polish on them. No one'll know the difference,' she soothed as she gave them to him, worried about his wounded pride.

'Don't be daft, Milly, there's nothing wrong with brown boots!' he argued.

'They may be all right in Dulwich, but they'll make your life a bleedin' misery if you go to the docks in brown boots! Haven't you ever heard of "Brown boots, no dinner"?'

He hadn't, but she wouldn't have the kids of Arnold's Place plaguing him with the familiar catcall, and she knew he'd be given no peace if he wore the boots as they were.

So Bertie wore his 'black' boots to sign on for the dole and continued his fruitless tramping for jobs. In the past he had been lucky enough to get called on at Hay's or Butler's Wharf, for half a day's work, trundling barrow loads of butter, bacon or tea from ship to warehouse. But now he began to be turned away day after day. Days turned into weeks of unemployment and Milly could see it was wearing him down.

As the year progressed and the economic recession deepened, smaller factories all over Bermondsey went to the wall. The dole queue outside the labour office grew longer and soup kitchens sprang up at every mission and church. Now was the year when Milly began to doubt that things could ever get better for them. She noticed that the women standing at doors with their children began to have a hollow look, their chatter seemed less light-hearted, their expressions less outgoing. But still there was a generosity of heart that could not be squashed by want. The collectors from the Labour Institute still came round for the miners' fund, even though they'd long ago been starved back to work. But they were much worse off than before the strike and still needed help to pay for basic food and medicines. She'd read in the local Labour Party newspaper, which Bertie sometimes brought home, that Bermondsey people had sent over £7,000 to the South Wales miners. Even her mother, who had little enough to live on and despised the strike, gave what she could.

One evening, after another fruitless day waiting at the call-on gates, Bertie came home looking more defeated than she'd ever seen him. 'I just don't understand it,' he said. 'There's men older than me, there's strips of boys, there's even known shirkers, all being called on, except me!'

'Well, you know what it's like, the call-on foreman's always got his favourites.'

'I know, love.' Bertie pulled off his boots, and Milly noticed the scuffs, where brown showed through the black polish. 'But if I didn't know better I'd say I'm being singled out for some reason. Even the other fellers have noticed. God knows what I've done to upset him, but that foreman doesn't even look my way, let alone chuck me a ticket now and then.'

Milly went to put her arms round him as he slumped forward over his boots. As a grocer, he'd been used to buying and selling all the foodstuffs coming out of London's Larder and, though he never complained, she could see that life on the dole was sapping him.

The next day she made a trip to Arnold's Place, carrying a small bundle. The time had finally come when she needed the services of Mrs Carney. She knocked hesitantly on her front door, which, before she could change her mind, was opened by the squat old woman, wearing her black pork-pie hat even at home.

'Milly! Got a bundle for me?' she asked cheerily. 'It's a wonder you ain't been before, you do marvellous!'

Milly stepped over the bundles destined for the pawnbroker, piled up in the passage, each one carefully labelled with the family's name and the amount of the pledge.

'Not so marvellous today, Mrs Carney.'

Mrs Carney's bright, button eyes lit up. 'Oh? Trouble at home, love? Come in, kittle's on.'

As the old lady slurped at her tea, Milly explained why she'd come.

'Don't get no luck, does he, your feller?' She cocked her head, as though calculating a set of pawn tickets. 'An' it's a bleedin' shame that foreman's took against him.'

So it was true, Bertie was being singled out. Fountainhead of all gossip, rumours, and occasionally even the truth, Mrs Carney was the one person who might have answers to Milly's questions, and though they would be common knowledge in Arnold's Place by this evening, Milly decided to risk it.

'But why? What's he done wrong?' Milly asked, sitting forward, ready for the pearl to drop from the old lady's toothless mouth.

The woman put a finger to her nose. 'I won't be certain, but that tubby bleeder with the loud gate, whas'is name?'

'Barrel?'

'Yuss, 'im. He told Rosie Rockle, it's been goin' on for months!'

'What?'

Mrs Carney looked at her pityingly, for her ignorance, and enunciated her words very carefully.

'*Someone's* been spreading rumours your Bertie's a tea leaf, that he's been lifting stuff off the docks. *Someone's* been taking a bung, to put it about to the call-on foreman.'

'And that's why he's been giving Bertie no work?'

'I won't be certain, but . . . yuss!' Mrs Carney's little hat wobbled on her head as she nodded vigorously.

'Do you know who's behind it?'

The little hat wobbled from side to side. 'No, but whoever it is, he wants shootin'. He does.'

Mrs Carney eased herself up with an audible cracking of joints and began putting on the long black coat that she wore in all weathers. 'Got to get me bundles off now, love, but you go and talk to that Barrel. I b'lieve he knows.'

The first opportunity to see Barrel came that evening when she went to pick up the children from her mother. At fourteen, he was a messenger boy at the docks. Though he still hung about beneath the gas lamp in Arnold's Place, now his companions were other working boys. Milly came upon them, smoking and exchanging football news, but as soon as she called to him, Barrel flicked away the cigarette. He was dressed in a man's waistcoat and jacket, but his face beneath the flat cap was still boyishly plump, his voice still penetrating.

'Oi, Mill!' he boomed back. 'Speak o' the devil.'

After her talk with Barrel she hurried to her mother's, finding her on the doorstep saying goodbye to one of the Irish priests from Dockhead Church. He nodded to Milly and smiled.

'G'night to you, Milly, see if you can't have a word with your sister now and get her to behave!'

As the priest left them, her mother turned a worried face to Milly. 'Our Amy's been hoppin' the wag, the little cow. I'll tan her hide when she gets in!'

Milly knew Amy's behaviour at school hadn't improved. As she'd grown older, she'd just become more brazen, though Milly hadn't realized she'd abandoned school altogether. But her mother's threats were empty. There was only one person in their family capable of tanning Amy's hide, and that particular leather dresser was mercifully absent from their lives now.

'Don't talk rubbish, Mum, you wouldn't touch a hair on her head, not your little baby!'

Milly laughed, and followed her mother into the house in search of her own children. Jimmy was sitting under the kitchen table banging on a saucepan and, hearing her voice, he emerged wearing the pan on his head.

'I'm a soldier!' he announced, banging the top of the saucepan with a wooden spoon he'd been using for a gun. He ran to greet her, the pan falling down over his eyes. She made a fuss of his new helmet while her mother went upstairs to bring down the sleeping Marie. Milly cuddled Jimmy on her knee, listening to his chatter. She never tired of his exuberant delight at her return home from work every evening. When her mother handed her Marie, Jimmy slipped down and returned to his camp under the table.

'Oh, have you been good for your nanny?' she asked her daughter, who flapped her arms up and down as though she might fly away with excitement.

'Anyway, Mum, you shouldn't worry about our Amy,' Milly said, returning to their conversation. 'She'll be going to work in a couple of months, and you're never going to turn her into a scholar now!'

'I know, but it's a right show up having the Father come round here, telling me my child's a truant, and what's more he tells me she's been going to the soup kitchen of a morning! Anybody'd think I didn't feed her.' Mrs Colman sat down, arms crossed over her pinafore. Milly was about to make light of the whole thing when she saw real distress on her mother's face. With trembling lips, Mrs Colman went on. 'The disgrace of it, we don't need charity! Wait till she gets in here, just wait.' And Mrs Colman looked as though she might burst into tears.

'Mum, don't get upset, no one will think any the worse of you. There wouldn't be soup kitchens if people didn't need them.'

'I know, love, but I feel such a drain on you, and the fact is when Amy goes out to work, then as God's my judge, I'm going too. I'll come cleaning with you, I will, and don't you try to talk me out of it!'

Milly wasn't going to argue. If the idea could keep the tears from her mother's eyes, then she would go along with it.

'Well, who knows what tomorrow will bring? As Bertie's always saying to me.'

'No luck?' This was the minimalist conversation being repeated in families all over Bermondsey these days, and no one mistook the question as being about a bet on the horses. Milly shook her head and her mother shook hers.

'And you're the poor old fucking donkey that carries the lot of us, gawd forgive me.'

Her mother was crossing herself when Amy burst into the kitchen. Her thatch of fair hair had been bobbed and Milly noticed the dress she wore, an Elsie cast-off, now fitted her perfectly. But her sister's appearance was less unruly than it had been even a few months ago, and the perpetual scabs on her knees from knocking about the streets with Barrel had disappeared. With such a growth spurt, no wonder the girl was hungry.

'What's that interfering old prat of a priest been saying about me?' she stormed.

'God forgive you, talking like that about the Father!'

Milly wondered who'd told Amy she'd been rumbled, and she admired her sister's strategy. It was always best to go on the offensive with her mother; it confused her somehow. She was a woman who lived by as many of the Church's rules as humanly possible, including some the Church couldn't stake claim to, like not putting new shoes on the table or throwing spilled salt over her shoulder. Her nature simply didn't understand rebellion, so when Amy denied her wrongdoing as Milly thought she undoubtedly would, then her mother would be stumped. Her imagination didn't run to anarchy.

'He's said you've been hoppin' the wag, and going to the soup kitchen!'

'Who told him that? It's that lying cow of a nun Sister Mary Paul, she's always got it in for me. If you must know, I've been helping Sister Clare out in the little ones' class!'

Mrs Colman tucked in her chin. 'Hmm.' She pondered, while Amy stared unflinchingly at her.

'Go up the school and ask Sister Clare, she'll tell you. She's the only bleedin' one there that knows how to tell the truth.'

Milly suspected that her sister was bluffing, but it was impossible to tell from the outraged look on her face.

'And what about the soup kitchen?'

'What's wrong with that? I've been getting soup on the way to school. I've not been half-inchin' it, have I? It's free! *And* I've been going up the Methodist Central Hall of a dinner time, for another load!'

Amy smiled, failing to see that this was an even worse sin than the truanting in her mother's eyes.

'Well, may I never move from this spot, if I ever thought a daughter of mine would go begging for a bowl of soup. You're not to go there no more!'

Amy clenched both fists and leaned forward, speaking slowly as though her mother was an idiot.

'Well, I'll promise not to go there any more the day you don't send me out starvin' 'ungry of a morning!' She spun round. 'I'm going out for me tea, they do a lovely oxtail over at Arthur's Mission.'

She slammed the kitchen door behind her and Mrs Colman began to cry, Milly suspected more out of frustration than hurt, then Marie joined in, and Jimmy poked his head out from under the table. He had pulled the saucepan tight down over his ears and now emerged as though from a bomb shelter.

'Mummy, Jimmy want to go home!'

Milly did too.

After reassuring her mother and soothing Marie, she set off for Stork's Road, looking forward to the peace of her own home. When she arrived, Bertie was already back. Sitting in his chair by the dimly glowing fire, he looked up at her as she came in, with Marie in the crook of her arm and holding Jimmy's hand. She noticed there were two Seville oranges on the kitchen table. He smiled. 'Ah, there's my beautiful girl, you're late!'

'Oh, there was a to-do with Amy.'

Bertie got up to help her with the children. 'What's she done now?'

'Hoppin' the wag and going to the soup kitchens, and Mum thought the soup kitchen was the worst of it!'

'Well, it's not something we'd want for our two, is it?' he said, lifting Jimmy for a kiss. 'Think how she must feel, living off charity.' He looked down at his black boots.

'Oh, don't look so glum. Everyone's in the same boat,' she said briskly.

'But don't you see how guilty we feel, Milly? All of us, not just your mother. We're all sponging off you!'

He put Jimmy down and reached out for an orange. 'Here, this is all I've got to show for a day hanging about at the docks, two oranges! A boy with a barrow load tossed them my way while I was waiting for the call on. I didn't earn a penny today.'

He sat back down. 'Oh, Milly, this is not what I wanted for you.' He rubbed his forehead. She lay Marie down on a blanket next to Jimmy and, exhausted as she was from her own day at the factory, she went to comfort him, putting her arms round him.

'It's all right, Bertie, you know, it's easier for the likes of me. I've been brought up to work hard, I don't expect anything else. I'm not one of your Dulwich ladies. Tough as old boots, me!' She tried to make him laugh, but the familiar whimsical look refused to be conjured.

'That's tosh and you know it. There was a time you had dreams of being something different than a jam girl; it's just you had to ditch them earlier than most.'

He was looking down at Jimmy, who was trying to interest Marie in her rattle. Milly didn't like this bitterness; it wasn't like him. She wished she could explain to Bertie just why his luck at the docks had been so bad of late, but it was something she would rather he never knew. For Barrel had told her it was Pat Donovan's doing, but the boy had also assured her he knew a way to stop him. He had asked her only to be patient. She straightened up.

'The oranges will come in handy. I'll take one to Mum's tomorrow.'

Not that Milly felt like handling oranges; she spent her days up to her elbows in the bitter fruits. She was sick of the sight of them.

Milly hadn't repeated last year's painful visit to Elsie. Her mother reported that she seemed resigned to her life in the asylum and had refused to listen whenever Mrs Colman suggested there might be a chance of her getting out of Stonefield when she reached eighteen. Milly tried to put Elsie out of her mind altogether. She'd once vowed that she would get her sister out of the asylum or die trying, but all her attempts had failed and she blamed herself for not doing more.

It was the beginning of spring when she was forced to think about Elsie again. Milly and Bertie had been invited to Kitty Bunclerk's wedding. Her friend was apologetic, she would have liked Milly to be bridesmaid, but as she explained, with so many sisters who wanted that honour, there simply wouldn't have been room enough in the aisle for them all. So instead she asked Milly to be one of her witnesses.

The service was at Dockhead Church, and though Freddie wasn't a Catholic, he had easily been persuaded on that point. His sister Nellie and her small family sat on one side of the church and the extended Bunclerk clan packed out the other. Milly noticed that the Clark side nervously looked at the Bunclerk side throughout the service for their cues as to standing, sitting and genuflecting. Afterwards in the Folly, where there were drinks and sandwiches for all the guests, there was no such confusion, and both families mingled happily. Freddie looked handsome, with his fair hair neatly swept back, and a new suit showing off his impressive physique. Milly thought he looked more like a film star than a lorry driver, and she was pleased for her friend because Freddie clearly adored Kitty. The only awkwardness in the whole affair was that Pat had been invited too.

She found herself looking away whenever there was any danger that their eyes might meet, and throughout the day he had seemed as careful as she was to avoid any contact. Now she had wedged herself behind a table with Bertie and a few of the jam girls, hoping that, here, she could enjoy the rest of the evening without bumping into him. But it was Bob Clark, Freddie's brother, who came over to them.

'Milly, can I have a word?' He leaned over, a little unsteadily she thought, for he'd obviously counteracted his best man's nerves with a few pints before and after the ceremony.

Bertie, deep in conversation about the slow retail trade with Peggy Dillon's butcher, looked at her enquiringly as he moved his chair to let her pass. Bob led her nervously to the side of the bar. Milly knew that Bob still worked at Stonefield and she could only assume there was news of Elsie. The young man pulled anxiously at his tie and carefully put his glass on the bar. His hand, holding the pint glass, was trembling a little, and Milly, suddenly alarmed, imagined the worst.

'Is it about Elsie? Has she had an accident?'

He put his hand on her arm. 'No, nothing like that. Honest, there's nothing to worry about, but . . . well, I know she gave you the cold shoulder last time you visited, but I just wanted to say, don't give up on her. She needs her family more than she lets on.'

He seemed so uncomfortable she felt sorry for him, but she was glad too that he seemed to care about her sister's well-being.

'Bob, I've tried with her. There were good reasons why I couldn't visit, but she seems harder on me than anyone. She never gives me an inch!'

A small smile played on his face. He wasn't so robust or handsome as his brother, but he had intelligent, gentle eyes which put her at ease.

'I don't want to put you in an awkward position, but . . .' He blushed. 'If you could just stick by her, she's going to need you, whatever she says now.'

'Of course I'll stick by her. She's my sister after all, and you can tell her that from me, if you like.'

He smiled, thanking her and looking relieved as he went back to join the Clark table. Milly wished it hadn't been such an ordeal for the shy young man to speak to her. God knows what tales Elsie must have told him about her, but she let herself be comforted by the idea that her sister had a friend in that awful place. She sighed and went looking for Bertie.

Her mother had offered to look after the children, insisting she and Bertie should have a night out enjoying themselves. Milly had been looking forward to having Bertie to herself for once. But when she returned to their table, she found it deserted. Bertie and the butcher had gone to the bar, while Peggy and the other jam girls were dancing to the latest jazz song that Maisie was belting out on the piano. The glass of beer on top of the piano jumped and slopped, and the floorboards of the old pub bounced to the rhythm of the Charleston. Milly sat down at the empty table, watching them with a smile on her face, when a handful of beefy constables came crashing through the old door of the Folly. One constable blew a whistle, while the other lunged across the small dance floor, scattering jam girls and bringing down Pat Donovan in a rugby tackle. Wedding guests grabbed their beers and cleared out of the way as more police piled on top of Pat, who was screaming, 'Yer breaking me fuckin' arm!'

As the police hustled Pat to his feet, he kept his head low, but at the doorway he turned suddenly and grinned at her. 'See you in a couple of years!'

But she heard the constable holding him mutter, 'You'll be lucky to get away with ten for this one, Patsy.'

And out of the corner of her eye, Milly noticed a face peering through the grimy pub window. Barrel grinned at her, winked, then ducked out of sight.

Suddenly Bertie was at her side. 'Strike me dumb, that's livened things up!' he said, putting his arm round her, and Milly leaned against him, filled with relief that Pat and his money could no longer do Bertie any harm.

The proceedings seemed to have given new life to the evening. Guests rearranged tables and chairs, glasses were refilled, Maisie started up on the piano, and soon the story was passing from table to table. It seemed that the police had raided the Donovans' on a tip-off, and found several thousand pounds of stolen banknotes and two handguns, hidden in the outside lavatory. 'The beauty of it was,' Barrel told her later, 'old Ma Donovan was sitting on the privy at the time!'

That year Amy started work. Her dream of making moisturizer and California Poppy perfume did not come true. Atkinson's was laying off women, not taking them on. With money scarce, housewives were choosing to buy cheap bread and jam to feed their families, rather than cosmetics. So Southwell's didn't turn Amy away, and she became a jam girl, just like Milly. In the end, she was glad of the seven shillings and sixpence a week. Seven shillings went to her mother; the extra sixpence, more than she'd ever had to spend on herself, she kept. Amy seemed to flourish outside school. The jam girls appreciated the rebellious ways that had scandalized the nuns, and soon her wicked impressions of the foremen made her even more popular.

Milly had taken Amy to Southwell's on her first day, showing her the cloakroom, standing next to her on the picking line, showing her how to sharpen the knife, teaching her what fruit was good enough to go into the jam and what needed to be discarded. Though Amy soon baulked at being in Milly's shadow and switched to a team of her own friends, she and Milly would still walk to and from work together, and one evening as they returned to Arnold's Place, Amy broached an idea.

'Look at the state of this frock, Mill. I need more than sixpence a week if I'm going to look decent,' she began. 'And all my mates can afford to buy make-up and face cream. Look at me. I look like a bleedin' nun!' She pointed to her unmade-up face.

Milly knew she'd started to go out in the evenings with other jam girls and she'd seen her a few times in make-up borrowed from them. Her sister had turned from a street urchin into a burgeoning flapper almost overnight, and was relishing the new role.

'It's hard, love, but Mum needs every penny, you know that.'

Her mother, as she had threatened, now joined Milly for an early morning office-cleaning stint. Jam and chars were always in demand it seemed, and while jobs for men were disappearing, lower-paid women were holding on to theirs. Many more men were to be seen around Arnold's Place during the day as unemployed men stayed at home, looking after the children, while the women worked.

'Yes, I know that. I don't want to keep any more of me wages. I was just thinking perhaps there's a way I could help make more money on your clothes sales.' The two sisters cut down tiny Farthing Lane and crossed Wolseley Street, rounding Hickman's Folly.

'How would you do that?' Milly asked, not quite seeing how Amy, who was all thumbs when it came to sewing, could help.

'Remember that time you bought a load of shirts from the wholesaler over the City?'

Milly nodded. 'It made me a bit extra, but I just haven't had the time to go back to De Jong's. I've got to rush home for my shift after the charring. And then there's the outlay to think of.'

'Well, I was thinking I could go to De Jong's Saturday afternoons for you . . . and I've got a bit put by I could use for outlay.'

Milly looked at her sister in astonishment. 'A bit put by! When did you ever have any money to put by?'

'Christmas sixpences and that . . .' Her sister blushed as Milly scrutinized her. 'And I used to run errands for Mrs Carney.'

Milly wasn't sure she'd got all the truth, but daren't probe further, for fear she might hear something about the neighbours' gas meters.

'So how much have you got?'

'Five pounds.'

'Five pounds! How long have you been saving up?'

'Oh, ages, I was keeping it for me escape fund, in case the old man ever come back.'

How was it possible to live in the same house as someone for all those years and never really know them? She had to give it to Amy – she might have been the smallest of the set of jugs, but she was definitely the canniest.

'Well, we could all do with the extra money . . . all right then, go and buy half a dozen shirts, but I can't afford to hire a stall this week.'

As they turned into Arnold's Place Amy grew more animated. 'I'm not just talking about shirts. I thought I'd get a couple of men's suits as well while I'm there. How many men do you know can afford a new suit straight off? But they might be able to pay two bob a week!'

'But you're talking about sixty bob for a suit, that's all your money gone and more.'

'No, it'd be nearer thirty wholesale, we could sell them for fifty-five and nearly double our money!'

'But if they paid back two bob a week, we wouldn't make anything for ages.'

'Not on the suit, but the shirts wouldn't take so long and the money from your clothes would tide us over.'

'And what about the stall?'

'We don't even need one! We'd run it like a clothing club, Mill. We'll just tell Mrs Carney and the neighbours'll be round to Mum's the next day, asking what we've got!'

Milly was trying to find something wrong with Amy's plan, but she really couldn't see any flaws. Amy had the money just sitting there and with her father long gone, there was no need for escape from anything except poverty.

'Well, love, you said that money you've been saving was for your escape fund. Looks like we'll all be escaping with you!'

30

Daughters of the Flood

January 1928

It was a steel-grey January morning in 1928. Milly had been up all night listening to a storm tearing over the rooftops and heavy rain beating on windows. That morning, peering out of the front-parlour window, she was alarmed to see a small river rushing down the road, overflowing the gutters with murky bubbling water. Bertie came to join her at the window and advised her to wait before leaving for work. In spite of her venture with Amy into the clothing club, she still desperately needed the eighteen shillings a week from Southwell's, and she wouldn't jeopardize that by being late, whatever the weather.

The Common Thread Clothing Club, as the sisters had decided to call it, had grown during the summer of last year, and by Christmas it had become a surprising life-saver, not only for Milly and her family, but also for many of the residents of Dockhead who'd been saved from the shame of being without a new suit for weddings or funerals. Many young factory boys had cause to bless the Common Thread too: those who'd worn ragged shorts to school were able to start work with a new pair of long trousers, or a hard-wearing working man's jacket. Mrs Carney was proving to be an excellent saleswoman and was paid in kind for getting the word out, either with a bottle of gin or a made-to-measure dress from Milly. Amy's five pounds was soon doubled and their profits, though small and intermittent, had been the difference between staying above the breadline or dipping below it into a life of misery and handouts. Bertie with his shopkeeping experience was the one who kept the books and opened a bank account in the name of the clothing club, and soon Milly had enough for a monthly stall as well.

She never ceased to be amazed that it was madcap Amy who had made it possible. True, it had needed her own desperation and skill with a needle to launch the endeavour in the first place, but without Amy's nous and her escape fund, it would have stayed a mere life raft, instead of an ark to float them all above the floods of privation. They weren't quite up on the mountain top yet, but Milly was hopeful that one day soon the dove would return with an olive branch and they would all reach dry land.

She threw on her mac and tucked the children warmly into the pram, with the hood up and the waterproof cover on. As she set off for Arnold's Place, the rain seemed to be easing, but at Jamaica Road she was brought up short at the edge of the pavement. She had to wipe rain from her eyes to make sure she was seeing properly, for spreading out before her, as far as she could see, was a vast sheet of water. Olive-green and evil-smelling, it blocked her way at every turn, all the way across Jamaica Road and beyond, into the low-lying riverside streets. The whole of Dockhead seemed to have turned into a flood plain. She looked around to see what other people were doing and began to run with the pram to the end of Jamaica Road, searching for any way across. Many people in the same predicament began wading out into the road, shouting encouragement to those on the pavement to follow them. She was wearing her wellington boots, so with no thought but to get to Arnold's Place, she pushed the pram forward. Soon the water was halfway up the pram's big front wheels and as she pushed further out, she was alarmed to see the water getting even deeper. Now it had reached the top of the wheels and the pram was in danger of turning into a boat. She couldn't risk going further; she had to turn back. Quickly pulling the pram back the way she'd come, she suddenly felt the swirl of the current tugging at the pram wheels. What a fool she'd been to blindly follow the others! She yanked at the pram handle, desperate to get back on to the dry side of the road, fighting the surging current with all her strength till she was back at the kerbside. Shaking with exertion and relief, she checked the children, making sure no water had found its way into the pram. Trying to quieten her panic, she stood still, breathing deeply, forcing herself to stop and think. But she could see no way through the flood to Arnold's Place. Opposite her was Neckinger Street, named after the lost river that had once run into St Saviour's Dock. For generations, the river had been nothing but a subterranean stream, running deep beneath Dockhead. Now, overnight, it seemed to have risen once more to the surface.

'Oi, missus, don't you try and get across there with that pram!' A docker, with his trousers rolled up and boots hung around his shoulders, shouted from the other side.

'What's happened, was it the rain?' she called across, not willing to believe she couldn't get through.

'Not just the rain. The Thames has burst its banks! It's all flooded four feet deep back there.' He indicated behind him towards Bermondsey Wall.

'Me mum's on her own over in Arnold's Place. I've got to get over there!' Her voice rose in panic.

'Only way you'll do that is if you get in the pram with the kids and paddle! Sorry, love, I've got to see to me own family, but I'll go up Arnold's Place and look in on your mother, what number?'

As the rain returned in great fat drops, she saw that he had floated an old door on the floodwater and was now stepping on to it. It toppled precariously as he balanced himself with a long pole. Another couple of dockers had joined him and were using boards of old fencing for similar rafts.

She gave the docker directions and he tried to reassure her. 'Don't worry, love,' he shouted across the floodwater. 'We'll see that no one's left trapped.'

And the men pushed off, navigating the old mill stream as the monks of Bermondsey Abbey must once have done, hundreds of years before, when the waters were pure enough to fish and the country round about was still marshland.

At least now she could be sure her mother and Amy wouldn't be left alone in the flood, but she could only imagine their terror last night, when the waters had poured into the house. Much as she wanted to go to them, she had to think of the children. Jimmy, who at first had thought the paddling pool spreading round him was fun, now picked up on her panic and began to cry.

'Mummy, I don't like the water!' He put his arms up, to be taken out of the pram. He was squeezed up under the hood with Marie and now his wriggling was upsetting his sister. Soothing him, she realized she had no choice but to return home. Spotting a policeman inspecting an abandoned car, she asked him how far the flood stretched.

'It's flooded all along the riverbank, right up to Hammersmith. It's chaos.'

'My family's in Arnold's Place, can't you get me over there?' Milly said, feeling fear scraping at her chest and throat.

'We've got police going through the streets in boats. We'll get your family out. Have they got an upstairs?'

Milly nodded, thinking miserably of her mother's few remaining possessions, saved from the old man's rages, only now to be ruined by Thames mud.

'Well, that's good, at least they're not in a basement. They'll be all right upstairs. Now you get your kids back home, love. There's nothing you can do till the water goes down.'

Milly's hands gripped the dripping pram handle and, leaning into the rain, she hurried back to Storks Road. All she could think of were her mother and sister, on the far side of that great lake. From what she'd seen of the houses beyond Jamaica Road, Arnold's Place would be half submerged by now. When she got home she would ask Bertie to try getting through the floodwaters to them. She knew she couldn't just sit at home doing nothing.

But when she returned, the house was empty and she remembered it was Bertie's day for signing on. He must have already left for the labour exchange. Damn, it *would* be today, she thought, stripping off her wet mac before parking the pram in the passage. She felt marooned here and if she hadn't had the children, would certainly have found herself a raft and paddled all the way to her mother's.

She had been home for about an hour, busying herself with drying out her clothes, when there came a knock on the front door. Bertie! Thank God he was back. She ran out from the kitchen and down the passage.

'Have you forgotten your key?' she called out, throwing open the street door.

But it wasn't Bertie who'd returned over the floodwaters like a dove: it was her sister Elsie, and the expression on her face told Milly that she had not come bearing an olive branch.

'I haven't come to stay,' she said, unsmiling. Her hair was plastered to her head and she wore a thin coat. Several sizes too small for her, it looked like the one she'd worn to go away to Stonefield. 'I've only come cos we can't get through to Mum's.'

'Of course you can't. Dockhead's flooded out, and what the bloody hell are you doing here?'

If she hated her so much, why was it that Elsie always ended up at *her* house every time she escaped? Milly was aware of the rain driving into the passage, soaking the mat, and she felt Jimmy gripping her leg, peering up at his aunt from behind her skirt. It seemed to take an age before she could act, then she grabbed Elsie by the shoulder. 'Get in here, before someone sees you!'

But her sister resisted, her bony frame immovable. She looked over her shoulder. 'I'm not on me own.'

Then Milly saw him, standing to one side of the street door, looking like a bedraggled orphan, his flat cap dripping, his gentle eyes staring apprehensively at Milly. It was Bob Clark, the young gardener at Stonefield, and he looked terrified. He seemed as though he were ready to make a run for it, or at least to stay out there in the rain, rather than face Milly's wrath. She'd imagined all sorts of reunions with Elsie, hoping one day she might build bridges, heal old wounds, but her sister had taken her by surprise yet again. Why did she have to turn up in this deluge, today of all days? Milly was in no mood for another crisis. She forced herself to soften her expression for Bob.

'You can come in too,' she said, standing to one side as the two of them traipsed the muddy floodwaters into the house.

With the fire banked, hot cups of tea and bread and jam in front of them on the kitchen table, the storm-driven pair began to lose their chilled pallor. Milly had taken her sister upstairs to find her a dress to change into. It swamped her skinny body, and as she changed from the sopping asylum-issue frock, she turned her back. Bony shoulderblades protruded like wings, and visible ribs ridged her back. Elsie didn't speak or look at Milly. It was as if all her sister's attention was turned inward, cocooned in an icy silence that Milly wouldn't attempt to break. She felt she might have a better chance of finding out what had happened once Elsie was back in Bob's company.

Downstairs, the kitchen window began to stream as Elsie's clothes dried over the range, joined by Bob's jacket, cap and socks. Milly sat down opposite them.

'So, are you going to tell me what happened?'

'You're not to jaw me,' Elsie said defensively, taking a huge bite out of a slice of bread and jam, followed quickly by another. She licked jam from her fingers and eyed Bob's plate. 'Don't you want your'n?'

He shook his head and pushed his plate towards her. 'No, you have it.'

Milly was astounded to see Elsie tuck into a third slice.

'Elsie, you must have worms!' She tried to make light of the fact that her sister was clearly starving.

Elsie carried on chewing with her mouth full, saying, 'There's nothing like home cooking.'

Milly smiled nervously. She couldn't work out if Elsie was criticizing her for not offering a cooked meal or if she was just being ironic. 'It's not cooked!'

Elsie inspected the slice. 'It's Southwell's jam and it's bread from Spa Bakery. That's what we'd call home cooking where I've been the last four years.'

There was so little expression on her face that Milly had no idea what she was feeling. Yet as Jimmy pulled on Elsie's skirt, whispering, 'Are you my auntie?' her face lit up.

Milly remembered that look of delight, from the days when her sister would gaze in pleasure at one of her grottos, and the captivated intensity that had played over her face as she sang at the Star. It was the old familiar Elsie who dropped to the floor beside Jimmy, and tears stung Milly's eyes when she saw her little boy drawing out the sister she knew. It didn't matter that Elsie was cold to her, so long as, somewhere behind that blank facade, she was still there.

Milly turned to Bob. 'Why on earth have you helped her run away again, when she'll only have to go back?' she asked in a low voice.

Elsie's head shot up. Peering over the table at Milly, she said, 'I'm never going back and I haven't run away. I got married.'

'Married!' Milly looked in astonishment from her sister to Bob, who shifted in his seat, and choked on his tea.

'What, to him?'

Elsie stood up and walked over to Bob, banging him on the back vigorously, before putting her scrawny arm round his shoulders.

Finally, he was able to speak. 'Yes, Milly, she's married to me.'

'But she's still only seventeen. She can't marry, not unless the old man signed the form.'

'We got the form signed,' Elsie said enigmatically.

'What, you've seen the old man?'

Bob blushed and Elsie stared stonily at her, as though she were an idiot.

'Oh, you dozy pair of sods, you've not forged his signature?'

The couple nodded simultaneously. Bob cleared his throat. 'It might seem stupid, Milly, but even if we could've found your dad, he'd never have signed the papers, would he? And getting married was the only way Elsie could get out of Stonefield.'

Milly didn't understand. 'But what about the charges against her?'

Bob shook his head. 'It's an open sentence, once you go in there. But the board has the choice to hand a married woman inmate over to her husband's care.' He looked up at Elsie, a shy smile playing on his face. 'I'm your gaoler now, ain't I, Else?'

Elsie's serious expression resolved itself into an intense focus as she looked into his eyes. 'More like my saviour, Bob Clark.'

'So she's free for good?' Milly asked Bob. 'And it's all legal?'

Bob nodded. 'Apart from forging your father's consent.' He grinned.

'Well, you two have got a lot of explaining to do. Start at the beginning 'cause it looks like we're going nowhere for a while.'

Heavy rain spattered the kitchen window, and the odd rumble of thunder announced that the storm was still overhead. They sat by the fire while Bob, with the occasional interruption from Elsie, told Milly how their love had blossomed in the unlikely gardens of Stonefield.

'At first I just wanted to protect her, poor kid. She didn't know what'd hit her when she first went in. It's a scary enough place if you're mad, but if you're sane, it's a bloody nightmare. Bad enough even for me and I only worked there! Anyway, I couldn't stand to see her going under, so I made sure she got assigned gardening duty.'

Milly nodded. She knew this but hadn't realized just what it had meant for her sister.

'It was the only thing that kept me from going off me rocker,' Elsie said, addressing Bob rather than Milly, whose eyes she still avoided. 'I knew I was stuck there forever, when that solicitor couldn't do nothing for me. But when I was in the garden with Bob, sometimes I could forget there was walls all round. I just used to look up at the trees and when the wind blew 'em about, I thought, well, they're beautiful and the flowers are beautiful, and

I could see a bit more sky there than I ever did in Bermondsey. So I lived for the garden.'

And for the gardener, Milly thought, as Elsie closed her hand over Bob's. The beauty of trees and sky may have saved her, but so had the boy with the kind face.

'Of course, at first it was just friendship,' Bob said, 'but later on, well . . . we both felt it. But neither of us was brave enough to say anything, not until last autumn.' Bob paused and looked at Elsie, as though asking permission. Milly saw a brief nod from her sister.

'She was really low, weren't you, love?'

With the faraway look Milly had seen on her face at the asylum, Elsie nodded again. 'Bob saved me.'

'I found her at her favourite tree, an old winter-flowering cherry, right at the end of the grounds . . . Luckily, she didn't know how to tie the knot properly . . .'

The heat from the fire couldn't prevent a chill from lifting the hairs on Milly's arms. 'Oh, Elsie, no!'

Elsie, at last, looked her full in the eyes, and Milly recognized that shameful, hopeless expression. She'd seen it once before, on her own face, staring back at her from the mirror after that night on Fountain Stairs.

'Bob promised me he'd get me free, if I could just live one more day,' Elsie said in a barely audible whisper, 'and I thought I could hold out another day, and then another, and before long, he'd got the special licence and we was married in Stonefield Chapel at Christmas.' She gave a wan smile. 'I'm sorry my family wasn't there, but we had to do it on the quick.'

Milly's heart broke for her sister then. She knew that desperate place, where ending your life seemed preferable to the pain of living it. She was about to wrap her arms round her, but in that moment Elsie's softness was veiled again, replaced by a hard blankness.

'Wait till Mum finds out you're married,' was all Milly managed to say. But the thought of her mother revived her anxiety.

'I wish Bertie would hurry up home, though. He's probably doing a good Samaritan somewhere and I won't see him till dark.'

She asked the two of them how near they'd got to Arnold's Place and their description of the road up from London Bridge was even worse than the flooding she'd seen.

Bob stood up. 'Why don't I see if I can get over there? It looks like it's easing up.'

Elsie jumped up and was at Bob's side. 'It might be dangerous!' She plucked at his sleeve, almost like a child who didn't want its mother to leave.

But he took her by the arms and said firmly, 'I can't drown in four feet of water, Else. You'll be all right here, with your sister, won't she?'

'Yes, 'course, and I could do with some help with the kids. I usually rely on Bertie to help me settle them down of a night. He's got the patience of a saint!'

With Bob gone, the awkwardness between the two sisters was even more evident. The old battleground between them was so familiar, she hardly knew how to talk to Elsie now, without being ready to deliver a barb or receive a blow. Stonefield may have scoured away her sister's dreams, leaving her with unimaginable nightmares, but being loved by Bob Clark had given her a softness that all her residual armour couldn't hide and Milly hoped eventually that the veneer would crack open, just enough to let her in.

Milly gave her the job of getting Jimmy ready for bed and she watched as Elsie sat him on the draining board, washing his hands and face carefully with the flannel, then coaxing him into pyjamas. She was equally patient with Marie, who at two was a slippery toddler and hated to be fussed over.

'You'll make a good mum yourself one day, Elsie,' Milly said as she took Marie from her. 'Let's get these two up to bed.'

Afterwards they sat and waited for the men to return, while Milly, trying not to be anxious about Bertie's long absence, asked Elsie about her plans.

'Have you thought where you two'll live?'

She knew that Bob lived in tied accommodation near the asylum, but presumed it was for a single man. 'Has Bob got a big enough place for the two of you at Stonefield?'

Elsie seemed to start at the very notion. 'Oh, we'd never live at Stonefield. I couldn't stand the sight of it! Anyway, Bob's had to leave his place.'

'Why?'

'They sacked him for fraternizing.'

'What! But you're not an inmate, and anyway he married you!'

'I know, but the governors said it must have been going on a while and that it wasn't a good example to the inmates, so he's out of a job.'

'Oh, Elsie, love, that's terrible. Believe me, it's not easy for the men to get jobs round here. He'll be lucky to get anything.'

'We'll be all right. I'll get a job.'

Elsie had been out of the world a long time and Milly tried to explain that the days of walking into jobs were over; even for low-paid women, it was getting harder and harder.

'I can put in a word at Southwell's for you, but I'm not sure you'll be up to lugging those stone jars around or standing up all day peeling oranges.'

In truth Milly thought the foreman would take one look at her frail frame and send her packing. But she was more worried about Bob. She feared if he didn't get work soon, Elsie could be swapping the asylum for the poor house.

'We could stay at his sister's in Vauban Street, but we'd have to sleep in the kitchen. They've only got two bedrooms and Bob doesn't want to turf out their kiddies. So I was thinking of asking Mum if we could stay at Arnold's Place. Amy could sleep with Mum, just till we get somewhere.'

'The place might not be in any fit state for anyone, not after this lot.' Milly looked out into the blue-shadowed evening. The rain had stopped, but the sky still threatened and as the clock ticked, the two sisters fell silent, each lost in their own anxieties.

The enforced incarceration in the warm steamy kitchen, and the long, drama-filled day, eventually had its effect and Milly found herself nodding off to sleep. Elsie must have joined her, for they both looked up with equally startled expressions as the kitchen door burst open.

'Look who we've brought home!'

Bertie and Bob walked in, followed by a mud-spattered Amy holding a bundle of clothes, and then Mrs Colman, with hair falling down and a searching look in her eyes. She held her arms wide open and Elsie ran into them.

Bertie looked at Milly and winked. 'Never rains but it pours, eh?'

31

Return of the Dove

January–October 1928

'You're not going back!' Milly was engaged in a tussle with Mrs Colman, who insisted on returning to Arnold's Place the morning after the flood.

'What else am I going to do? Sit here and let me home go all mouldy?' Her mother was already putting on her coat. 'Amy!' she called upstairs. 'Ain't you up yet?'

Amy was exhausted after her ordeal during the flood, which had involved carting every one of her mother's few possessions up to the bedrooms. As the water level rose in Arnold's Place, surging up the passage and eventually pouring through the front window, she'd waded back and forth to the scullery, retrieving as much food as she could.

'Oh, let her have a rest, Mum. You should too, just for today.'

'Amy! Stop sweatin' in the bed, get up and fetch the bundle!' Mrs Colman shouted up the stairs.

Milly heard protests from upstairs, but eventually Amy appeared. The bundle proved to be a pair of curtains, containing most of their wardrobe, together with the penny policies and the framed photos of their brothers and the three sisters.

'I had to save the photos, couldn't leave me boys and me set of jugs behind!' her mother said, carefully cleaning the bespattered glass with her coat sleeve.

'I hate that bleedin' photo. Look at the state of me, dress all tucked up! You should have let Milly shorten it,' Amy said to her mother, quickly pushing the photo back into the bundle.

Ignoring her daughter's jibe, Mrs Colman picked up her bag.

'We'll help you clean the house up. Just sleep here for a few days,' Milly pleaded.

'No, it's my home. It might not be much, but I want to go home, thanks, love.'

So, in the end, Elsie was left looking after the children, while Milly went with them to Arnold's Place. They spent the day sweeping out vile-smelling green mud, scraping it from walls and scrubbing cupboards with carbolic soap. The lino had to be thrown away, but eventually some semblance of normality was restored. Still it was obvious, by the end of the day, that the downstairs would take a long time to dry out and her mother and Amy would have to live upstairs until it did. Elsie and Bob couldn't possibly stay there, and though it wasn't a prospect she relished, Milly realized that, when he found out, Bertie would immediately offer them a home at Storks Road. She'd been hoping for a chance to get to know her sister again, and it seemed she would be getting her wish sooner than she'd expected.

Over the next few months Milly's predictions proved true, and neither Elsie nor her new husband were able to find work. Even with Milly's influence at Southwell's, her sister wasn't taken on, and although Elsie was convinced it was because of the stigma of Stonefield, Milly knew better. Tom Pelton had told her the girl simply wasn't strong enough for long hours in the boiling or picking rooms. He'd suggested it would be cruel to take her on, when he knew she couldn't cope, though Milly suspected economic necessity played its part along with compassion as he simply couldn't afford to take on dead weight. With machines increasingly taking over jam processing, even topping and tailing was now automated, so those girls who were taken on had to be built like workhorses.

Fragile Elsie would never make a jam girl, and it was Milly who finally hit upon the idea of something else she could do.

For though Stonefield had robbed her of much, it had given her three things: a husband, a love of gardening and an ability to sew. True, it had been mostly flat sewing, but her hours in the asylum laundry had included making aprons and overalls, as well as sewing sheets and pillowcases.

'What about helping me and Amy in the Common Thread?' she asked Elsie one day in early March, when the girl had exhausted every factory in Bermondsey in her search. Up until now Elsie had shown no interest in her sisters' enterprise, other than to be grateful that it bolstered Milly's income enough for her and Bob to live rent-free at Storks Road.

'I know sewing's not your cup of tea, but . . .' Milly began, half expecting Elsie to pull a face at an activity she found boring, and to turn her down flat.

'I'll do it,' Elsie said, in an instant. 'Poor Bob hates not paying his way.'

Bob had found that Bermondsey had very little use for gardeners. In a borough of thirteen hundred acres, the only open space to speak of was Southwark Park, and it had a full complement of groundsmen already. He'd managed to get some odd jobs in the local churchyards, but even though he was willing to do anything, so were a thousand other unemployed men. Even if Milly sometimes questioned his sanity in marrying Elsie, Bob, it turned out, was a thoughtful young man, who insisted his dole money go into the common kitty, which fed and housed the family at Arnold's Place as well as Storks Road. Though he had no obligation to them, he'd immediately made himself one of the family. He was as different from his brother Freddie as chalk from cheese, but in one respect they were identical – they both had the same generous heart.

Bob and Bertie now went out together every morning, either to Butler's Wharf, hoping to be called on, or following leads for any odd jobs that might crop up. But as far as Milly was concerned, Bob earned every bit of his keep, for since his arrival, Bertie's spirits seemed to have lifted. Perhaps it was just that he wanted to buoy up Bob who, never having been out of work, suffered great humiliation at his first visit to the labour exchange. But she suspected it was easier for Bertie, now that he was not the only male in the household unable to provide for the family. Having company might have diluted her husband's sense of failure, but Milly worried for him still. It was almost two years since Bertie had been in full-time work and she wished that, with her fabled strength of hand, she could simply wrest him from the grip of this monster that the newspapers were beginning to call 'the Great Depression'.

Milly spent her evenings teaching Elsie how to sew the simple shift dresses that were still fashionable. With their unfussy, straight lines they were easy enough to make, and if there was a collar or a bit of fringing required, Milly added them afterwards. The two sisters would go to the Settlement together and Florence Green let them use the machines for buttonholing and fancy stitching. Her sister was a docile pupil, hemming and tucking exactly as she was instructed, but without the enthusiasm she showed when working with Bob in the Storks Road garden, for Bob had turned half of it into a vegetable plot. Milly hoped that as she and Elsie sewed together and lived together, or as Elsie helped with her children, there might at least be some thawing between them. But her sister, though polite and grateful, stayed distant and Milly remained, she knew, completely unforgiven.

It was a fact she couldn't escape. It faced her at the breakfast table, it faced her as they did the laundry together, snapping the sheets tight, holding each end and folding them concertina-like till they met in the middle, when, inches from her sister's face, Milly could still get no answering look from Elsie, who was as cold as the day she'd returned with the flood.

It was a day they had been waiting for. After the winter deluge and a damp spring, the reluctant summer arrived in a flush of sweltering days and thick humid nights. In the boiling room at Southwell's, the heat, always intense, now threatened to melt Milly into a cloud of strawberry-flavoured steam. When Saturday afternoon came, determined not to spend a moment longer indoors, she hurried back to Arnold's Place, dodging her way down shaded alleys and across sun-slatted courts, assailed by the concentrated scent of humanity oozing from close-packed, overheated streets. She needed air, and the nearest place to find it was by the river. Though much of this stretch of the Thames was hidden behind blank warehouse walls, there were secret stairs and alleyways, down which the locals could find a clear stretch of water, a shingle beach and a vaulted sky, entirely innocent of slate and brick. Now, as she collided with some boys chasing each other to Horsleydown river stairs, she knew she wasn't alone in the desire for a cooling breeze off the Thames. Every house in Arnold's Place had windows and street doors open and, outside, most women sat on chairs, chatting to neighbours across the narrow alley or watching their children play marbles or alley gobs on the hot paving stones.

A musty smell hit her as she entered the dim passage of her mother's house. Even though five months had passed since the flood, the walls were still damp. Sunlight striped the new lino that Milly had bought for the passage and she made sure she left the street door wide open, to let in the drying warmth of the day.

'Anyone at home?' she called to the seemingly empty house.

'We're in the backyard,' her mother called.

It was a fenced-in, airless square of cobbles, which seemed to cut the sky above it into a cube. A foot of earth down one side, which her mother named the 'mould', was dotted with self-sewn love-in-a-mist and Welsh poppies, the blue and yellow splashes brightening an otherwise workaday patch, dedicated to the outside lavatory, the big old mangle and the oval tin bath. This last object, which was usually hanging on the fence, had been taken down and now Jimmy was sitting at one end of it, with Marie at the other, while Elsie and Amy took turns pouring jugs of water over them, each dousing bringing forth excited squeals for more. Her mother sat on a kitchen chair, seemingly unconcerned that her slippered feet were being periodically soaked as water spilled over the edge of the bath. Sun bounced hotly off the wet cobbles, painting them with liquid gold.

Milly was greeted with a wet embrace from Jimmy and an indifferent splash from Marie, who at two years old was taking over from her brother in stretching Milly's patience. Now four, Jimmy had returned to a state of grace. His untroubled eyes seemed always to be observing the world closely, and his observations had turned him into a mimic. He could make them laugh with impressions of Father Mallone holding forth from the pulpit and he had learned to ape Amy's version of the Black Bottom dance, which she practised endlessly in the kitchen. Always a pretty baby, now his head of fair hair and broad smile drew answering smiles from strangers in the street.

'Anyone fancy coming to the river with me this afternoon? If I don't get some air I'm going to faint.' She flopped on to her mother's lap in mock exhaustion.

'Gawd, *Jesus*, Mary and Joseph, get off me, yer great lump!'

'Yer great lump!' Jimmy mimicked.

Her mother said she preferred to stay at home and Amy was going out with friends, but Elsie seemed anxious to escape the confines of the backyard, so after their dinner, they set off with the children for the jetty at the end of Southwell's Wharf. When they arrived the river was low, leaving exposed a narrow band of muddy foreshore, studded with mossy stones, broken bricks and pebbles of ground glass, which tinkled like bells beneath long rippling waves that moved in with the tide. The wooden struts of the jetty dripped with strands of emerald-green algae, and long loops of iron chains clanked with every passing boat.

'Ohhh, that's a lovely cool breeze!' Milly smiled, narrowing her eyes against the glare off the water. Her gaze followed the chains to a group of covered barges, moored six deep, which formed a floating platform reaching far out into the river.

'Can I paddle?' Jimmy asked, his hand wriggling to escape Milly's firm grasp.

'No, we've got Marie in the pram,' Milly said.

But seeing his disappointed face and unable to refuse him anything, Elsie said quickly, 'Oh, let him. I'll take the pram on the jetty.'

As Elsie walked to the end of the wooden pier, Milly helped Jimmy descend the slippery river stairs to the little patch of uncovered muddy sand. She stood just out of reach of the small curling waves, watching while Jimmy happily splashed, barefooted, up and down the foreshore. In the shade of the river wall, where the sun never reached, there was a damp chill, at odds with the bright blue sky and Milly, after ten minutes in its shadow, stepped out into the sun again.

'Come on, Jimmy, let's go up on to the jetty, eh?'

Jimmy ran away, splashing and giggling, till she caught up with him and swept him up on to her shoulders.

'Gee up, donkey!' he said, patting her head.

Once back on the jetty, she and Elsie sat with their legs swinging over the edge, watching a group of boys running across the covered holds of the barges, leaping from one vessel to the next. When they reached the furthest barge, they stripped to their underpants, if they had any, or went naked if not. Then, throwing their white-limbed bodies off the barge in careless fluid dives, they disappeared for alarmingly long periods, only to re-emerge far off, like sleek-headed seals. Then they clambered back on to the deck, pausing only to flick their wet hair in arcing sprays before diving back in.

'What are they doing?' Jimmy asked. He was lying flat on his stomach, staring intently at the group of boys. Milly held his ankle and prepared to give him the lesson all riverside children received and habitually ignored.

'They're jumping the barges. But they're being naughty boys, because it's dangerous and you must never ever do that, hear me?'

'They're naughty.'

'They are.'

'What are they doing now?' he asked.

Finally tiring of their game, several of the boys had moved to the back of a barge, where they'd uncovered the stored cargo of coconuts. With whoops of joy the boys each pulled out a netting bag of coconuts, and holding them close to their chests launched themselves, one by one, off the back of the barge. The buoyancy of the coconuts created ready-made rafts on which they floated downstream to the next group of barges.

'The little buggers are floating on the coconuts!' Milly said to Elsie.

'Little buggers!' Jimmy said, pretending to leap on to an invisible net of coconuts, but landing with an *oomph* on the wooden boards instead. Milly pulled him back by his ankle.

Elsie laughed and Jimmy lay flat again, putting his eye to a gap in the boards.

'I was always jealous of the boys, being able to swim in the river,' Milly said. For girls, however strong they were, couldn't strip off like the boys and swim out into the tide. It wasn't considered decent.

Milly was convinced she could have been as good a swimmer as any of the boys, given the chance, but she supposed it was too late to learn now. Only Amy had secretly defied the convention in the days when she had played Run Outs with Barrel and Ronnie. Milly knew she'd joined them in their barge-hopping, and swimming too, for there were summer afternoons when she'd come home with wet hair and a bundle of damp underwear beneath her arm. She'd probably got away with it because, by that time, the old man was taking up all her mother's energy with his tyrannies. Amy had been allowed to run free like a little savage, in a way that Milly and Elsie never had.

'I never wanted to swim in it. It always looked to me like it was waiting to swallow me up,' Elsie said.

'Probably because of that boy in your class, you know, the one who got sucked under the barge.'

'The nuns put the fear of God in us about it. I didn't even want to paddle after that.' Elsie looked dreamily down into the deceptively sluggish, eddying ripples, as the incoming tide rose rapidly up the wooden pilings.

'I always loved the river. It's the only place round here you can breathe.' Milly put her head back, enjoying the breeze lifting her hair. She squinted over the water, sunlight crinkling in watery whorls, revealing the hidden currents, and she remembered the time when she would have let the river take her into its cold embrace.

'There was a time I almost did what you tried to do,' she said suddenly. 'You went to the cherry tree, and me . . . I went to the river. Funny we both went to the place we loved best.'

Elsie stared at her with a look of disbelief. 'You?'

Milly nodded. 'It was soon after I brought Jimmy home and I didn't know how I was going to live. I just gave up, but my Bertie saved me, same as Bob saved you.'

Milly wasn't sure why she had wanted to tell her secret to Elsie now, perhaps because it was the only thing they had in common, and she was tired of the great gulf between them. But now she saw that her sister's lip trembled and tears had begun to trickle down her cheeks. Milly leaned over and put her arms round Elsie. This time the sharp-edged body gave in to her embrace and the two sisters clung to each other.

'Oh, Elsie, I'm sorry I let you down.' She could feel the front of her dress wet with Elsie's tears, but her sister shook her head.

'You couldn't have done nothing about it, Mill.' Elsie looked up and their eyes met. 'I know that now. I did blame you for a long time, but Bob made me see sense. It was like they locked up my whole family when they sent me in there, and there's only the old man to blame for that.'

Milly cupped Elsie's face with her hands. 'Well, the old bastard's gone for good and you're safe home now.'

Jimmy had silently squirmed between them and patting Elsie's cheek said, 'Don't cry, Auntie Elsie, old bastard's gone.'

They laughed as they wiped away their tears, and Elsie gathered up Jimmy in a tight embrace.

After sharing her secret, Milly noticed a change in her sister. For the first time in her life, she'd allowed Elsie to see her as weak, and the revelation, far from calling forth her scorn, had resulted in a common bond. Both sisters now knew that they had visited the same dark depths of hopelessness, and both knew that it had taken the love of another to bring each of them back from the brink. Neither could claim to be stronger than the other, and the sense of isolation they'd felt growing up, islands cut off from each other in the sea of fear generated by the old man, began to dissipate, receding just as the floodwaters had earlier that year. For Milly, it felt as if the dove had finally returned with the olive branch in its beak, and that at last Elsie was her sister again.

And in the long, dark nights of autumn, as they sewed together, they began to share confidences. One evening while making some baby romper suits that had been particularly popular, Elsie put down her needle, with a worried look.

'Milly, don't jaw me, but I think I'm expecting.'

'Oh, love, I'm so happy for you!' Milly's response was unfeigned. 'But why would I jaw you? The way you are with my kids, I know you'll make a lovely mum.'

Elsie's brows knitted together as she plucked at a loose thread in the romper. 'Well, it's just another mouth to feed, and if we can't feed ourselves, how will we find the money for a baby?'

'It don't cost nothing to feed a baby, well, not at first, and I've kept all Marie's baby things, so that'll help out.' She paused, feeling sad that such joyful news should only be the cause of another worry. 'Oh, Elsie, be glad about it. You've got Bob now, and me. You're not on your own. Besides, you can't stop living, just because you ain't got two ha'pennies to rub together. Wasn't Bob pleased?'

Elsie shook her head sadly. 'He seems more ashamed than anything.'

'Ashamed! But why?'

'He says we've got no business bringing a child into the world. He says it'll have no future, not the way things are, with no jobs and no money. And the thing is, Millie, I think he's right. We should be able to give our kids a better life than we had . . . but we can't,' she finished flatly.

Milly felt herself getting angry. Stonefield had knocked so much of the fight out of Elsie, it had tamed her beyond recognition.

'Well, God knows we were poor enough as kids *and* we had the old man bashing us about, but you think back to that cherry tree – would you rather Bob hadn't come along? Would it be better if you didn't have your life? I know when I think back to the Fountain Stairs, I bless my Bertie every time. Life's sweet, darlin', no matter how poor you are, so you just think of that little baby inside you, and give it a chance to live, will you? It's all any of us get.'

Milly picked up her sewing again, the clock ticked, Elsie was silent and Milly wondered if she'd been too stern. But then her sister dropped her sewing, and sinking to the floor beside Milly's chair, she laid her head on Milly's lap.

'Oh, Milly, I want to be glad. I know it'll be the best thing that ever happened to me.'

Milly stroked Elsie's hair. 'It will be, love, I promise.'

Elsie's news was just what they needed to brighten their lives during an autumn bleached by mists and thick fog. Day after day, yellow pea-soupers rolled off the Thames and collected like grimy cotton wool in all the courts and alleys of Dockhead. The air was perpetually full of the mournful foghorns of passing vessels and the sharp, shrill warnings from the tugs. It was on such a foggy evening in October that, as Milly made her way to Arnold's Place to collect the children from her mother's, she sensed a figure shadowing her. All the way down Hickman's Folly, she had felt a darker shape, brown against the jaundiced mist surrounding her, moving as she moved, pausing when she paused. Yet each time she stopped to listen for the footsteps she was sure she'd heard, she was met only by silence. Dockhead was her home and behind each shabby, peeling door, in every crumbling alley or court, were friends and neighbours; the place held no terror for her. Yet she knew there were sometimes strangers passing through, casuals off the docks, who came from outside Bermondsey, looking for work at Butler's Wharf, or sailors, Yankees and Chinamen, from the moored vessels along the quaysides, searching out the nearest pub. Sometimes they would see a rare, dusky-skinned, turbanned street vendor, but the only terror she'd ever experienced in these streets had come from inside the walls of her own home: the old man.

Crossing Parker's Row, she again had the sense of being watched, and whirling round, caught sight of a dark figure disappearing into the momentary glow of the Swan and Sugarloaf. The door banged shut, but putting her jitteriness down to tiredness, she pulled her coat tightly around her for warmth against the chill damp. She was grateful for the mist-shrouded halo of light around the gas lamp on Mrs Knight's wall, spreading out to greet her.

But over the next week, try as she might, Milly could not rid herself of the feeling that she was being followed. It was only ever when she was walking home from work, once she was alone, and had said goodnight to Kitty and the other girls. One evening after she'd arrived home and was hanging up her coat, still damp from the fog, a sound behind her startled her, so that she cried out and jumped back.

'Good gawd, Milly, it's only me!' said Elsie. 'What's put the jitters into you?'

'Oh, you made me jump! It's probably just the fog, but I keep feeling there's someone behind me.'

She expected her sister to laugh at her, but instead Elsie's face grew serious and once they were in the kitchen she turned to Milly with a worried expression.

'Funny thing is, Milly, I've been feeling that too. When I've been shopping, or going round to see Mum.' The two sisters looked at each other for a long moment, not wanting to voice their suspicions. Milly was the first to speak. 'You don't think he's back, do you?'

Elsie sat down at the kitchen table and began to rock ever so slightly back and forth. 'If he is, he'll come after me. Oh, Mill, what if he finds out I got married and forged his signature? He'll shop me and I'll be put away again!'

Milly rushed to soothe her sister. 'We're probably getting ourselves into a state over nothing. Even if he's back, love, he can't know when you got married, can he?'

But Elsie's brow was still furrowed and she shook her head. 'But what if someone tells him?'

'I'm telling you, he's not come back. He's got it too cushy over in Whitechapel, all the beer he can drink. Why would he give that up?'

'I don't know. But I've got a bad feeling about it. I haven't said anything, but I've even been dreaming about him lately. I dream over and over that he's back at the leather mills and I see him floating in one of the lime pits, all bloated, and when I wake up, I feel so guilty.'

'Why should you feel guilty?' Milly whispered, chilled by the image.

'Because I feel so happy . . . happy that he's dead.'

'Well, we've all felt that one time or another, and you've got more reason than all of us.'

'I don't think I could stand to go back to Stonefield, though.'

'You won't have to,' she patted Elsie's hand, 'because he's *not* back.'

But it was Kitty who proved her wrong. They met up as they were both walking along Jacob Street the next morning, and after they'd clocked in at Southwell's Kitty linked arms with her. 'I've got some bad news, love. My Freddie says your old man's been seen at the Swan.'

Milly froze. It *had* been him, then, all along, silently shadowing her and Elsie. It felt far more frightening than the prospect of an open assault.

'I thought as much. I don't know what he's planning, but he's been following me and Elsie, and she's scared he'll get her put away again.'

'How can he do that? They let her out when she got married.'

414

Milly reminded her of the circumstances of Elsie's marriage, which Bob had confessed to his brother.

'Oh no, I didn't think of that!'

'Does Freddie have any idea what the old man's doing back? He must want something.'

'From what he heard, the old cash cow in Whitechapel chucked him out. Fed up with him pissing all the profits up the wall.'

'Well, if he turns up at Mum's, he'll find the cupboard's bare.'

Kitty nodded sympathetically. She knew that it was Milly and Amy keeping the two families afloat. 'When he gets no joy there, he'll sling his hook soon enough, I reckon.'

'I hope so,' Milly said uncertainly.

32

Sweet Thames Flow Softly

October 1928

It was as if summer had suddenly returned. One day the world was shrouded in fog and gloom; the next, unclouded blue skies arched over Dockhead and set the river sparkling again, in mild October days reminiscent of high summer, when Elsie's and Milly's bond had first deepened. The dark shadow stalking them disappeared from the riverside streets along with the mist, and they relaxed into an Indian summer, when Milly dug out her cotton frocks and took the warm flannel liberty bodices off the children.

On a bright Sunday morning towards the end of October, Milly and Elsie left Storks Road early, to walk with the children to Arnold's Place. They were going to Mass at Dockhead Church as they usually did, with their mother and Amy. On this particular morning their talk was all of the plans for Elsie's baby, which was due in two months' time. Elsie's pregnancy had been straightforward and, in spite of her fragile constitution, she had kept going with daily chores, shopping and sewing, as well as helping out with the children. Milly had been impressed but not surprised by her hidden resilience, forged, she had no doubt, in those dark days at Stonefield.

'Have you thought of a name yet?' Milly asked her sister.

'If it's a boy, I think we'll name him Charles George, after our Charlie, and Bob's dad George.'

'Ah, that'll please Mum,' Milly said, remembering their eldest brother, killed at the Battle of Loos. 'I was only nine when our Charlie died, and you must have been about six?'

'Five.'

'I still think of him. It's only now I realize how young he was when he died, twenty-two, same age as me!' Milly sighed. 'He was a good brother. It was different when he was at home, do you remember?'

Elsie nodded. 'I remember him always bringing home an orange or something from the docks for us, and he used to swing me about like a sack of potatoes, till I got dizzy.'

'I don't know if I'm imagining it, but the old man seemed different then. He was still always at the pub, but it just felt more like a home when the boys were around, and then when Jim died too, that's when everything seemed to go to pot.'

They had never really talked of their soldier brothers' deaths. Two years apart, they had come like dull hammer blows into their young lives. Milly knew now that their mother had protected them from the consequences as much as she could. But thinking back, she could see it had been those two events that had shattered whatever fragile home life they'd had. After that, it had been the start of another war – in the Colman household, when they'd all begun pulling in opposite directions, with only their mother trying to capture each unravelling skein as the fabric of their lives pulled apart. Now Milly hoped that as the wounds between her and Elsie healed, there was a chance of another common thread to bind them all, the tie of sisterly love. Even Amy had begun to circle their newfound closeness with a wistfulness that gave Milly hope.

When they arrived at Arnold's Place, Milly was surprised not to find Mrs Colman and Amy ready and waiting at the doorstep, for her mother was a stickler for being punctual at Mass.

'Someone's overdone it!' She pushed at the front door. 'Better bring the kids in,' she said to Elsie, lifting Marie out of the pushchair. 'Looks like we'll be waiting for them to get ready!'

'You all still sweating in the beds?' she called. 'Come on, you lazy—' She stopped short at the kitchen door, silenced by the scene that greeted them. Her mother sat white-faced and rigid. Behind her, holding the curved blade of his double-handled tanner's fleshing knife to her throat, stood the old man. Amy leaned like a frozen, toppled statue against the mantelpiece, her lip cut, blood oozing from a gash in her forehead. She shot Milly an unnecessary warning look. She had fought him.

He looked a wreck. Two years of unlimited booze had coarsened his features, so that nose, mouth and eyes had swollen into a bulbous, undifferentiated mass, the colour of raw meat. He was unkempt, long greasy hair falling to the collar of his stained, worn jacket. Whatever he was, he'd always been meticulously clean, but now the unwashed smell coming off him was obvious even to Milly, standing across the room. His lip curled in a snarling smile when he saw her.

'So, Lady Muck's arrived, still looking like a slut. How does your drip of a grocer like the leftovers?' He licked dry cracked lips and Milly felt revulsion replace the initial fear that had stopped her. Only her mother's obvious terror prevented her from taking two steps across the room and flattening his swollen features.

'And you look like a filthy tramp. I can smell you from here.'

The old man yanked her mother's hair, pulling her head back to expose her throat. The curved blade nicked loose flesh and a thread of crimson appeared. All three sisters started forward, but their mother called out, 'No! He'll kill me, he will!'

'What do you want?' Milly asked carefully, standing her ground, for she'd edged a little nearer to her mother.

'I only come for what's mine. I left money here and a full bottle of drink, but she's a fucking wicked liar, says she's got nothing in the place.' He tugged her mother's hair. She whimpered.

'We didn't think you'd be back for your brandy after all this time, and I swear I haven't got a penny!'

'She's telling the truth! If you must know, I drank your soddin' brandy!' Milly hoped to draw him off, anything to get him to let her mother go.

He looked at her with contempt. 'Still leeching off me, houseful of women, fuckin' useless the lot of you, when I've got two sons in the grave worth ten of you!'

'And another son who'd rather go out to get killed at sixteen, than stay home with a bully like you!'

'Shut yer trap! You're a fuckin' liar, just like your mother!'

'He told me himself, and that's why he stayed in the army too. It's you drove him away!'

'He went to war out of respect for his brothers, something a whore like you wouldn't understand. And when he come back, there was nothing for him 'cause the women had took all the jobs!'

Milly gave a bitter laugh. 'I can just see our Wilf peeling oranges all day. He wouldn't work for the pittance we get anyway.'

'Looks to me you're set up all right. I'll have some of it off you. Gis yer bag over.'

He stuck a hand out and she saw the knife wobble in his other trembling hand. His strength must be sadly diminished, if he could barely hold the fleshing knife that he used to wield with such skill and speed. Her father had boasted of dehairing a hide in under a minute. She took her chance and lunged forward, swinging her bag to knock the knife from his hand, but stumbled to her knees as she did so. The scimitar-like blade skittered across the floor, landing at Jimmy's feet. Instinctively he picked it up and handed it to his grandfather. Before she could scramble up, the old man had bundled Jimmy under his arm. He swung the knife in a wild arc around him, edging towards the door.

'You want to see what it's like to lose a son? Do ya?' he screamed at her, veins standing out in his neck, as if they might burst.

Barging Elsie out of the way, he charged up the passage and out of the front door. The sound of Jimmy's long wail galvanized Milly into action and she shot up from the floor, like a sprinter from the blocks. She ran like the wind, pounding along Arnold's Place, long legs pumping, following the old man's lumbering flight, till she lost sight of him at Dockhead. She slammed to a halt. Which way? Then she heard Jimmy's cries; they were coming from the direction of Hickman's Folly. As she entered the narrow alley she caught a glimpse of the old man disappearing into George Row. He was heading for the river. She cut through a gap in the houses, skirted the Ship Aground and ducked down Farthing Alley, trying to cut him off. But by the time she reached Bermondsey Wall he was already on Southwell's jetty. Now he stopped. Turning on her like a cornered wild beast, he held Jimmy above the water like a kitten in a sack.

'Leave him be, Dad! He's done nothing to you!' she pleaded. But she had little hope, for by now she was certain that whatever sanity or humanity the old man ever possessed had been obliterated by his years of drinking, all decency pickled and stripped from him, like a hide in the lime pits.

As Jimmy's little legs flailed, the old man's grip tightened. High tide was turning and the thick, oily water was dappled with huge flat pools of current slapping lazily into the jetty, before crashing into the foot of the river stairs. The old man backed to the end and suddenly leaped on to the nearest barge, one of six moored parallel to each other.

'You don't deserve a son!' he called from the barge, which bobbed and dipped in the fast-running tide. 'Why should you have one and mine all dead!'

'You've got Wilf, you've got Wilf, please, Dad!' Her voice, high-pitched and taut, sounded like a stranger's.

'Dead to me.' He shook Jimmy, looked from him to Milly, then, almost as an afterthought, tossed her son high into the air. Milly screamed.

But instead of hearing the splash of Jimmy's body hitting the water, there was a dull thud. He had landed on the barge furthest out into the stream. The old man began scrambling across the barge towards Jimmy, who looked as if he was trying to hide himself beneath the tarpaulin covering the hold. Milly leaped from the jetty to the first barge, springing over each vessel as, with feet barely touching the gunwales, she threw herself headlong at the old man, who by now had almost reached her son. The knife fell to the deck, and she caught it mid-air, swinging it up without pause in a slicing arc, catching the old man behind the knees. Toppling forward, he lunged for Jimmy, but the little boy had found a netting bundle in the hold and was heaving it up on to the gunwale. Hugging it tightly to him, he used all his remaining strength to roll with it over the side, and into the fathomless, soupy waters. The old man howled, for Jimmy was floating away from his grasp, buoyed up on a raft of coconuts, imitating the forbidden game he'd witnessed earlier that summer.

Milly didn't hesitate for an instant. Thought no longer existed; nor fear. Her precious child was being washed away and where he went, she would go too. Stepping over the old man, lying hobbled in a pool of blood, she picked up another net of coconuts and launched it, and herself, on to the mercy of the great river.

The shock of ice-cold water winded her and she swallowed a mouthful of scummy foam. Jimmy was still within sight, but being carried further off by the minute. She struck out. With one arm draped over the coconut raft, she used the other like an oar, paddling furiously and kicking her legs in a doggy paddle. She was astonished at how fast the tide took her downstream. She began gaining on Jimmy, but even if she caught up, with the river running almost at the top of the wall, she could see no exposed foreshore where they could land. When it came to it, she would just have to grab for a piling or the next group of barges. With a surge of strength, she ploughed the water as though it were air, and calling to Jimmy, saw him turn his head. The bright morning sun bounced light around him and his dark eyes, surreally calm, locked on to hers. He held out his hand in a gesture as trusting and commonplace as if they were about to cross the road together. She gave an almighty kick, which propelled her forward on the running tide, so that she was within touching distance of him. Straining forward, her extended fingers caught his hand, gripped it tight, held him fast.

'Mummy's here!' was all she had time or breath to utter, before the water entered her mouth and the notorious Fountain current sucked them both under, in its whirling embrace.

She had always known it would come to this. As the waters tugged at her hair and clothes, the coconut raft was ripped from her hand and she felt a certainty that whatever god inhabited the river was exacting his due. She had offered herself and her child to it and then drawn back. How stupid she'd been to think that the river god would be denied its tribute. Holding her son tightly to her chest, she gave herself up to the depths.

The strong undertow dragged Milly and Jimmy beneath the opaque waters, so that they were invisible from the foreshore. But standing on Fountain Stairs were two witnesses to their struggles, and now the eager eyes of Elsie and Amy scanned the surface of the water. They had followed Milly as she'd pursued the old man from Arnold's Place, and had arrived just in time to see her plunge into the river with Jimmy. The two sisters had run the length of Bermondsey Wall, with Elsie lagging behind, and had tracked Milly downstream, desperately trying to keep up as the tide took her and Jimmy; waiting only for the chance to get close to the river. At Chamber's Wharf they had glimpsed mother and son shoot by, seen Milly getting closer and closer to Jimmy, but they'd arrived at Fountain Stairs only to witness them both being sucked under by the current.

Now they clung to each other, shivering and terrified, while the river sloshed and boiled up the narrow stairs, soaking them. Suddenly Amy pulled out of Elsie's arms.

'I'm coming, Milly!' she shouted, launching herself through the foaming waves slapping against the stairs, and out into the fast-flowing tide.

Elsie's cry was lost in the noise of water rushing against the river wall. She saw her sister's arms whirling in an ungainly crawl which, however untutored, had been acquired in this same treacherous stretch of water. Amy's forbidden Thames swimming expeditions with Barrel had taught her the secret of the Fountain and she was heading for the exact spot in the stream where the spout spewed out the lucky ones. She began treading water, but the tide's pull threatened to bear her downstream – only by swimming against the current was she able to stay in the same position. Desperate seconds passed as Amy's head whipped back and forth, willing the surface to break. Then there was a burst of air bubbles, and the thick green waters broke, as the river like some liquid leviathan opened its maw and shot forth Milly and Jimmy, with such force that they were propelled clear of the water. Today, the old river god had chosen to be merciful – they were free! Amy was on them in a heartbeat. Grasping Milly under the armpits, she shouted in her ear, 'Hold tight to Jimmy!'

But the instruction was unnecessary, for though Milly could no longer hear her sister, she had Jimmy in a death-like grip, which not all the mighty force of the old river had been able to loosen. Amy turned on to her back and, supporting the two bodies, kicked out for the Fountain Stairs, but the force of water shooting over them and sucking back down threatened to break all three of their bodies on the stone steps.

'Elsie!' Amy called as she was dragged back by the undertow. 'You've got to help me. I can't get them out on my own!'

But Elsie was frozen, her deep childhood fear of the river rising up now, as it caught at her feet and smashed against her legs.

'Elsie! I'm losing them!'

This time Amy's cry seemed to unlock something in Elsie, and she began to descend the river stairs. Her skirt billowed out and her hands reached forward, feet slipping as water covered her legs, she toppled back on to the steps. Now, sitting up to her swollen stomach in water, she braced herself, made a grab for Amy and with an almost animal roar, pulled her up until she too was on the stairs. She strained her heavily laden frame, till, one step at a time, she hauled up Amy, who held fast to Milly and Jimmy. Finally, they were all at the top of the stairs, coiled in a sodden spiral of bodies, the sisters intertwined like a three-cornered triskele around the child at its heart.

The light was too bright, the air too thin. She must be in the wrong place. She knew she had surrendered herself to the river, opening her mouth to fill her lungs with its thick opacity. Drowning was heavy, she knew that, a slow strangling, bursting weight, that crushed the chest and dragged on the body. So why, now, did she feel so light? She knew she couldn't be in heaven. Her mother had always said she made a bad Catholic, and at the end it wasn't either the caddywack or the proddywack God she'd turned to, but the old river god – and even he hadn't heard her prayers. The light hurt her eyes and she groaned, pulling her arms more tightly round Jimmy. But they closed around empty air. He was gone. Her groan turned to a soft whimpering, then a long moan.

'Jimmy!'

She felt hands exploring her face, soft as butterfly wings brushing her cheeks. She opened her eyes. He gave her the smile she loved, broad enough to dimple his cheeks, bright enough to light his eyes.

'Mummy's awake!' Jimmy said.

Gathering him into her arms, she squeezed so hard he protested, then the room seemed suddenly full of noise. Amy, draped in a huge grey blanket, sat on the edge of the bed where Milly lay and engulfed her in a scratchy embrace, then Elsie, wearing borrowed clothes, joined them.

A voice she recognized said gently, 'Give her some air, girls.' And she turned her head to see Florence Green at her bedside. The young woman took her hand, seeming to understand her confusion. 'It's all right, Milly, you're back safe on dry land. Thanks to your sisters; they pulled you out of the river. You're at the Settlement and we've sent for Bertie, and your mother will be here soon. Just lie back and rest now.'

Florence pulled the cover up over her and Jimmy, as Milly felt tears of gratitude begin to trickle down her cheeks. Her child was alive, here in bed with her. *She* was alive! As her sisters obediently moved away, she pulled them back.

'No, let my sisters stay.'

She looked up into Elsie's serious, sharp-chinned face and at

Amy's careless beauty and felt nothing but gratitude, realizing now that they'd both risked their lives to save her and her child. She pulled them closer, remembering something her mother had once said, in another lifetime or so it seemed.

'Be friends with your sisters,' she'd begged. 'You'll need each other one day.'

It was many days before Milly realized the full extent of Amy's heroism. She learned it not from Amy, but from Bertie, who, once she was back in Storks Road, nursed her and Jimmy as tenderly as though they were both children. He told her how Amy had braved the strong currents and deadly undertow at Fountain Stairs, and how Elsie had found a superhuman strength to pull all three of them up the stairs. When she tried to thank her sisters, Amy had shrugged and reminded her of all the times Milly had told her off for coming home with wet underwear and dripping hair. Elsie insisted she'd done nothing, but Milly remembered how fearful she'd been of the river, sometimes not wanting even to look at it. She could only guess at the courage it had taken to immerse herself in its waters.

Jimmy wouldn't leave her side and she didn't want him to. Her strength had been sapped and the quantity of filthy Thames water she'd consumed left her with a fever, but in spite of Bertie's protests, after three days she determined to get up from her sick bed. Her life and her child had been given back to her. She wasn't going to waste it lying in bed. Besides, she wanted to see her mother. She'd been vaguely aware of her presence at her bedside at the Settlement, and had battled to keep her eyes open, and she remembered glimpsing the thin cut at her mother's throat. She'd tried to raise herself up.

'The old man?' she'd managed to ask, before collapsing back into sleep.

Now as she moved slowly around her bedroom, being helped by Bertie into her clothes and shoes, she realized with a start that her mother hadn't been to see her and Jimmy since their return to Storks Road.

'Has Mum been round, while I've been laid up?' she asked Bertie.

'No, love.' He was fumbling with her buttoned shoe strap and she bent to do it herself, but her head swam and she found herself gripping his shoulder to steady herself.

'There, you're not ready to get up!' Bertie said.

'I'm fine, just a bit dizzy. Why hasn't she been round?'

'Who?'

'Mum! She'd normally be here wanting to take over.'

'Amy's been giving her the news. You haven't really been up to visitors.'

Something in his tone made her suspicious. Bertie was an open book, his mobile features reflecting every emotion. Now she could see him struggling to hide his blushes as he bent his head and started buttoning the other shoe.

'Bertie Hughes, you're a terrible liar. What's going on?'

He moved to sit on the bed beside her. Taking her hand, he stroked it gently. 'I haven't told you anything because you've barely been able to lift your head from the pillow. You've been in no fit state.'

His characteristic slowness was agitating her even more than usual. 'Has something happened to her? Just tell me!'

He paused for a moment, then sighed. 'Your mother's had some troubles of her own, love.'

33

Trees of Heaven

October 1928–May 1929

'Dead? How? At the river?' If she had been the cause of it, she would have to live with the consequences, but she wouldn't have, *couldn't* have done anything differently. Her mouth had gone dry and all her determination to get up and face the world had drained away. Her legs were weaker than the beef tea Bertie had been spooning down her mouth for the last three days. She wished her brain felt more connected to her body and she wished her feelings were more connected to her brain. It was as if the river had melted all the normal everyday connections that allowed her to function properly in the world, and she realized, with a jolt, that she had begun to cry. The old man was dead, and she was crying. How could that be? The truth was, she had so often wished him dead it had become second nature, but now she began to suspect that all along, she had only really wished him – different. The old man had been her father . . . once.

'It wasn't your fault,' Bertie said, reading her mind.

'No?' But she had left the old man lying in a pool of his own blood; she had sliced the back of his legs and hobbled him. She had left him, bleeding to death for all she knew, on that barge.

'No!' he said with emphasis. 'You did what you had to do to protect our son and I'm proud of you. Your father killed himself.'

'How?'

'We don't know if it was deliberate or an accident, but he drowned.'

'In the river?'

Bertie shook his head. 'Not the river. It was at Neckinger Mills.'

'In the lime pit,' she whispered, a shiver raising every hair on her body as the image flashed into her mind of the old man, face down in a square pit of liquid lime; hairless, bloated white flesh already pulpy and softening.

'Strike me dumb, how did you know that?'

'Elsie had a dream, ages ago, that he'd drowned in one of the lime pits.'

Bertie whistled. 'Looks like Polly Witch got it right this time!'

Milly put her hands to her face, rubbing at her eyes, wanting to erase the horrible image. She shuddered. 'I wouldn't have wished it on him, not even after everything he's done to us. It's horrible, Bertie.' And she leaned into him, letting the bitter tears fall for her unloving father.

'But how could he have even walked, after what I did to him?' she asked after a while.

'I think all the blood made things look worse than they were. Some people saw him later on Sunday, walking past Neckinger Mills. He was bloody and hobbling, and looked half mad they said. Then later on, some kids saw him climbing *out* of the tannery, over the wall next to the pits.'

Milly knew the place. It was a fairly low wall they had used to run along as children, and the grid of lime and tanning pits beyond were visible from there.

'They said he looked drunk, had a bottle in his hand, started shouting at them to clear off, but then he just fell back and disappeared. We think he must have toppled back into one of the pits.'

'But why would he go there of all places? There's no reason to it all.'

'Oh, there's a reason, Milly. It turns out he'd been hanging around the place for weeks on and off, even asked for his old job back, and when the foreman refused him, he started getting abusive, saying he'd torch the place.'

'I'm not surprised he's been back for a while. I never told you, but I felt as if someone was following me, back when we had all that fog.'

'Why didn't you say anything?'

'Well, I never saw anyone, but now I know it was him.' She shuddered, thinking of all the times when she'd been at his mercy, whirling round in the fog to find nothing there at all. 'But he never damaged anything at the tannery?'

'I think he probably got distracted. After they fished out his body, the police found the offices broken into and the directors' drinks cabinet empty.'

It was a pitiful end, and now she was no longer at the old man's mercy, she found she had room for her own. Being turned away from the tannery must have seemed the last nail in the coffin of whatever dignity he still possessed.

'Do you know what he said to me on the barge, while he was dangling my poor baby over the side? He said it was living in a houseful of women that ruined him.'

'Oh, that's a load of old tosh, Milly.'

'Not really, he blamed us for being alive, while our two brothers were dead, and he blamed Wilf going away on us too, said the women had taken all the jobs . . .'

Bertie held her tighter. 'Wilf left because he couldn't stand your father. And there's only one thing ruined the old man, my love, and that's the drink. So there's to be no more talk of blame, hear me?'

'I need to go and see Mum. She's had to go through all this on her own and I wasn't there to help.'

'Not alone, she's had your sisters.'

Her sisters. Suddenly she felt lighter, suddenly the phrase sounded full of promise. Now their common enemy was gone for good, perhaps they really could be bound together by something other than fear.

'Where are they?'

'They're at the undertaker's.'

*

The old man's funeral was discreet and painful. Her mother had insisted everything be done properly, just as though he'd been a real husband and father. And Milly understood that it was as much for her own sake that her mother wanted it this way. Her life with him had been one long humiliation, always to be referred to as 'poor Mrs Colman', always to have been powerless, fighting for a respectability that he inevitably sabotaged; it had eaten away at her native pride, but hadn't destroyed it. Now the burying of him was perhaps the first independent act she'd carried out in her adult life, and Milly had to admit, she did it well.

Everyone was decently dressed in black. The men's suits came out of the Common Thread Clothing Club, and Milly and Elsie made every other black garment. There was a Mass and a proper Christian burial, as his death had been ruled an accident, not deliberate suicide. Milly stood through it all with a rigidity that made her muscles tremble and her jaw ache. The few tears she'd had to spare for her father had already been shed. There was no crying at the old man's funeral.

After the burial they went back to Arnold's Place, where a few of his more sober workmates, and some of the neighbours, were given sandwiches and nothing stronger than tea. Admittedly the crockery and furniture had to be borrowed from Storks Road, but afterwards Milly could see a sort of grim pride in her mother's face, when Mrs Knight said her goodbyes and added, 'All very respectable, Mrs Colman, very respectable.'

The baby's cries were insistent and piercing. Milly rolled over in bed and curled against the curve of Bertie's back.

'Thank gawd I don't have to get up for this one.'

'Your turn'll come again soon enough.' He was awake.

She pulled him over and laid her head on his chest. She was happy. Elsie had brought home her new baby girl just before Christmas. They had called her Ivy, not just for the season, but because, as Elsie said, it was a plant that would flourish almost anywhere. The baby had certainly thrived and if her lungs were anything to go by, she had the constitution of an ox. Milly could only think it came from the Clark side, for the child had very little of Elsie's fairy-like fragility.

But Milly's happiness had another cause, for shortly after the new baby arrived she found that she was expecting another child herself. Bertie's happiness, she knew, was tinged with worry. She had tried to reassure Elsie that babies didn't cost much, but now the reality was hitting home. Bob had been out of work for a year and her own husband hadn't worked full time for almost three. If she was honest, her own happiness was sometimes interrupted by fear that their precarious ark would spring a leak at the worst possible time. But she took strength from the fact that the Common Thread was still thriving.

This morning, the two men were going to try for some labouring jobs with Bermondsey Borough Council. Their slum clearance programme was well under way and the dilapidated houses around Cherry Garden Street had been demolished. Finally, the area had begun to reflect a little of that old pleasure garden, filled with cherry trees, which had once graced the banks of the Thames centuries ago. Soot-encrusted hovels had been replaced with an incongruously pretty estate of cottages, boasting their own front gardens – the result of a long-held dream of their MP, Dr Salter, to replace all the slums of Bermondsey with something that people could be proud to live in. Milly and Bertie had walked around the flagship streets of Wilson's Grove, marvelling at what previously had seemed an impossibility: in the shadow of factories and wharves, a little garden village had grown up.

But, not long after the cottages were finished, Bertie had heard at the Labour Institute that the economic Depression was threatening to put an end to Dr Salter's dream. The council had no more money to build garden estates, and though the worst of the slums were continuing to be demolished, from now on they would be replaced by flats. Neither of the men were skilled bricklayers or carpenters, but if they couldn't contribute to building the new, they could certainly help demolish the old. That task was easy, as the old houses were collapsing under their own decrepit weight anyway.

Today they were going to look for demolition work in the area known as Downtown, in Rotherhithe. Here the houses lining the river had been amongst those worst hit by the January floods. The high waters had poured through already broken windows, undermining foundations dug more than a century before. Nothing could save them and nobody wanted them to be saved.

When she heard a soft snore coming from Bertie, she nudged him. 'You can't go back to sleep.'

A pearly February light was beginning to filter through the net curtains and the men had to make an early start of it.

'I wasn't!' he protested.

'Come on, move yourself. I'll go and get the breakfast started.'

She saw the two men off with high hopes, but that evening when they returned, weary, wet and caked in what looked like Thames mud, their news wasn't encouraging. They had been lucky to get a day's work; there were hundreds of skilled bricklayers, carpenters and plumbers queuing up in front of them just for the chance to wield a sledgehammer. Milly could see they were both crestfallen.

'Let's get the bath in,' she suggested.

Later, after the water had boiled in the copper and the grey tin bath had been filled, she leaned over to soap Bertie's back. His hands rested on his drawn-up knees, but they were not the hands of the man she had married, soft, white, sensitive hands, used to weighing out flour and jam and sugar, used to writing entries in the ledger. Over the past two years, his hands had turned into those of a casual labourer; she felt their calluses when he cupped her face or stroked them the length of her back. His hands were not the only thing that had changed. The relentless rejections had sapped him of so much of that irreverent jauntiness which had made her love him. But she thanked God for that optimistic core, which remained. Suddenly overwhelmed with love for him, she embraced his wet, soapy body.

'You'll have better luck tomorrow, Bertie, I know you will.'

He let himself be kissed and then said, 'If Bob wasn't waiting for his turn, I'd have you in here with me, so think yourself lucky!'

It was next morning as she walked to Southwell's that she got the idea. Why hadn't she thought of it before? Trees! Trees had been springing up all over Bermondsey, the result of yet another of Dr Salter's seemingly impossible dreams. When Bertie had first heard the MP give a speech about his plan to see every street in Bermondsey lined with trees, and every house with a flower garden or window box, he'd come home so excited she had to sit him down and get him to repeat the speech to her. The doctor had the idea that arid streets were good for neither body nor soul, and that the health of both would be vastly improved if the rows of terraces that criss-crossed the borough were turned into avenues. And now his vision was being implemented, the results were plain to see, for as she walked along Storks Road, trees of heaven lined the pavement. Saplings still, but already softening the harsh lines of brick and slate. Even now, in their bare winter state, a black filigree of branches laced the leaden sky. Somehow, the trees made you lift your eyes, Milly thought, and for some reason the sky seemed bigger because of them. And it wasn't just trees; old graveyards in the churches had been transformed, with gravestones moved aside so that beds of tulips or dahlias could be planted, splashing the borough with blocks of colour. When she'd last taken Jimmy to the joy slide in St James's Park, the beds were full of bright winter pansies. It gave her some of that old 'hopping' feeling, brought on, she knew, by that indefinable smell of green-sapped, growing things. And it was all the work of the Beautification Committee, run by the doctor's wife.

Milly stopped outside the Salters' house. It was early, but Bertie had told her the hard-working MP's wife was as dedicated as her husband. 'They work triple shifts in that household!' he'd said in admiration one day. The woman had proved a good neighbour once before. Perhaps she might again. So Milly, gathering up her courage, adjusting her hat and checking her shoes, breathed deeply before knocking on the front door. To Milly's surprise, Ada Salter answered the knock herself. She held her hands in front of her like a surgeon waiting to scrub up, but they were filthy, nails rimed with dark soil.

'Oh, Mrs Hughes, how lovely! I'm potting up seedlings. Do come in.'

Milly walked into the carpeted hallway. The house was the same layout as their own, but as she passed the parlour she glimpsed good furniture with the patina of age upon it, and looking slightly too large for the room.

'Come into the garden, Maud!' Mrs Salter laughed. 'Forgive me, but I must just see to my seedlings, before they wilt.' The back garden was a green oasis. A little like Bertie's, its walls were covered in climbing roses and ivy, but towards the back was a greenhouse, stuffed with seedlings and plants in various stages of growth.

Mrs Salter continued her task of potting up what looked like tiny trees, listening intently, while Milly explained the reason for her visit.

'My husband hasn't had a proper job since he was locked out after the strike, Mrs Salter, and my brother-in-law's out of work too. I was wondering if you needed any more men, planting all the trees?'

The woman looked up from her task, bare hands plunged deep into the tray of potting compost. 'Oh yes, I do remember, your husband was such a stalwart during the strike! I wish you'd come to me before. I'm sure there's useful work he can do for the Beautification Committee.'

Milly, breathless with excitement at what she'd just heard, grasped Ada Salter's dirty hand and squeezed it. 'Oh, thank you, Mrs Salter!' But, eager to put in a word for Bob too, she pressed on. 'And our Bob can reel off the names of *every* tree your Beautification Committee has planted. I know we've got trees of heaven in our road, and when we walked round Dockhead the other day, he was pointing out London plane, poplars, acacias, and he said there's even cherry trees in Cherry Garden Street again!'

Mrs Salter beamed. 'How wonderful, someone with as much enthusiasm for our trees as my husband and I have!'

'Oh, we all love the trees. It's nice not to have to go down hopping just to see some!'

For some reason she felt at home in the little garden, glad that Mrs Salter hadn't left her sitting in the parlour, but had invited her out, as if she belonged there.

'I can understand the draw of hop-picking. It's not just for the income, is it?'

Milly shook her head and smiled. 'It helps! But no, it's not just for the money. When you're a child, it's the freedom and the open space. We loved it.'

'Alfred and I love Kent. We bought a house there.' Milly knew of the large manor house at Hartley that the couple had given to the borough, to be used as a convalescent home.

'Oh, I've heard of Fairby Grange, I know women who've been grateful to stay there after their babies were born. Once they're back home, they don't get much rest, so it sets them up.'

Mrs Salter nodded and said softly, 'Well, perhaps when your little one's born, you can go there yourself.'

Milly didn't think her pregnancy was that evident, but somehow the woman had guessed. Milly blushed. 'I'd like that, but I've got two other children at home.'

'Well, they can go too!' Mrs Salter laughed, then went on. 'You may not know that we use the grounds of Fairby as a nursery for all the trees we plant in Bermondsey, so you see, you have a little bit of Kent right on your doorstep!'

Milly was delighted with the idea. No wonder the very sight of them reminded her of hopping.

'Well, my dear, I'm sure the Beautification Committee can find work for your gardener brother-in-law too, especially now it's planting season. We have hundreds of saplings just waiting to be put in the ground. And I have an idea for your husband. Back in twenty-six, Bertie drove the motor van delivering the strike bulletin, didn't he?'

Milly nodded.

'Well, my dear, all the saplings and bedding plants have to be driven from Fairby Grange to Bermondsey. Do you think he might like the job of transporting them?'

'Yes!' she said quickly. 'He'd *love* to do that!'

'Do you think you'd better ask him first?'

'I don't need to, Mrs Salter.'

For Milly knew that he would indeed love nothing more than driving out to the countryside every day, bringing back green pieces of Kent, and delivering beauty to Bermondsey.

It was May, and the three sisters were walking away from the polling station. The adult suffrage law, passed the previous year, meant that at twenty-three Milly was finally able to vote, in what was being called 'the flapper election'. Amy and Elsie had waited outside the polling station with the children, almost as excited as Milly, while their sister had cast her very first vote. The trees of heaven lining the road were hung with all the promise of unfurling fresh green, and as they turned into St James's Road, Milly pointed out a row of young, frothing cherry trees.

'Just think, Elsie, Bob might have planted those.'

'They're beautiful!' Her sister reached up to stroke the lowest pink blossom, setting it dancing on the slight branch.

Jimmy ran ahead into St James's Churchyard, which they were cutting through on their way to Dockhead, and Milly expected a tussle with him when she told him they couldn't stop at the slide. But something else had caught his eye.

'Mum, look at the flowers!' The five-year-old was pointing to a bed of early flowering yellow roses, planted in a sunburst pattern. 'It looks like sunshine!' He looked up at her, his eyes bright.

'Yes, it does, love, just like sunshine.'

'Quick,' she said under her breath to Elsie, 'let's get a move on, before he remembers the slide!'

They quickened their pace as much as Milly's heavy pregnancy allowed.

'So, who'd you vote for?' asked Amy. She was in charge of Marie's pushchair, while Elsie pushed Ivy in the handed-down, big-wheeled pram.

'Who do you think? The one who gave my Bertie and Elsie's Bob a living wage, Dr Salter, of course!'

'Well, I guessed that, but at least you've got the choice. You can have your say now, instead of having to wait till you're old!'

'Thirty's not *that* old!' At twenty-three, Milly's idea of old clearly differed from fifteen-year-old Amy's. She saw the wicked gleam in her sister's eye and realized the jibe had been deliberate.

'Cheeky cow,' Milly said, shoving Amy's arm.

'But she's right,' Elsie chimed in. 'I'm glad I'll have my chance next time. I wouldn't want anyone but good old Alf for Bermondsey, would you? Not the way things are going with the unemployment.'

'My Bertie says if the others get in they'll cut the dole, cut the wages, cut everything . . . and things look like they'll get worse before they get better.'

Elsie gave a little shudder. 'Just more hard times – you'd think we'd be used to it by now. Do you think we'll be all right, Milly?'

Milly, slipping her arms through theirs, drew her sisters in close as they turned into Arnold's Place. 'We'll be all right,' she said, 'as long as we've got each other.'

Their mother was outside, talking to Mrs Knight, and seeing her daughters walking along arm in arm, she smiled. 'Look at 'em!' Mrs Colman announced proudly as they reached the front door. 'Me set of jugs, best of friends!'

And Milly felt a surge of joy as she realized the truth of it. How often had she despaired that her broken family could be healed, believing that she and her sisters would forever be at odds? But now she understood. Hard times had forged a bond between them that was stronger than all the wounds of war, stronger than the mighty old Thames itself. Whatever the future held, she had no doubt that the set of jugs would indeed remain friends for the rest of their lives.

Acknowledgements

Grateful thanks are due to my agent Anne Williams at Kate Hordern Literary Agency and to my editor Rosie de Courcy, for their invaluable advice and expert guidance. Thanks also to all the team at Head of Zeus for their enthusiasm and dedication.

Thanks to all the Bexley Scribblers for their continued support; to Violet Henderson and Jim Munday, for their stories about life in Bermondsey before the Second World War and to Roger Metson for sharing his childhood memories of Hop Picking in Kent. I would also like to acknowledge the work of Theresa Tyrrell in preserving the oral and pictorial history of Bermondsey through the Bermondsey Memories project.

Many thanks to my ever supportive family and friends, especially to Daniel Bartholomew for giving me the character of Jimmy. Lastly, my special thanks to Josie Bartholomew, without whom this book could not have been written.

A letter from the publisher

We hope you enjoyed this book. We are an independent publisher dedicated to discovering brilliant books, new authors and great storytelling. If you want to hear more, why not join our community of book-lovers at:

www.headofzeus.com

We'll keep you up-to-date with our latest books, author blogs, tempting offers, chances to win signed editions, events across the UK and much more.

If you have any questions, feedback or just want to say hi, drop us a line on hello@headofzeus.com
or find us on social media:

@HoZ_Books

HeadofZeus

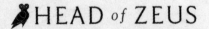